THE
VEINS
OF THE
OCEAN

Also by Patricia Engel

It's Not Love, It's Just Paris
Vida

THE
VEINS
OF THE
OCEAN

Patricia Engel

Grove Press
New York

Published simultaneously in Canada
Printed in the United States of America

FIRST EDITION

ISBN 978-0-8021-2489-0
eISBN 978-0-8021-8999-8

Grove Press
an imprint of Grove Atlantic
154 West 14th Street
New York, NY 10011

Distributed by Publishers Group West

groveatlantic.com

16 17 18 19   10 9 8 7 6 5 4 3 2 1

For my mother and my father

"Más allá del sol, más allá del mar,
más allá de Dios, poco más allá."

—Carlos Varela

THE
VEINS
OF THE
OCEAN

ONE

When he found out his wife was unfaithful, Hector Castillo told his son to get in the car because they were going fishing. It was after midnight but this was nothing unusual. The Rickenbacker Bridge suspended across Biscayne Bay was full of night fishermen leaning on the railings, catching up on gossip over beer and fishing lines, avoiding going home to their wives. Except Hector didn't bring any fishing gear with him. He led his son, Carlito, who'd just turned three, by the hand to the concrete wall, picked him up by his waist, and held him so that the boy grinned and stretched his arms out like a bird, telling his papi he was flying, flying, and Hector said, "Sí, Carlito, tienes alas, you have wings."

Then Hector pushed little Carlito up into the air, spun him around, and the boy giggled, kicking his legs up and about, telling his father, "Higher, Papi! Higher!" before Hector took a step back and with all his might hoisted the boy as high in the sky as he'd go, told him he loved him, and threw his son over the railing into the sea.

Nobody could believe it. The night fishermen thought they were hallucinating but one, a sixty-year-old Marielito, didn't hesitate and went in after Carlito, jumping feet first into the dark bay water while the other fishermen tackled Hector so that he couldn't run away. The police came, and when all was said and done, little Carlito only had a broken collarbone, and Cielos Soto, the fisherman who saved Carlito, developed a permanent crook in his back that made him look like a big fishing hook when he walked until his death ten years later.

Hector Castillo was supposed to spend the rest of his life in prison—you know the way these things go—but he killed himself right after the sentencing. Not by hanging himself from the cypress tree in the front yard like he'd always threatened since that's the way his own father had chosen to depart this life. No. Hector used a razor purchased off some other lifer in a neighboring unit and when they found him, the floor of his cell was already covered in blood. But Carlito and I didn't hear about all that till much later.

Since Carlito had no memory of the whole disaster, Mami fed us a story that our father died in Vietnam, which made no sense at all because both Carlito and I were born years after Vietnam, back in Colombia. But that was before we learned math and history, so it's no wonder she thought her story would stick. And forget about the fact that Hector was born cojo, with a dragging leg, and never would have been let into any army.

In fact, the only clue we had about any of this mess was that Carlito grew up so scared of water that Mami could only get him in the bathtub once a week, if she was lucky, which is why Carlito had a rep for being the smelliest kid on the block and some people say that's why he grew up to be such a bully.

But then, when he was fourteen and our Tío Jaime decided it was time for Carlito to get drunk for the first time, only Jaime got drunk and he turned to Carlito over the folding card table on our back patio and said, "Mi'jo, it's time you know the truth. Your father threw you off a bridge when you were three."

He went on to say that Hector wouldn't have lost it if Mami hadn't been such a puta, and next thing you know, Carlito had our uncle pinned to the ground and smashed the beer bottle across his forehead.

He was asking for it, I guess.

Mami had no choice but to tell Carlito and me the real story that same night.

In a way, I always knew something like that had happened. It was the only way to explain why my older brother got such special treatment his whole life—everyone scared to demand that he go to school, that he study, that he have better manners, that he stop pushing me around.

El Pobrecito is what everyone called him, and I always wondered why.

I was two years younger and nobody, and I mean *nadie*, paid me any mind, which is why, when our mother told the story of our father trying to kill his son like we were people out of the Bible, part of me wished our papi had thrown me off that bridge instead.

All of this is to tell you how we became a prison family.

It's funny how these things go. After Carlito went to jail, people started saying it was his inheritance—que lo llevaba en la sangre. And Dr. Joe, this prison shrink I know who specializes in murderers, told me that very often people seek to reenact the same crime that was inflicted upon them. I said that sounded a lot like fate, which I am strictly opposed to, ever since this bruja on Calle Ocho, a blue-haired Celia Cruz knockoff with a trail of customers waiting outside her shop door, told me no man was ever going to fall in love with me on account of all the curses that have been placed on my slutty mother.

What happened is that Carlito, when he was twenty-two, heard that his Costa Rican girlfriend, Isabela, was sleeping with this insurance guy from Kendall. And that's it; instead of just dumping her like a normal person would, he drove over to her house, kissed her sweet on the lips, told her he was taking her daughter by her high school boyfriend out to buy a new doll at the toy store, but instead, Carlito drove over to the Rickenbacker Bridge and, without a second's hesitation, he flung baby Shayna off into the water like she was yesterday's trash going into the landfill.

But the sea wasn't flat and still like the day Carlito had gone in. Today it was all whitecapped waves from a tropical storm moving over Cuba. There were no fishermen on account of the choppy waters, just a couple of joggers making their way over the slope of the bridge. After Shayna went in, Carlito either repented or thought better of his scheme and jumped in after the little girl, but the currents were strong and Shayna was pulled under. Her tiny body is still somewhere down there, though somebody once told me that this water is actually full of sharks, so let's be realistic here.

When the cops showed up and dragged my brother out of the water, Carlito tried to play the whole thing off like it was one big, terrible accident. But there were witnesses in sports bras who lined up to testify that Carlito had tossed the child like a football into the angry Atlantic.

If you ask him now, he'll still say he didn't mean to do it; he was just showing the baby the water and she slipped out of his arms—"You know how wiggly little kids are, Reina. Tú sabes."

I'm the only one who listens because, since they arrested him, Carlito's been in solitary confinement for his own protection.

If there's one thing other inmates don't tolerate, it's a baby killer.

This is Florida, where they're cool about putting people to death. After the Supreme Court banned capital punishment in the seventies, this state was the first to jump back into the execution business. I used to be one of those people saying "an eye for an eye," even when it came down to my own father, who was already dead, God save his soul. But now that my brother is on death row, it's another story. Mami doesn't go with me to see Carlito. She's over it. Not one of those mothers who will stand by her son till his dying day and profess his innocence. She says she did her best to make sure he grew up to be a decent man and the day he snapped, it was clear the devil had taken over.

"Out of my hands," she says, smacking her palms together like there's dust on them.

The last time the three of us were together was the day of the sentencing. I begged the judge for leniency, said my brother was young and could still be of use to society, even if he got life and was stuck banging out license plates for the rest of his days. But it wasn't enough.

After she blew Carlito her last kiss good-bye, Mami began to cry, and her tears continued all night as she knelt before the altar in her bedroom, candles lit among roses and coins offered to the saints in hopes of a softer sentence. I heard her cry all night, but when I tried to comfort her, Mami brushed me off as if I were the enemy and told me to leave her alone.

The next morning she announced her tears had run out and Carlito was no longer her son.

Mami's got a dentist boyfriend in Orlando who she spends most of her time with, leaving me in the Miami house alone, which wouldn't be so bad if I had any kind of life to fill this place. But I use up all my free time driving down US 1 to the South Glades Penitentiary. We're lucky Carlito got placed in a prison just a few hours' drive south and not in center of the state or up in the panhandle, and that he gets weekly visitation rights, not monthly like most death row killers.

I want to say you'd be surprised by the kind of people who go visit their relatives and lovers in jail, but really you wouldn't be surprised at all. It's just like you see on TV—desperate, broken-toothed women in ugly clothes, or other ladies who dress up like streetwalkers to feel sexy among the inmates and who are waiting for marriage proposals from their men in cuffs, even if they're in maximum security and the court has already marked them for life or death sentences. There are women who come with gangs of kids who crawl all over their daddies, and there are the teenagers and grown-up kids who come and sit across the picnic tables bitter-lipped while their fathers try to apologize for being there.

Then there are the sisters, like me, who show up because nobody else will. Our whole family, the same people who treated my brother like he was baby Moses, all turned their backs on Carlito when he went to the slammer. Not one soul has visited him besides me. Not an uncle, a tía, a primo, a friend, anybody. This is why I take visiting him so seriously and have spent just about every weekend down there for the past two years, sleeping at the South Glades Seaside Motel, which is really a trailer park full of people like me who became transients just to be close to their locked-up sweethearts.

I'm not allowed to bring Carlito snacks or gifts since he got moved to the maximum-security prison. If I could, I would bring him candy bars because, back when he was a free man,

Carlito spent a big cut of his paycheck from his job at the bank on chocolate. I mean, the boy was an addict, but you could never tell because Carlito was thin like a palm tree and had the smoothest complexion you've ever seen. Carlito got it together late in high school, and even made it into college and graduated with honors. I'm telling you, even Mami said it was a milagro. He got into a training program at a bank and was working as a teller, but they said after a few years he'd be a private banker, moving big money, and his dream was to work at one of the Brickell banks that hold the cash of all our Latin nations.

Carlito would move our family up—make enough so that our mother wouldn't have to paint nails anymore. That was the plan.

Carlito, now, is fat like you'd never have predicted. He says it's a prison conspiracy given all the mashed potatoes they feed the inmates, and he thinks everything is laced with hormones meant for cows. He has to eat his meals alone in his cell and not in the chow hall like the regular lifers. He doesn't get to work out in the yard with the other prisoners, he just gets an hour a day to walk laps around a small fenced-in concrete cage with a chicken-wire roof they call "the kennel."

Sometimes he gets his rec time deducted because a guard decides to write him up for some made-up offense. So he mostly does his routines in his little cell—push-ups, sit-ups, and squats—but he still looks like a two-hundred-fifty-pound troll because Carlito's hair started to fall out the day of his sentencing. That luscious, shiny Indian hair went straight into the communal shower drain and now my brother, barely twenty-five, looks like he's somebody's grandfather, with anxious creases burrowed into his forehead and a nose that turned downward into a beak the day he lost his freedom.

He's not your typical inmate; he doesn't try to act remorseful or even say he's innocent anymore because really, after the first appeal to overturn his conviction was denied, we sort of lost hope. He did the whole thing of writing letters to Isabela before the trial, apologizing even though he says it wasn't his fault, but even then you could tell Carlito's heart wasn't in it.

He blames Papi for all this, and then Mami. Says maybe Tío Jaime was right, if Mami hadn't been such a puta all those years ago, none of this would have happened.

I don't tell my brother that Dr. Joe, who works in Carlito's prison and sometimes meets me for drinks in the lounge of the South Glades Seaside Motel, told me it probably all comes down to brain chemistry and Carlito may have just been a ticking bomb, and that homicidal tendencies sometimes run in families. I pretended not to be worried by this, acted nonchalant, and even went so far as to lie to Dr. Joe and say, "I guess I lucked out because Carlito and I have different fathers." I believed this for a while, but Mami said, "Lo siento, mi corazón. Hector was your papi too."

Dr. Joe is familiar with Carlito's case. Not just from the newspapers but because he reviewed his files when assigned to the Glades prison, hoping Carlito was in need of some kind of counseling. He says he's doing research on the ways solitary confinement can change a person's mind over time. He got permission to scan lifers' brains to compare the ones who are segregated from the main prison population and those who are not. I asked him if it's right to run them through tests like they're animals, but Dr. Joe said, "It's for *science*, Reina," and he can already prove being in isolation makes inmates nearsighted and hypersensitive to sound and light. Solitary can also make a person psychotic, paranoid, and develop hallucinations, he says, but it's hard to tell who is being honest about their nervous breakdowns because, even if lots of inmates check into prison as mentally ill, some just want to be labeled crazy to take or trade the free pills.

Carlito wants nothing to do with Dr. Joe or the other prison shrinks and refuses to talk to any of them. Dr. Joe tried playing the insider, standing outside Carlito's cell door, peering through the small reinforced glass windowpane, saying he knew Carlito was innocent, and he was on his side. If only Carlito was willing to talk, maybe he could help him with his next appeal. Carlito didn't bite.

Sometimes I suspect Dr. Joe only acts interested in me so that I'll soften Carlito, convince him to hand himself over for Dr. Joe's research, persuade him the way Dr. Joe tries to persuade me that since they won't let Carlito take classes or socialize like other inmates, submitting to his study is a small way to feel useful, give something of himself, and it's also a way to have interpersonal contact those weeks when he doesn't exchange words with a single human besides the prison guards, and me.

"All of this has to be so hard on you, Reina," Dr. Joe said to me the first time we met at the motel bar. "You must be overwhelmed with so many feelings."

Dr. Joe thinks I have anger toward my brother because when I was nine he locked me in my bedroom closet for hours, told my mother I'd gone to the neighbor's to play, and I had no choice but to pee in a shoebox. Also, because when our mother was at work, he would make me take off my clothes and sit around watching TV naked, or sometimes he'd make me get up and dance, and when I refused, he'd pull out a knife from a kitchen drawer and hold it to my neck.

But I tell Dr. Joe my brother was mostly a good brother because he never did dirty things to me like the brothers of some of my friends. And when a girl from school started bullying me in the eighth grade, saying I was an ugly junior puta, Carlito went over to her house one night with a wrestling mask on his face, crept into her room, and beat her out of her sleep.

Nobody ever found out it was him.

He did that for me.

Joe—he told me to stop calling him *doctor* but I keep forgetting—thinks I'm confused. He buys me beers and told me he's thirty-two, which is really not much older than my age, twenty-three. He's from Boston, which he says is nothing like South Florida. He might even be cute if he got a normal haircut, not his side-parted dusty brown shag, and lost those round glasses that look like they belong in 1985. He has a condo in Key Largo and sometimes invites me there. Just yesterday he said I could sleep there if I wanted, so I don't have to spend all my money at the prison motel. I said thanks, but no thanks. I make good enough money to pay for this piece of paradise.

"You're real pretty," he said last night when I walked him to his car on the gravel driveway outside the lobby. "You got a boyfriend up there in Miami?"

"No, I come with a whole lot of baggage, if you know what I mean."

I was thinking specifically about the last guy, Lorenzo, a plastic surgeon who picked me up at Pollo Tropical. We went for dinner a few times and when we finally fucked at a hotel, he told me he'd do my tetas free if I promised to tell everyone they were his work. Then he wanted to take me to Sanibel for a few days, but I said my weekends were reserved for Carlito.

I still remember his eyes when I explained.

"You're Carlos Castillo's sister?"

That was the end of that.

Joe laughed as if I'd meant the baggage thing as a joke, and then swallowed his smile when he realized I hadn't.

"You're a great girl. Any man would be lucky to be with you."

I smiled at Joe, even though I feel like people only say shit like that when they know you're already a lost cause.

I paint nails just like my mother and her mother before her. I just realized as I'm telling you this that we're a family of all sorts of inheritances. Between us, we still have the house. Mami owns it free and clear even though she pawned all her jewelry years ago, and if you were to ask her, she'd say the only valuable things she has are her santos and crucifixes. After Carlito went to prison, Mami converted his room into a shrine to the pope, which is fine with me. She replaced all of Carlito's football trophies and car posters with framed prints of His Holiness, books, and postcards of the Vatican. Her big dream is to go to Mass at St. Peter's one day and I think that's good for her. It's good for you to dream about things that will probably never happen. That's why I still have this picture in my head of the prison board recommending clemency for Carlito, and the governor waking up one morning and deciding to give a pardon to my brother, as if in his sleep God wrote onto his heart that there's this boy down in the Glades who deserves a second chance, commuting his sentence to life, and maybe even with the possibility of parole. But stuff like that just doesn't happen.

I work at a fancy salon in the Gables. On Fridays, I pack up my bag, stuff it in the trunk of my Camry, and, after my last client of the evening, get on the turnpike and drive south so I can spend the night at the motel and get up at four the next morning to be among the first visitors to check in for the day visits at the prison. Each visit is only an hour long and has to be approved in advance. Sometimes we get to stretch it longer if the guard is feeling merciful. Carlito is allowed two visits a week. That's my Saturday and Sunday. The other girls at the salon tell me I should take a weekend off, do something for myself for a change, but I say, "What kind of person would I be if I abandoned my brother?" I'm the only thing that reminds him he is human and not a caged animal.

After I drive through the prison gate, past the twenty-foot walls topped with razor wire, the barren valley marked by gun towers; after the searches, filling out forms, the X-ray machine, the patting down by guards, and checking my bag into a locker, I'm sitting in a windowless concrete room, at a small table across from my brother. Most death row guys get strict noncontact visits, forced to sit behind a Plexiglas partition. But we're fortunate that we get to sit face-to-face and he cups his hands around mine, strokes my knuckles with his fingertips, and asks me what's going on in the world outside of this place.

"I think Mami and Jerry are going to get married. If she does, she'll want to sell the house, which means I've got to find my own place."

"You should move out of that house anyway. Start fresh somewhere. That house is full of bad spirits."

"No, after you went away, Mami had it blessed by a priest."

He shakes his head. There are more tiny wrinkles around his eyelids and buried in the corners of his lips than ever before.

"How's work?"

"The same. I'm getting famous for my acrylics. Better than Mami ever was."

"That's my Reina."

My brother drops his face onto the table and I stroke the back of his bald head, his bare neck, run my fingers on the edge of his blue prison suit.

"I'm dying," he says without lifting his head.

I kiss the back of his head, and the guard who's been watching us from his perch along the wall steps forward and slams his hand on the table.

"No contact," he says. "I always let it slide with you two, but you always push it."

Carlito pulls his head up and sits as erect as a man about to be executed.

"She's my sister, man."

I give the guard my prize eyes that make him soften and say, "One minute."

He always does this for us.

Carlito stands and I rise and go to him. Before his cuffs get chained back to his waist, he lifts up his arms so that I can slip under them and then he drops them so I feel the bulk of his cuffs sitting on the curve of my back, on top of my hips. I press my body to his chest and Carlito's biceps tighten around me, his head drops into my hair and I press my cheek to his neck. We stay like this until the guard bangs the surface of the table again.

"Enough, Castillo. Your time is up."

I give my brother a kiss on the cheek before the guard pulls us apart. It's always like this. We say good-bye with a little push of the rules. I slip out from under his cuffs and the guard leads my brother through the back door of the visiting room, down the corridor to the solitary cells.

Later, at the motel, Joe, who's just gotten off work, asks me how my visit with my brother went.

"Same as always. But today he told me he's dying."

"As far as I've read in his files, he has no serious illnesses," says Joe.

And then, "Reina, would you like to go for a walk on the beach with me?"

We take his car and Joe pulls off the road onto a winding path and tells me there's a perfect patch of beach just there, beyond the mangrove trees. It's night but with the moon so full and bright, I still feel the comfort of daylight, every breathing ripple of the sea on display—not one secret out here. I leave my sandals on the sand and Joe rolls up his khaki pants and takes off his loafers revealing pale feet with crinkly leg hairs and long toes that make me embarrassed for him. We walk along the water's edge, the current mostly quiet except for the occasional rush of the rising tide.

I see a flutter in the sand and, as we approach, notice a gull tossing about in the shallow water, struggling to breathe, its small black legs limp under its body, its wings unable to span and lift. I scoop it up, pull it toward my chest while Joe looks on with disgust, telling me those birds carry diseases and to be careful or I'll get bitten.

"He was about to drown," I tell him, the bird frozen like a toy in my arms, "We need to find help for him."

"Reina, you can't be serious."

My eyes tell him just how serious I am. We head back to his car and I sense his regret for having invited me. He mutters something about me thinking it's my job to save every living creature from itself.

I insist he pull up next to a parked police car. The officer recognizes Joe immediately and looks to me. My face is familiar to him from standing in the long lines outside the prison waiting for visiting hours to begin, or arguing against parking tickets when I leave my car overnight outside the Glades Motel because the lot is full, and for those times I speed down US 1 to get to the Keys before sunset because my mother always told me that's when the crazies come out.

"Do you know where we can find help for an injured bird?" I ask the officer from my place in the passenger's seat.

The cop looks skeptical, his eyes land on the limp seagull in my lap, and he shakes his head at us, looks to Joe disapprovingly before telling us to try the marine reserve a few miles down.

"They have a bird sanctuary down there. Might be closed at this hour, or might not. Someone down there may be able to help you."

As it happens, the place is closed, gates locked and chained. I press my face against the metal grill, call out to see if anyone is still around who can help us.

"I think you should just let the bird die a natural death," Joe says, leaning against his car, arms folded across his chest, with a look of contempt.

I hold the bird out to him. "Does this look like a natural death to you?"

"We should put it out of its misery. Drown it or something."

"You mean put *you* out of your misery because you don't want to deal with him."

Joe sighs at me like a father would at an unreasonable child. "So what do you want to do with it?"

"I'll take him home with me and bring him back here first thing in the morning."

"Reina."

"I don't need your help. Just drop me off back at the motel."

"Why don't you stay with me tonight? We'll put the bird in a box in the bathroom and I'll drive you back here at sunrise."

"You don't care about the bird."

"But you do. And I care about you."

I go with the doctor because, really, I'm sick of the knotty green carpet of the Glades Motel, the sad-looking people who putter around the trailers, the stragglers like me who take up the rooms in the main lodge, and the women who come down here to visit their men by day but spend their nights with the teen-age hustlers who hang around the gas station on Hickory Key.

Dr. Joe's condo is nicer than I expected. Looks like it belongs on South Beach and not in the crummy Keys. Stark white like a hospital, chrome and leather furniture, huge abstract paintings on the walls—the kind of stuff only rich boys buy.

"Shit," I say when he leads me through the door.

"Cost of living is so cheap down here," he says, as if I caught him in a crime. "Nothing compared with life up north."

"Why would you leave Boston to come down here and work in a prison?"

He smiles bashfully and offers what sounds like a false confession that he just needed a change of scenery. I suspect the doctor is running from something, and he came to the Keys to hide out. I decide not to hold it against him, though, because we all have our shadows.

Joe goes off to look for a box for the bird, which I want to believe is napping in my arms but really, he looks like he's just about had it with this world. I think his legs are broken by the way they keep bending and folding as if made of string.

Poor bird. If life were fair, the bird and I would both be living in Cartagena, not in Florida where all of the world's crap seems to accumulate.

Joe returns with an empty box that looks like it was meant to ship electronics. I put the bird in and we take it to his guest bathroom together, rest it on the floor, and I tell the bird goodnight while I feel Joe's hand on my shoulder.

"Let me fix us some drinks. How about a screwdriver?"

I ask him to make us some tea instead.

We sit together on his leather sofa. I can't decide what I feel for Joe. He seems like a lonely man and this makes me like him, see bits of myself in him. But part of me also sees him as the kind of guy who gets turned on by tragic people.

"You inspire me, Reina. The way you always reach out of yourself to care for others. Your brother. Even that dying bird. You give so much."

Hearing him talk about me like I'm some kind of saint makes me uncomfortable.

"You've given up your life to be present for Carlos. It's so admirable. I don't know anyone with that kind of loyalty."

"There's a whole motel full of them right where you found me."

"You're different from them."

"No, I'm not."

He takes advantage of my parted lips and puts his mouth on mine and next thing you know, we're making out like junior high kids right on Joe's leather sofa. His hands fumble with my blouse buttons and I reach for his belt. He's telling me he's been dreaming of kissing me since he saw me that first day going through the metal detector at the jail when Carlito got transferred to the federal prison.

He's telling me to wrap my legs around him, pulls off my bra, and I rip the nerd glasses off his face. Then Joe says to me, "Tell me about the first time you got fucked, how old were you?"

"Thirteen," I sigh into his ear while he feels around me and then he wants to know with who, where, how did I like it?

I whisper that it was with my brother's friend Manolo and when it was over, I found out my brother had been watching the whole thing from his closet because he told me I looked good, like a real woman, finally, and I felt proud. After that, I started sleeping with all my brother's friends. But my brother told my mother and she told me to be careful because a woman who is a good lover can make a man insane, just look what happened to our father.

Dr. Joe pulls me closer and just as we're about to do it says, "Talk to me like I'm your brother."

I freeze. Stare at him. His mouth wet with my saliva, his cheeks red. A loose eyelash on his nose.

"You're really sick, you know that?"

"Reina, come on. I didn't mean it like that. Come on."

He's trying to pull me back to him but I've already got my legs on the ground, straightening myself out, clipping my bra back on.

"Come on, I was just playing."

He stands up, tucks himself back into his pants, and follows me toward the bathroom. I pick up the box with the bird and push past him.

"Where are you going?"

"Me and the bird are leaving."

This is how it goes: I make it far down the road with Dr. Joe on my tail shouting, "I just want to be close to you and all I get from you are walls!" until the same cop who told us where to take the bird pulls up beside me wanting to know if there's a problem.

The cop has one eye on me and one on Joe, who's disheveled and looking way too desperate and guilty to be out in the middle of the night.

"You need a lift back to the motel?"

I nod and when we're sitting alone in the cop car, Dr. Joe way behind us, walking back to his condo, the officer turns to me and says, "You know, if you want to pitch something like an assault or harassment charge, I'll fully corroborate. I never liked that doctor guy. Not one bit."

M y seagull was poisoned.

That's what the bird expert at the marine center told me when I brought him there this morning.

"I think his legs are broken," I told the woman, who had a permanent-looking sunburn and wore men's overalls.

She shook her head. "Sorry, honey. This bird's dying. A nice thing you did keeping it from drowning and all, but we're going to have to euthanize it."

"You're not even going to try to save him?"

"He's beyond saving. Look at him. He's suffering."

"Suffering means you're still living," I told her, but I knew the bird's destiny had been decided.

She picked him up with one hand, crushing his wings together, and left me with the empty box.

I tell the whole story to my brother during Sunday visiting hours at the prison. Everything except the flesh scene between Joe and me on the sofa. Carlito really doesn't need to hear that. He has women writing letters to him, but he's not allowed to meet any of them like some of the other inmates with normal privileges.

When he was still in county jail, I started sending my brother books because, believe it or not, Carlito was the biggest reader you ever met, even during the years he was doing crappy in school, before he went to a real college. My brother was the smartest guy I knew—could talk to you about ancient wars, religions, all sorts of stuff that you'd wonder what a guy like him had any business knowing. But my brother said knowing about the world was important. He said by reading you develop ideas of your own and ideas are what keep a brother alive.

I'd pack boxes full of books about whatever I could find to send him. When this old guy on the corner died, his widow said I could have all his books, which she left in boxes out on the curb, so I sent those too. Biographies, historical shit. Everything. And within those packages I'd sometimes sneak in a batch of porno magazines even though they'd likely get confiscated—I thought it was worth the effort—because I understood that a guy in jail might have urges of the kind my mother often described, and nobody to take care of them.

One day Carlito said, "No more books. No more magazines. Nothing."

When I asked him why, he repeated what he'd said years earlier, that books give a man ideas, they make him want to live. But ever since the judge put Carlito's last minutes on the clock, having ideas and hope were making it even harder and more painful to be alive.

My brother kisses my hand and rests his cheek on the back of my palm the way he always does.

He tells me he loves me and I say, "I love you too, hermano."

"You know what tomorrow is," Carlito says, and I nod, surprised that he's still keeping a calendar.

September 8. The anniversary of the day our father threw him off the bridge.

What kind of a man can do that to a child, is what we used to say until Carlito did the same thing.

Five days later, I'm on the same journey, edging down the turnpike with the scrim of sunset lowering in the west, passing through Florida City, strip malls and car dealerships melting into swampland and fishing tackle shops, past Manatee Bay onto the Overseas Highway. It's drifter territory, where people go to forget and to be forgotten. I've come to think of this land as a second home. The prison motel; familiar faces though few of us have exchanged names. Each of us serving our sentence, waiting, waiting, because prison has made us more patient than we ever knew we could be, until we get the call that it's time; the end of the sentence, or just the end.

About a year ago, I saw Isabela at a wake for Miguel, one of Carlito's old friends, a guy she eventually married. I waited until midnight thinking the mourner crowd would dissolve, then go to someone's house for a meal or a drink, but there she was, sitting in a folding chair near the casket with her mother cradling her shoulders. I stood in the doorway, crossed myself, said a five-second prayer, and asked God to take Miguel straight up to heaven because he was pretty special to me when I was sixteen, and we did more talking than screwing, which back then was a rare thing. Miguel was a cop and he and Isabela fell in love during Carlito's trial because Miguel was the type of guy to lend support. He was shot on the job by another cop during a robbery at the Dolphin Mall. Friendly fire.

I didn't want Isabela to see me. Not that night. It's bad enough that she has to run into me at the supermarket, the pharmacy, and the gas station. She's never been cruel to me like other people in the neighborhood. She always smiles, tells me she prays for my family and for me. That she forgives Carlito and she doesn't want him to die. I believe her, too, because on the day of the sentencing, Isabela cried through her victim-impact statement with a picture of her daughter clutched against her chest—one of those department store Christmas portraits— Shayna in a new red dress; a face just like her mother's in miniature. Isabela faced the judge, then turned from him to Carlito, who was handcuffed to a table beside his lawyer, and through her tears asked the court to go easy on him because Isabela said no matter Carlito's crime, and no matter how much she believed in justice, one death is no cure for another.

Isabela and I were close friends once. She was a few years older but we were in the church Youth Group together and she took me for my first abortion when I was fourteen because she said it wasn't right to bring that kind of shame on my mother who'd already been through so much, and Isabela knew of a doctor who didn't require parental consent.

A few years later, Carlito fell in love with her.

I was jealous. Isabela with her soft smile, a blanket all the boys wanted to be wrapped in. No boy ever looked at me that way.

My brother used to say he saw a family in her gray eyes and I'd grow furious, tug on his sleeve, and say, "You already have a family."

Something I've never admitted: I was the one who told Carlito about Isabela's cheating when he was beer-drunk in front of the TV one Saturday afternoon, wondering why she took so long to return his calls.

I pumped him full of rage, told him she was giving him horns, that he was letting her play him like some kind of cabrón.

I lied.

Said everybody in town knew about her easy ways but him.

Sometimes when we run into each other Isabela invites me to her house for dinner because she knows I spend most nights home alone watching the local news, just me and a tin of pollo asado from the cantina. I never go. I appreciate the charity, but despite their daughter's graciousness Isabela's parents probably wouldn't let me through the door if I showed up.

She always hugs me when she sees me, hums into my hair that even though people say we're on opposing sides, we're in this mierda together and her baby is an angel now watching over us all.

There was a time when Mami called my brother and me her angels.

Carlito and I would cram into bed with her at night and she'd tell us stories about Cartagena before our papi dragged us away from our grandmother's home, across the sea to Miami, before this house with the iron security bars on the windows.

"Mis angelitos," she'd whisper, kissing our cheeks as we curled under her wings.

We'd pretend Mami's bed was a raft and we were castaways adrift together, floating through the Caribbean, and Carlito would point out dolphins, sea turtles, manta rays, and sharks while Mami and I played along like we could see them too. Until Carlito declared that there was land on the horizon and, at last, we were saved.

We were saved.

Like everything down here, the park used to be Tequesta land. It sits on a crusty peninsula jutting into the bay like an accusatory finger, a tropical hammock overgrown with invasive Australian pines, foreign flora that killed off the indigenous trees, keeping in all the bugs and blocking out most of the sunlight. To Carlito and me, suburban kids normally confined to small yards and patchy lots, it was a jungle.

Our mother liked to take us there on weekdays, avoiding the weekend crowds, even if it meant calling in sick at work, declaring it un día de fiesta, pulling my brother and me out of school. Mami said we all deserved our little breaks once in a while. And we were just little kids, so it's not like we were learning anything important.

I was seven and Carlito, nine. Best friends. Still innocents.

It was a weekday morning. The sun wasn't yet at its highest, and the park was quiet except for a few tourist families and lonely fishermen along the seawall, standing between the pelicans lined like guards on the edge of the pier. We parked the car and walked past them to the other side of the narrow cape, to the beach beyond the forest. I wore a red bathing suit that was getting too small for me, elastic pinching my nalguitas. Carlito wore swim trunks handed down from a neighbor, too big and hanging low enough to show an inch of crack, and Mami complained he should have tied a rope around his waist to keep them up.

Our mother took to the beach like it was her temple, finding a piece of shore far from the lifeguard stands, boom boxes, and smoky portable grills, spreading a blanket, smoothing the sand lumps underneath before lying down and shutting her eyes to the sun. Sometimes she forced me, never Carlito, into the ocean with her and I felt guilty leaving him behind on land. Mami said the salty air purified the lungs and seawater nourished the skin. She'd pull me in by the hand, take my head into her palms, dunk me under the surf like a baptism, and let me float in her arms. I let her because these were some of the few times I had my mother's full attention.

"Listen to the water, Reina," she whispered as I let myself be cushioned by the soft rush of waves. "If you trust the tide, it will always return you to shore."

We didn't yet know about undertows and rip currents, the many ways the ocean can turn on you.

Carlito hated getting wet and stayed away from the beach, kicking a soccer ball around on the concrete walkway toward the seawall, down dusty trails through bendy pines, dodging the swarms of mosquitoes and spiderwebs that kept most people out of those paths. I was a faithful little sister, reluctant to go anywhere without him, so I'd always pull myself out of the water and away from Mami, towel off, and follow my brother.

Sometimes Carlito let me kick around with him, but most of the time he just wanted me to cheer him on while he battered the ball, shouting, "Go Carlito! Viva Carlito!" and after he'd kick an imaginary goal, he'd do a little dance and I'd scream so hard I'd almost make myself cry.

I was shouting and clapping so loud that morning that we didn't notice the rattle of the planes right away. It was a slow burning buzz steadily rising over the shrill song of the cicadas. We felt the vibration over the roof of the forest and saw the bowing of the treetops before we knew what it was. Through an open patch of canopy we saw the belly of a chubby gray propeller plane, the quiet, old-fashioned kind. Behind it, another plane, and the two looped over us. Carlito grabbed the ball and I knew to follow him.

Mami was already by the seawall waiting for us to appear. She pressed me into her hip but Carlito hung back, embarrassed at her affection. Our uncle had put it on him that he had to be un hombrecito, the man of the house, since our father was dead and couldn't be referred to even in passing—our mom forbade it—not even as the kind of myth of a dad that fatherless kids like to tell, the guy who may or may not ever show up at your door one day with presents and an explanation for his absence.

The lifeguards and park rangers made everyone get out of the water, then cleared the beach, and people gathered by the pier to gossip about the commotion. Someone said it was a drug bust; a cigarette boat registered in the Bahamas had unloaded a bundle of packages into the bay once the crew spotted the Coast Guard in their wake. Someone else heard there'd been a drowning, but if there had been, I guessed they would have pulled all the beachgoers into a human chain to comb the water like they did a few years earlier when Mami thought I'd gone under but really I just went to use the public bathroom.

Someone else said it was a suicide; one of those fishermen had gotten too drunk while minding his lines, staring out at the Stiltsville houses, and decided it was his time to end things. But the water along the seawall and beneath the pier was shallow, folding into barnacle-and-urchin-covered rocks that would needle you bad while breaking your fall. It was no place for a final jump.

Then we saw the vehicles arrive. Trailers unloaded ATVs. Another truck spit out a line of cops in special gear ready to mount them and take them into the woods. I didn't realize I was scared until I noticed a stocky green-uniformed park ranger standing next to our mother, and that somehow made me feel safer even if strange men were always trying to stand next to her. She was still beautiful then, wearing no makeup, just the sheen of humidity, her hair in natural black curls, not the coppery straightened look she took on a few years later along with a smoking habit that hardened and sallowed her golden complexion.

"You know what they're really looking for," he muttered to Mami like he was an old friend.

She gave him a blank look. She could appear very naive when she wanted.

"Refugees."

I remember his tone, as if the word itself were illicit.

"How do you know?" she asked.

"We got a call from someone who spotted a boat dropping them off."

The search vessels arrived. Official-looking ones that weren't Coast Guard but something else with a crested seal painted onto the sides. *Jail boats*, Carlito called them, plowing parallel to the seawall, though it seemed to me that between the rocks and the water, there was nowhere to hide. I knelt to get a better look, but the sun was high over the bay now, water reflecting like a mirror, yet I could still make out thousands of tiny fish gleaming like blades in the current below us.

Carlito complained that he wanted to go home but the ranger warned us that the Border Patrol had the park on a hold and nobody was allowed in or out. Not till they found who they were looking for.

"For all we know, somebody's been waiting to pick them up and drive them out of here. They'll be checking cars and trunks before they let anyone out."

He put his hand on Mami's shoulder and she let him, which I didn't like.

"Best to wait till this whole thing clears and they got those folks all accounted for. This stuff happens at least once a month around here."

Carlito and I sat on the wall watching the planes circle overhead, the cops rushing the vegetation like soldiers at war. Then came the dogs. A parade of angry-eyed canines, eager to enter the forest to find their prize.

I looked at Carlito and he looked to the ranger, who was standing even closer to our mother now, asking her where she was from, where she got that lovely accent.

"Colombia," she said, and the guy let out a hoot.

"We got one right here!" he shouted, pointing to Mami, then to Carlito and me. "No, we got three! Quick, bring the dogs!"

Carlito and I didn't get that he was joking till Mami let out a soft laugh, the kind everyone believed was authentic but us. We knew it was her decoy laugh. The one she used to get people off her back, and by people, I mean men.

We heard from another bystander who heard it from another ranger that four people had been caught already and were sitting offshore on a jail boat waiting for whatever came next. There were eight more out there, they said, but those who were already in custody wouldn't say if the others had made it to land, were on another boat, or were just floating out on the water, clinging to a buoy or an inner tube or, worse, drowned. They probably weren't Cubans, though, someone said, or the police wouldn't be trying to smoke them out of the park like this.

An hour or so passed. The three of us sat in a patch of shade on the seawall. I laid my head on my mother's lap while

Carlito held the soccer ball in his. She told us the story about the náufrago who washed up on the beach in Cartagena when she was a little girl. That was in the time before jail boats and police planes, when the people in charge just let castaways land where they may and stay if they felt like it. The guy told everybody he was a Spanish prince and all the girls wanted to marry him, but it turned out he was just a gambler running from debts in Panama, and his enemies eventually caught up with him because, Mami said, nobody can run from anything forever.

Enough time passed that Carlito became bored with our mother's stories. He took up his ball and started kicking it again.

"Come on, Reina," he called for me, and we went back into the base of a trail already swept by the cops and rangers.

"Don't go too far," Mami said. "Stay where I can see you."

Carlito zigged and zagged and I tried to steal the ball from him, but he was too quick, his legs were too long, and mine felt rubbery and knobby as I tried to keep up.

"I'm tired," I moaned, squatting on the ground, my butt just shy of the dirt.

Carlito relented. "Just try to block my shots, okay?"

I stood up, ready to play goalie. I was small for my age, but my reflexes were quick. Carlito had trained me to read body language, to know which way a kick would come before the kicker even knew it. I watched and I waited and I blocked the first three kicks with a hand, with a foot, with my belly. But the fourth flew past me into the trees and because I was the loser, Carlito insisted I be the one to go into the bushes after it.

I should have been scared. But the need to please my brother overpowered all the terror stories we'd been raised on to keep us out of woods and jungles and swamps: legends of Madre Monte, who gets revenge on those who invade her territory by making them get lost; La Tunda, the shape-shifter, luring people into the woods in order to keep them there forever; or El Mohán, who simply loves to barbecue and eat children.

The twigs cut into my ankles and shins but I pressed through, negotiating rocks under my feet, pebbles wedging into my sandals, pushing branches from my face, slapping away bugs, slicing through spiderwebs until I was so deep into the woods that I came to the other side of a hidden inlet, a silent, still lagoon framed by mangrove trees with roots like ribs in the pooling green water.

I stood on the dusty embankment unsure of my discovery. A gray heron swooped over the water before me, and the only sound was of the planes, still rumbling over the far side of the park. A few turkey vultures and crows gathered by the edge of the brush and some instinct told me to run into them to scare them off, and search the shadowy wood behind them.

My brother called from the other side of the forest wall, "Reina, hurry up!"

I wanted to find the ball before he did, to avoid hearing him call me a useless slug, to prove I was a worthy teammate, that I was as good as any boy at keeping up a kick-around with him so he'd finally stop threatening to take me to the pulguero to trade me for a television.

And there it was: Carlito's ball, its black-and-white mosaic waiting for me among the knotty roots of a lonely banyan smothered by prickly pines. I pushed in closer, until the ball was just beyond my reach, but behind the plastic ball I noticed a meaty form that looked to be a shoeless human foot.

It's no secret that dead bodies turn up all over South Florida, floating in canals, along the swampy arteries of the Everglades, or tossed to the side of a road. In this very park our mother had found, washed up on the beach, what she swore was a real human jawbone, and was so moved by its white smoothness that she took it home with her, bathed it in holy water, and buried it in our backyard until the raccoons dug it up, and then Mami just surrendered and put it in a drawer somewhere.

But this foot was dark and fleshy and my eyes followed it up to a bare leg in frayed denim shorts and a shirtless torso. It belonged to a boy—a teenager, I should say—thin, crouched like an animal. He turned to me. His eyes were wide and his young face was worn and burned from seawater and sun.

He watched me and I watched him as I heard my brother's voice grow clearer, his feet crunching through the brush, "Reina, Reina! Where are you?" until he was finally beside me, his hand closing around my wrist.

My brother's gaze moved from me to the boy, who stared back at us, trying to make himself even smaller.

I heard Mami calling for us, heard the worry in her voice, and the cops behind her shouting for us kids to come out of the woods and stop goofing around.

I heard the dogs barking, the weight of more footsteps walking over the dried leaves and broken branches carpeting the forest floor.

I knew he was one of the ones they were looking for. I knew he didn't want to be found. I didn't know which was the right side or the wrong side. I only knew that I never saw eyes like that before, so dark with fear, so aware that my brother and I could betray him.

"Get the ball," Carlito whispered, releasing his grip on me.

I stepped closer to the boy, who watched me, pulling his hand from the curl of his chest to push the ball at his feet toward me.

I picked up the ball and looked back at my brother. He turned toward the woods and called out to whoever could hear us not to worry, that we were coming, and rushed ahead while I stayed behind.

I stared back at the boy until he hid his face from me again. I wanted to help him and felt confused because in school I'd learned that police were people you went to for help, but something told me the best thing I could do for him was to leave and pretend I'd never seen him.

"No le voy a contar a nadie," I said, assuming he understood, and ran out of the forest toward my brother and mother, but was intercepted by a dog, barking frenetically, its sight set on the ball in my hands like it was a piece of raw meat.

The cop took the ball from me and held it close to the dog that snapped and howled at it, but the cop just looked frustrated and stared at Mami, who'd come to my side with Carlito behind her.

"This is your ball?" he asked me.

"It's *my* ball," Carlito said defiantly. "She's my sister."

"You brought it with you to the park today? You didn't find it here?"

"I bought it for my son myself," our mother said, slipping a hand onto each of our backs. That wasn't really true. Tío Jaime had been the one to give Carlito the ball, but it gave us a kind of thrill to see her lie to a man of the law.

The officer yanked the dog by the leash away from the trail and started back toward the seawall. I looked at Carlito but he looked away from me, away from the woods, and sighed to our mother, "Can we go home now?"

We never found out what happened to the rest of those migrants or even where they came from. When I was old enough to fool around with cops and academy cadets, they told me loads of people washed up on South Florida shores in crafty sailing vessels from all over the Caribbean, even after the laws changed and it became much trickier to be let in: Cuban balsas with Soviet car engines, Haitian and Dominican rafts held together with tarps and tires. Some people were just dropped off by speedboats or yachts that shuttled across the Florida Straits in the night. Some slipped right in before dawn, forever undiscovered. If they were among the lucky ones, a dry foot on land would get them amnesty or asylum. But some had the misfortune of arriving in daylight and being spotted on the water, ratted out by citizens, booked into Krome within hours, and set for deportation. But I guess that's not as bad as drowning along the way.

The park terrain, with the way it poked into the edges of the Atlantic and the silence and blackness that fell over it after sunset, was an easy drop-off point for those Caribbean arrivals, but also one of the more obvious and heavily patrolled ones. They came from all over, not just the northern half of the Caribbean, but from as far south as Colombia and Venezuela, as far west as Honduras and Nicaragua. But we rarely saw that stuff on the news anymore. The public had already heard enough about boatlifts and refugees and now preferred to hear about murders and cocaine busts and corrupt politicians instead.

After the day of the planes, we stopped going to the park as often. Mami got roped into relationships with men who didn't like having Carlito and me tag along on their outings, and Carlito and I grew old enough not to care. My brother was into bicycles and forming boy gangs with the neighborhood kids, and I was happy to be their mascot, until we got to the age when our bodies started to divide us—girls over here, boys over there—and then the rough waters of puberty when I figured out the boys didn't mind keeping me around as long as I agreed to be their toy.

We never told our mother about the boy in the woods. And Carlito and I never spoke of it to each other after that day. But there were times I'd wanted to bring it up to my brother. Sometimes I'd see a young guy around town or at the supermarket who looked just like the boy by the banyan and I wondered if it was him, if he'd ever made it out of the forest and into our world or if they'd hunted him into the night. I wondered if the dogs had finally sniffed him out. I thought if he'd managed to stay hidden, we could have gone back for him the next day. The planes and boats would have given up the search, and it would be old news among the rangers. Mami could have pulled up the car close and we could have sneaked him into the trunk and out of the park, taken him home, and given him food and clothes and a place to rest. Why hadn't we done that?

A few months ago, they made Carlito's execution date official. They'd be moving him up to the death row prison in Raiford and I was planning to move up there too as soon as I got the matter of selling our house settled. I'd heard rents were cheap because nobody really wants to live around a bunch of murderers, in a town that's only known for its executions, except maybe their families or their fans. I figured I could get a job easily enough because no matter where you are, there will always be women who enjoy the small luxury of having their nails painted, and it would save me the hours I spent driving south each week to see Carlito down at the Glades.

Our mother moved up to Orlando to be with her boyfriend, Jerry. He makes enough at his dental practice for her to stop working. This is the kept-woman gig she's been praying for all her life. She suggested I join her up there. Said I'd benefit from starting over in a city where nobody knows me or my last name. I thought she was inviting me to live with her since Jerry's townhouse is big enough and there's a room specifically for guests they never actually have. But she explained I could rent an apartment nearby and find a roommate or, even better, maybe with a little effort, I'd get lucky like her and find a man to take care of me.

I told her I had to follow my brother.

During one of my last visits at the prison with him before his transfer, I was trying to be positive about things, saying it would be a good change for Carlito, who was so sick of his prison down in the Keys, the smell of the ocean so close as if taunting him, reminding him of his crime. I didn't acknowledge that a date had been set for him. It was still years away and I knew more appeals could push it off even further. I was already writing to law school groups, advocacy programs, doing all I could to get things delayed or hopefully overturned. And everyone knows it can take decades for the governor to sign the death warrant to put someone in the chamber.

In this case, I told Carlito, time was on our side.

We were in the private family meeting room where we sometimes had our visits, sitting across a wide table from each other. Carlito was in his red jumpsuit. Most of the inmates wear orange, but death sentence cases have to wear red. I was in a loose T-shirt and jeans because they're picky about what women can wear when visiting prisoners. Nothing too tight, not too much skin, no shorts or dresses. I've seen ladies get turned away for pushing it with their too-sexy outfits, or forced to change out of their tube dresses and borrow sweats from another visitor who already knew better and came prepared. Here they were even strict about jewelry, so my earrings had to come off before I went in, left with my purse in one of the visitors' lockers.

I held Carlito's hands in mine, my fingers wedged between the cuffs and his wrists because I hoped that at least for a moment he would feel me and not the cold metal against his skin. Those are things to which he'd become too accustomed. I saw it in his posture. The way the years of walking with his hands chained to his waist, his ankles shackled together by leg irons, had sloped his spine, causing him to walk with his head tilted down, in short steps, so different from the way he moved when he was free, with rhythm in his gait, a walk more like a glide.

"Reina," he began. "Do you remember when we were kids . . ."

"I remember everything."

Sometimes Carlito liked to reimagine our childhood and I played along. He'd talk about how Papi used to play the guitar and sing us boleros or put on a record and while Mami danced with Carlito, our father would sway around the room with baby-me in his arms. I didn't contradict him even though he was only three years old in those days and couldn't possibly remember such things. I wanted to believe it was as he said, but I once asked Mami if any of that had ever happened and she shook her head slowly before changing her mind and simply shrugging: "I don't know. It's been so long, mi amor. Ya no me acuerdo."

But there were things she did remember and she'd wait until she was angry at me about something to unleash them on me like a wolverine. How my father never held me when I was a baby, either the cause or the consequence of my relentless crying—there was no way to know. When he was drunk, he'd deny he was my father, or worse, say I was a bad-luck baby, that my crying had driven his own father to suicide after his wife died and Hector brought him to live with us. When my grandfather hanged himself in our front yard one night, my father blamed me.

Some guy Papi worked with, a part-time yerbatero, warned I was an abikú, the wandering spirit that incarnates in children and makes them die. I'd taken the soul of the baby my parents lost between Carlito's birth and mine, only to be reborn in the form of another child because the spirit world didn't want me either. The yerbatero warned my father an abikú that doesn't die carries the dark spirit and has the power to make future siblings or others around them die in their place. Abikús, he said, are the children that come to destroy a family.

Mami claimed not to believe in those pueblerino superstitions, clinging to her crucifixes and escapularios, but to satisfy my father she did as the yerbatero advised to lift the maleficio. She put a silver chain around my ankle to help with my crying, carved my footprint into the skin of a palm tree, and even let

Hector clip my ear himself, with metal pliers and a blade, on the tip and though the cartilage, just as the yerbatero instructed, so they would recognize me if I were to die and be reborn again.

These, my mother said, were reasons my father did not love me.

But Carlito had his mind on something else that day. Something other than our family.

"Do you remember"—he lowered his voice—"that day in the park when they were looking for those people? That kid . . . hiding?"

I nodded. "By the tree."

"I think about him."

"You do?"

"I've thought about that kid every day I've been in this place. I see his face." Carlito inhaled deep, letting it all out through his nostrils. "The fucking terror. Qué mala suerte. El pobre. He knew . . . he knew . . ."

"Knew what?"

"He knew they were gonna get him."

I looked at my brother wanting to see the same in his eyes, because if there is terror there is still hope that things might work out the way you want them to, but my brother's eyes had gone dead long ago.

"Do you think he made it out of the park before they got him?"

"Not a chance."

"I do." I said, maybe for myself more than for my brother. "He's probably a citizen by now, with a good job and a wife and a family."

"Maybe he's right here in this prison."

I shook my head. "He didn't come all that way to fuck shit up."

Carlito sighed and I realized I'd made him feel bad.

"I didn't mean it like that, Carlito. I didn't mean you fucked things up. I know you're not supposed to be here. Everybody knows it was a mistake."

I'm not sure why I was the one apologizing. Sometimes I wished my brother would take the blame, admit that he was the one who ruined everything, drove all of our lives so far off course that we'd never find solid ground again.

I thought maybe, in that moment, since his final hour was already on the calendar, he'd take the opportunity to say something about it, not that he was sorry, but just that he knew what he'd put us through for seven years, and that he understood it hadn't been easy for us. That would have been enough. But he was quiet for a while and when the guard told us our time was up he only said, "Te quiero, hermanita," like he always did, but this time he didn't look back at me as the guard led him away back to his cell.

Carlito never made it to the prison in Raiford. They found him limp and suspended from a ceiling pipe the morning he was scheduled to be moved. He hanged himself with the cord from the fan they let him keep to alleviate the sweltering Florida Keys heat because he'd never been classified as a suicide risk. He didn't leave a letter for me or for anybody. He'd met with the prison chaplain the day before, but that was nothing out of the ordinary for Carlito. He liked to talk to preachers and nuns from time to time, though he said that in prison, religions are just another gang to join for protection, like the Latin Syndicate or the Aryan Brotherhood. He liked to ask questions about life and death and sins and souls even if he didn't agree with the answers. The chaplain says Carlito repented for his sins, which I think sounds really nice and of course Mami was happy to hear that, but I'm not sure I believe him.

I was in the middle of showing the house to a prospective real estate broker when I got the call. I'd been hoping our house would be adopted by another family that could bring to it new happiness, but the broker, a gringa recommended to me by one of my salon clients, said investors were buying up houses all over our neighborhood to renovate and flip for profit, and that ours was run-down and ugly enough to have that kind of appeal. They'd gut it completely, she said, maybe even tear it down. When they were through, it would be unrecognizable. She was smiling when she said this, but it made me uneasy. And the best part, she said, was that most of these investors were people from other counties or from up north, unaware of our family reputation and less likely to shy away from the lore of our home.

Then the phone rang.

Normally phone calls from the prison start with a recording saying you're getting a call from an inmate and asking if you'll accept the charges, but this time it was a man's voice saying he was the warden and I should go somewhere quiet before he said what he had to say. I thought it must have to do with the logistics of Carlito's transfer up to Raiford. Something like that.

"Okay," I said, once I'd stepped out of the kitchen into the yard. "Let's hear it."

"Miss Castillo, you'll want to sit down for this," the warden told me, but there was nowhere to sit; our patio furniture had rusted beyond function and I'd managed to get rid of it before the broker came by.

"I'm sitting," I said, though I was just standing in the middle of the last surviving scrap of grass in what used to be our garden. Our old swing set was still at the back of the property where our father had erected it, corroded and shaky, and only used now to hang laundry on its rails.

"Your brother has expired, miss."

"What do you mean he 'expired'?"

"I mean he's dead, miss. The officer on duty found him this morning. I'm sorry for your loss."

He explained how Carlito hanged himself and I closed my eyes, feeling the pressure of the sky pushing me down into the earth.

I should have seen it coming. Our mother got a similar call when our father died, but the warden at that particular prison had been more sympathetic, even offering Mami some pocket-psychology nugget that men tend to express themselves through violence in suicide and she shouldn't take it personally.

Prisons only want their inmates alive so they turned my brother's body over to my mother and me so we could give him a funeral, along with a few boxes containing all his worldly possessions—a few notebooks with cartoonish pencil drawings, books, letters from women, and photos I'd given him over the years of happier times before his crime, when it was him and Mami and me and we still celebrated Nochebuena and birthdays.

Somehow, in death, Mami became Carlito's mother again.

We thought we could keep my brother's passing private, but the headline hit the front page of both the English and the Spanish newspapers the next morning: CONVICTED BABY KILLER FOUND DEAD, over a picture of Carlito in his red suit, thirty years old and bald, staring at the camera as if he'd already decided it would be his final portrait.

There were no phone calls of sympathy. No flower arrangements. Except from Isabela, remarried with two more little ones of her own, who sent us a Mass card and a note saying she'd always pray for Carlito's soul.

If we'd left his body with the prison, they would have buried Carlito in a state cemetery along with the other dead inmates who went unclaimed by their families, beneath a wooden cross marked not by his name but by his prison number. But we couldn't afford our own hole in the ground for Carlito so we decided on cremation because it was cheaper.

My mother still considered herself super Catholic—except for occasional visits to brujas, psychics, and espiritistas, and that phase when she became obsessed with the Ouija board and played with it for hours every night—but neither of us had been to church in years, maybe because those wooden pews reminded us too much of being in the courtroom, and she was too ashamed to look for a priest or minister to preside over a suicide funeral.

She let this short guy from the funeral home read a standard prayer over Carlito's coffin and we did our crying over his swollen and stiff body in the rented casket privately, praying for his salvation, asking that my brother be forgiven, and may we be forgiven too.

A few of our relatives eventually showed up—Tío Jaime, his wife, Mayra, and some distant primos—which Mami appreciated, but I got the feeling they just wanted to see if Carlito was really dead and it wasn't just a rumor.

The bedroom that used to be Carlito's was empty now. Mami had packed up all her saints and candles and prayer cards and taken them with her to Orlando, but most never made it out of the cardboard box because Jerry told her only ignorant peasants believe in "esas tonterías," and I guess she decided she didn't really need them anymore.

At first we couldn't figure out what to do with my brother's ashes. They returned them to us in a heart-shaped tin and Mami wrapped it in what had been his and my christening gown, sewn by her mother's hands. But she didn't want to take the ashes back to Orlando with her, and I didn't feel right keeping them either.

In the end, we decided to return Carlito to the earth in our own way, tying a brick to the tin with the same rope Hector's father had used to hang himself. I didn't know until that day that all this time, Mami had kept it in a box in the garage. My grandfather's body had been shipped back to Colombia for burial, but Hector had been cremated just like Carlito. Mami hadn't wanted his ashes so Tío Jaime kept them and when he traveled back to Colombia he sprinkled them over their own parents' graves in Galerazamba. She admitted to me that before turning them over to Tío Jaime, she'd pulled out a thimbleful for herself, which she now stitched into a sachet and placed in the tin with Carlito's ashes.

Around sunset, Mami and I drove to the bridge that had sealed both my father's and my brother's fates, walked halfway across to its highest point, and with both our hands clutching them, tossed the tin and brick and rope into the bay water, watching them disappear under the current, hoping the ashes and relics of the men of our family would be pulled down and buried in the ocean floor.

That night Mami asked me to sleep with her in her room like I'd sometimes done as a little girl.

I didn't sleep. I only watched her, wondering how she could slip into such a calm slumber when even the hum of the ceiling fan blades hit me like a torrent of screams.

She was small under the blanket, and halfway through the night she awoke, and I pretended to sleep as she touched my hair, my cheek, and whispered my name, though I didn't move.

In the morning, we had our coffee together at the kitchen table and then she took a long look at me standing by the front door before leaving me alone in our house for the last time.

The house in Miami never felt like home even if it's the only one I remember. A brown concrete cube with a red Spanish-style teja roof, and white iron bars over the windows and front door that didn't do their job very well because we were robbed four times. Each time, the thieves just took the TV and broke some stuff. We didn't have anything else that anybody would want. Any extra money we had, we kept in a cigar box under a broken floor tile in Carlito's room, even after they took him away. When I was packing, I dug out our little wooden case. The family savings. There was nothing left.

There was a time when we knew all our neighbors: Nicaraguans, Peruvians, Dominicans, and Venezuelans—everybody on the run from some dictator, broken currency, or corrupt government regime—and other Colombians like us looking to find some peace away from the narcos and guerrillas that had hijacked the country.

They lived in houses just like ours, painted pastel colors. They took pity on Mami, the single mother of two kids, the victim, wife of "ese loco" Hector Castillo. But those neighbors stopped inviting us to their backyard parties and asados after Carlito's arrest. It was understandable. I'd probably have done the same.

Mami was never short on male company though. Any guy who got a look at her wanted to stick around, from the mailman to the surgeon who performed her hysterectomy, and she was equal opportunity, giving most of them a shot.

I packed up the things in the house. There were only a few photographs I'd take with me wherever I ended up next. The rest

I left to my mother, but she didn't want most of them either, so now they're sealed in boxes held in a storage unit in a warehouse behind the airport along with the other crap we didn't bother trying to sell because nobody wants anything de mal agüero, that might carry the DNA of a convicted killer.

There were no photos of my father. Mami got rid of them after he died. Only Tío Jaime kept a framed shot of Hector on the mantel of their artificial fireplace, a blown-up version of what was either his passport photo or his government ID. Hector, who was ten years older than our mother, sitting square in an unironed white button-down shirt, staring at the camera with his round wrinkled eyes and bulky lips over his blockish yellowed teeth. Con una mirada de chiflado, if we're being honest about it, the kind of look that would make nice ladies make the sign of the cross, and even though I couldn't describe him to you beyond that photo, just his face made me tense; the same guy Tío Jaime talked about with tears in his eyes, the little brother who, even with his bad leg, dreamed of one day becoming a champion boxer like his hero Kid Pambelé.

Before I knew the full truth, or at least as much truth as I've been able to piece together so far, I used to hope that Hector's bad leg made him somehow virtuous, that he was a patapalo like the original Mediohombre, Blas de Lezo, who, missing a leg, a hand, an eye, and an ear, managed to defend Cartagena through countless battles against the British. But Mami said I was wrong. Hector's bad leg only made him a cagalástima, self-pitying and bitter.

"He was no hero, mi'ja," she said. "Not for one day of his life."

From the photos that remained, I kept one of Mami that our father took just after they were married. She's standing on a beach in Rosario, wearing a frumpy bathing suit, looking shy and modest. Her hair was long and dark, tied into a loose braid. She was pretty back then but nothing remarkable. People said she was the sort of woman who got more attractive with age, all that experience worn into her expression. Another photo of Carlito and me when we were toddlers, when our mother used to bathe us together, up to our necks in bubbles, laughing like stupid.

Then, a photo of the three of us on our last trip together to Cartagena to see Mami's mother when she was dying. An abuela I only knew from our summer visits to Colombia, because she refused to leave her neighborhood even to visit us, convinced that in her absence the authorities would steal her home away like they'd done to the people of Chambacú, flattening their community on the marshes to fill the waterways with more traffic-filled avenues and shopping malls, and Abuela would be forced to live in some shanty in the hills.

We stayed with her all night, holding her hand until she passed away. Mami said the greatest gift you can give someone you love is being with them as they die. I'd always planned on being at my brother's execution for that same reason. I reminded Mami of what she'd told us, but she said this case was different, then added a prayer of thanks to God for taking her mother from this world before people from her barrio had the chance to talk about her with shame and blame, mock her, and say she was like La Candileja, the fabled and disgraced grandmother of a boy who became a murderer.

The most recent photo: my brother, ashy and washed-out in his red death row suit, and beside him, me, looking like the gray-faced commuter-zombie I was, taken at the prison against the blue cinder block wall in the visiting room that some inmates had been given permission to paint with a mural map of Florida. I asked the guard to take the photo from the elbows up so the cuffs on my brother's wrists wouldn't show. You can't see in the photo that Carlito and I are holding hands.

With the sale of the house, my mother leaves me with half the profits, a small chunk of change she says is meant to be my herencia and help me start a new life. She pushes for me to follow her to Orlando, but I tell her living so far inland feels unnatural to me and Miami, the city I've lived in all my life, now feels vacant.

I want to be forgotten.

I want it to feel as if I've never existed.

I want to be a stranger. Rootless.

For weeks, I try to think of where I might live now that I don't have ties to any one place. I buy a road map at the gas station and stare at the state of Florida, drawing my finger up along the red and white highway lines, across different counties, trying out the names of towns on my lips.

Pensacola. Sebring. Valparaiso. Apalachicola. Carrabelle.

But my finger keeps dragging southward, even farther south than where I live now, closer to the equator, down to the strand of islands held together by a series of thin bridges, the ones scientists are always saying years from now will be covered by water when the seas rise and drown all the edges of earth.

There, I think, I might be able to disappear.

Before I leave our house for the last time, before the final days when I hand over the keys to the real estate broker, and before the new owner arrives to demolish our dilapidated kitchen and peel out our tile floors, I decide to go back to the park on the bay for one last look.

Years after the day of refugees, Hurricane Andrew wiped out those promiscuous nonnative pines and the state used the luck of the barren park to restore the vegetation, repopulating it with trees that were meant to be there.

The forest is no longer a forest but a garden of palms and various types of poinciana and ficus trees, and blankets of blooming flowers mined by iguanas and chameleons; the crows and turkey vultures replaced by parakeets, cormorants, and flycatchers.

Now there are neat trails for bicyclists and people out for a stroll, nature paths with marked signs providing brief histories of the flora and fauna.

I hardly recognize the place but walk down one of the trails, now a wide tunnel through gently arched palms.

It's spider season. The path is laced with wide webs, thick golden silk spiders ready to birth at their centers, waiting for prey. I spot a baby lizard dangling by its tail from the edges of a web, still wriggling. I pluck a leaf from a tree and place it under the lizard to cushion its fall, pull it out of the web, and set it on the ground, free.

I walk, until I remember the passageway I once took.

I'm taller now and it's harder to push through the undergrowth, but I manage, and soon find myself on the other side of the woods in a clearing by the lagoon and its jointed mangroves, and see another lone long-legged heron, this time a white one, perched on a rock, watching the water.

I was brought to the United States as a baby. If you want to blame someone, you can lay it on my father's brother, Jaime. He was the first one to cross over. He left Cartagena de Indias as a crew member on a cargo ship and spent years on Panama Canal crossings until he ended up at the Port of Miami. They gave away visas more easily in those days. Green cards too. It didn't take much for him to convince Hector to join him on the other side.

Our father had always been looking for a way out of Cartagena. If you weren't rich or light-skinned, there wasn't much for you there. Hector was a mechanic who specialized in spray-painting cars to look as new as they could against the salty corrosion of the Caribbean, a good enough skill, he thought, to take to a place like Miami. He left his new bride where he found her in her neighborhood of San Diego in Cartagena, and only came back in time to get her pregnant once a year.

Between Carlito and me there was the lost baby, stillborn, a girl who refused to be a part of this world, and when I was bad, to punish me, my mother would say I was not an abikú after all; that dead baby was her true first daughter, and if she'd taken the breath of life like she was supposed to, Mami wouldn't have bothered going on to have another.

Hector came back to Cartagena to collect us all when I was three months old and Carlito was approaching three years—still long-haired because people said if you cut a kid's hair before he speaks full sentences, he'll be mute for life.

Mami panicked when it was time to move. The only world she knew was there in San Diego and she was scared about the life that awaited us across the sea, but her mother told her it was her duty to follow her husband anywhere and she should be grateful because most men who leave their country alone never return for their families.

Hector had found solid work at a body shop in West Miami and bought the crappiest house on an underdeveloped stretch of road, without sidewalks or streetlights, bordering the orange groves of Southwest Dade that have since been bulldozed and converted to housing developments and more strip malls. The house had two bedrooms but with Tío Jaime's help he put up a thin wall to make it three. Mami didn't work in those days. She stayed with her babies and hardly left the house. No English and no car left her dependent on the men and Jaime's wife, Mayra, who couldn't have children of her own. But Papi became jealous, always imagining her sneaking away to meet men. Who knows how it started? I'm not going to pretend my mother was guiltless even though she will say in those days she was only ever with our papi.

There must have been preludes to the disaster that broke us. I think violence must have been churning in my father like the August wind. I think he must have hurt my mother. He must have hurt us all. But when I ask her, Mami only shakes her head and says Hector's dead now and there's no reason to remember those days.

We were a complete family for just nine months before my father took off with my brother for the bridge.

When the three of us went back to Colombia to watch my grandmother die, our mother slept in the bed with her mother, Carlito took the sofa in the living room, and I slept in the bed that was Mami's when she was a child and later became her marriage bed with my father until he left, promising he'd return for her.

I would lie stiffly, watching the ceiling cracks, taking in the voices from Calle de la Tablada, the sounds of horseshoes dragging carriages behind them, hitting cobblestones, and the morning bells of the Santo Toribio church echoing against the apartment walls. It was a bed that wouldn't be fit for a child back in the States, with a mattress so thin each plank supporting it pressed against my body, but it was the bed where my parents had made my brother and me and the girl in between.

The apartment had belonged to our grandmother's parents and before that, nobody knew. You could hear every whisper, every sneeze, every limb's turn on a creaky bed or chair. The interior walls were of peeling plaster, the exterior walls of chipped stucco and stone, and the wooden windows were always open to dilute the humidity, hoping to catch a breeze coming over the city walls, off the Caribbean.

When we were kids and others asked about our father, Carlito would say, before any crumb of truth had a chance to slip off my lips, that our father was a millionaire. If we were in Miami he'd make up alibis, saying our father lived in a mansion in Cartagena, and when we came back to see our abuela, he'd say our father had stayed behind at our estate in

Coconut Grove and gave details about the life he imagined for us, straight out of *Miami Vice*, full of fast boats and sports cars and money.

Till one day, during a summer visit to see our abuela, we were cooling our butts in a patch of shade in the Parque Fernández de Madrid with some other barrio kids when Carlito started on one of his favorite lies about how our papi owned hotels that we could run around in like they were our own playground, way better than the dumpy old streets of Cartagena's walled city, which were still dusty and dirty, webbed with wiring and antennas, buildings sun-flushed and water-stained, untouched by the colorful restoration that would follow years later.

One of the boys, Universo Cassiani, scrawny, shirtless, and juggling a rubber ball, laughed at Carlito, happy to have a chance at revenge for the times my brother had mocked his name in front of the other kids, and howled that Carlito was a cochino mentiroso and our father was no millionaire. He was kind enough not to elaborate that day, but several summers later, when I was fifteen or sixteen and found myself making out with the now eighteen-year-old Universo, tall with stringy muscles, in the night shadows of the muralla overlooking the sea amid shuffling drunks and beggars, he confessed his mother had told him the story of our father as a warning of the madness that afflicts men when they leave for Gringolandia.

"It's better down here," his mami warned him. "Here, women know their place. Up there, they become wild and their men go crazy trying to contain them."

He knew Hector had tried to kill my brother. He even had an explanation for it.

"Boys are the ones who carry a family name. Girls get married and fade away from a family tree. Your father probably did it to avoid the shame of your descendants."

His words hurt. But serves me right because back then I still had the habit of scavenging for memories even if they were false ones.

Sometimes I'd look at old photos and invent stories for them. Sometimes I heard relatos of things that really happened, like the way Hector proposed to our mother, which wasn't really a proposal at all but a deal: "Let me marry you and I will help you get away from your mother." Then I'd invent a cover-up; tell myself that he met her when she was out buying food for dinner. Not the truth my mother once confessed to me, that he'd forced himself on her in an alley one night when she came home from a long day of painting nails for society ladies in Manga. But they didn't call it rape back then, and because las malas lenguas had already anointed my mother with a reputation as a loose girl, people wouldn't have been surprised he took liberties with her even though she tried to fight him off. So instead of being known as her attacker, because she was afraid she might already be pregnant and because he said he could take her away from this life, he became her boyfriend and then her husband.

Universo Cassiani was probably the first and only boy who ever came close to being a boyfriend to me. He would hold my hand as we walked along the streets of El Centro, kiss me in the archways of the muralla once used to hold cannons shooting against invaders, tell me my lips were sweet like granadillas, and that I was different from the other girls of the neighborhood who were prudish and protected by their papis.

I was with Universo just before the final hours of my grandmother's life. Mami sent my brother out looking for me, to bring me home because she knew her mother's last breath was coming. Carlito ran down the seawall shouting for me until I heard his voice echo against the stone. I pulled back from Universo, who was biting at my neck, but he persisted so I let him continue until Carlito appeared next to us in the alcove where we'd been hiding. Carlito pulled Universo off me, informing me that Abuela had announced she was waiting for me to be at her side before transitioning, which may or may not have been true. I went with my brother and left Universo by the sea.

My mother, brother, and I held hands across my grandmother's body. She wasn't even that old but she was a shrunken stump of a viejita with cropped white hair, a fleshy nose, and a tropic-charred complexion. Her palm was cool in mine and I tugged at her papery skin, counted the dark spots, compared it with my own, and thought nature is a real beast, the way it robs a body of its dignity.

She was ready to quit this life. Until a few days prior, she could still walk around okay, even without the help of the neighbor who'd taken on the role of her nurse. She survived alone with the money her daughter sent from Miami and ate well even if her body didn't show it. She always smoked hand-rolled tobacco, and that evening kept her cigar on a porcelain plate on her nightstand. She'd been praying all her life for a good death, como buena colombiana, and knew tonight was the night. When I showed up in her doorway, she tilted her head my way and nodded slightly as if to say, *Now we can get on with things.*

It took a while, but was still faster than I expected. Her breaths became longer, then shorter. Her eyes drifted to the farthest point in the room, a corner between two windowless walls.

"Open the door," she said, and Mami looked to Carlito and me and to the bedroom door, which was already open.

"It's open, Mamá. The window is open too. Are you hot? Should we bring in the fan?"

"No," Abuela shook her head with more force than we'd seen in a while from her. "Open the door. I want the door open."

Carlito stood up and closed the bedroom door and opened it again, narrating to Abuela as he did so, "It's open, Abuela. As open as it can be."

"Open the door!" Abuela cried, but her voice was growing faint so it came out like a whisper.

Her breath quickened, her eyes widened. She looked at each of us, closed her lids, and left us in the room without her.

We did things the traditional way. That's how I learned how to mourn the dead. We prayed over our grandmother all night like she was a saint and not the cold and rancorous woman our mother secretly hated for not defending her against the father and stepfather who'd put their hands on her; the woman she'd wanted to escape so badly she married our father; the woman she'd hoped would, in her final days, tell her daughter she was sorry, admit to having failed her in some small way, though that didn't happen.

We cried over her; spoke of her; as if she'd been a holy woman; waited for the priest to come administer blessings; gave her a somber funeral Mass in the Santo Toribio church, attended by all her neighbors; and buried her in the Santa Lucía cemetery, facing the ocean.

Universo lives in Miami now. The funny thing about immigration is that people from your old neighborhood often end up right around the corner from you in your new one.

We ran into each other at El Palacio de los Jugos and made eyes at each other through some small talk.

"So you finally got the courage to leave your mami behind," I teased.

"No, they increased the taxes in San Diego so much we had to move. She went to live with her sister in Santa Marta, so I came here."

It was just as Abuela feared—the return of the rich to edge out the poor. Local folk who'd lived there for generations, unable to pay the higher taxes, forced to sell their homes and move.

Universo followed me home on his motorcycle for a welcome-to-Miami bang on my couch. He told me he'd heard about Carlito's crime through the inter-American gossip wires as soon as it happened. We saw each other for a while. Not in a meaningful way but in one that was easy because, even though years had passed between us without contact, he already knew the things I never tell anyone. He knew why my house was always empty and why I didn't have friends to go to parties with in pretty-girl clusters, wearing new dresses, shiny with makeup and iron-curled hair.

But he was no longer the Universo who looked at me like I was a special creature. The one who'd write me long letters in between summers saying he missed me, begging me to come back to Cartagena over the December fiestas, promising one day he'd defy his mother and move to the other side of the Caribbean and we could be together every day.

He was casual about me now, more like the boys I'd grown up with around the neighborhood, Carlito's friends, who came looking for me when they had nothing else to do. It was okay, though. I never asked to be taken anywhere so it was always a nice surprise when Universo suggested we go out to eat instead of me cooking up some rice and warming over whatever leftovers I had in the fridge. He had another girlfriend, a rich rola, which I thought was funny considering Universo always claimed he wasn't colombiano but cartagenero, as if it were its own nation, because, he said, what does Cartagena have in common with Bogotá other than being manipulated and ignored by its government? Here, equally displaced on neutral ground in Miami, they were novios. Sometimes he'd talk about a new movie and say we should go see it together that weekend, but we never did. I knew stuff like that was reserved for the official novia. And Universo knew my weekends were reserved for Carlito.

I lost touch with Universo. In the years since, I've hardly dated anyone in the sense that he likes me and I like him and the guy makes an effort to treat me nice by consistently taking me to public places like restaurants or movies or to a park, not just home or to a hotel room. I've only had that sort of treatment two or three times in my life and it's always been short-lived, never a meet-the-parents situation. The last time was with Pedro the Peruano, who worked in the electronics store next to my salon in the Gables. He came on strong, bringing flowers to my job, until I agreed to go out with him. He took me to a steak house in the Grove and then we walked along Grand Avenue and he bought a rose for me from some guy selling them from a plastic bucket. We had a few more nights like that and I thought it was nice, this slow pace. It was something new for me. But then he stopped calling and when I went to his job to see if he was still alive, he pretended I was just another customer and asked a coworker to help me.

There have always been other men. I don't go out looking for them. They just sort of appear. But I'm good at figuring out what they want right away, and it's usually a quick turnaround. They want me in bed. They want the feeling of love and lust, but confined to an hour or two, or maybe, once in a while, a whole night. Sometimes I know they're juggling me along with a few others, or maybe just just shuffling the deck with me and a wife or a girlfriend. I'm not picky about marriage or those kinds of rules. I would be if I were the married one. I think I would be the most faithful woman in the whole world. But I've never been given the chance.

I don't believe in maldiciones but I have to admit, so far that old bruja has been right about my lovelessness. Maybe somebody did a trabajo or hechizo on me to make sure I stay alone.

I don't want to sound like one of those girls crying about boys leaving me. I told my mother once, when she asked why I never keep a regular boyfriend, joking that all I need to do is find a guy with an even messier life than mine, that I'm like one of those dealers at the Magic City Casino blackjack tables. I know there are only a few ways for the cards to fall. I don't like to lose, so I give only pieces of myself away. The pieces I know they like, the pieces they can handle. The girl who smiles in spite of everything. The one who can shimmy out of a bra without undoing the hooks, who knows what a guy wants even before he knows it.

The rest, the life I lived only for my brother, the life locked in memories of what we were *before*, I keep only for me.

But then Universo reappears. He hears I've sold the house. He stops by on one of my final days here to see for himself. He looks older, but I guess we all do, his thinning hair smoothed back with gel and about thirty new American pounds on him. He's upgraded from his motorcycle to an old Jeep and tells me he's now working as a forklift operator at the Port of Miami, loading and unloading the cargo of ships from China. I invite him in and it isn't long before old habits take over. He's not wearing a ring but tells me, once we're both already naked, that he's married, not to the rich girl but to some caleña who works at a day care in Doral.

"I don't care," I say, so his guilt won't get in the way.

Afterward, he's in no hurry to leave my bed and holds me against his chest like we're supposed to be falling in love or something.

"You're like no other girl I've ever known, Reina."

"I'm like *every* girl you've known if she'd been stuck with my life."

He starts getting turned on and wants to go at it again but stops abruptly, as if he's suddenly remembered who I am and that he came here to say good-bye.

"So where are you going to go?" He glances around my room, all packed up and spare as a cell.

"I don't know."

"You could go back to Cartagena."

"There's nothing there for me anymore."

"It's the place where you were born. You'll always have that."

There was a time when we dreamed of returning there to live, Mami, Carlito, and me. We idealized Cartagena all year long as Mami saved up for our summer trips, but when we got there, it was never the way we wanted it to be—too hot, too rainy, too full of pueblo chisme, too grim, too hopeless. Still, during our prison visits, Carlito liked to conjure stories from the Cartagena of our nostalgia and made me swear that if he never got the chance to go back, I'd go for him.

When it was time to release his ashes, I told our mother maybe we should scatter them in Cartagena, spread Carlito onto the beaches of Bocagrande, or mix him into some concrete and push him into the pavement on our old block, mold him into the plaster or bricks of the bedroom where we slept as babies, or dust him into the trees along the hillside of La Popa.

Maybe we should have buried him next to Abuela in Santa Lucía, or at least grounded him into the soil over her grave. But Mami insisted it was better like this—it made more sense to let him go at the bridge where he and Hector had each found their end—and by releasing him into the ocean here in Florida, we could still be sure his ashes would somehow find their way across the Caribbean back home to Cartagena.

I will go back one day.

For him. For me. For all of us.

But not now. Not like this.

"I want to go someplace where nobody knows me," I tell Universo.

"If things were different, I would go away with you. We could have an adventure."

"But they're not different," I say, because I hate it when men start the fantasy thing in bed. All kinds of impossibilities hardly worth contemplating.

"Make sure you tell me before you go."

"Why?"

"So I'll know where to find you."

I don't tell him the point of my leaving is that I don't want to be found.

We kiss because it seems like the thing to do, and lie together a while longer while night falls. Outside, I hear the cars of the neighborhood people pulling into their driveways, husbands, wives, and children home in time for dinner.

Universo starts to fidget beside me.

"It's okay. You can leave if you want to."

"I don't want to," he says, and I believe him until he sits up, gives me his bare back, grabs his rumpled boxers from the floor, pulls them on, and then his jeans.

His is a body that I knew thin and boyish, and now, thick and mannish. In some way, I think it's nice our bodies have grown up together.

He says he'll come see me again before I clear out for good.

He doesn't, but neither does anybody else.

My coworkers at the salon see me off on my last day with a cake as if we are celebrating a birthday. From Tío Jaime and Mayra, I get a phone call. "We just want to wish you well," Mayra says. We don't talk much these days. I think when they see me they see a souvenir of pain. So it's not like I expect a farewell party, but I'd hoped somebody would be there to watch me go, to somehow mark the moment of my leaving my lifelong home.

Instead, nothing happens.

The sky is cloudless and empty except for the autumn sun and a sliver of daytime moon, the neighborhood hum uninterrupted by my loading the car trunk with two suitcases like I'm going on vacation, not shopping for a new life, locking the house behind me, and pulling out of the driveway for the last time.

I am my only witness.

The Everglades are on fire on my final drive down to the Keys. On the curve of the turnpike where the pineapple groves end and marshland begins, I watch the green horizon burn with helicopters bobbing overhead, fighting the flames. It's too late in the season to be a wildfire. The radio says some thrill-torcher is responsible.

I don't believe in omens. I believe we choose our own signs, so I take this one as my own: with this blaze, I leave my old life up here on the mainland in ashes.

*   *   *

Because, for now, I've got no other place to go, I take a room in the South Glades Seaside Motel, dingy as ever, but I still feel a kind of loyalty to the place.

It's Friday and the motel is already filling up with the old crew, familiar faces, the women I grew up with as a prison sister even if we never shared more than a few words. Women I waited in line with, all of us watching each other as we exited the penitentiary at the end of visiting hours with that same look of aching hope and fatigue, making our way back to the motel. Women who, unlike me, are still serving their time with the ones they love.

People have this idea that it's hard to start a new life but it's actually pretty easy. I tell myself if my parents could change countries without speaking the language, I can migrate too. I circle ads in the local paper and take down numbers from the bulletin board at the Laundromat, and hit a string of appointments to see a series of moldy, desolate concrete apartments in high-rises that sprouted during the housing boom and were left empty by the recession, some beachside motel efficiencies, and a couple of garden park trailers along the water that wobble under the slightest November breeze, forget about when the hurricanes come. But I know there has to be something better around here.

Before I left, a client from the job I quit back in the Gables told me to visit a friend of hers, Julie, a Canadian transplant who caught "Keys Disease" and decided to stay, running one of those shops on the Overseas Highway in Crescent Key that sell shined-up conch shells and mailboxes painted to look like flamingos. Crescent Key is one of the smallest islands, halfway down the boa of the Keys, between the marshes of Card Sound Road and the cruise ship crowds of Key West. It's small enough to feel like an afterthought of an island, one that most people driving down the Overseas Highway don't even notice passing through, but close enough to Marathon, one of the larger and more developed islands with big chain stores and twenty-four-hour pharmacies, and far enough from Carlito's prison for me to sometimes forget it's there.

"I heard you were coming," Julie smiles at me when I arrive, as if with her whole body, from her rumrunner-paunch to her perma-flushed cheeks.

My client vouched for me. Told Julie I was clean-living and responsible. Turns out her friend Louise Hartley is looking for just that sort of tenant for a cottage on her property, a former coco plum tree plantation on the tiny island of Hammerhead that breaks off just before the bridge at Crescent Key Cut.

Julie gives a call ahead and sends me right over to see her.

Mrs. Hartley is waiting on her pebbled driveway when I pull up. She's got straw-blond hair, wears waxy makeup, and is dressed in tennis whites. She wants to know if I've ever been arrested (no), if I do drugs (no), if I've got a husband or kids (no and no).

She leans in close and lowers her voice like she's hoping for a confession.

"You got a man on your tail? Maybe a boyfriend you're trying to keep away from? Anything like that?"

"There's nobody. Only me."

She twists her thin lips like she's still deciding on whether to give me a shot.

"You got a job down here yet?"

"I'll start looking once I'm settled."

"Where are you staying for now?"

"Up at the South Glades Motel."

"The one by the prison?"

I nod and she looks scandalized.

"Be careful. Lots of strange people pass through there. People you'll want to avoid, if you know what I mean."

I raise my eyebrows at the revelation.

"You got to get out of there, honey."

"That's what I'm trying to do."

"How do you plan on paying rent if you don't have a job lined up yet?"

"I've got some money saved."

"I'll need three months' rent up front."

"That's fine."

"All right then. Follow me."

She leads me down a path framed by banana trees and palms to a cottage on the far end of the property facing the ocean and a small dock.

"I should mention the cottage has never been rented out," Mrs. Hartley says, adding, in a tone that I think is supposed to resemble modesty, "Our family doesn't really need the money. We just want someone on this side of Hammerhead to keep out squatters or vandals who come in on boats through the canal. I'm here alone most of the time. My husband works in Philadelphia and only comes down a few times a year."

The vegetation is so thick it's almost eating the cottage, which is small and yellow, with white shuttered windows and a small veranda that opens onto a narrow beach. As we get closer, the sounds in the trees grow louder, caws, the rustling of animals crossing branches. I see two flecks of red swoop through a patch of light from one tree to another.

"Holy shit."

"Parrots," Mrs. Hartley tells me proudly. "We've got a few pairs. God only knows where they came from, but they've made themselves right at home. Like those huge iguanas you see around, the African rats, or even those pythons everyone's hunting in the Everglades. It's easy to forget what's natural to the area anymore."

The cottage is one room with a small bathroom built into a corner and a kitchenette along one wall, definitely a step up from the places I've seen so far. It comes furnished too, with wicker furniture and a double bed pushed into a corner. I won't have to take any of my own furniture out of storage. It's a relief to start fresh.

"Don't mind the stink," she says, opening up all the windows and doors, though I don't notice the faint smell of sewage till she points it out. "That's from outside. The tide's low and sometimes seaweed accumulates under the dock. It'll wash away soon. That's island living for you."

She watches me as I poke around, open cabinets and closet doors, peek out the window, see the ocean spread beyond the thicket of trees.

"The water pressure's good and the kitchen is stocked with more pots and pans than you'll probably ever need. You'll have to get a PO box in town and garbage collection is every Thursday by the main driveway. There are flashlights, flares, and a blow horn in the broom closet. You know, for the storms. But for most hurricanes we have mandatory evacuations. I assume you've got somewhere on the peninsula where you can go in that case."

I nod, though I'm not sure I do.

She works a little harder at the sell, but I know this is all I need.

My first night in the cottage, I wait to see what sounds fill the evening as the sun slips behind the Hammerhead coco plum forest into the gulf. I step out onto the veranda to get a dose of sunlight before nightfall and make my way down the stone path toward the small cove of beach. Beyond it, on the other side of a coral wall and past a row of leggy mangroves, the Hartley house towers over the shoreline.

A flock of pelicans glides over me, probably some of the dozens that gather to hunt for fish and rest their wings along the valley of wooden boat stumps by the bridge at Crescent Key Cut, landing on my dock as if it already belongs to them too.

I sit on the beach and stare out at the water. Facing east, the sun disappearing behind me, I watch the sea darken with shadows, feel the sand cool under my feet.

The ocean is different down here. On the mainland, the curling bay water is a deep blue and even on the shallow edges of shore it only clears to a pale green. The waves folding into the open ocean grow thicker and peak higher as you head farther north, a menacing rush in the current, the wind splitting waves that could push you under with the force of a hundred men.

Down here the tide is calm, pulsing softly even under a heavier wind. The water bleeds turquoise and only darkens out past the reefs.

I sleep with the window slats open, something I never would have done back home. I hear only the sounds of the night animals. Owls. The wrestling of branches by raccoons or possums. There are no police sirens. No car horns or screeching tires. No shouting neighbors. No arguments between the old couple living next door or screaming teens. No sounds of a creaking older house, leaking pipes, no rain beating on a roof in need of repairs. No television reporting the crimes of the city, no radio voices of late-night advice shows where people call in with their sad stories: the noise my mother relied on to fill our emptiness. No sounds of Mami in what used to be my brother's bedroom, on her knees at her homemade altar, saying prayers, making promises, bargaining with her saints to set us all free.

TWO

When Carlito was sixteen and had saved enough money working at the car wash to buy his own ten-year-old cockroach of a thirdhand Honda, he and his friends would pack in and drive up to the MacArthur Causeway where the paroled sex offenders had set up their own tent village since the law didn't let them live anywhere near parks or schools. If you drove past it, you'd never know there was a colony of ex-cons living there beneath the traffic, under tarps, cooking with mess kits over open flames. I saw the place myself once when Carlito dragged me there with him. He wanted to scare me because I was fourteen and the sort of girl who'd identify what others called *danger* and walk right into it just to see what would happen.

Like the time I went hitchhiking, the one thing they always warn kids about in school since society is full of predators and pedos. I'd gone to the mall to meet a boy who ditched me within the hour for a girl he met at the doughnut stand. I remember I was feeling sick that day, but it was another month before I'd figure out the fool had already gotten me pregnant. I only wanted to get home, but Mami was at work and Carlito, off in his new ride. It was before the age of cell phones and there was no way to reach him. So I walked out to Kendall Drive and put out a thumb. A shiny black Audi pulled up a few seconds later. I'd never been in a car so nice so I got in.

Sometimes you can tell a degenerate right away and other times they slip past even the most cynical folk. I didn't smell this guy's perviness until I popped into the seat next to him and the car was already rolling. Then it hit me heavy: the wetness of his grin, saliva gathering at the corners of his mouth, sweat forming on his lip and within the folds of his hands, which went right for my thighs, and it didn't help that I was in a short-shorts phase that summer. He asked where I was headed and I told him home, and to turn onto the Palmetto. He didn't, and next thing I knew we were flying down the Snapper Creek Expressway, his fingers inching into my crotch, and when I slapped them away, he took it as a tease and pushed farther.

When we slowed into some traffic, I pushed the door open and jumped out. I tumbled, concrete ripping my skin like cloth, and huddled against the highway divider. It's kind of a miracle I didn't get killed, but the bigger mystery is why nobody stopped to ask if I was okay or why I'd jumped out of a moving car.

I made the mistake of telling Carlito what had happened, and to scare me straight, like my torn-up elbows and legs weren't enough of a reminder, he took me to the sex offender colony to show me some real depravados. I knew he and his friends liked to go there to throw rocks and yell at the guys that they should be castrated. I thought that was cruel even if they were society's worst. I mean, you do the time, you should be able to get on with your life, but people are especially touchy when it comes to children.

When I mentioned it to Dr. Joe, the prison shrink I used to hang around with, he said maybe Carlito was projecting his anger toward our father onto those men since most of the ex-cons were old and run-down-looking, the way I imagined Hector would look if he were still alive. I don't think it goes that deep though. Those were years when Carlito and his posse of gangly bros would bench weights and beat speed bags in somebody's garage, roaming around Tropical Park at night, jumping people for kicks, not even for their wallets. Theirs was a casual violence, yet they managed never to get caught.

When we got to the sex offender camp that day, the boys started their usual taunts and I walked a few yards off while they went looking for targets because I didn't want the pervs to think I'd just come to be mean. They weren't so bad looking. Most of them appeared to be regular guys, like they could be somebody's sick grandfather or borracho uncle. A few were dressed pretty normal, in pants and button-down shirts, looking like they could live in a real house or something, but others resembled rag-wearing swamp people, crusty-haired with dirt tattoos on their faces. Most actually looked sort of gentle and sad to be there and didn't give me a second look as I toed the camp periphery. Only two or three did what you might expect and pulled out their penises when they saw me, but I was on their turf so you can't really blame them.

One of the guys walked over to me, asking me where I was from, and said he was originally from Mississippi and wanted to go back but he lost track of his family. I said that was unfortunate, but felt a yank on my arm and there was Carlito rudely pulling me away when the guy was just trying to tell me a piece of his story. Carlito called the guy a rapist, a pedophile, all kinds of things, and yelled at me the whole drive home for being such a tonta.

Both of us were the type who cracked up at horror movies. Monsters, demons possessing houses, masked killers. We thought it hysterical that there is an industry of artificial horror when real life is so much more lethal. The secret is real murderers look like anybody else and you might even have one living in your own home. For all you know, the person you love most in this world might one day try to kill you. But that day Carlito's goal was to teach me a lesson in practical fear and I had failed.

"What's wrong with you?" he sounded desperate to understand. "I take you to a zoo of psychos and you're trying to make friends like some kind of bobita? You're going to get yourself killed one day, Reina."

I was quiet, but I knew he was wrong, and that it was just the opposite. Making friends with danger is the only way to survive.

It's a good thing I didn't let myself become traumatized by the hitchhiking experience or Nesto and I never would have met. Though you can't really call what I did to meet him hitching. And he wasn't looking to pick anyone up.

I was at the full-moon party at the Broken Coconut, a beach bar where all the Crescent Key area locals hang out. Since my arrival, I've found the island population strangely skewed—a lost generation of North American retirees, and most of the younger folks are their children or grandchildren, down for a visit, or service industry people in life-limbo. Like Ryan, the lanky Nebraskan pool boy at the Starfish Club Hotel I'd gone to the bar with that night, whom I met when I got a job doing nails at the hotel spa. He was part of a tribe of recovering cruise ship employees and seasonal nomads buying time working as charter boat jockeys or in hotels and restaurants till they figured out their next move.

Maybe I misled Ryan, hanging out with him a few nights a week like we were on our way to becoming some kind of couple, even spending Thanksgiving together, along with the other holiday orphans right there at the Broken Coconut, eating conch fritters and blackened hogfish. But by then I'd been in the islands almost a month and with new winter darkness setting in early, I didn't have much else to fill my evenings.

All my years of solitude back home hadn't prepared me for this type of loneliness. Even being ignored or avoided in an unfriendly community is its own sort of companionship.

The night of the full-moon party, Ryan was especially grabby, pawing at my waist, my thigh, throwing his wormy lips close to my face. Until that night, he'd been careful with me, and I hadn't made myself easier for him like I sometimes do when I can tell a guy is moving slow. We hadn't even kissed, so the tension was high and maybe, if his approach had been different, though I'm not sure how, I would have been into it. Maybe I would have even let things get started there in the parking lot and gone home with him to the canal rental house he shared with four other guys, and slipped out in the morning in time for work. But something held me back.

I'd been reflecting as of late that in this new life down here in the Keys, I wanted to try things differently. So I told Ryan as kindly as I could that we were not going to fuck that night. He looked both defeated and angry, tried arguing that there was no reason not to and we both wanted it, but I insisted I didn't want it, *trust me, I really don't*, which insulted him and he left me alone on the bar stool while the herd of drunks tried to push past me with their plastic cups waiting for refills of rum punch.

I wove through the crowd to get out, but found my car was blocked into the parking lot by a dozen others, and there were no taxis on this end of the Overseas Highway. My cottage on Hammerhead was a few miles away, but it's not the kind of walk you want to take alone at night—*I'm* not even that bold—so I hung around the parking lot entrance for a while waiting to see if I could catch someone on the way out to give me a lift home.

That's when I saw Nesto walking through the moonlight toward his blue pickup, conveniently parked beside the road. I approached him. He was wary of me. I mean, who wouldn't be—a girl alone in the middle of the night asking for a ride— but he agreed with an accent my Miami education told me was distinctly Cuban, the freshly arrived kind, not yet watered down by years of exile, and in the sea of gringos that was the Broken Coconut that night, this somehow felt comforting.

Plus, stuck to his dashboard there was a small faded stamp of a little pilgrim child saint holding a staff that I recognized right away from a similar depiction Mami kept on a table in Carlito's old room.

"El Santo Niño de Atocha," I said when we got on our way, pointing to the mini Jesus. He was big in Colombia, especially for those who left the country, said to protect wanderers and travelers. He, San Antonio, and La Virgen del Carmen were the last santos Mami had petitioned for mercy and her son's freedom. Even if she'd disowned Carlito by day, she still prayed for him every night. My mother was especially devoted to this little guy because he was also said to be the patron saint of the imprisoned.

Nesto tipped his chin at me and shook his head. "No. That's Elegguá."

"Oh, I didn't know that."

I would have liked some conversation on that ride home, but he didn't offer much. I tried questions on him. I noticed he'd been dragging a pulley with a toolbox behind him when I found him in the parking lot, so I asked him about it and he told me he'd been at the bar to fix a pipe leak, not for the party.

"You're a plumber?"

"No. I just fix things."

"What kind of things?"

"Anything."

He turned onto the road to the Hartley estate on Hammerhead slowly, dimming his beams as we approached the main house.

I thanked him and hopped out of his truck onto the gravel path.

"How are you going to get to your car in the morning?" He asked as I started to walk off.

I shrugged. "The bus."

"I'll take you."

"You don't have to."

"I know. But I will."

Crescent Key is a small enough island that after a week or two, you'll see the same faces, and default to hello smiles at the familiar ones at the Laundromat, post office, and mini-mart, even though you've never properly met. But it's also the kind of place where you can go days without seeing a single nongringo, which doesn't mean there aren't any, it just means you can't see them.

I would have remembered Nesto Cadena's face if I'd ever seen him before. I thought about it early the next morning when I stepped out onto the dock behind my cottage. Though I sleep badly, awakened in the night by my own thoughts, I was never a naturally early riser in my old life. I was never late to work, and often had to open the salon, but it cost me to wake up early for another day of the same tired life.

Here, though, the sounds of the thicket around the cottage are gentle shoves and I wake up with the sun and birds, the morning dew slick on the planks of the veranda. The animals fall into a routine with me; the iguanas who live in the bushes discover the row of sliced grapes I leave for them along the path and I watch them peek out of the shrubbery and drag themselves over to their treat.

That morning, I stood out on the dock behind the cottage, watching a couple of lionfish—another invasive species Mrs. Hartley warned me to watch out for, since they're poisonous—whirl around its posts, and then two dolphins as they folded through the current in the distance.

An old sport-fishing boat belonging to one of the neighbors down the canal came puttering out of the inlet toward the open water, a burly bearded guy behind the wheel.

He waved as he passed me standing on my pier, and his beard parted with a grin.

"Beautiful morning."

"You just missed the dolphins." It seemed like the neighborly thing to say. They'd disappeared with the buzzing of his boat coming out of the waterway.

"I know where to find them." He tilted his head toward the sun. "There's a whole nation just a few miles out."

A little while later, I headed down the path from the cottage to the driveway hoping Nesto would come through with the ride he'd offered me the night before. Where I usually parked my car, I spotted the blue truck, Nesto leaning on the edge of the hood.

I paused on the path before he noticed me coming, enjoying the sight of him for the first time in daylight.

I can tell you what he tells me now: his blood is wildly blended, the product of generations of clandestine encounters until it came down to his mother, the morena-mestiza from whom he inherited his wide smile and a bronzed complexion he likens to seven-year añejo rum, and his father, a guajiro from whom he got his sharp nose and slanted black Taíno eyes.

My mother often said she was grateful that neither of her children carried any of their father's features. In fact, we both looked so much like her, with her small eyes and small mouth, high forehead, and heavy brows, she joked it was as if we had no father and she'd had us alone.

Nesto wears his hair in ropey locks tied together by a band, whipping across his shoulder blades, hair he says he started growing long the moment he began to plan his defection and will only cut the day ese, el barbudo Fidel, finally dies. He's tall and muscular, with strong legs because he says milk was still plentiful when he was growing up, not like after the Soviets pulled out of the island and everything became scarce.

We're both of the invented Caribbean, Nesto says, a Nuevo Mundo alchemy of distilled African, Spaniard, Indian, Asian, and Arab blood, each of us in varying mixtures. He likes to compare our complexions, putting his arm next to mine, calls me "canelita, ni muy tostada ni muy blanquita," showing off his darkness, proof, his mother told him, of his noble Yoruba parentage and brave cimarron ancestors, la raza prieta of which he should be proud no matter how much others have resisted mestizaje, hanging onto the milky whiteness of their lineage like it's their most precious commodity.

It makes me think of my grandmother and the way she would have me stand on the wooden stepping block in her apartment so she could measure me for dresses she'd make me, how she'd examine me, warn me against sitting in the sun so I wouldn't darken my already trigueña skin; she'd pick at my hair, "coarse as a rat's, black as azabache," she'd say, just like my mother's and a remnant of our Karib roots, complaining, in the way of her generation, that such evidence of our family's past would take generations for the bloodline to clear.

"Nobody cares about my rat hair in the United States," I'd tell Abuela.

She'd shake her head at me. "You *think* they don't care, Reinita. But believe me, they do."

My grandmother was poor. We have only ever been poor, any way you look back at those who came before us. But Abuela was ashamed of that fact and often tried to pass herself off as de mejor familia because she somehow shared a last name with one of the most distinguished families of Cartagena. But Mami says people borrow and steal last names all the time, "as easy as a Santero stealing a Mass," and a fancy last name doesn't mean anything anymore; the only thing that proves where you really come from is your blood.

That first morning, Nesto was waiting for me with a plastic cup in hand. He gave it to me. I saw it was filled with thick orange liquid.

"I brought this for you. It's guarapo de caña. Try it."

I'd had sugarcane juice before and didn't like it, but I accepted it, because Nesto was smiling, all his chunky teeth on display, and told me about the old guy in the trailer park where he lived, who takes the bus up to the Mexican market in the Redlands every weekend just so he can buy real caña to make guarapo for himself and for his Caribbean friends, to ease the homesickness, la añoranza.

I had some time before I had to be at the spa and Nesto was still waiting for his first repair call of the day, so we stopped by Conchita's. Conchita is a dominicana who sells coffee, pastries, and sandwiches from a little shop she built out of her front porch complete with a few tables in the adjacent yard. She's married to a Coast Guard guy who's never around and you can often catch her having full conversations with the chickens and stray cats that hang out on her property. I bought Nesto a cafecito of gratitude for delivering me home the night before, then back to my car today.

That morning, I noticed the pale seams of scars around his fingers, thick as cigars. In our initial weeks as friends he would tell me his body was all marked up with clues of his youth, pointing out the map of history all over his body. His leathery feet, rough from years of playing basketball on the concrete cancha because there was only one pair of sneakers passed around among all the boys of his barrio and he never had the patience to wait his turn, his toes scarred from cuts and infections. His knuckles chafed, palms callused, from fixing, fixing—*inventando*, he calls it—using wires from a bicycle tire to repair the ignition on a 1952 Chevrolet, breaking down rocks to turn into fresh cement to repair a collapsed wall, or stealing bricks from an abandoned factory in Marianao to turn one room into two, two rooms into three, to accommodate his home's growing population; fine purplish lines and keloid tracks marking where a mismanaged blade or a jumped fence pierced his skin.

"Look at you," he said to me when he grew more comfortable around me, telling me the stories of some of his marks, taking my wrist between his fingers and holding up my arm as if inspecting me. "It's like you've been living in a glass case all your life. No marks, no scars whatsoever. How is that possible?"

"Oh, I have plenty," I said, amused because nobody's ever thought me perfect in any way.

Even though Carlito once told me our father used to hit us bad—even me, and I was just a tiny baby—I don't have any memory of it, and no evidence on the flesh to make me wonder.

From the day I hitchhiked, when I jumped out of the perv's car, I've only got a tender, shadowy patch that shrank to the size of a quarter on my knee where the pavement dug into my bone. Other than that, it's kind of funny how immaculate I am.

I pushed my hair back to show Nesto where my father sliced my ear to break the curse he was convinced I carried.

"What is that from?"

"My father marked me. They said I was an abikú."

"Is that so?" He looked surprised though he didn't ask me to explain.

I nodded.

"That can't be your only scar."

"I have more."

"Where are they?"

"They're the kind you can't see."

When Carlito was still among the living, I'd drive back up from my weekend visiting him down at the Glades and find my mother waiting for me at home on Sunday night with some warmed-over dinner, usually just back herself from a weekend with her boyfriend. It was the only day of the week she cooked. She wasn't a talented chef. Her meals were always the same: sancocho that would last us for days, or some kind of fried fish or pork with arroz con coco, and maybe some empanadas or carimañolas she picked up at a bakery on the way home.

We'd sit together at the kitchen table, and she'd tell me about the nice restaurants Jerry took her to up in Orlando, show me things he bought her, brag about the promises he made to buy her a new car, a new wardrobe, to take her to Rome so she could finally see Saint Peter's Square. She never asked about Carlito. We'd made an agreement years before that I wouldn't talk to her about him, even to relay the messages he'd ask me to send her, his pleading questions about how a mother could forget her son, deny him, turn her back on him—he said it was as unnatural as murder. She'd just stare at me when I walked through the door and tell me I looked tired, stroke my hair, and set my plate on the table before me.

Sometimes the visits were particularly tough, like when Carlito would tell me about days he spent in "the hole," a solitary confinement even worse than the one he was already used to, in an empty, unlit, windowless cell with nothing but his hands to talk to. He got sent there for fighting with a guard who taunted him as he pushed the food cart down the death row hall every morning around five, saying, "Enjoy the taste of my piss in your grits, Castillo," as he slid Carlito's breakfast through the door slot, purposely breaking the plastic spork that came with it. The same guard who complimented the thickness of my lips when I came to visit, saying he'd like to see what I could do with them, and who once left a note for me at the Glades Motel front desk saying that he'd like to take me out sometime.

I can guess what sort of things he said to provoke my brother into trying to attack him with his bare hands while being led to the shower room in handcuffs. The thought of my brother crouched on the dirty floor of a prison dungeon made me ill for days but I never told Mami about these things because it's not what she wanted.

I never understood how she could cast Carlito away, forgetting he was the baby she'd coddled and kissed, fed from her breast, and whom she always favored above me.

I wished she could be more like Isabela, almost pathological in her grace, sending Carlito a birthday card every year saying she knew that beyond his hardened heart, he was still the boy she once loved and believed she'd marry, and she forgave him for killing her daughter.

My mother was a woman who was capable of performing happiness no matter what. There were times when I knew she felt sorrow, her body withering away from anxiety, but she put on her painted smiling face and no stranger could guess what she carried within. Only I knew. But she never permitted the kind of closeness that would allow us to commiserate, to help each other, to give each other strength. We were each on our own.

Now, instead of meeting me in the kitchen with a plate of food on a Sunday night, she gives me a phone call. She always calls on the cottage line and rarely my cell phone since the reception is spotty out here on Hammerhead.

She says she wants to know that I'm okay.

"It's not normal for a girl to be living on her own in the middle of nowhere, Reinita."

She thinks I should move to a city, somewhere where there are cultured people, people going places, and I know she means people with money.

"Have you met anyone?"

"I've made a few friends." I'm lying, and my mother knows it. We can leverage men well enough, and maybe keep a few women as acquaintances, but never real friends. The only contender here is Nesto, who, so far, hasn't made a move on me, which makes me both grateful and suspicious. But maybe that's how real friends happen.

I watch him sitting on my sofa, thumbing through an old copy of *National Geographic* from a stack that was in a corner of the cottage when I moved in. I twist the plastic telephone cord around my finger while my mother moves on to the next item on her agenda: Nochebuena.

"We're expecting you. I hope you can stay with us at least a few days this time."

"I don't think I can get the time off from the spa."

"Nobody works on Christmas."

"It's a hotel. They're open every day, and I just started. I can't go taking vacation days anytime I want."

In truth, I haven't even tried asking for the day off and I don't plan to. Mami knows I'm no fan of Jerry, whose real name is Jerónimo. He came over from Puerto Rico as a teenager but when he's around people he deems real gringos, pretends he doesn't speak Spanish, as if English is the language of the gods. He treats his generic townhouse like a palace, shoes off upon entry, constantly running his finger over ledges, checking for dust the weekly cleaning lady or my mother might have left behind. He's no beauty either, a real carechimba with smushed features like they put him facedown at birth, and teeth veneers that look like he bought them at a hardware store.

"So you'll spend Christmas all alone?"

I've still got an eye on Nesto, absorbed by some photo spread on orangutans.

"I'll figure something out."

There's a pause. The obvious thing would be for my mother to offer to visit me, see how her daughter lives, spend a little time together during the holidays. But I know Jerry won't travel this far for me and Mami has entered the stage in which she's reluctant to go too far for too long without her man. Age has made her a little paranoid. Ahora que consiguió marrano, no way is she going to risk letting him get away.

Instead she changes the subject. She tells me Jerry's been saying this might be the year he finally proposes to her. Why he'd bother is a wonder. She's already as wifey as she's ever going to be, and it bugs me how he hangs it over her, like having to serve his pinga for life is some kind of honor.

Mami never had a real wedding—not the kind you celebrate. She was nineteen when Hector claimed her in Cartagena and she was already pregnant with Carlito when they had their marriage ceremony at a church in Barranquilla, where nobody knew them. There was no party because her mother thought it shameful that Mami was already showing barriga. Now, with Carlito gone, there's no reason to remember that day, and at fifty, she might finally get her dream of wearing a white gown. She's talking venues and color schemes, never mind that she's got hardly anyone to invite. She says I'll be her maid of honor. She'll buy me a special dress and everything. I want to tell her that we are not that kind of family. We're not of rituals or celebrations. We are people who live day by day. But I remain silent.

When we hang up, I sigh long and look out the window to the darkness over the ocean, no delineation between water and sky. It's always disorienting when I speak to my mother, that pull of her voice back into our old life even though both of us have tried to move beyond it.

In her soft Caribbean accent I hear my brother's laughter, see us both as children playing together in the backyard when it was still covered in crunchy green grass and our toys were new.

Mami's voice was the song of our home, even with no father, even as we lived with that black mass of the unspoken, even with the marks on our bones we didn't know we carried.

Through all life's uncertainty, we felt anchored by the love in her voice.

Carlito worshipped her, always picking flowers for her, and when he was old enough, stealing jewelry for her from the local Walmart and later even nicer stores. He never dreamed that one day she would take her love away from him, that the love of a mother is not unconditional or eternal the way they say.

The voice we were raised with, the voice that lulled us through the night, was just a voice, not a promise or a prayer.

Mami was just a woman trying to take care of two kids she'd had by a man she hated. That's all.

"¿Todo bien?" Nesto asks from behind me when I hang up the phone.

I turn to him and nod. "Yeah. Everything's fine."

He made his own Sunday family phone call this morning. I met him for coffee at Conchita's and then waited for him by the post office as he used a phone card to call Cuba from a pay phone. I watched him lean into the vestibule, press his fingers to his temples, his hands moving animatedly at one point, and then his head sink while he nodded as if the person he was talking to could see him. When he came back to me at the plastic table where I was sitting, I'd asked the same thing. "¿Todo bien?"

He smiled but sighed. "Normal. Everything is *normal.*"

"Come on, Reina," Nesto says to me now. "Let's go for a walk."

We step down the stone path toward the beach. There's no wind so the December chill doesn't penetrate our clothing. We walk to the water's edge, stand on the wet sand, hard from the low tide, cold through my sneaker soles.

Nesto lives on the beach too, over on the northeast end of Crescent Key, in one of those trailer park motels I checked out when I first arrived, a single-occupancy efficiency in the main building with little furniture but a great view of the open Atlantic. The only problem is that the property is full of drunks and drifters, each night is a symphony of arguments and shouts, and he always wakes up to a garden of broken bottles.

He likes my little chunk of the Hammerhead peninsula better. Out here it's like the world forgot us, or like we can forget the world.

I sit on a mound of dry sand while Nesto walks along the shoreline, as if looking for a road with which to cross the water.

"Reina. Can I ask you why you came down here? I mean, why did you leave where you're from?"

It takes me a moment to respond. We've managed to talk around certain things so far, but I decide to try the truth tonight, or at least a part of it.

"I had no reason to stay after . . ."

"After what?"

"After my brother died."

"How did he go?"

I like the way he says it, as if Carlito just left on a trip and might still return.

"He killed himself. Our father went the same way. And our father's father too."

He nods as if he's not all that surprised.

"How . . . how did . . ."

"My brother? He hanged himself." I leave out that the pipe he used belonged to a prison. "Our grandfather hanged himself too."

"And your father?"

"He slit his throat."

Nesto draws in his breath. I can tell he's trying not to look shocked for my sake.

"So they're good with ropes and knives, the men in your family."

"Good enough, I guess."

"You must be descended from sailors . . . or mercenaries."

"All I know is that mother says I come from a long line of bastards on both sides."

"We all do."

He leans over and dips his palms into the tide, pulls them out, and runs his wet fingers over his face and hair, water dripping off his shoulders like feather plumes.

He walks back over to me and bends over, touching one hand to my cheek so I can feel how cold the water is on his skin.

"You know why I came down here, Reina?" He steps back toward the water.

"To get away," I say, figuring Crescent Key is the kind of place people just turn up, coughed up from some other broken life.

"No. I came to get closer."

"To what?"

"To there." He points to the black horizon. There is no moon tonight. "Home."

There's the sudden rumble of thunder above us. Nesto looks to the sky and raises a hand, then brings it back down to cover his heart.

"Bendición, Changó."

He turns to me with a wide smile.

"That thunder means he hears me."

When Carlito was first taken into custody, to punish myself for being the one who pushed him into his madness, I didn't let myself sleep. I closed the door to my room so my mother would think I'd gone to bed, but I'd sit in a chair in the center so that I couldn't even tilt my head back to lean against a wall. Sometimes I dozed off. So I became stricter with myself, tying a string around my neck connected to the ceiling fan, taut, so if I slumped over into sleep, the tug on my neck would wake me up. But sometimes nothing could stop me, and I'd fall into a walking sleep during a break between clients at work. My boss took me aside and asked if I was on drugs. I realized this might jeopardize my source of income, so I decided to find another way to punish myself: I stopped eating.

I was satisfied by my silent hunger strike for a while. The pangs pass, the mind settles into a soft fuzz that buffers you from the world around you. My flesh shrank, my features sharpened, but these are things people compliment in women, so nobody noticed I'd only wanted to imprison myself in solidarity with my brother.

I felt Carlito's hunger in the county jail where he was held without bail until his trial because the judge considered him a flight risk, and then when he was moved down south to the prison. I felt his disgust every time he looked at a plate of prison food, some of which Dr. Joe once told me came from bags and barrels marked NOT FOR HUMAN CONSUMPTION.

I felt the inescapable noise of intercoms and alarms and howls and whispers permeating the prison walls and bars that kept him from ever getting real sleep, the hard boot steps of the guards checking his cell every fifteen minutes, the fluorescent overhead lights that never went completely out.

I stopped bathing as much to keep up with the three ten-minute showers my brother was permitted per week.

Even as I eventually let myself sleep, I kept the lights on in my bedroom to remind myself of my brother's suffering and often only let myself rest on the floor because my brother slept on a thin plastic-coated pad set on a concrete slab with only a prickly blanket for cover.

I had a fear of forgetting, as if I ever could.

I saw my mother, with her patchwork amnesia about our father, the way she tossed out memories of Carlito too, and I thought, *someone has to remember*, for the sake of our family, if only to tell someone else one day what was, what could have been, and what never will be again.

And there were the dreams.

I think I was born having nightmares. My mother tells me I refused to sleep as a baby, fighting off fatigue by crying until my body gave out, and even then, my sleep was always short-lived and I'd awake in screams, a look of terror on my face.

The nightmares have stayed with me all my life, but I'm not afraid of them anymore, like an old film on repeat, scenes from our family's darkest moments: a baby dropping from a bridge, my brother's face when he received his death sentence, the sounds of our mother's wails filling our house.

Sometimes I dream of my father. Though in the dreams he's not my father but a man who looks like him and is calling my name from far away.

I dream of the old house; me, a child, sitting on the dirt patch my mother called a garden even though it refused to give her any flowers, digging into the soil with a plastic shovel, pulling out worms and lining them up as if I were reuniting them. Sometimes I would dare myself to eat dirt. Mami warned us that children who ate dirt grew up to be crazy, but I did it anyway, stuffing a handful into my mouth, telling myself she would never know.

I dream of Cartagena. Of playing in the grimy streets with my brother, of him leading me by the hand up the hidden steps to the roof of Abuela's building where the whole city stretched out in front of us and we could see as far as La Matuna and Getsemaní. Or when he'd take me down to the third floor to spy on Doña Gabriela, who had regular male visitors. From the stairwell we could hear them grunting, pounding against the furniture, and we'd laugh and imitate them, watch the men as they came out of the apartment and wobbled down the stairs rubbing sweat from their foreheads with a kerchief, and then we'd give them dirty looks when we saw them at Mass at Santo Toribio on Sunday mornings, sitting among the church pews with their wives and children, and receiving Communion.

I dream of my grandmother. How she used to sew blouses for me with embroidered flowers on puffy sleeves while my mother watched, and when the blouses were finished and she gave them to me to wear, she would tell me she loved me better than anyone else in the world while my mother looked on, shaking her head.

For years, when we were small, Mami would talk about going back to Cartagena to live, as if this North American life were just some interlude and we ended up here by accident. But when we'd ask, "When, Mami? When are we moving back?" she would never give an answer. When Abuela died, instead of keeping her apartment in the family like Carlito and I begged her to do, Mami sold it and said now there was no need for us to ever return.

I didn't miss Cartagena anymore in my waking life, but in my sleep I still longed for it, and sometimes wandering those city walls in my dreams was the only peace I got.

In the old house in Miami, I'd wake with the feeling of a hand on my chest, my eyes open to the murky blue half-light of my bedroom. Everything quiet, though still feeling noise all around me, through my ears, behind my eyes, under my skin.

In the cottage, I fall asleep slowly, counting the sounds of the night animals—crickets, frogs, squealing raccoons, a cat in heat somewhere beyond the coco plum trees.

But mine is still a loneliness that shakes me from my sleep.

I can forget my solitude all day, through my working hours, through errands, the evening housecleaning ritual I've made up for the cottage.

Yet night remains a tomb, when I'm most vulnerable, lying down for rest without distraction.

Only this body and that darkness, the whispers of the never-ending noche:

You belong to no one. No one belongs to you.

Nesto says he never knew silence until he came to this country, that there is no quiet to be found in Havana. In his barrio of Buenavista in the high folds of the Playa district, he lived in a concrete house that tunneled from the street down a long corridor with a patio and garden running alongside it, home to a mango and an avocado tree. It was a good house, he says, in a not-so-good neighborhood, a reparto people would never go to if they didn't have to. The house had belonged to his mother's father, who owned a grocery store until it was seized by the Revolution. But he and his family had been eager to support what was then believed to be a democratic turning of the tide, certain it would be an improvement from life under Batista, when streets in every neighborhood echoed with screams from the dictator's secret torture chambers, bodies of the executed left lying on sidewalks for days as warnings against dissent.

For submitting to the cause and keeping in line with the new property redistribution policy, the family was able to remain in their house in Buenavista if they gave up their beach cottage in Guanabo, and it became Nesto's mother's, where she lived through three marriages, three children, and now, three grandchildren. Nesto says it was a malleable enough house, like everything else in Cuba. Walls could be added to make more rooms, the long house extending, growing wider, like bacteria: a second floor added above, a separate entrance created to make room for the widowed aunts, the children and cousins displaced by divorce and broken affairs. Just like that, a simple family house becomes a commune, full of voices, footsteps, doors opening and closing, and outside, a row of houses enduring the same overcrowding, a simple street becoming its own restless city.

He says life in Havana was a series of house swaps, permutas, since buying or selling property was still illegal, and he'd only left his mother's home in Buenavista to move a few streets away, to live in the house that belonged to the family of his new wife, who he married at nineteen.

"You're married?"

I'm surprised he hasn't mentioned it until now, though maybe I shouldn't be.

We're sitting on the deck outside the Lobster Bay Inn, picking over our last bits of stone crab from the permanent all-you-can-eat seafood buffet. It's an obnoxious spread made even tackier by holiday lights, miniature snowmen adorning the display, employees in Santa hats; artificial reminders that it's holidays season in the tropics.

"I *was* married. It ended a long time ago."

Before I can ask anything further, he turns the question on me.

"Have you ever been married?"

"No way." I don't know why I'm embarrassed by the question.

"Nobody ever wanted to marry you?"

He's teasing me and I know it. I turn away from his grin to a table of tubby tourists with plates piled high with crab legs and seafood slaw.

"No," I say, coolly. "Nobody ever wanted to marry me."

He pinches my arm the way Carlito used to do to get my attention.

"I'm sure somebody wanted to marry you. You just didn't know it."

Later, I follow him back to his place, where we sit on the patio outside his door, on a pair of shaky plastic chairs planted half in the sand facing the ocean. It's getting chilly so he lends me a sweatshirt so I won't have to go back to my car for mine. He's been anxious because there's hardly been any work for him this week—few calls for anything to be fixed. And this is the high season, just before the holidays. If it's this quiet now, he worries about what will happen when the snowbirds go back up north. He lives simply and frugally enough that I wouldn't have thought it an issue until he tells me about the clan of people he supports back home, waiting for their monthly remittances.

I say something about hearing that everything—food and necessities—is provided for over there, but his expression dims and he says that's a myth, what's provided by the government is only enough to keep hearts beating, not to keep people from hunger or from suffering through sickness.

"That's not a life." His voice falls so low I can barely hear it over the tide. "It's not a life at all."

When it's dark, he shows me his room, a block carved out of a row of identical efficiency apartments, with a low ceiling, gray as a puddle. His bed, a futon covered with a blanket and a coverless pillow, an old armchair pushed into a corner beside a stack of worn books. A guitar rests upright in a corner and I notice a small stack of photos atop the sole wooden dresser.

The bareness between the painted-over concrete walls reminds me of how I've always imagined my brother lived during his years away from us. But Nesto has a pair of windows. Carlito told me all he had was a three-inch-wide slat carved out of the thick wall angled toward one of the gun towers. He could only see out of it if he stood on the toilet and crooked his neck so far to the left he thought it might snap.

I sink into Nesto's armchair while he pours me a glass of coconut water made by the same old guy who prepared the guarapo de caña, then fumbles through his only cabinet to see what else he can offer me to eat even though I insist I'm not hungry.

"I'm guessing she was pregnant," I say.

"Who was pregnant?"

"Your wife." The word *wife* feels strange on my lips. "I mean, the girl you married."

I try to sound half-bored by the topic already, not like it's something I haven't stopped thinking about since he mentioned it at the restaurant.

He nods. "She was."

"You're a father."

"I am."

"To how many?"

"Two. A boy and a girl."

"Both with her?"

He laughs. "Yes, both with her."

I watch him shake a bag of plantain chips onto a plate. He brings it over to me and finds a place on the floor at my feet, his legs crossed.

I can't picture him holding a child.

Nesto is thirty-five. Seven years older than I am now. As night seems to swallow the ocean outside his window, I wonder what he was like at nineteen, the age he became a father. I listen as he tells me about the girl who was his high school love, whom he'd first met at fifteen during one of his required stints at Escuela al Campo when the whole school was transplanted to the Pinar del Río province for forty-five days of tending govern-ment crops—potatoes, coffee, strawberries, tomatoes—farming for the State in exchange for their "free" education.

"Yanai was so pretty even the teachers were trying to be with her. I was a skinny, shy thing. And she was much whiter than I was. Not as white as an egg, more like flan or bread crust. But still much lighter than me and people always reminded her of this—'¿Qué tú quieres con ese tinto?'—I didn't think she would ever want to be with me. But she did."

By eighteen, he'd grown into an athlete, went to do his mili-tary service, and was assigned to guarding the gate of a general's home in El Laguito, where mansions once inhabited by Havana's wealthiest families were now the homes of pinchos, high-ranking military officials. It was during a visit home, in his second year of service, that Yanai became pregnant. Their mothers agreed they should marry and he and Yanai agreed, for the sake of the baby—a son they'd call Sandro after a Brazilian musician Nesto once saw perform—and because they loved each other enough, and because there was no reason not to.

They tried for ten years to sustain their marriage, through occasional separations, and had their daughter, Camila, until he eventually left Yanai's house for good and went back to live with his mother and family in Buenavista.

I thought of my own life and the times I'd been pregnant, and the men, most of them boys at the time, who made those never-born babies with me.

When I was eighteen, Carlito took me to the clinic. He thought it was my first time but it was really my third. Until the very last minute before they called me in he tried to convince me to keep the baby. He said we could raise it together, that as a family, we'd been through harder things.

"A baby will brighten things, Reina. Maybe it's your destiny."

"Fuck destiny," I said, and he warned me not to tempt bad fortune by talking that way.

Till he got locked up, Carlito was a churchgoing guy. First, with Mami, even when I refused to go with them, then with Isabela and her daughter. They'd sit side by side in one of the front pews. The perfect little family.

"Don't you ever want to be a mom?" Carlito asked me that day.

"Not by some huevón who won't even talk to me now."

When it was over, he drove me home and helped me into bed. I slept for two days.

"¿Y a esa qué le pasa?" Mami asked.

Carlito lied, told her I'd eaten some rotten bistec and just to make me some caldo to settle my stomach.

With Nesto in front of me, talking about his family, I consider for a moment all the times I might have created a family of my own, and where I would be now if I'd let that happen.

The only certain thing is that I wouldn't be here now, on this island, with him.

"Why did you leave them to come here?" I ask. "Your children, I mean."

"I didn't leave them. I just took the first step. So I can throw out the rope and they can come behind me."

Nesto left Cuba three years ago but he tells me he'd been trying to get off the island long before that. Like so many, he says, he was just waiting to find a way.

As a boy he'd dive with the other kids from the rocks below the Malecón, practicing holding their breath underwater, counting the seconds, the minutes that passed, timing each other, seeing how deep each could go, vowing one day they'd be brave enough to swim to La Yuma on the other side of the Straits.

But life passes quickly, he tells me, even when the days are all the same—*especially* when the days are all the same.

One day he was already a man, sitting on the same seawall, watching the younger boys launch themselves from the rocks below as he'd done, taking in the ocean, that slippery surf, thinking of those who died trying to cross, many of whom were the parents, uncles, brothers, and friends of people he knew, who left the island full of hope yet never made it across the water.

His generation had been raised on horror stories of how bad it was in other countries, how the world, particularly the yanquis, hated Cubans, and if they were to leave and actually make it to a foreign land, they'd only suffer and starve and beg to come back. But by then their assets would have been seized, their identities erased, and in Cuba, the land they'd forsaken, they would no longer exist.

Through the whispers of Radio Bemba, they heard when bodies washed up on the beaches, bodies of those who tried to get away and failed, and the people who would drift for days in the open sea and touch land only to realize the serpentine current had played with them, taking them far out only to deposit them on another part of the island.

They'd hear how the fattest sharks in the world are the ones swimming between their island and the Florida shores. Havana's cemetery is not the Cementerio Colón, he told me; its real necropolis is the ocean floor, covered with the bones of those who went to rest with Olokun, orisha of the deep.

Even so, when the rods and planks of broken balsas smashed against the rocks or turned up on the sand, and even though getting caught trying to leave could get you a year in prison, it wouldn't be long before someone picked up the scraps of those broken rafts and used them to build another.

Nesto was a good swimmer, with strong limbs and large lungs. He knew about tides and currents, and could read clouds and wind as easily as the alphabet. But he respected the sea too much to challenge it.

If you go to the city of Regla, Nesto says, you will find people at the church of the Virgin that keeps vigil over the Havana harbor, placing flowers at her altar, asking Yemayá, orisha of the living part of the sea, to help them find a way across. Nesto went there himself many times.

"But if Yemayá answered every petition that came to her feet," he tells me, "the island would be empty."

Both his parents were teenagers when the rebels came out of the Sierra Maestra, and they grew into faithful socialists. They were believers in the dreams and promises of the Revolution and wanted their children to grow up with blind devotion to the regime. His mother went from being a grocer's daughter to joining the literacy brigades in the campo to teach peasants how to read, and later working for the Ministry of Agriculture, helping to broker sugarcane deals with Canada and the Eastern Bloc. His father, the guajiro who joined the army after the cows of the family he worked for in the campo were nationalized, proudly went to battle in Angola and made it back alive only to die a few months later in a crash while riding in the sidecar of his brother's motorcycle. Nesto was seven. The family conspired to hide the truth. For the funeral week, he'd been sent to stay at the home of a cousin in Alamar. For another year, the family would collectively lie, saying that Nesto's father had gone back to Angola. Until he thought to ask, "Is my father dead?" and his mother reluctantly nodded yes.

They'd always been a proud communist family. Like everyone else.

"I didn't have a father so people said I should think of Fidel as my father," Nesto says. "And I was a good little pionero. I studied my Russian lessons in school. I wore my blue scarf with pride and couldn't wait until I got old enough to wear the red one. Like every other kid, I chanted ¡Por el comunismo, seremos como el Che! and I believed those words. I wanted to be like him, so brave and intelligent and charming, a hero who died for his ideals. I was named Ernesto for him, after all. It was the most honorable name you could give a boy in those days. Now it's the name I'm embarrassed to have. But at least I didn't get stuck with a Russian name like my sisters and many of my friends."

His parents had dutifully abandoned God for the State, as was encouraged. They were exactly the kind of young people the Revolution hoped for—soon bewitched by the teachings of Marx and the doctrine of Lenin, devout believers in the promises the regime made for the future of the island—and thought there was nothing old religions could offer anymore. But Nesto's grandmother was a follower of La Regla de Ocha and had managed to have him and his sisters baptized Catholic as babies, even if Christmas was still illegal, and eventually paid for him to go to a babalawo and receive his orishas when he was sixteen even though his mother was opposed to it.

That's how Nesto learned he'd been claimed by the orisha Elegguá, controller of destiny, and by the warrior Ogún, protector of orphans and orisha of tools and labor. The babalawo divined that Elegguá would show Nesto his path and Ogún, machete in hand, would help him to clear it. From a Santero he received his collares, elekes, beads of devotion, black and red for Elegguá, and black and green for Ogún, which he now wears around his neck so they fall over his heart.

An iyalocha later told Nesto, through a divination guided by Orunmilá, that his future lay on the other side of the sea and the orishas would help him find a way to cross it.

She said he was lucky to be claimed by Elegguá, identified as the Anima Sola, the lonely spirit, one of the souls suffering in purgatory, enduring purification by flames until being freed to heaven, because for Nesto there would be struggles too, she warned, but in the end, there would be salvation, and the promise of paradise beyond his dreams.

There are ways to get here, Nesto tells me, beyond the balsa. A ride on a boat ferrying people across the Florida Straits would have cost an impossible ten thousand U.S. dollars in a peso economy, and he didn't have anyone abroad who could pay it for him. Even if granted an exit permit, a legitimate visa through the U.S. Interests Section took years to process through waitlists and bureaucratic delays. The rumor was the twenty-thousand-visa quota was more likely filled by white Cubans rather than Afro-Cubans and the only way to move ahead in the line was with bribes.

"As we say over there, in Cuba one has to wait in line even to die."

Even with the long-gone relatives in Miami filing the paperwork for him on the other side, Nesto knew that boys like him—healthy, strong—were rarely given permission to leave, too obvious a risk for immigration, and the aging Revolution needed its youth.

He still played basketball almost every day on the un-paved, rock-pitted court a few streets from his family's house in Buenavista, shooting at a backboard with no hoop. One day the priest from the church where Nesto sometimes went for English classes came looking for him. He told Nesto the church's basketball team had been invited to play in an inter-diocesan tournament in Mexico City.

Nesto understood what the priest was offering.

He played the match, helped the church team win, and defected the night of their victory, thanking and saying good-bye to the priest, who also showed Nesto the way to sneak out of the dormitory. He slept on church steps and park benches until he made his way to Matamoros, where he walked across the border to Brownsville, identifying himself as Cuban at the customs office, and was given asylum.

From there he bused it to Miami, where his father's eldest brother, who'd fled in the sixties, waited for him at the station, took him to buy clothes, showed him around, and helped him find a job with a friend repairing air conditioners and refrigera-tors in the bodegas and cafeterias of Sweetwater and Hialeah.

He made some friends. Guys who taught him how to open a bank account and write a check, taught him about credit and car payments and insurance, and how to use the Internet—things he never had to think about back home. They were guys he would play basketball with on Saturdays at José Martí Park, who spoke the same chabacanería spoken back home, who took him to see bands perform at Cuban clubs, who introduced him to their sis-ters and other girls also from La Habana—some recently arrived, some who came as children, though they rarely encountered the ones born here to long-settled exiles, those who, when he did meet them, mostly looked down on him for being the son of failed communists, a little Soviet puppet, un recién llegado, a reffy, un cubano más.

He was supposed to be an exile now, too, but didn't feel like one.

Maybe, he says, because he left the greatest pieces of himself back home.

There were things he liked about Miami: the quimbe and cambalache, the way things could be bartered and traded in daily negocios just as they were back in Havana, a stand-in economy of exchanges and favors, and anything else could be found for cheap at ¡Ñooo! ¡Qué barato!, or the Opa-Locka market and the local pulgueros. But there was much that shocked him: the abundance of electricity, the entire city lit up through the night, where the government doesn't cut the power with no warning; the excess of American supermarkets, so much of everything, so much going to waste.

Sometimes he ran into people from home who'd crossed over before him, already settled with new houses and new families, who seemed so content with their lives over here that they didn't give much thought anymore to all they'd left behind.

Miami was just as described back home: "Cuba con Coca-Cola." He liked the sight of fresh paint on buildings and homes, how it seemed there was a factory-fresh car for every person to drive on the smooth paved roads of Miami, lined with palms and working streetlights, everything so new it was as if the whole city came out of a box.

Even if the beaches were not as beautiful as back home, there were neighborhoods that reminded him of Tarará, a shiny fabricated seaside community where primary school kids were taken for an enchanted fifteen days a year, unaware that the residences they stayed in would eventually house the kids who came to Cuba from Chernobyl to heal, and children like Nesto who played in the fields and bathed in the surf would age into the adolescents who had to work for their education out in the campo. There were neighborhoods in Miami lined with imitation Italian and Spanish villas almost as grand as the palaces lining Quinta Avenida, around Vedado, spread through Miramar and Siboney. If he closed his eyes, he could almost convince himself the air was the same on the continent as it blew in off the Atlantic, but he missed the ruffle of the tropical trade winds, and the thick salty mist wafting in from the Straits and from the Caribbean.

The cubanía and cubaneo had eased the shock of his arrival, but after a year, he felt alone, adrift in the last generation's exiles' secondhand nostalgia for a country that hadn't existed in over fifty years, and by street corner rants about what had become of their country by those who refused to go witness it as it was now.

In Cuba, he'd loved to go on long drives to the hills of Viñales and Las Terrazas, to Artemisa, to the beaches beyond Varadero and Matanzas Bay, but gas for the car was expensive, and when things were hard, he went months, even years, without leaving Havana. But once he began making money in this country, enough to start payments on a truck of his own and fill up its tank, he took to the Florida highways, tracing the peninsula, sometimes sleeping on beaches the way he liked to do back home, driving as far north as Virginia, where he saw snow for the first time, then found himself heading farther and farther south, past the edges of the Everglades down to these small islands and, one day, he called his uncle in Miami and told him he'd decided to stay.

Nesto came of age in the eighties, at the height of what he calls the Soviet colonial era in Cuba, fluent in Russian, practicing military exercises in his school at Ciudad Libertad in case of U.S. bombings, and educated like every other child to serve the State. But he grew disillusioned by the Revoluntion's inconsistencies; everyone was supposedly equal, but when a distant cousin of his father's had come to visit from Spain, the family wasn't allowed to enter the hotel where he stayed. And when that relative sneaked Nesto in, at age twelve—and bought him a chocolate bar in the gift shop, with its kiosk full of candies and snacks Nesto had never seen in his life; and sent him home with a sandwich from the hotel restaurant made with a thick, grainy delicious bread so different from the bland, airy white bread made available to regular citizens, wrapped in aluminum foil he'd never seen before either—he understood that nothing on the island was as it appeared.

Nesto realized with the taste of that chocolate bar that he'd been hungry all his life, though it would be a few years until he came to know real hunger, he says, with the institutionalized famine that overtook the island when the Soviets pulled out, what *ese* called "a special period in time of peace."

Even the Santeros rationalized the food shortages with the old Yoruba proverb, *There is no renewal without decline*, and recounted the pataki of how Poverty and Hunger used to walk the earth together, hand in hand, striking in every town as they looked for a place to settle, until the great orisha Obatalá chased them away so that they would have to wander the earth forever. "Poverty and Hunger may have come to visit," the Santeros said, "but we won't let them stay."

Sure, they were already accustomed to periods of vacas gordas and periods of vacas flacas, but this period was different; now there were no cows at all.

With the State-run bodegas empty, his entire family growing thinner by the day, Nesto put his ability to hold his breath for several minutes underwater to use and made a spear out of an old antenna and scrap metal with which he and some friends would fish off the Malecón, taking their catch home to their families, and selling what was left over. But the police caught on and warned that if they kept at it they'd have bigger problems.

"How absurd," he tells me, "that on an island, it's illegal to fish without a license. Even the creatures swimming in Cuban waters belong to the State."

Later, as a young soldier doing his military service, stationed to guard the home of a high official, Nesto witnessed the banquets enjoyed by those in high government ranks, while the people outside El Laguito's walls starved—food was so scarce that cats and dogs disappeared off the streets and pigeon coops kept on building roofs were, depleted; the terrified yet resigned faces of the young guajira girls brought from their villages to the estate's metal gates for officials' entertainment, and the parents who sometimes showed up looking for their daughters, crying to Nesto for mercy until a more senior guard came to scare them off with threats of jail or worse.

Why, he often asked his mother, hadn't she or her husband left, taken the family away from the island when they had the chance?

Because with the Revolution, they'd had more to gain than to lose, she'd reasoned; because it wasn't right that on their island there could exist such obscene wealth alongside such crushing poverty. And because, under Batista, with nobody safe from being hunted by his police, life was so much worse.

But why then, Nesto insisted, when the failures of the Revolution became clear, hadn't they tried to leave later, even on one of the boatlifts? So what if they'd be called gusanos and vendepatrias, shunned by neighbors, even having rocks thrown at them? He insisted to his mother those were things they'd forget in their new life.

"Ay, mi amor," she'd said. "It's hard to leave, and even harder to break up a family. May you never know how hard."

He'd been a gifted athlete, and good enough in school that he was tapped to join the young communists of the UJC, which at eighteen would have secured him a carnet del partido and he'd have been a full-fledged Party member, but Nesto refused to join, disappointing his family and making neighbors suspicious.

After his military service, he could have gone to university to be a lawyer like both his older sisters, or even to be an engineer. He'd passed the entrance exams. But ten miles on a bicycle each day since the camello buses didn't come out to Buenavista, and so many years of study just to give his life to serving the State, defending laws he didn't believe in, and earning next to nothing for it? Even his sisters, with all their education, earned just over twenty dollars a month. Nesto wanted no part of it. He'd completed his military service as a young father and newly married, and had a future other than his own to think about now. He was raised to believe a man should serve his country before anything—¡patria o muerte!—but knew he wouldn't pass that obedience on.

Everyone had one job the government saw; but another, the job that truly fed and provided, was the job the government didn't see. He opted to be an obrero and went to a trade school to learn to repair things so at least he could earn some money, that which he'd declare, and that from side jobs which he'd hide, so his family could live better, supplement the food rations of the Libreta de Abastecemiento, perpetually scaled back, the government grocery depleted of just about everything but beans, diluted coffee, stale bread, and maggot-filled bags of rice. Anything else cost extra, and in fula—dollars—not the pesos the locals earned, and was sold in the diplomercados and shopping malls meant for diplomats and foreigners.

They were poor, like everyone else, but he didn't want his kids' bodies to show it with skinny, enclenque legs and rickets, so he did all he could, resolviendo, inventando, to make money for better food, for milk beyond what they were rationed only to age seven.

"But there are eyes all over the island," Nesto says. And eventually the neighborhood snitches of the Committee for the Defense of the Revolution turned him in for fixing cars—Russian Ladas or discontinued Korean imports left behind by foreigners, when only cars manufactured before 1959 could be bought and sold—to sell for a personal profit.

After the Cederistas reported him, police arrived at Nesto's door to arrest him.

"So you went to jail?" I ask him.

We're at the Crescent Key marina watching the fishermen come in with the day's catch. Nesto wants to buy a couple of fillets to char on the grill behind my cottage, which he helped me clean out and get working again. He says once he has enough cash, he's going to buy himself a real spear gun, the fancy mechanical kind, and start catching fish himself again. For now, the fish from the marina market will do.

"Yes. Three times. For three days each. But that's nothing on the island. Anybody can be arrested for anything. They make honest work a crime. Everyone becomes a criminal because everything is illegal."

"You weren't scared?"

"Not really. Not until the last time when they said if I got arrested again, they wouldn't let me go. Then I knew they were serious."

"What was it like in there?"

He looks at me with a hint of impatience in his eyes.

"¿En el tanque? They put me in a big cell with all kinds of people. Some were real delincuentes, thieves, pandilleros, jineteros. Some were guys like me who got turned in for nonsense: a guy who sold mangos from his garden, a tailor who made somebody a suit for his wedding, a baker who sold someone a birthday cake, a guy who bought a microwave."

"They can arrest you for buying a microwave?"

"They watch how much each person spends. Everything is assigned to a name and nobody is allowed to buy more than his share. It's called *Illicit Enrichment.*"

"Where do they put the murderers?"

He laughs. "Somewhere else. With the rapists, subversives, and spies."

I can tell he thinks me naive because of my questions, that maybe he's shocking or even thrilling me with the intrigue of his time in jail, but really, I'm trying to decide if I should tell him about Carlito.

The fishermen lay out their fish and Nesto leans over a table picking out a bonito for them to fillet for us. I turn away when the fisherman pulls out the blade to cut off its head and start the skinning and pulling of bones.

The fisherman with the knife asks if we want to keep the head.

I say no just as Nesto says, "Of course. The head is the best part. The eyes are what give you wisdom."

When we have our wrapped fillets in hand and are headed back to his truck, I tell Nesto, "My brother was in prison."

"What did he do?"

I wait until we're in the truck, his key in the ignition, to answer.

It gives me time to rehearse my words in my mind. But there really is only one way to say it.

"He killed a baby."

Nesto pulls the key out and turns to me, but I look away, out the window toward the marina.

"A baby?"

"It was his girlfriend's daughter. He threw her off a bridge into the ocean."

Somehow, I believe it doesn't sound as bad as if he'd stabbed Shayna or shot or even strangled or poisoned her, maybe because Carlito's public defender put that notion in my mind. We were hoping he'd be charged with voluntary manslaughter, but the prosecutor went straight for murder in the first degree with malice and intent to kill. Carlito pleaded not guilty and his attorney tried to prove to the jury it had been a lapse of sanity, not some premeditated thing, that he hadn't driven over to Isabela's that day knowing he would soon end her daughter's life. The jury didn't buy it though. I'm not even sure I did.

I watch the image burn across Nesto's face in revulsion.

I always expect people to ask why Carlito did it. But they never do. Once, I mentioned to my mother how I was always prepared to come to my brother's defense, to say that it had been a momentary psychosis and it wasn't the real Carlito who committed that terrible crime. But the opportunity never came up. Mami told me that's because most people believed the only explanation for Carlito taking the life of an innocent child was that he was evil; whether he was born or bred that way didn't matter. And even she was starting to accept that this might be the truth.

How could she say that, I'd screamed at her, when the same people, all those Judases who now called my brother a monster, had once called him "the miracle baby" because God had chosen to save him from the hands of his own murderous father, sending that angel Marielito into the water after him. It was a proper divine intervention, there was no doubt, and the baby, they'd said back then, would grow up to do great things.

"We were wrong," she said. "Y fíjate que the Bible is full of bad children born to nice parents. Look at Cain and all of Joseph's brothers, los desgraciados."

"He's your son, not some cuento. And if you want to talk about the Bible, it also says, 'Remember those in prison, as though in prison with them.'"

I learned that much in our Youth Group scripture study, but Mami didn't want to hear it.

"How can you turn your back on him? Where's your compassion?"

"I didn't have it for your father after he did what he did, and I don't have it for your brother after what he has done."

I told her I had faith in Carlito even if she didn't. I would not abandon him but remain with him through his darkest periods, be there waiting for him when he was finally redeemed. I didn't know how it would happen. But I was hopeful it would.

I didn't talk to her for weeks. She didn't care that I was furious at her, that in speaking of my brother that way, she was also breaking my heart. She didn't try to soften me up or reason with me. She only stuck to her position that we shouldn't let ourselves be held hostage by the actions of yet another madman.

"Ay, Reina. No es fácil," is all Nesto says, as if we're still just talking about fish eyes or a slow day at work.

"You're not going to ask me why he did it?"

"Only he could know that."

"They were going to execute him."

"They execute people in this country?"

I nod. "All the time."

"How do they do it?

"Injection. Or the electric chair. They give you a choice. But everyone picks injection since one guy they electrocuted caught on fire and flames started coming out of his head. That's why my brother hanged himself."

I've always believed it was to avoid his own murder, to deny the state the satisfaction of killing him, an act of rebellion, to at least keep the black-hooded executioner from getting paid his hundred and fifty bucks for putting Carlito to death.

It never occurred to me until now, hearing myself say so to Nesto, that my brother's suicide maybe had something to do with his conscience, with guilt, with surrender.

Nesto watches me. I still can't meet his eyes. After a few moments, he slips the key back into the ignition and we are on our way, under the last threads of daylight, moving toward Hammerhead.

I don't know what I hoped for from this conversation. Maybe I wanted to confess, to testify. Maybe I wanted the chance to share my whole history, even if in fragments, the way Nesto has offered me pieces of his.

I thought I could shake these shadows when I moved away, skin my old life from this new one as swiftly and bloodlessly as the fisherman at the marina did when gutting our fish for dinner. But if Nesto is to know me at all, he has to know I am my brother's crime. I am that baby's murder.

When Nesto pulls into the path to the Hammerhead estate, careful to park his truck on the side driveway Mrs. Hartley prefers the service vehicles use, I tell him how I visited Carlito at the prison every weekend for the seven years that he was there.

He doesn't say anything, but later, after he's grilled our dinner and we're sitting on the floor across the coffee table from each other, an unopened bottle of wine between us, the bonito devoured down to the last tiny thin bones the fisherman let break off the spine, Nesto tells me he understands why I was so loyal to my brother.

"But the thing about loyalty," he says, "is that it always has a cost."

"What do you mean?"

"For example, I am here with you in your home eating this nice fish we bought together, but I can't look at it without thinking of the money we spent on it, knowing this is money that would have fed my family for one week. I can't eat a meal without thinking of the food I've taken out of my children's mouths. I can't spend a dollar without calculating the pesos it would put in my mother's hands. I can't eat a piece of beef without remembering it's something my family hasn't tasted in years, since I was last able to pay a beef broker for a steak he would smuggle from the government slaughterhouses in a briefcase all the way to Havana. Every time my stomach fills, I only remember the emptiness I felt all those years, and I know, if not for the money I'm able to send them from here, they would still be feeling it.

"That's one of the reasons I left Miami," he goes on. "There, people told me I was lucky I made it to the other side and this was my chance to start a new life, borrón y cuenta nueva. I could find a new woman to marry and have a new family. But I can't start a new life when my life is still back there. I didn't want to leave. Everybody thinks everybody wants to leave—but who would *want* to leave their home, their family, everything they love? We leave because we have to. I left because there came a point when I had no choice. They depended on me, and with my arrests, not being able to make my money on the side, I was failing them. So I am here. Not because I was looking for an adventure or because I had dreams of becoming a rich man in this country. I came for them. So they can live better. Only for them."

I don't know what to say so I stay quiet, my eyes on him.

"I can understand why you were that way when your brother was alive, Reina, living half a life out in the world, free, and half a life locked in that prison with him. This is what family does. What love does. It chains us together."

Nesto knows plenty of people in Crescent Key and the neighboring islands. He's been here for three years already and everywhere he goes, someone gives him at least a nod or a wave. Sometimes he gets pulled over for a handshake and some banter, and his English is pretty good—accent-heavy but fluid—since one of the benefits he received upon arriving in the United States as part of the Cuban Adjustment Act was free English courses at the local community college. Even Mrs. Hartley smiled big when she saw him pull into the driveway the first time, then turned her grin on me when she realized he was there to see me. Since I moved in, we hardly ever cross paths. I slip my rent checks under her front door on the first of each month, and the only regular evidence of her is the land crabs crushed by her car on her end of the driveway.

Nesto also has a few friends from Cuba that we sometimes run into who turned up in the Keys for the same reasons he did, that gravitational pull back to native waters. Guys from his Malecón days with whom he swam and fished, including Lolo, who grew up around the corner from him in Buenavista and whose father, a former navy diver, taught scuba diving out in Playa Baracoa and let Nesto take his course under a fake tourist name since it was illegal for Cubans to dive if not for military purposes.

Lolo defected from Cuba by way of the Dominican Republic ten years ago; bald-headed and square-chested, he now runs his own dive shop in Key Largo. At least once a weekend, and sometimes during the week, when work is slow, Nesto will go out with Lolo on his boat, not even to fish but to throw himself into the ocean, hold his breath, and go as deep as he can, something he couldn't do back home without watching his back for police. Sometimes they go after sunset and I asked him once why he bothers swimming in darkness.

"I go to see," he said.

"What can you see at night?" Even with flashlights and boat lights it seemed like something better saved for daylight.

"You don't see only with your eyes," he told me, like it was the most obvious thing. "You see with your whole being. One day I'll take you and you'll understand."

I kept quiet because I didn't want him to know that the idea of being out in the middle of the ocean scared me. It was one thing to wade out to our waists in the waters off the Hammerhead beach under the moonlight where we could still feel the sand under our feet and I could run to shore if I felt some creature rush against my calves, and something else to plunge into the black ocean where, should anything happen, nobody could even hear you scream.

I'm with Nesto when Lolo calls to invite him to his place up in Key Largo for a Nochebuena party. We're at the supermarket in Marathon buying some food for our own Christmas Eve dinner at my place, and Nesto wanders down the aisle away from me, but Lolo is so loud I can still hear his end of the conversation coming through the phone.

"Ven, asere. What, you're going to spend the night alone down there?"

"Not alone," Nesto mumbles, his back fully to me, while I pretend to examine pasta boxes.

I think it's sweet that he's chosen my company, even if sometimes it seems like Nesto comes over to spend time with the cottage magazines more than with me. He says I take them for granted. The beautiful paper they are printed on. The fact that I can go to a newsstand and buy a magazine anytime I want when back in Cuba, there are hardly any magazines beyond *Revolución y Cultura,* or *Trabajadores,* and *Bohemia*—if you can get your hands on a copy—and if you want to read one of the international magazines foreigners have left behind and brought into circulation, you've got to rent it on the gray market.

Later, I take our plates and wash them off at the sink, and he uses my absence to dip back into the stack. He's made a pile beside it of the ones he's already read. Tonight it's the leopards of Londolozi, South Africa.

"Can you imagine," he asks, showing me an image of a mother leopard with her cub, "seeing one of these animals in real life?"

"Haven't you ever been to a zoo?"

"It's not the same. At the zoo their eyes are full of sadness. It's unnatural."

"You think it's natural for them to be followed around by some guy with a camera?"

"Haven't you ever wanted to go anywhere, Reina? You, who have the freedom to go anywhere in the world, and you've never been anywhere. I've only been in this country three years and I've already seen more of it than you."

The phone rings and I know who it is before I answer. My mother. The only person who calls me besides Nesto. She wants to know how I'm spending Nochebuena, if I've at least been invited to a party.

"I'm home, Mami. I just had dinner."

"¿Estás solita?" She sounds worried.

"No." I glance his way and see he's hypnotized by another photo spread. This time, the Great Wall of China.

"You're with a man?"

I mutter affirmatively.

"Does he have a name?"

"Nesto."

Mami's in the mood for chisme. She wants to know what he does for a living, if he's married, and if he's a real novio or just a peor es nada.

"Ya," I tell her. "No more questions. He's just a friend. Someone to pass the time with."

That last part I know Nesto hears, because he's closing the magazine, slipping it back onto the stack, and looking right at me.

I realize my words might have sounded harsher than I meant them.

My mother tells me she's had Jerry's mother and his son from his first marriage over for dinner. She cooked them a churrasco and pernil. Even la suegra was impressed.

"You never cooked things like that for us."

"Ay, por favor, Reina. You're always looking backward. I don't know how you manage to get anywhere in life without running into walls."

When we say good-bye, I return to the kitchen area and start cleaning the counter. There's no dust, no smudges. It's already clean, but I rub it until the paper towel disintegrates between my fingers.

Nesto turns the television on to a documentary about butterflies, possibly the only nonholiday-themed program on tonight. When I'm finally satisfied with the counter, I see a tiny sugar ant slip out from a crack between the countertop and the wall. Behind it, another ant, then several more. I watch them, the line they form, so certain of their direction. I could kill them with the paper shreds in my hand, but I let them go on their way, even as a dozen more emerge from the seam in the wall.

My mother kept the old house full of poison. In every corner, a mousetrap or a roach motel. The counters lined with a clear gel meant to annihilate a population of ants. The poison was why we could never have a pet, she insisted, even if we argued a cat would do a better job of getting rid of the mice and lizards that found their way into the house. We could bring in one of the strays that hung around our block that she yelled about every time she caught me bringing them our leftovers.

But poison wasn't the real reason we couldn't have animals. When Carlito went to trial, to ease the silence of the house, I told her we should get a puppy, something to love, to love us back. But she refused and finally confessed it was because she suspected that with our luck, any animal we took into our home would eventually turn on us just like all the men in our family did. She didn't want us to become *that* story, the survivors of an already broken family who were mauled and eaten by their dog. She said in her house we did what she wanted and when I had my own house one day, I could do what I wanted.

So in my cottage, I let the ants live. I admire their instincts. Their intrepid way of staking out the counter until they detect no more movement, and make their way across the surface, down the side of the cabinet, all the way to the top of the garbage can, its lid slightly upturned and reeking of fish bones. They know how to live, these ants. Even with all the poison Mami put out for them, their colonies persisted. Even when she got so frustrated she called professional fumigators, pest killers. The mice died. Even the roaches manifested upturned, on their backs, feet curled into the air. The lizards shriveled into crusts we'd find pressed into the rugs. The spiders dropped off the ceiling, landing on tabletops, turned inward like buttons. But the ants lived.

Carlito told me that in jail, the only free beings are the in-sects that fly in through the window slats and back out at their own will. Sometimes a lizard would creep in and he'd watch it. He knew some other inmates tortured the life-forms unlucky enough to find themselves in their cells, even smashing the rare unlucky sparrow that made its way in, but Carlito wanted to befriend them, invite them to stay, even make pets out of them. He made a fly trap on a sheet of paper out of some gravy left over from a prison meal just so he'd have treats for the lizards, the crickets, the brilliant roaches, but they never stayed. Once he grew so angry at their abandonment, so jealous of their freedom, he killed a grasshopper by pulling off its legs but he swore he heard it scream so loud the walls of his cell vibrated. He set it on the window ledge and hoped it was strong enough to find its own way out. Then he started watching the ants, the way they dug into the holes in the concrete, and when he grew impatient and started pressing his thumb on them to kill them one by one, he could hear them scream too.

"Everything cries, Reina," he told me. "There's not one living thing on this planet that doesn't scream to survive."

I turn back to Nesto, but he's fallen asleep on the sofa, his head dipped into his shoulder. I've never seen him sleep. Never seen him with his eyes closed longer than a blink.

I've thought about him spending the night. Sometimes when he touches me, brushes up against me for no reason other than I'm in the way, I think about what it would be like to have his hands on me because he put them there, because he wanted to touch me. I've watched his lips move when he tells me one of his stories, wondered what it was like for his ex-wife, Yanai, who got to kiss him for so many years, or for the other girl he lived with for a time in the barbacoa loft of a solar, a tenement by the Parque Trillo in Cayo Hueso where there was often no electricity for days and the entire building shared a phone line and a bathroom with water pulled from a tank.

Nesto learned to ignore the smells. "A person can get used to anything," he said. "That's our island's biggest problem."

But he went back to Yanai after a few months and the girl from Cayo Hueso eventually found an old Italian man to marry and is now living somewhere in Rome.

Maybe it's because I haven't been kissed in so long, the longest I've gone since I was a girl and boys started reaching for me. But Nesto doesn't. Sometimes I wonder if with a little effort I can sway his interest, change the way he looks at me. Those are skills I've had as long as I can remember, but with him I hold back.

His lips part, air slips out of them. His long lashes press against his cheek and his hair fans out on the cushion behind him.

So this is what he looks like when he's alone in his little room by the beach, when he takes off his clothes at night and rests his body on that flimsy futon. When he dreams of his family. His life. His island. This is his face wearing the freedom of sleep.

I've never invited him to stay, not explicitly, but I hoped he could sense my wanting him to be my companion in the night, to maybe make the hours pass a little faster, easier, with fewer throbs of loneliness.

In the old days, I never had to ask men to stay with me. They'd usually leave before the night was over, but I never had to work to get them to want me. Seduction was intuitive for me. Even when I was the one who wanted it more, I could make them think it was all their idea.

But with Nesto, I'm different.

I let him sleep. I turn the television off, but not even my nearness or footsteps stir him awake. I take only myself to bed. I lower into the blankets, turn off the light.

Then, I hear his weight shift.

He must have opened his eyes, maybe he even forgot where he was for a moment and then realized I'm across the darkness under the same roof, in my bed.

"Nesto?"

"Go to sleep, Reina."

"You don't have to leave."

"I know."

I hear him kick off his shoes and the sound of them hitting the floor. I hear the removal of his collares. He once told me that because his beads are sacred—strung on delicate cotton, blessed over seven days, and washed in a river with an ofrenda to Ochún—he must take off the necklaces to shower and to sleep, kissing them, giving thanks for their bendiciones and protection, placing them on a white handkerchief he keeps folded in his pocket, so I know that Nesto is staying with me in the cottage, at least for tonight.

Carlito was hated in a way that can only happen with the help of the media. Beyond the nature of his crime, he was made more of a celebrity as the youngest of the nearly four hundred inmates on Florida's death row, until a few years into his sentence when a nineteen-year-old in Jupiter killed both his parents with an ax. We used to say we had the bad luck of geography. Only sixteen states allow capital punishment and we had to live in one of them. Too bad we didn't live in Wisconsin, Carlito once joked, where not even a guy who murders seventeen people and eats their remains is sentenced to death. At least Florida only gets around to executing someone a couple of times a year. Not like Texas or Ohio or Alabama, where they're much more efficient about these things.

There are killers who sit on death row for decades before they get their date. I suspect Carlito's execution was fast-tracked because his was one of those crimes that became public obsession. Dr. Joe said people had a morbid fascination with Carlito's case—a guy driven insane with jealousy, the stolen child, like it could happen to *anyone*—and watching his trial gave them a sickening, voyeuristic pleasure. People petitioned for his death more than for your average murderer's. Joe said execution is less about the crime and more about extinguishing a social nightmare, part of the collective unconscious, like capturing the boogeyman. When Carlito took his own life before the government could, people called him a coward. I guess he ruined their fun.

It used to be that I could hide out at home and pretend the world had forgotten my family and me. Time would pass and the newspapers would get thrown out and the only remnants of our story lived in stale gossip on the tongues of old people in the neighborhood. But the Internet is the world's biggest backyard freezer, keeping everything fresh, and I can always count on someone finding me through the electronic portals, wondering if they can ask me a few questions about my experience as the sister of a killer. Usually these nudges come from law, criminology, or psychology students. Sometimes they come from other women trying to form networks to share stories and complain about the justice system together. Sometimes it's a weirdo who came across an old photo of me archived online, walking outside the courthouse, on my way into another day of Carlito's trial, wanting to know if I'm lonesome wherever I am and if I'd like some company. That's why I don't go on the computer much.

I used to think that was enough to draw the line between my old life and my new one, especially down here in the Keys where the only news people care about is the daily tide report.

Nesto wakes up before me. I hear his steps on the wooden floorboards, walking into the bathroom. By the time he gets out, I've pulled myself together a bit, splashed water on my face at the kitchen sink, brushed through my mess of slept-on hair. I take in his morning face—flushed, smooth, his eyes still small with sleep. I make some coffee and we take our mugs out to the veranda. He puts his arm around my shoulders and pulls me half into his chest, but I stiffen in reflex and he gently releases me.

"I almost forgot it's Christmas," I say.

"Feliz Navidad, Reina." He smiles at me, but as he turns toward the ocean, his smile disappears.

A week ago, he sent a box full of gifts for his family with the courier agency, things they'd asked for—a pair of soccer shoes for his son, a bathing suit for his daughter, diapers for his niece's baby, blood pressure medication and eyedrops for his aunt, the vitamins his mom requested, along with creams for his stepfather's vitiligo since the island pharmacies were forever depleted. His mother was jubilada, retired with distinction, but her pension wasn't enough to live on, so she made extra money as a seamstress and even had a permit to sell her creations at the Fin de Siglo department store. But it wasn't enough to compensate for the eternal lack on the island. And even though Nesto sent a box full of his family's requests every few weeks along with the monthly remittance, it always fell short of their needs.

When he calls home, his kids always ask the same question: "When are you coming to see us, Papi?" and he tells them, "Soon, mis amores. Soon."

He doesn't have any jobs lined up for the day but I'm due for my regular morning shift. He drives me to the hotel and says he'll come by for me when I get off so we can do something together in the afternoon, maybe go to the beach or take a drive down to Bahia Honda. I expect it will be a slow day at the spa. I'm the only manicurist on shift and the hotel isn't even at capacity. I check myself in the mirror in the employee locker room, my hair pulled into the required bun, dressed in my pink scrubs looking like I'm on my way to deliver a baby.

"Your client's at the table already," Gemma, my boss, sticks her head in to warn me. She's a mostly kind Trinidadian lady but her voice holds a kind of schoolteacher severity, like she might send you to detention.

I step out into the manicure area and, before she even lifts her head up or shows her face through the curtain of caramel hair falling into the folds of her plush white spa robe, my chest tightens in a familiar but forgotten way; I know with absolute certainty that the woman waiting for me at the table is Isabela.

I step back into the locker room and feel my throat closing. I sit on a bench and count until I've got my breath under control. I don't know why my body reacts this way. I've seen Isabela plenty of times over the years and even during the worst moments of the trial, like the day she was called to testify against Carlito, and the following week, when it was my turn, and I lied under oath saying there was no way Carlito could have done what he was being tried for while she watched me from her place on the wooden bench between her parents, the three of them shaking their heads at me.

"It's wrong to lie with your hand on the Bible, you know," my mother warned me as I drove us to court that morning.

"So is asking a sister to testify against her brother."

"It's not just a sin, it's a crime. You could get into very big trouble."

"I don't care," I said, because Carlito would not be taking the stand in his own defense and I knew my testimony would be his only hope.

So I lied, as the judge, jury, and spectators watched me, but the only eyes I felt on me were Isabela's.

Even then, I never felt so stunned by the sight of her.

Gemma pokes her head back in the door. "Reina, what's taking you so long?"

I don't answer so she comes closer, standing over me on the bench, a small woman with a suddenly large shadow.

"Are you all right?"

"I'm sorry. I can't take care of that client."

"Why not?"

"I know her."

"What's the problem? If you know her, all the better."

I picture myself going back into the spa, sitting down across from Isabela, taking her hand in mine to clean and prepare her nails, how I'll try to avoid her eyes, make the burden of small talk pass as quickly as possible. She'll ask what I'm doing here. I'll ask what *she's* doing here, especially on Christmas, which she always spent with her parents, forever la consentida, and when she was still Carlito's girlfriend, she even invited Mami and me to join them for their Christmas lunch. I refused to go, saying I was no arrimada and didn't need her charity, but Mami and Carlito went without me.

Or we'll talk about the weather, the island scenery; she'll ask about my mother, and I'll ask about her parents, her new husband, and the kids she had after Carlito killed Shayna.

The thought of it all makes me dizzy.

"You don't understand," I say to Gemma. "That lady and me. We have a complicated history."

"I told you when I hired you, I don't want to know anything about your personal life, and I don't want it in my spa."

"I can't go out there."

"I don't have anyone else to do it, Reina. You either go in there and take care of the client or you take your things out of your locker and I'll notify H.R. of your refusal to work. The choice is yours."

I keep quiet but stand up, open up my locker, and pull out my bag.

"I'm warning you," Gemma says as she watches me. "We don't do second chances around here."

I consider telling her the truth. But what can I say? I don't want to paint Isabela's nails because my brother threw her daughter off a bridge?

I hate Carlito more than ever at this moment because, even though he committed the crime, and even though he's dead, I'm still the one who has to do the confessing.

"So?" Nesto says when he pulls up to the lobby. "What happened?"

I didn't explain anything when I called to ask him to come back for me.

"I don't want to talk about it," I say once I climb into the truck.

I try to be tough about it, bite my tongue and chew my inner cheeks until I taste blood. I don't cry. It's not that I'm incapable. Tears only come every few years and the last time was over Carlito's coffin, which wasn't so long ago. But here in Nesto's truck, pushing along the Overseas Highway though I have no idea where we are going, I feel my throat swell and my eyes sizzle with restrained tears. I ask Nesto to pull over—command him, really—and he eases onto a patch of road by some mangroves suspended over the marsh. A couple of bird-watchers squat a few yards down, their binoculars fixed on an ibis wading in sea grass.

I couldn't be further away from my brother, from the old life, but it's as if I'm still sitting across the table from him in the visitors' room at the prison, studying his face, looking for those features that were once identical to mine, trying to see him as he was now without forgetting who he used to be.

And there was Isabela. Once my friend. Once my brother's enamorada.

Years ago, when both our families were awaiting the judge's sentencing, Isabela came to see me at work. The jurors had already found Carlito guilty. It only took a day of deliberation.

Seven out of twelve of the jurors had recommended he be sentenced to death, and in Florida you only need a majority even though practically everywhere else they still execute people the jury has to be unanimous. Mami and I were still hopeful the judge would at least offer Carlito life and maybe even with the possibility of parole. Isabela's parents had given a statement to reporters that appeared on the front page of the newspaper that morning saying they and all their relatives prayed for my brother's death every day. Isabela apologized to me for their hatred. She said she didn't want Carlito to die and no way would she ever go to witness his execution, even if her parents dragged her. She said she would never wish for me the pain he'd caused her by taking her daughter away, and even though he'd never taken full responsibility and had never asked for it—not yet at least—she'd already forgiven Carlito because she had faith he could not have understood what he was doing up there on the bridge that day, to baby Shayna, to her, to us all.

"We'll get through this, Reina," she said, putting her arms around me, but I'd remained limp, unable to hug her back. "You and I are like swans. We swim though shit, but we'll come out clean."

I wanted to believe her.

I wanted to confess to her the words that filled my mind when I saw her.

Isabela, I'm the one who did this to you.

Nesto puts his hand on my shoulder and his touch, the warmth of his large hand, feels like an unbearable weight on me and I crumple forward into my palms, until I am breathless. I open the car door, lowering myself onto the grass below. Nesto's footsteps follow me but I hide my face, swallowing hard, trying to mute my sobbing, rubbing away the tears before they hit my cheek.

I feel his body shell around me, holding me, until I finally whisper, though it comes out more like a moan, that I saw her, Isabela, and Nesto asks who that is.

"The mother," I say. "The mother of the baby my brother killed."

I tell him I am ashamed, so ashamed, of who I am because it's not who I am, it's who my brother made me.

"It's not your fault, Reina. You're not responsible for what he did."

"Yes, I am," I manage to mutter, unable to meet his face.

My cheeks press into my knees until my eye sockets ache and when the tears finally let up, I look up to see my shoes in the grass, a beetle making its way up my pants leg.

Nesto and I sit together in the dirt until my breath becomes even again and the doom of the day seems to lift with the noon sun rising high above us.

He doesn't press me to say more, or tell me what he thinks about anything. He only sits with me, the gentle pressure of his arm around my back, and me, finally at ease enough to let myself lean into him.

There were no especially happy Christmases in my past. They were always marks of something broken in our lives. My mother told me that during our first holidays in this country, she yearned for home, the music, the lanterns that lined the streets of Cartagena, candles lit in every window, from the sixth of December to el Día de los Reyes. After Hector was gone, although we always went to misa de gallo at Our Lady of Divine Providence and celebrated with Tío Jaime and Mayra, the day was just another yearly reminder of our dishonor. And when Carlito left us, it only cemented our sense that as a family, we were a failure.

I decide I should go back to the cottage but Nesto insists there is nothing but my own thoughts waiting for me there and I should stick with him for the day. It happens that he gets an urgent repair call from the dolphinarium down on Cloud Key because it's Christmas and their regular fix-it man is taking the day off to be with his family. Lolo is friendly with the manager of the place and put in a good word for Nesto since he'd done some work repairing tanks and plumbing at the Acuario Nacional back in Havana.

The dolphinarium is supposed to be some kind of sanctuary, not your typical aquarium, all about bucks and flash, or one of those shabby spots littering the Keys, mom-and-pop businesses built out of canal houses with a pair of captive dolphins for tourists to swim and take pictures with. The place claims it's no water circus, but a well-funded private research facility with a mission to better understand dolphin intelligence. But it still looks to me more like an aquatic farm, with pens carved out of Florida Bay by chain-link fences, joined by a wooden walkway from which visitors can stare down at the dolphins, and a wooden shack on a tower at the center of it all that the staff uses for broader observation.

Before you make it out to the dolphin pens, you have to pass the sea lion enclosure, and before that, a long artificial river coiling around the front of the property, with walled-off sections of barracudas, stingrays, and sea turtles. The turtle stream is the one with the problem today, with a backed-up filtration system.

Nesto and I watch the turtles while the manager, Mo, a bald guy in his fifties with the body of a fifteen-year-old, explains the problem. There are at least a dozen loggerheads and leatherbacks, and among them, three or four wearing partially inflated life jackets like they're part of a gang, bobbing through the current, unable to dive deep or glide as smoothly as the turtles without jackets. I ask Mo about it and he explains that before hatching, those turtles' eggs were disturbed while in their nests, probably by beachgoers, causing air pockets that made the shells grow deformed, top or bottom heavy, which, without the jackets, would make the turtles sink and drown.

Just a few days ago, Nesto told me about his kawama-catching days during the Special Period, when he'd drive east to Corralillo where local fishermen draped a net across the bay at Playa Ganuza to trap turtles as they came in from the sea to lay their eggs. Nesto would arrive in the early morning with a scuba tank borrowed from Lolo, and dive under to bring up whichever turtles had already drowned in the netting. "You can never kill a turtle," he told me, "because they can be the size of tables, strong as bulls, and it would also be cruel to the animal and disrespectful to their guardian, Yemayá." So he'd pray to the orisha, explain his family's hunger, thank her in advance for any turtles she would give him since he knew they were sacred to her, and promise to pay the debt as soon as he was able, because he said Yemayá can have a terrible temper if you take from her without asking, but she is also fair and understanding. He waited for the turtles to drown from the struggle, and once he carried one to shore, the fishermen chopped it up for its meat and took their share, throwing the shell out to sea so there would be no trace of it for the police to find and arrest or fine them for stealing from the ocean.

Nesto took his portion of the meat with him back to the capital to sell on the bolsa negra for three dollars a pound. His entire family could live off the profits of one turtle for over a month.

"Pobres tortuguitas," I'd said, with a horrified expression.

"You don't know hunger, Reina. You don't know the things people will do to feed their family. I hope you never know."

And here he is now, ironías de la vida, assigned to fix the pump so these lucky turtle refugees in life jackets can have a nice habitat.

While Nesto gets to work, I walk around the rest of the facility. There are just a few tourist families roaming around, gathering at the big lagoon up front where a trainer is getting ready to do some kind of show. I walk down the stone path toward the back of the property past a pen with the pair of resident sea lions sunning themselves on a wooden platform. And just past their pen, there are nearly a dozen other fenced enclosures, each holding two or three or four dolphins.

I walk from enclosure to enclosure till I come upon one where a guy in a wetsuit sits on a platform with a dolphin poking out from the water at his knees, doing hand motions to which the dolphin responds with some behavior like nodding or shaking its head, and the wetsuit guy rewards it with fish from a bucket at his side.

I wander farther up the dock to look in the other pens. Dolphins swimming around, some just parked by the dock with an eye on me or another visitor, others doing quick loops around the fence periphery. In another pen, two mother dolphins swim with their babies in their slipstream, and I stand for a while watching them press against each other, slicing through the soft gulf tide penetrating the holes of the fences.

I'd tell Carlito about this place if he were still alive.

When he died, the hardest thing to get used to was the end of his phone calls. I could count on them once or twice a week. The buzzing recording of the prison announcing a collect call from an inmate, my accepting the charges, then his voice: "Reinita, hermanita. Tell me about the world."

He joked that I was his scout, his eyes on the outside, his little guerrera on the front lines. I felt like an informant, relaying to him entire conversations I had with other people, a fuller kind of gossip because he'd have me set scenes, describe a place in detail. He trusted my vision of the world, the way I told stories with my own judgments interspersed, because our first impressions of life had been shaped together; we'd been taught the ways of humanity by the same misguided tribe, were fruit of the same knotted and twisted family tree, and had walked through the world together until he lost his place in it.

He feared he couldn't picture life beyond the prison walls anymore, that his memory was unreliable, and said he was forced to live in his imagination like any loco in an asylum. In prison he could watch some TV and movies, but it only made him more aware of his shrinking picture of life and the fact that he'd likely never walk under the open sky again.

I knew he gave up some of his rec time to call me. The prison chaplain once advised him that if he declared himself a smoker, he could negotiate to get an extra thirty minutes in the kennel each day. But that would require me to deposit even more money in his commissary account, and I was already putting in as much as I could afford just so Carlito could buy bags of chips, cookies, or powdered soups, anything to avoid eating the prison food, and so he could keep calling me collect, though the calls always cut out before we'd have a chance to say good-bye.

They let Carlito have a CD player with headphones. But he told me his ears had become so sensitive from the solitude that even listening to music was painful. He talked to himself, he confessed to me, something he used to think only the most pathetic insane people did. He didn't get to interact with the other inmates since he was permanently in segregation. Most inmates only got put in solitary for days, weeks, or months, not years, but committing a crime against a child put him at the bottom of the prison hierarchy, and if left among the main population, chances were he'd be dead in an hour.

But the tedium of his confinement was so unbearable that Carlito once told me he could spend hours biting his arms, palms, thighs, calves, any part of himself he could reach, testing the threshold of his pain, until he made a solar system of pink and purple spheres across his body, dabbled with red pinpoints in places where he managed to puncture the skin, just to see how long it would take for the teeth marks to fade from his flesh.

And when the marks cleared, he would do it again.

Dr. Joe told me those in segregation sometimes act out, saving their feces or piss to ambush the guards with, deliberately clogging their toilets with shit, or flooding their cells with water from the faucet.

"You remove an individual from society and they lose their ability to be social. Normal behavior falls away."

"So why do they do it?" I'd asked him. "Why do they put them in solitary?"

"Someone long ago figured out it's the worst kind of punishment."

Ignoring inmates was one of the guards' favorite games, but at least it wasn't as bad as when they were really in the mood for cruelty, locking inmates in a lightless storage room with no food or toilet for days. Other times, since the guards were heavily rotated, the new guys often forgot to let Carlito out for his scheduled kennel time, to make a phone call, or even to give him his mail.

"It's the monotony that's so destructive," Joe told me. "For some in solitary, the only constructive activity they can come up with is to plan their own suicide."

I used to think I was the only person Carlito ever used his phone time to call, till he let it slip that there were a few women he had regular conversations with on the phone. Women who'd gotten his photo and profile off one of those Internet directories where strangers can write to inmates. I looked up his profile myself and there was my brother, in his prison reds, crouched against a gray concrete wall, a headline under his photo: *Looking for a friend.* I thought women who seek out attachments to a convicted murderer when they don't have to must be some kind of nutty, but Carlito said they were like angels, and in a way, those lonely women, feeling irreparably wronged by life themselves, were like prisoners too.

When the jail turned his cadaver over to Mami and me, they also gave us a box with all his possessions, junk he'd accumulated during his prison life that hadn't been confiscated: a small radio, a photo album I'd made for him, books he'd held on to rather than donated to the prison library. There were also the letters from women, but I wouldn't read them. Even if he was dead, I thought Carlito deserved his privacy.

A few days after he hanged himself, one of those women called the house.

"I know you're his sister," she started. "I haven't heard from Carlos in a few weeks. I called the prison but they won't tell me anything."

"You haven't seen the news?"

"I'm in Utah."

I told her Carlito had died but before I could go on she whimpered, "They killed him! I knew something like this would happen. He told me they were poisoning him. He was afraid to eat or drink."

"He hanged himself."

"How do you know that?"

"The warden told me they found him in his cell."

I had begun to wonder how the cord didn't tear from the beam with the force of Carlito's weight, how he could have remained dangling like they said, or if they'd found him on the floor, choking, or already dead.

"Did you have an autopsy done?"

"No."

"They're lying to you. They killed him. I know it."

She started to cry and I thought about trying to console her but just said I had to go.

After I hung up, I considered her words.

Carlito sometimes talked about how it cost the state hundreds of thousands of dollars to keep a single inmate in prison and his execution would cost taxpayers even more, so it was cheaper to keep him alive than to kill him. Still, he never said anything to me about being poisoned. I guess it wasn't totally out of the question. I knew the guards had a thing for exacting revenge, like the time I made the mistake of openly referring to one of them as a "guard" and he became indignant as he reprimanded me. "We are corrections officers, ma'am, not security guards. We are *law enforcement.*" I said I was sorry for the mistake, even though what they called themselves made no difference to me, just like they could call the building Carlito lived in a "correctional facility" instead of a prison or even a purgatory, but I guess my apology didn't come off as sincere enough because that guard kept Carlito from calling me for a week.

Carlito knew I kept a record of every instance of incarceration injustice and prisoner mistreatment for the sake of his appeals and stays of execution even though most of it couldn't be proved since it was always his word against an officer's.

He'd never mentioned anything about being poisoned.

I wondered whom he'd been trying to protect: the woman on the phone or me?

I still feel the impulse to report to my brother on life on the outside. Sometimes I narrate things in my mind as if he can hear me—always the good things, never the bad—because I can never shake the feeling of not wanting to disappoint him, even if it means embellishing or inventing the world as I see it.

Look where I am, Carlito. Look where I've taken my life.

Look at this ocean, and these animals. Look at these baby dolphins, the way they swim tight with their mamis.

Look at this sky, feel that sun, smell that air, taste that salt.

Forgive me when I hate you.

Don't think I've forgotten you, hermano, even if you've forgotten me.

I take you everywhere with me.

I'm still your little guerrera. I'm still your Reina.

THREE

Years ago, back in Havana, Nesto says he sometimes felt so confined in the city that when he couldn't afford to put gas in the car, rather than take a guagua, he'd stand by the road haciendo botella, waiting for a local car to give him a ride on its way out of the capital, with nothing but the clothes he wore and a few pesos in his pocket. On one of those trips, he started on Avenida Maceo and caught a lift in a Pontiac to the Vía Blanca highway. The other people sharing the ride got off at the Playas del Este or Guanabo, but he stayed on, wanting to go as far as he could out of Havana.

They only made it to the Bacunayagua Bridge before the car broke down and all the travelers had to make their own way. But Nesto didn't look for another ride. Instead he walked down from the mirador point overlooking the canyon that sank into the Straits flushing toward the Matanzas province. There were no defined trails on the slope of the hills, just some slightly foot-worn paths made by the few people who lived down in the valley. He walked and walked until he came across a bohío in a clearing near the shoreline. An old man sat in a block of shade under the grass roof overhang with a scraggy dog curled like a horseshoe at his feet. Nesto greeted him and the old man asked what he came down there for. Nesto wasn't in uniform so the old man knew he probably wasn't with the police, but he could have just as easily been undercover. Nesto told him he'd just come to take a look around, and asked if the old man minded if he stayed by his hut to rest for a while.

Nesto stayed for four days. He says most of the time he and the old man hardly spoke, just navigated their shared space in silence. The old man invited him to sleep on the floor of his hut, and gave Nesto a blanket and a bag of frijoles to use as a pillow.

During the day, they went for walks together. Took hikes up into the Yumuri Hills, and down toward the rocky inlet where water poured in from the Atlantic. Here, where the ocean pushed through two slabs of land, one could forget, at least for a little while, that they lived on an interminable island, with a coast that led nowhere but back to itself. A small, solitary body of earth, strangled by its own umbilical cord.

On the third day, Nesto admitted to the old man that the reason he'd come this way was that he wanted to feel like a boy again, free to wander, to get lost. He was a husband to a girl he hadn't particularly wanted to marry, father to a boy he hadn't been ready for. He wouldn't trade any of it, he said, because the reward of the love one has for a child is far too great to ever give up, but there were days when he woke up to the ever-burning Cuba sun with a feeling that his life had been stolen from him before he was even born. Not by the marriage or the improvised family, but by his mere existence on that island—pilfered and poached centuries over, until its latest incarnation, as a museum of failed ideals and broken promises.

There was no past, no future, only the repeating days, dawn and the arrival of the daily mission to secure the family's dinner. His dreams lay on the other side of an invisible bridge, but every bridge he came across, just like the famous Bacunayagua, which Cubans believed to be one of the Wonders of the World, led nowhere but back to itself.

That's why he left his city and his family that day without a good-bye, without letting them know where he went or if he'd ever come back. It wasn't the first time—after all, he was a son of Ogún, the lonely orisha who dwells in the forests from whom he inherited his need to flee, to clear new paths—and of course, it was hard to get very far on the island and he'd always come back so he didn't fear his family would worry too much; a neighbor or official would have notified them if he'd been arrested or worse. He didn't expect it would be the last time he wandered off either. It was the price of finding a little solitude and silence, for the illusion of freedom even if just for a short while.

The old man listened to Nesto and when he was done he shook his head at him the way Nesto imagined his own father would have done if he'd lived to see his son grow into a man.

"Compañero, how do you think I ended up here forty years ago? Go back to your family. And think twice before you ever leave them again."

In the days after Christmas, I am restless. I wake before the sun, just a little while after I've managed to fall fully asleep. With no job, vacant hours swelling my day beyond scouring classifieds, submitting job applications, I spend time with Nesto, in between his repair calls, waiting for him in the truck when he's on a job.

I consider going up to Orlando to see Mami. I picture her hugging me as if we are old friends, bringing me into her home, showing me the new things she's bought, sitting me down on her new department store sofa, and offering me tea off a tray in the rehearsed way she practiced in the years of my childhood, when we'd sometimes get visits from social workers the school sent to check on my and my brother's well-being. We were mostly normal children, but in class, I tended to go silent when spoken to and a school therapist tried to convince my mother I had selective mutism, while Carlito had a habit of back-talking his teachers, kicking over desks, and storming out of class, and they briefly tried to diagnose him with some kind of rage problem. But that was nothing; we knew boys his age who were already throwing punches at the principal, pulling knives on the lunch ladies, flashing guns they kept in their lockers, and getting sent to juvie.

In junior high a guidance counselor started calling me into her office, convinced I was being victimized or at least coerced by the older boys who trailed me in the halls trying to get me to ditch class to go fool around with them in the boys' room or behind the school gym. The lady didn't believe me when I told her not to worry, that everything I've ever done I did because I didn't mind it, not because someone forced me. I had this idea that it was on the older boys to teach us younger girls what to do with our bodies, the same way they taught us how to dance salsa and merengue at block parties and asados.

I could tell I'd stumped her.

The school board required us to go see a therapist a couple of times. We each had to talk to the guy, a grandfather type, individually and then the three of us went in together, but I don't think he got very far because, even back then, none of us were dumb enough to trust a shrink, and we eventually stopped going.

When Carlito was arrested, the papers mentioned those things. He was never a full-fledged delinquent but there were enough flags in Carlito's past and people willing to be quoted for articles, saying there'd always been something "not right" about my brother, árbol que nace torcido, jamás su tronco endereza. But Carlito had been the one to graduate from high school and even go to college and get a good job, so what if people who knew him would later say he shot up like a palm tree, only to fall like a coconut.

I didn't get so far. My grades were okay and I hung out with both the remedial crew and the jocks. But halfway through senior year I dropped out. It was right after the Christmas break and I was tired of it all. Mami and Carlito didn't try to talk me out of it. They both said that this meant I had to find a full-timer to earn my keep. Till then I'd just swept hair off the floor of a salon after school and on Saturdays. Mami was pretty good in school herself when she was growing up, even wanted to be a teacher, but that took time and teachers didn't get paid much in Colombia, always going on strike, and she had to work to help her mother maintain their home; they were women on their own ever since her father left them for another family in

Turbaco and the stepfather that came after him got stabbed to death over some money he owed, which Mami always counted as a miracle. She said life doesn't wait for education, and work is always the answer.

The same guidance counselor who'd tried to convince me I was victimized by the junior high boys was now an assistant principal at my high school and, after I quit, she came by the house trying to persuade me to reenroll. She didn't say I was smart or anything, she just said that I could do better in life than be a dropout. But I told her I'd had enough. I'd get my GED and start cosmetology school. If I'd been smarter about it, maybe I'd have put in some time trying to date athletes or drug dealers like other girls I knew and get myself set up that way. But I've never been what they call *forward thinking*.

In these in-between hours, I think about those faces from my old life.

Universo, the summers in Cartagena when we'd disappear together, sneaking off on his scooter to the beaches in Boca-grande and Castillogrande, when he'd tell me, like he was an expert, one of those fancy newspaper columnists or TV news commentators and not a kid who barely finished bachillerato, that the sand and sea were dark around Cartagena's edges because it was contaminated, not from the volcanic ash or even from the pollution of cargo boats and coastal factories, but by the blood that pooled together on its beaches from all over the Caribbean, the million souls lost on the journey to these shores. "It's a sea of death," Universo said. "But the water remembers what civilization tries to forget."

Or when Universo would take me to his favorite pool hall outside the city walls in San Fernando and he'd play for pesos until he had enough to buy us ice cream on the way home. By the time we'd make it back to El Centro, it would be dark, the prostitutes already out, old-timers standing in doorways of Getsemaní while the younger crop waited by the port or around the fancy hotels hoping to "coronar," find a foreigner to take them out of Cartagena, and Universo would joke that his mission was to coronar with me.

Sometimes I wish I'd held on a little longer, but my mother told me from the day I started running around with him in Cartagena that I should never fall in love with a boy like Universo, much less marry him. It would be like going backward, she said, and she always hoped I would at least have enough sense to marry for progress.

I wonder if he's still with his wife. If they've had kids or bought a house.

I wonder if he ever thinks of me or if he tries to guess where I went because I never told him.

What would he say if someone from the old neighborhood in Cartagena were to ask what happened to me?

Esa Reina. No dejó ni la sombra.

She didn't even leave a shadow.

Sometimes I even think about that dopey shrink, Dr. Joe. He left his job at the prison long before Carlito died, and even though I'd avoided the guy since the night with the dying bird, I asked the friendlier guards by the metal detectors about him, but nobody knew where he'd gone.

He came to mind again just yesterday when I asked Nesto, why, if he'd been such a reluctant father the first time, he'd gone ahead and had another kid. He'd already told me abortions were just about the only things in surplus in Cuba, and condoms—after a shortage in the eighties during which men got used to not wearing them—so plentiful they were often used to substitute as balloons for children to play with, or to make ice packs and sandbags, and during the Special Period, their plastic was even melted down to simulate cheese on pizzas.

He shrugged. "We both wanted another child, even if we couldn't stand each other. We went to see a Santero who threw the caracoles and he said we would have a girl. Every man wants a daughter."

I wondered if that was true.

Nesto watched me. I'd hardly mentioned Hector to him, but maybe that's why he was able to read my thoughts in that moment.

"I'm sure your father loved you."

It struck me because it was the exact opposite of what Dr. Joe had once told me—that the deep weight of sorrow I'd been born with was the unconscious awareness I had that my own father had never loved me, long before my mother even started telling me so, a trauma almost as severe as birth itself.

"I don't know about that, Nesto."

I thought this would be the end of the conversation, but he continued.

"All men love their daughters. It's a special love. Different than that for a son."

"Look, you can't speak for all men any more than I can speak for all women."

"You could if you wanted to."

"I wouldn't."

"It's the fear men feel. Sometimes it grows so big inside us, we can't help but hurt ourselves and the people around us."

Part of me wanted to laugh at how Nesto was comparing his failings to a part of my history unknown to him.

"You really shouldn't be so quick to defend a man you never knew."

"I'm not defending anyone." He sounded disappointed at my rejection of his wisdom. "Least of all myself."

I can guess what Dr. Joe would have to say about Nesto. He'd probably tally up his life's errors, blaming his early promiscuity, just like he did with me, saying it arrested my development and that's why I was so confused about normal human relations, but he argued that it wasn't my fault since I inherited the family female burden of early puberty.

Never mind that Nesto says sexual openness was just another tool the Revolution used to get kids to warm up to its doctrine and abandon the traditions of the past, the religion of their elders, and that Escuela al Campo was a free-for-all, where secondary school girls and boys were fair game for the teachers and staff, and students quickly learned sexual favors could earn them not only better grades, but more than the small share of putrid parasite-infested food they got after hours tending crops since their parents could only make the trip out there to visit them on Sundays, walking hours in the heat to bring their children home-cooked meals to keep in their lockers throughout the week though they were usually stolen by bullies or even by the school guards and teachers.

It was a brutal life training. This was the reason Nesto gagged at the smell of strawberries and cringed at the sight of tomatoes. For the months he spent picking them, and the shit he got kicked out of him in the filthy bathroom each night by the dorm thugs. By the next year's labor term, he came up with a plan to throw himself off the roof of his house so his ankle or arm would break or at least swell enough for a doctor to vouch that he was unfit for working the fields and give him permission to stay home. But the next year, they warned, even with a broken leg, he'd have to go back.

If there is one thing Nesto is grateful for now, he tells me, it's that the island has depleted its resources so much that there are no crops left to be tended and kids are no longer sent away each year to work out in the campo. No more coffee. No more sugar. The only thing the island has left to export now, he says, is its people.

Dr. Joe would have things to say about Nesto's infidelities to Yanai, too, which Nesto talks about like it's just another fact, nothing to brag about or hide. He told me he wasn't flagrant about it. He says he was no matatán or pinguidulce, just that sometimes he'd get caught up with other women who were between novios or maridos themselves and spend time at their homes; descargas, really—no vows or promises required.

Yanai figured it out, of course, as all women do.

Nesto says there is no room for secrets in Havana, no privacy to be had. Outside, there are the spying eyes of the DRC and surveillance cameras on street posts. Beyond the *Granma* newspaper propaganda, local chisme and chanchullo occupy the space of news of the rest of the world. Years pass and few things change but the lovers and pairings of the neighborhood folk.

You can't be modest over there, he tells me. Walls are thin. Windows are always open to let in a breeze. Alleyways echo. Everyone hears everything. Every moan, every pleasure cry. Sometimes the only place a couple can go to be alone is the roof of the building, ripping into each other on a dirty azotea, under the scorching sun or maybe protected by night shadows, but even then, you can be certain somebody, from some window on some building that's just a little bit higher, is watching.

Nesto says Yemayá was always good to him because he's a son of Ogún, to whom she was once married. When he was a boy diving off the Malecón, he says it was Yemayá, mother of all life under the sea, who kept him safe and out of Olokun's realm at the bottom of the ocean. She protected him from the insidious contracorriente that could pull him out to sea, and she kept the rough tide from slamming him against sharp rocks they called dientes de perro. When he was a teenager hunting in the water with only blurry goggles made out of melted boot rubber and beer bottle bottoms, Yemayá brought fish to him so he could catch them with his net or pierce them with his spear. She saved him from drowning more than once, Nesto says, always delivering him to the surface with her gentle power.

Nesto was never fully initiated to make Santo. He never had money to pay for the rites or the white wardrobe he'd have to wear for a year, all of which would have run in the thousands. Back then he'd sometimes stop in at an ilé ocha; go to a bembé or a toque de santo; watch as the musicians pounded the batás, calling to the orishas, before making their petitions and laying down their ofrendas. But he never did kariocha and was nobody's ahijado, and he didn't keep a canastillero or soperas for his orishas. In his room, he only kept a pair of candles, a dish full of candies, and a glass of rum he'd change every Monday in front of an image of Elegguá, master of fates.

On the last night of the year, Nesto pops open a bottle of rum inside the cottage, spilling a few drops behind my front door for Elegguá, who he says lives behind hinges, and more drops in every corner of the cottage, in remembrance of the ancestors.

I follow him out to the beach behind my cottage and sit on the sand as he steps to the water's edge, looking to the sky, palms up, asking for the blessing of the Great One, recognizing the dead who accompany him, known and unknown, the camaché, and looks down at his feet, asking Elegguá, who controls the flow of aché, to guard his health and for his specific request, the same thing he always asks for: to bring his family across the Straits to be with him and to intercede on his behalf to Obatalá, creator of mankind, and his wife Yemayá, mother of the ocean that separates him from his children.

Then Nesto reaches down to the white cloth at his feet where he's spread out pieces of watermelon, berries, and coffee beans, picks them up, carries them to the water's edge, and places them in the ocean. Rather than push the offering up to the sand, the tide takes it out with the current.

When he returns to my side on the beach, we take turns sipping from the bottle and he tells me that since he received his green card almost two years ago, he's started the paperwork to bring his kids over to be with him. But after waiting a year for their appointment to get their tarjeta blanca exit permit to leave the country, they've been denied and told to make another appointment, which they did, for the first available opening, three years from now. Even paying secret fees and bribes has only managed to bump the appointment up from three years to two.

Nesto gulps the rum. I've never seen him drink like this. He complains every other Caribbean rum tastes like candied piss compared to Havana Club, but that doesn't stop him from swallowing more and closing his eyes, and, as if he's forgotten I'm beside him, he whispers to the sky, "I don't know how much longer I can live like this."

It's not yet midnight but we can already hear firecrackers in the distance. The Broken Coconut put out word that they're launching fireworks from a barge offshore. I thought maybe Nesto would want to go see the display, but he said he just wants to be with the ocean tonight, and with me, if I don't mind.

He hands me the bottle and I take a few sips. I hold the rum in my mouth for a few seconds before letting it slide down, stinging my throat.

"What about you, Reina? Isn't there anything you want to ask for?"

"Ask who?"

He touches the sand and kisses his fingers before saying, "Olódumare."

"I don't know who that is."

"God. The supreme one. Owner of the day and night."

"I know you believe in that stuff, Nesto. But I don't."

"You don't need to believe to ask."

"Then I would be a hypocrite."

"No, you would be honest."

"I've learned asking for things doesn't work. You have to just accept what's given to you. Make the best of it."

"You don't believe in praying for things?"

I shake my head.

"You know, there was a time when all the birds of the world had feathers but no wings. They lived on the ground and leopards would come and eat them. The surviving birds prayed to Elegguá, asking him to find a way to protect them from the leopards. So Elegguá spread the birds' feathers and gave them wings with which to fly away from all the creatures that wanted to eat them."

"I don't need wings."

"I am sure there are other things you need. The only way to get what we want from life is to ask for it."

I smile but I can see it isn't enough for him; he wants me to say I'm willing to believe one can petition the sky and the sea and be heard.

Instead I say, "I believe there is what happens and what doesn't happen. Hoping or praying won't change that."

"If that were true, I wouldn't be here. I'd still be stuck on that island."

"Nesto, if there were such a thing as answered prayers, *I'm* the one who wouldn't be here."

"There are worse places you could be."

"If my prayers had been heard back when I used to say them, life wouldn't have taken the turns it did. I wouldn't have had to come here. I'd be somewhere else living some other life."

I mean that I would be with my brother, but Nesto takes it differently.

"You would be living somewhere with a wonderful husband and many children."

"Maybe."

"Is that what you want?"

"I don't *want* things the way other people do. I just take what I have, what's already in front of me."

"It's good to want things, Reina. We have to want things or we'll die."

"I don't think so."

"What makes you get out of the bed every morning?"

"The fact that being awake is better than being asleep."

"Why is that?"

"I dream too much."

"Your dreams are messages. They are telling you to pay attention to the world around you."

"Nesto. You have all the answers."

"Just look out there at the sea. We can't see below the surface but that doesn't mean that there's not a whole world under the current."

"If we go for a swim we'll see it."

"No, we'll see just a small piece of it. And you don't have to see all of it, so immense it's beyond our comprehension. You just have to know it's there. It's the same with everything else. If you take a chance believing, you'll see what can happen."

I consider telling him I once had faith. I was, for a brief time, a young girl who prayed and believed in the unseen, perhaps as much as he does, but it all fell away from me.

Instead, I shove him gently.

"You live in your world. I'll live in mine."

He stands up quickly and stretches his hand out to me to pull me to my feet as well.

"What is it?"

"Come on," he says "We have to bring in this new year with happiness, not with such gloomy talk. It's bad luck."

"What are we going to do?" I'm standing in front of him now, still holding his hand, which he holds up, putting his other hand on my waist.

"We're going to dance."

He starts swaying gently, guiding me with his hands and steps, following the slow rhythm of the tide washing up the shore just inches away, and he adds his voice to it, humming the tune to "Lágrimas negras," which he once told me was his mother's favorite bolero. With each step he leads me a bit closer to the surf, until the cold foam covers our toes and then reaches above our ankles. He's close enough for me to feel his warm breath pass my cheek, but his body is far, his long arms between us. I step in closer, without thinking much about it, but he steps back, and I try it again, and again he steps back.

"It's not so bad where you ended up, Reina, is it?"

"No. It's not."

I lean my face forward to kiss him, but he pulls back before my lips reach his, though he never stops dancing.

"What are you doing?" I say, because he says nothing.

"I'm dancing with you."

"You don't want to kiss me."

"I do."

"But you won't."

He drops my hands and steps away, leaving me alone with my feet in the water.

He turns his back to me to face the moon behind us.

"Lolo invited me out on his boat tomorrow. Do you want to come?"

I walk up on the beach and sit on a mound of sand a few feet from him.

"Okay."

"I'll sleep here tonight, if you don't mind."

"No problem."

He walks up to the cottage but I remain behind on the beach, digging my feet into the sand.

When I go back inside a while later, Nesto is already stretched out on my sofa, asleep or at least pretending to be.

I don't fall sleep for a while though. I sit on my bed with the nightstand light on beside me and think back to the end of last year, when I still lived in the Miami house, and Carlito was still alive and waiting for my next visit. I brought him chocolates that morning but the guard took them away at the security check because someone got caught a month or two before smuggling pills inside a similar box. When I got to the visiting room to see Carlito, I only had a corny Christmas card to give him. I'd bought it at a drugstore and planned to write a nice note inside but no words came to me, so below the printed message, I'd only signed my name.

When he opened the card, Carlito traced his fingers over the letters.

"Did you know I was the one who picked your name? Mami wanted to call you María Reina de la Paz after Abuela's favorite Virgin, but I convinced her to just call you Reina. I said you were *my* Reina. My little queen."

"Carlito, how is that possible? You were only three."

"Ask Mami. She'll tell you."

And for once, when I asked my mother about one of Carlito's stories of our childhood she nodded, turning her face from me to the ground.

"Sí, Reina. Your brother named you. That much is true."

Nesto can't believe I've never been on a boat. I grew up close to the Atlantic, not on an island where you need a permit to take a boat offshore like he and Lolo did. But I've never even been on one of those Everglades airboats that blow through the swamps on gator tours. I've never even been on a canoe.

To ease my introduction to the open ocean, on the way to the marina to meet Lolo and his Boston Whaler, Nesto tells me one of his favorite patakís:

"In the beginning, the earth was made of only rocks and fire. So Olódumare in the form of Olofi, the all-powerful, turned the smoke of the flames into clouds, and from the clouds came down water, which put out the fires, and a new world was born. In the holes between the once burning rocks, oceans formed. What remained above the water was known as *land*. Olofi gave the oceans to Olokun and the land to Obatalá with a small pile of dirt that a chicken scratched out with its feet to form the continents. But Obatalá was jealous of Olokun's vast domain, so he chained her to the ocean floor where she remains with a great serpent that only peeks out its head with the new moon. Olokun is vengeful, though, and still tries to steal parts of Obatalá's land for herself, by shaking the sea floor, sending up tidal waves and tsunamis from the deep.

"When it was created, the ocean was massive and empty of life. At this time, Yemayá lived in the heavens with Olofi, complaining that her womb ached. It's Yemayá who gave birth to the sun, the moon, the planets, the stars, and to the rivers, the lakes, and to the orishas, becoming mother to all life on earth. To show his love for her, Olofi made Yemayá queen of the oceans and gave her the rainbow to wear as a crown, which appears only when Yemayá shows herself to the world in the form of rain."

We are only a few miles offshore when my stomach starts to quiver.

I feel the vibration of the engine under us, watch the marina shrink, the darkening of the crystalline waters bordering the islands, from my place on a padded bench on the back of the boat with Melly, Lolo's wife, while Nesto has joined Lolo by the wheel.

Melly has already peeled off her shorts and is down to her string bikini, posing on the edge of the boat like one of those rubber truck flap girls. She's twenty-two and Lolo's third wife, though they have this running joke that he only married her because she's Canadian and wanted to get her U.S. papers. She calls herself a wildlife artist, but I saw her work when Nesto and I went to meet them at Lolo's dive shop earlier this morning, and her paintings aren't what you'd call *natural*—they show dolphins and stingrays paired with big-breasted mermaids touching the animals in lusty ways. Nesto and I had to keep from spitting our laughter when we saw them all over the dive shop walls next to posters for wetsuit brands.

I'm thinking about Melly's paintings when I throw up the first time, all my breakfast into the white waves spiking against the side of the boat. Nesto has his back to me so he doesn't notice until Melly makes a fuss, running to my side, rubbing my shoulders. I push her away and keep on vomiting, which would be embarrassing if I were to stop and think about it, but I can only focus on the churning of my stomach and the burning of my throat as stuff keeps coming up and up.

I hear them all behind me, Lolo saying we're hardly two miles out and I'm already tossing up hasta el último tetero. Then

Nesto is beside me, telling me to concentrate on the horizon, but when I try to it looks lopsided to me and the only thing that helps is closing my eyes and forgetting where I am if for just a second.

"Do you want us to turn back?" I can tell by Nesto's tone that he wants me to say no, so that's what I give him, while steadying myself on the railing, and he goes back to Lolo and tells him I'll be fine.

But I am not fine. I feel a confusion of my senses. On my back, the sun is warm and delicious; the sea salt is calming and aromatic; and the splash of the boat cutting through waves, sprinkling cool drops on my face, is a relief from the convulsions I feel from the neck down, my intestines twisting, exorcising themselves even when there is nothing left to push up. I want to forget where I am. Forget I'm on a boat heading to nowhere in the ocean, with Nesto, who, at this moment, seems more of a stranger to me than the night I met him, and his friends, who I sense mocking me as they trade glances.

And then I am not there anymore.

I am still under the winter sun, still surrounded by water, but now I am a child again, maybe five or six, swimming at the public pool Mami sometimes took us to during the free family-swim hours since Carlito didn't hate pools as much as he hated the ocean. One afternoon, Carlito and I made friends with another kid, a girl there with her father. She had inflatable tubes, floating toys, all for her, but she shared them with us. I was drawn to this father-and-daughter twosome, mystified by the gentleness with which the father handled his daughter and how she hung on to him, her arm around his neck. When Carlito got out of the pool to sit by our mother on the lounge chairs, I stayed in the water with the girl and her father. She would invite me over to her house one day to play with her dozens of Barbie dolls, she said. I didn't have any.

Her father picked her up and tossed her across the water and she landed with a big splash. He must have seen the envy on my face because he told me to swim over and lifted me up to do the same. I never felt such big hands on me. I never knew a person could be so strong. I didn't remember ever being carried off the ground by anyone. He tossed me up and away and I crashed into the water. When I came up for air, I looked over at my brother to see if he'd seen me soaring but he hadn't.

Then the father was carrying his daughter and pulling her toward the deep end, where I wasn't allowed. "Do you want to come?" he asked, and I looked back at my mother, lying on a plastic lounge chair, reading a magazine, and back to the man, nodding. He picked me up in his other arm and we glided, all three of us, two little girls in a father's embrace, to the deeper water, and I felt the thrill of knowing the floor was too far below for me to touch. I felt safe in this father's arms. He led us over to the wall and we perched there, the three of us, each girl straddling one of the father's knees. The daughter was talking about the new dress her father had bought her that morning—long and lavender with a ruffled bottom. It sounded like the most beautiful dress in the world. I could not imagine what it would be like to have a father buy me nice things and I watched her and her father and the way they loved each other. I felt something poke my leg and when I looked down, through the gloss of the pool water, I saw the father's penis had grown and popped out of his bathing suit. I knew what a penis was because I had a brother and during our early years, we took our baths together. I said to the father, "You should fix your bathing suit," and he looked down and said, "Yes, I should," and put himself away. But it happened again and when

I told the father this time, he said, "Why don't you fix it for me?" I looked at the girl, who didn't react, and then at my mother, still buried in her magazine pages, and my brother drying off with a towel on the chair beside her. I called to my mother, but she only looked up and when I said nothing else, she turned back to her magazine. I tried my brother. I called his name. He looked at me, and again I said nothing, but he stood up and came to me. He knew something was wrong. The man squirmed beneath me, and I reached my hand out to my brother and let him pull me out of the water. I said nothing and my brother saw nothing, but still looked at the man with suspicion. We went back to our mother, who still hadn't noticed a thing.

"I want to go home," I told our mother, afraid to look back at the girl with her father, afraid of what I'd seen under the water.

It's a memory that hasn't come to me in years. One I've never spoken of. But here it is, laid out before me in the delirium of my seasickness, until we are so far out that there is no land and no other boat to be seen in any direction. We are beyond the buoys, the pale shallow waters and sandbars along the coast emptied into to a watery lapis plateau.

Lolo drops anchor and the boat gives into bobbing over the waves that makes me lurch over the side, its engine fumes conjuring another vomit spell.

Nesto kneels beside me.

"I'm sorry, Reina. If I'd known you would get so sick, I never would have asked you to come."

His words aren't any consolation. I pull back, lie on the boat floor, hoping it will feel steadier, focusing on the sky above, but it doesn't help.

"You've got to get in the water," he urges me. "It will make you feel better."

He pulls his shirt over his head and is down to his shorts, which he steps out of too, and there he is, all of him crammed into a small swimsuit—the kind most guys, except professional swimmers, avoid.

I've never seen so much of Nesto. So much of his skin, his limbs, the length of his legs, bare toe to bare thigh. The stretch of his waist, hip folds to armpit. I remember him telling me that in Cuba, it's common for guys to shave their bodies from the waist up or even all over, because the weather is so hot, sometimes the water supply is cut, and it's a way to keep from stinking between showers: Nesto, hairless except for some stubble on his chest and that mane, which he pulls back with a thick rubber band. He catches me staring at him and waves his hand at me, as if I am hypnotized, and I look away, prop myself on my knees and over the boat railing again, eyes back on that unreliable horizon, and throw up some more.

When I look back up, Lolo is stripped down to an equally small bathing suit, and I notice a tattoo across his back of what has to be one of Melly's mermaids. He pulls a bottle of shampoo out of a bag and pours it all over Nesto's shoulders, and then onto his own chest and they each begin rubbing themselves down. I don't want to ask what they're doing. I just watch as Nesto's dark skin turns slick and shiny, but then it becomes clear they're just lubricating themselves to make it easier to get into their wetsuits.

When he's all wrapped in neoprene, Nesto reaches for me. "Come, Reina."

I take his hand and he leads me along the railing to the back of the boat, where he helps me sit down beside him, our feet hanging over the edge into the cold water.

He dips the mask he's been holding in his other hand into the ocean, fills it with water, then puts it up to my face.

"Close your eyes," he says, and I do.

He says some words in Lucumí, then, so I can understand, says, "Yemayá, take Reina into your arms," before pouring the water over my head.

I feel it run down my face, cooling my neck, my back, and my chest.

When I open my eyes, Nesto is watching me.

"Get in the water. Swim. It will help you, I promise."

He starts putting some long fins on his feet while Lolo tosses a large inflatable red tube on a long cord off the back of the boat.

"And when you get in, you do it like this."

He launches himself sideways off the back of the boat, disappears under the water, then breaks through the surface again, grinning.

"You'll only feel worse if you stay on board, Reina. Come in. I'm waiting for you."

Melly lets me use her wetsuit since she's decided to stay on the boat to work on her tan, and helps me lotion up, then pull the neoprene up over my thighs and around my hips, which is much harder than it looked when I watched Nesto do it. When I have it on properly, she zips me up from behind and I feel the suit push against my ribs up to my neck.

"Breathe," she tells me. "You'll get used to it. It'll feel better in the water."

She gives me her fins and mask too, and leads me to the ladder at the back of the boat to help me as I put them on.

"Are you scared?"

"Of what?"

"Of this," she points to the dark water all around us.

"What do you mean?"

"Out here is where the ocean floor drops off. Didn't you notice how clear and light the water is when we're closer to land? That's because it's not so deep. Then the ocean floor takes a big hit hundreds of feet down and you're out here, in the blue."

"Should I be scared?"

"You'll be fine as long as you don't panic and start swallowing water."

Nesto and Lolo are on the line by the buoy calling for me to come in, so Melly helps me push off the ladder into the cold water, sideways, just like Nesto said, and I feel it slip between my skin and suit. I push the fins with my legs, propelling myself along the surface, pulling myself along the line toward the buoy where Nesto waits with Lolo.

"Are you still sick?"

"I'll be okay." But as soon as I say it, a wave pushes against me and my stomach goes up with it, then back down, and the sickness returns.

"Put the mask on and go under," Nesto instructs me, and I do as he says.

Nesto and Lolo have weight belts on and lower another weighted line off the tube and start timing each other, doing ventilation patterns, so they can better hold their breath to dive on air. I don't have a weight belt, just the mask and snorkel and fins, so I remain on the surface but once I turn my face downward, I gasp at the immensity of the realm below, slivers of sunlight shooting through the blue like lightning.

I don't see small fish like the ones you see in tropical aquariums or when you snorkel by the reefs or close to the beach, with the stripes and dots. I see nothing, really, just a big slow-moving fish several meters under me, the outlines of a few small jellyfish bouncing along. Otherwise it's quiet, still, shadows and blueness and emptiness as far as I can see in any direction, which isn't very far, it turns out, because Lolo later tells me no matter how good the day's visibility, sunlight only penetrates the first two hundred meters of the ocean and beyond that it's an eternal midnight.

Even on the most perfect sunny day, the ocean lit up like a chandelier, Nesto says there is an underworld of inverted mountains far beneath the shimmering surface sea, valleys and canyons miles beyond the faintest trace of light.

I feel a tug on my suit and pop my head up to see Nesto tying a rope around my waist.

"You're drifting. I don't want to lose you out here."

Maybe it's because I feel a little safer knowing I am tied to him and to the tube that I spit the snorkel out and try to dive under, though my wetsuit makes me buoyant and I don't go very far. But being underwater soothes me. My stomach and my nerves calm. The boat fumes dissipate. My body turns and curls as it wants, weightless, with the ease of an acrobat.

I think of my mother and how, when I was a child, she'd take me into the water with her and I felt time suspended in her embrace. How badly I've wanted to return to those moments. We remained under the same roof, but the years pulled us apart, so we could never recover the softness I felt from her under the sun, amid the waves.

Here, in the open ocean, with nobody to hold me at the surface but myself, I become sad for what's become of my mother and me, the ways life hardened us to one another.

I turn and see Nesto a few meters away, lowering himself headfirst down the line, one hand on the rope, the other pinching his nose. A pair of sea horses comes into my line of vision, then floating close, just in front of my mask. I've never seen them swimming free like this. At the dolphinarium, there is a display near the entrance with a few sea horses that usually coil their small tails onto the seaweed at the bottom of the tank. They're supposed to prefer shallow waters, but here, this pair glides along, tails tied in courtship, and I almost do what Melly warned me against, swallow water, in my effort to call to Nesto, who is back up on the surface, gasping for air.

He gathers his breath and swims over to me, looking concerned, while Lolo waits on the line rig behind him. I take his hand and guide him to where the seahorses seemed to dance under a strobe of sunlight a moment ago. We go under together and the seahorses are still there, twirling beneath the current. We watch them for a few seconds. When we come up for air, Nesto looks pleased.

"Seahorses are a sign," he tells me.

"Of what?"

"You don't believe in signs, remember?"

"Tell me, Nesto."

"It's Yemayá. She's welcoming you. She's giving you a place out here."

On the way back to shore, Lolo stops the boat by the Key Largo hump where the continental shelf rises into a little mountain that pushes the smaller fish to the surface and larger fish come after them. That's what he tells me when I ask if I can get off the boat again and go for another swim. I'm not sick anymore. Ever since I got in the water out in the blue, I feel calm, and the feeling remained even when I climbed back in the boat and it started up again, skipping and splitting waves.

Out by the hump, there are a lot more boats, most outrigged with multiple fishing poles, hoping for bites from bonefish, tarpon, or snook. As Lolo sets up a couple of poles off the back of the boat, I know we'll be here a while. But he says I can't go for a swim because along with barracuda, there are plenty of sharks out in the hump and once in a while even a wandering great white makes an appearance. I settle onto a bench with Melly. She's been nice and helped me out of her wetsuit just like she'd helped me into it. She ran the freshwater hose all over me to wash off the salt and shampoo residue, and brushed out my hair.

"I've never seen Nesto with a girl before," she tells me when the guys are out of earshot and deep into some story about the old days spearfishing in El Salado. "Whenever he comes around, he's always alone. I tried to set him up with friends of mine a few times, but he's always said no. How long have you known him?"

"About two months."

"I knew Lolo three months when I married him. And that was three years ago."

"Really?"

"I came to his shop looking for a job. He said, 'I can't give you no job if you don't have no papers.' I said, 'Well, how am I supposed to get papers if I don't have a job?' so he said, 'You can marry me.' And he leaned right over the counter and pulled my face to his and kissed me right there with customers all around. That's how he got me to go out with him. I didn't think I'd marry him, but I like a guy who goes after what he wants."

I remember being on the beach with Nesto last night. How he treated kissing me like I was asking him to walk off a cliff.

There's a tug on one of the lines and Lolo rushes to it while Nesto looks at the others, but they're all slack. Lolo reels in his line and, after a small struggle, a fish turns up, flapping and fighting against the hook and line until the poor wahoo is flopping to its bloody death on the floor of the boat and Melly claps and cheers like it's a party, as Lolo grabs the fish, ramming his fingers into its gills. I look at Nesto, who also looks pleased with the massacre, then turn my eyes back to the horizon because I know I might be sick again.

Later, at Lolo and Melly's house, the guys skin and gut the fish for dinner out on the patio while I help Melly make a salad in the kitchen. It's a small house, with a lanai that opens onto a narrow canal on the edge of the ocean, and Melly's interspecies orgy paintings cover the walls. She sends me out back to ask if we should put some rice on the stove too. I slip out the screen door, to the block of patio around the side of the house where they are filleting the fish, and that's when I hear Lolo ask Nesto, as if he's been waiting for an update, "¿Qué vuelta, asere? Tell me, what's going on with the family situation?"

I wait behind the corner of the house, curious how Nesto will respond.

"Nothing's happening, 'mano. They keep telling us to wait. But I can't anymore. I have to figure something else out."

I stand there a moment longer to see if they'll say more, but they don't. When they see me come around the bend they both look at me, surprised. I ask about the rice and Lolo says it's a good idea, but Nesto just stares at me as if we're meeting for the first time, or as if he's forgotten I've been along for the ride all afternoon.

I leave them and go back to Melly in the kitchen. By the time we sit at the table under the sunset to eat the fish Lolo grilled for us, I've put the conversation I overheard out of mind, until I notice Nesto's eyes leave me, leave all of us at the table, to stare across the Atlantic as if it holds some kind of answer.

I'm used to disappearances.

I'm never surprised when guys take off. It's the opposite. I never expect them to stick around.

I don't hear from Nesto for a few days.

Then I run into him, though it's not a complete coincidence because I know he goes to check his box at the post office every Tuesday and Friday afternoon, after he fills his gas tank. I go check my mail at around that time, and there he is, pulling his blue pickup into the parking lot. I pretend not to see him right away. I want him to be the one to decide if he's going to approach me or if we're going to do that thing where we ignore each other until it's clear one of us wants nothing to do with the other anymore.

I park in front of the post office and pretend to fumble with my purse for a while, getting out of the car before walking up to the glass post office doors extra slowly to give him time to finish up and hopefully catch him on the way out. I'm a good planner because it happens exactly that way and he spots me easing out of my car, walks over like he's not at all surprised to see me, and pulls me into his chest.

"I'm sorry—"

"You don't have to be sorry for anything." I cut him off, ducking out of his arms. "We don't owe each other anything."

He looks a little confused at my words but goes on. "I'm sorry I didn't tell you. I went up to Miami for a few days. I just got back."

"I thought you hated it there."

"I had to take care of some things."

"Things?"

"Family things."

"You couldn't do that from down here?"

"No."

We watch each other for a moment until Nesto asks, "Aren't you going to go in and check your mail?"

I shrug. "You know I hardly ever get anything."

"Then let's get out of here. I did some work for a friend in Miami." He pats his wallet in his back pocket. "Let me invite you to dinner."

I leave my car back at the cottage and go with Nesto in his truck. We don't say much. He pops a disc of ballads into the stereo, singing along, and mutters between songs that he should have tried a little harder to make something of himself when he was younger and still had the chance. As a teenager, he and his friends would strum guitars and sing through apagones that shut down the city through the night until the electricity came back on. He was always told he had a good voice, rich and raw. He could have gone to a conservatory, he says, maybe even made a career of music. It would have been the smartest thing since the only Cubans who can get rich legally these days are artists and musicians.

He drives south till we're on the far end of Marathon, pulls off the road to a thatch-roof restaurant built on the waterfront below the start of the Seven Mile Bridge, stretching as far as anyone can see over the glassy shallows, an occasional fishing boat pushing through below its columns. The hostess, a girl who looks both faded and burned, seats us at a plastic table by the water's edge and drops laminated menus between us.

When Nesto is done fumbling through his menu I say, "You want to tell me something. I can feel it."

"You're right."

"So what is it?"

"I've been thinking of ways to say this." His nostrils expand with a long sigh. "I wanted us to be friends when we met. You know that. But things are different from what I expected."

He stares at me like I'm supposed to finish his thought.

"You understand what I mean, don't you?"

I shake my head.

"I know you like me. You know I like you. More than I would like any other girl at this point."

He looks out to the water, up to the sky, and mumbles something I can't make out to the clouds, then turns his eyes back on me.

"I do not want to burden you with my shit, Reina. I've told you about my life. It's a disaster. The situation with my family . . . está en candela."

"Everyone's life is a disaster."

He's shaking his head and I know no matter what I say, he's decided I've got it all wrong.

"Since I left home, I've been like a lone wolf in the hole I live in. Go to work alone. Go home alone. Eat alone. Sleep alone. I don't keep track of anyone and nobody keeps track of me. That's the only way I can be until I restore things, until I get my kids out of there. Until that happens, I'm not a real person. I'm not even *half* a person. I'm a maldito shadow."

He looks out to the water again, as if he can see them on the other side of the sunset.

"I like the time I spend with you. You've become important to me. And I think I've become important to you. But listen to me when I tell you this: I can give you nothing. I *am* nothing."

"Don't say—"

"You don't know, Reina. You can't understand what it is to be separated from my children. Lives you have watched since birth, that you brought into this crazy world. To have them cry to you every time you call because they don't understand why you left them. They have this idea of this country that everyone is a millionaire and lives like a movie star. They don't know how hard it is. They don't know that everything I do, every day I work, everything is for them. I did everything right. I adjusted my status to get political asylum, got the green card. I filed all the papers for them to come and they still can't get out. Every year it's another denial. They tell everyone there to wait, wait, because there is nothing else to do, and there's *nobody* better at waiting than a Cuban. But I'm here and I can't wait anymore. Maybe I made the wrong choice. Maybe I should have stayed with them. I wonder about that every single day that I'm here without them. I would still be eating shit over there, but at least I'd see them every day and we'd still spend birthdays and holidays together. You don't know what it is to have your family broken by a system, by old men who refuse to die, all because we were born in the wrong country at the wrong time in history, and to be able to do nothing about it."

The waitress appears to take our order.

"Reina," he says when she's gone, impatiently, as if my own name irritates him. "You think I don't want to kiss you? I'm there in your house, sleeping on your sofa, and you think it doesn't occur to me to get in your bed with you?"

I feel heat rising to my face. So *this* is blushing. Something I don't ever remember happening to me. I turn to the dock lining the water, the pelicans settling onto its posts.

"Mírame a los ojos, Reina. Why do you always look away when I have something important to tell you?"

I turn to face him.

"I do want to do all that and more with you," he says sternly. "But it wouldn't be right. You've got your own life and your own problems. You don't need to endure mine too."

I don't say anything and he goes quiet too.

No more arguing against this idea of him and me. I don't know if he expected a debate or some pained expression from me. Either way, I don't give it.

Night's fallen completely and the bridge is just a silver beam shooting over the ocean, dotted with car lights heading to and from Key West. I can barely see the contours of his face but the waitress sets a hurricane lantern at the center of the table and then he's back, fuzzy in the golden light.

I think we're at the point in the confession where we should begin to feel absolved, expectations relinquished, but none of the heaviness has lifted from his side of the table and instead Nesto exhales so long and airy I feel his breath brush my lips.

"Reina, you know me, and pretty well in the short time we've spent together. But when you're with me, you're not with only me. There are other people I carry with me everywhere I go. People you can't see. People I left behind. You don't know what that's like."

"I *do* know," I whisper.

I want to tell him I am the same, with my own army on my shoulders, guarded against my chest, those I can't shake even when I try.

"I won't be whole until I'm with them again," he says. "It's all I think about."

Something in me tightens. A sudden awareness. I feel it deep within, the same way I felt it when I entered the courtroom the day of my brother's sentencing; despite our hopes and endless prayers that the judge would override the jury's recommendation for capital punishment, before he even began his remarks, before he slipped on his bifocals, cleared his throat, and turned from Isabela to Carlito and said, "Mr. Castillo, you have committed one of the most monstrous acts that I have come across in my very long career," I knew that my brother would be sentenced to death.

Maybe this is not a premonition but just an impulse for cruelty or even jealousy, my wanting to grab Nesto by the shoulders and tell him not to count on it, there is no such thing as redemption, and the day of the great reunion of his dreams may never come for him, just as mine never came for me.

The ride back up to Crescent Key is just as silent, except for Nesto humming along to "Corazón partío," which he plays on repeat. When he pulls into the Hammerhead driveway, I hop out of the car, but his reflexes are quick and he catches me by the wrist.

"Wait, Reina."

"I think we said everything already."

"Not everything."

"¿Entonces?"

"I mean it when I say I have nothing to give you. Not for a while."

"I never asked you for anything."

"So what are you doing with me?"

I shrug.

"Just passing time, like you told your mother the other day on the phone?"

"I just want to be here, with you, now."

"Just tonight?"

"I don't know. Tonight is tonight. Tomorrow is tomorrow."

I turn and we watch each other through the shadows, but it's too much for me, and I leave him there to make my way toward the cottage.

I stop behind the trees to watch him drive off, but he doesn't. Not right away.

He stays parked in the driveway for a while as if waiting for something, maybe for me, to come back to him, but I don't. Not tonight.

I find my way through the dark path I've memorized until I'm at my door.

Home.

There are footsteps. Soft taps at the door.

There is Nesto. A determined look in his eyes that throws me a little, but he's already stepping through my doorway and I can't describe the play-by-play, I just know that all at once, his lips are on me, his arms are around me, heavy and crushing, and we fall onto my bed so hard it shifts from its place along the wall. I feel his heaviness, the sharpness of his muscles and bones against mine.

Normally, I disappear into my body, into another plane of blindness where I see nothing, not even the face hovering over mine. In the tension, the rising pleasure, I feel disintegration, crumbling, and release, and I float in the nothingness, the physical exchange, the affirmations that it feels good, that he wants me. I remember nothing afterward. No longing, not even residue desire; like the moisture on my skin, once washed off, it's gone.

Nesto finds the deepest places in me, his lips never leaving me, his lashes soft against my cheek, his breath warming me. I want to say Nesto is the first man I was ever with. He's not. Not even close. So then I want to say he is the last. And by being the last he is the first.

Since the first night, there have been many more like it. And mornings. And afternoons. In my bed, on the sofa until we drop onto the floor of my cottage, against the hard corners of the shower stall, out on my beach under the discreet cover of night, shells and twigs burrowed into our backs. At his place, testing the wobbly futon frame, in that run-down chair, on the cold metal of the back of his truck parked out on a desolate road at the end of Indigo Key. And on Lolo's boat, on days when there is no dive group for him to take out to the wrecks and reef, when he lends it to Nesto, so that he can break me of my seasickness forever.

He wants me to feel as at home on and in the water as he does, he says, and once we are docked, far enough that no other human can lay eyes on us, he drops anchor and tosses out a float and a line. He kisses me while the water holds me up to him. My senses are amplified. When I open my eyes, instead of wondering what we're doing out in the middle of the ocean, I feel I don't need land or even air anymore, as long as I am with him.

"Why did we wait so long for this?" he says.

And then, "I don't understand how you ended up so alone in this world, Reina. I don't understand how anybody ever let you go."

Our only promise is to not make any, never to speak of tomorrow, only this day and this night.

Now, when my sleep breaks, instead of falling into memory, I'm pulled only as far as the body sleeping beside me. He stirs, eyes closed, to reach for me, to wrap himself around me, pulls me into him. He always wakes before morning comes, so we can enjoy the last bits of each other before the day pushes us apart.

My mother taught me to read hands at the same time she taught me to apply polish. Not by reading the lines of a palm, but the way she'd learned from her mother and her mother before her, by touch, decoding the curves of the hand without looking. Carlito never knew about our ability. Our mother never shared those things with him. She said there were some things that were meant to stay between mothers and daughters. It was by holding my brother's hands, once when I went to see him at the jail during the first days after his arrest, running my fingers over the rough swells at the base of his fingers, that I knew that even though Carlito was still screaming injustice, he was guilty and would never again walk free. I lived my life differently, always wearing the costume of hope, but that's just an example of how easy it is to ignore intuition and betray oneself.

I asked my mother once if she ever read our father's hands. She thought about it before admitting she didn't remember ever feeling his hand in hers. He was always grabbing her, touching her, but always on her body, or pulling her by the arm down the street, as if this might be the moment she'd flee. There was never intimacy, the sort you assume exists between married people. The more she considered it, the more she was sure she'd never touched his hands. Not until he was dead and she saw him in the morgue when the prison turned him over. She'd gone with Tío Jaime and Mayra. She didn't want to, but they'd forced her to go to bid him a proper adios since she was the wife and there were vows between them. Tío Jaime and Mayra thought that was the moment Mami should have told Carlito and me the truth about our papi, and given us a chance to see him off ourselves, but Mami refused, and held on to the secret for a few more years.

After Hector, though, Mami started reading the hands of every guy she dated. And when Jerry came onto the scene, she fingered his palm across a restaurant table on their first date and knew right away that he had enough money for two, plus square fingertips, which any clairvoyant worth a dime knows are given to those who are born to count cash. She didn't care about love or romance. She only wanted a guy who could make her life a little easier.

She never read my hands and I wasn't allowed to read hers. She warned me that to do so was courting bad luck, like burning the wings of a butterfly. But I didn't listen, always trying to read my own palms, but then my intuition grew cloudy, and I could only sense that the solitude I lived with, even before my brother left us, the loneliness I felt even when surrounded by my own family, would never leave me.

Then I went to the blue-haired bruja because I figured she was a professional and people came from other states to see her and she even had her own international hotline. And she, with her tarot cards, candles, and long fingernails painted with chipped purple polish, pushed hard into the lines of my hand and told me my mother was cursed because of her sins and I, as the daughter, would pay her debts; that the devil had followed my family all the way from Cartagena to Miami, and then, what I had suspected for a long time:

"Love is not meant for you. You will always be alone."

"You need a manicure," was all I replied.

I thought the reading was finished so I pulled my hand back to reach for my wallet to pay her, but she held my wrist firm in her swollen, arthritic fingers and told me to wait, there was more.

"Your mother didn't want you," she said.

"Neither did yours."

She let go of my hand and told me I owed her two hundred dollars.

I dropped the cash onto her table and left.

I try to resist reading Nesto's hands. But in the early morning, when the cottage is washed with white light, when his arms are draped over me and he is snoring into my shoulder, I can't help closing my eyes and letting my fingers touch their way to the truth on his skin.

A faraway sensation comes over me. I don't know what to make of it at first, but then I understand that despite his closeness, his chest so tight against my back that we are sharing sweat, his mouth resting on my neck just like last night and dozens of nights before, there is still a nameless void between us that will never dissipate.

That's what I get, I decide, for trying to peek at the future when it seems the present is just starting to be kind to me.

So I stop myself and focus again, not on my touching and reading him, but on his touching and reading me.

When we were kids, Carlito and I ate the crummy lunch provided by the school's public assistance program. We faced our butter and baloney sandwiches and waxy apples while other kids ate lunches their parents packed for them, full of treats and last night's dinner. Carlito would identify these kids and take their food from them, giving me half of everything, until the lunch lady caught him and turned him in to the principal.

"I don't care how much you hate the food they give you, stealing is wrong," Mami told him after she got the call from the school.

"How am I supposed to get what I want if I don't take it?" Carlito asked.

Mami never answered him.

When Carlito was an altar server at the church, he started a little side business taking the flowers people left at the feet of different statues of saints, selling them outside the supermarket or at gas stations, or just to other boys from school to give to the girls they liked. One of the priests confronted him but Carlito argued he was doing no harm, and those flowers got thrown out at the end of every week anyway. The priest never told our mother, but Carlito decided to move on to cemeteries, picking bouquets off tombstones and out of the vases on the walls of mausoleums.

Instead of selling the roses and carnations himself, he put me to work. I'd stand by gas pumps, tell people I was selling the flowers to raise money for our school so we could buy new books and pens and art supplies, while Carlito watched and waited nearby. He gave me a dollar for every five that I made.

He'd be ceremonious about it when he later counted the bills on his bedroom floor, making me hold out my palms until he placed the bills on them.

"Bien hecho, hermanita."

Or on days I didn't sell so much, he'd shake his head disapprovingly.

"You can do better, Reina. Make your big brother proud."

He always gave me a bonus of a few dollars to make sure I kept my mouth shut about the whole operation and didn't start feeling guilty, confessing to Mami what we were doing. Carlito taught me there was a price to be paid for my silence and complicity, and I was honored to be his secret keeper.

For all the new people who turn up each day in the Keys, looking for a new life, there are even more people leaving. But that doesn't make it any easier to find work. I try every salon on Crescent and all the neighboring Keys, but I'm told there is no room for new hires. I apply for a few waitressing jobs, but they say I have no restaurant experience. I try stores up and down the islands, even ask Julie if she needs a hand selling painted coconuts and Lolo if he needs help in his shop. But people say with low season coming, they're better off short-staffed than taking on a new employee. Nesto counts himself among the lucky ones. After he fixed the turtle habitat, Mo, the manager of the dolphinarium, kept calling him for more repair jobs until he finally offered Nesto a permanent position, since something there needs to be fixed every day.

I spent plenty of time going along to work with Nesto before they took him on full-time, passing him his tools, just being an extra set of hands to feel useful in my unemployment. Nesto complains about working under the sun but I like the warmth, the breeze, so different from the stale recycled air and nail polish and acetone fumes I'm used to.

I decide to apply for a job at the dolphinarium too.

"How are you at math?" Mo asks during my interview.

We are alone within the wood-paneled walls of the back office. Between us, a wide desk covered in a mound of loose papers and manila folders that makes him look even smaller as he sits in his swivel chair.

"I've never had a problem calculating tabs, counting tips, or paying bills."

He looks down at my résumé in his hands. I printed it out fresh though it's already denting in the blow of the air conditioning.

"I see you don't have a proper high school diploma. You'd need at least that for me to put you on the register in the gift shop."

"It's never been an issue before."

He looks over the list of my past employment again and I notice the cut in his cheek that makes a shadow across half his face.

"How about I put you with the cleaning and feeding crew, and just rotate you around wherever you're needed? You'll help prepare the animals' food barrels, clean the pens. What do you think?"

"I can do that, if that's all you've got."

He watches me, a bit of pity in his eyes, and I remember something big mouth Lolo told me; even though it's supposed to be anonymous, everyone in the islands knows Mo is practically president of the AA chapter at the local Protestant church. He's not married and nobody knows if he's got a woman; people just know that he lives with a cockatiel named Dorothy. I stare at him. I used to be pretty good at appraising men. By the way he looks back at me, I estimate it's been more than a few years since he's slept with someone who didn't charge him for it.

"I'll tell you what, Reina. You've worked in salons so many years you must be good with people. I can offer you a slot in our Guest Relations department. You'll do rounds of the park property, making sure visitors are having a good experience; you'll make sure nobody is breaking any rules like throwing trash in the habitats, touching animals, smoking, or drinking on the premises. You'll have to always be chipper. Ready to answer any questions guests might have for you. Anything you can't handle, you send them over to me or a senior staff member. What do you think?"

"Sounds good to me."

I'm proud of myself for getting hired, even if it's entry level. Even if the last girl who had the position, who quit to go work at the big aquarium up in Largo, the dolphinarium's main competition, was ten years younger than me.

On my first official day on the job, I'm wearing my new uniform of blue shorts and a blue polo shirt. Mo stops me out on the patio and tells me that as part of my job, I'm also supposed to let management know if any activists show up.

"Activists?"

"Animal rights people, specifically. They come around from time to time."

"Why? This place is way nicer than the other dolphin parks around."

I mean it. There are places where you can find a dolphin in an aboveground backyard swimming pool or in a fountain behind a motel, kids tossing in pennies to make a wish.

"They won't accept that we take great care of them here. Sometimes they just want to make some noise, give the trainers a hard time, but we've had cases of more serious things happening. Even vandalism. We've found holes cut into fences and the way we usually find out isn't because the animals get out, it's because others get *in*. Last month we had a lemon shark swimming in one of the pens scaring Wilma and Betty half to death. All because of the damn activists who don't know nothing about nothing."

It's kind of a funny thing for him to say given that Lolo told Nesto and me that before he came down to the Keys to run the dolphinarium, Mo managed a sneaker outlet up in Ocala.

"We are an accredited institution here, not some home-grown fish pen," Mo continues. "We've got all our permits. These aren't market dolphins. Most are rescues, or retired from other aquariums or circuses, and we take them in. We love these animals like family. If it weren't for us, they wouldn't have anywhere else to go."

"What about back to the ocean?"

I can see from Mo's expression this is the wrong thing to say.

I try again. "I mean, if they're retired, why don't you just release them?"

"They don't know how to fend for themselves. You put any of these creatures out there in that wild ocean and you'll see they won't last a day. They don't have their instincts anymore. And they sure as hell won't feel like hunting again when they get their meals here free. If these animals could talk, they'd tell you how happy they are here."

I don't say anything.

"I want you to talk to the trainers and techs, Reina. They can explain the research we do here. We're trying to learn from the animals. See what they have to teach us. We do a lot of good work, especially with our interaction programs. I see miracles happen every day when people with disabilities get in the water with the animals. That's what the activist folk don't understand. The dolphins here aren't just for show."

He says this just as a show in the front lagoon is getting started, rockabilly music coming on loud over the speakers. Through the window behind Mo, I see a trainer cuing a dolphin into a tail walk to the small crowd's collective *wow*.

Mo looks over his shoulder to the show and back to me. "They love to perform. They love to make their trainers happy. And we love to look after them. It's in the good book, Reina.

Genesis 1:26. 'God gave man dominion over animals.' We know what's best for them and the animals are so smart, they know it too."

"All right. I'll keep an eye out for trouble."

When Mo leaves me to start my rounds, I walk along the dock from the lagoon holding the "family pod" at the front of the pen grid to the rows of pens behind it, containing pairs and trios of dolphins usually divided by gender, down to the nursery pen holding the mothers and the babies near the end. I notice one of the larger dolphins tucked into one of the front pens, its eyes following me as I pass through, floating half on its side in a way that makes it look like it's dying or something, and when I ask Luke, one of the trainers, if the dolphin is okay, he just laughs and says that's Sunshine's way of spying on me.

"How do you know that?" I ask.

"We know these guys real well. Each animal has its own dolphinality. Sunshine likes to spy, just like Strawberry, over there, likes to fling wads of seaweed at us to get our attention sometimes. They're having fun with us."

"But how do you really know that? It's not like they can tell you."

"From our research."

I watch as he calls a dolphin over to where he stands on a platform at the center of the pen. Luke signals with his hand for the dolphin to open its mouth, and then he shoves a long tube down its throat.

Luke calls over to me on the deck. "I'm doing this 'cause she's thirsty. They need water just like we do."

Nesto later tells me that wild dolphins get their hydration from catching live fish, and the frozen food diet captive dolphins get can leave them dehydrated, so the trainers supplement it by

shoving a lubricated hose down the dolphins' throats, dumping ice into their mouths, or feeding them gelatin cubes. He
learned that during his days working at the Acuario Nacional
in Havana. He said that back there some of the dolphins, the
ones they didn't snatch out of local waters, were from the Black
Sea, imported like so much else by los bolos, the Soviets. Just
another island absurdity, he told me, Russian dolphins in the
Caribbean, and it was only fitting that the aquarium was right
across the road from the Soviet embassy plunging like a sword
through the heart of Miramar.

When the Russians left, they didn't take the dolphins with
them. But they'd die, of course, because around there, Nesto says,
there's no Reina walking around making sure people don't throw
garbage into the tanks, and sooner or later necropsies revealed
plastic bottles in their bellies or too many mackerel jawbones.
Some of those animals, people would say, were former military
dolphins, trained to drop grenades on submarines and inject
enemy divers with poison.

During my first days at the dolphinarium I hear from a guy
called Sonny on the maintenance crew that this country once
had a similar project going on, and those secret navy dolphins
eventually made their way onto the aquarium circuit too.

"Might even be some here," he says with a raised brow.

I mention it to a couple of trainers who laugh, dismissing it
as an urban myth, adding that Sonny's a full-blooded Seminole,
raised not to trust the government, so I shouldn't listen to any
of his theories.

He's in charge of emptying all the garbage cans and pulling
seaweed and fish out of the pens. He points to the little bio the
facility has posted by each pen with a picture of each animal
and a cute little story about its origins, like that it's retired from

aquariums, or rescued from a mass beaching in South Carolina, and found paradise in these here pens. Lies, he says.

I think it's strange that Sonny has to spend half the day catching fish that swim through the fence holes from the ocean when dolphins are supposed to eat fish, but he explains they don't want to tempt them with being able to hunt for their own catch.

When I later ask Mo about it, he tells me to leave matters to the people who really know about this stuff; the vet techs with their diplomas, the trainers with their slick wetsuits and chirpy voices reciting a litany of facts about the species to visitors while the dolphins wait at their feet for a mouthful of dead fish.

"And you, you're just a newbie, sweetheart." He takes a piece of my cheek between two knuckles. "You don't know a dolphin from a dog off the street."

When my brother was old enough to get real jobs, first as a restaurant dishwasher, then as a stock boy at a grocery store till he got fired for swiping steaks, and then at the car wash where he stayed until he finished high school, he would still hit shops in his free time to see what he could take without paying.

Sometimes he'd aim low, going for drugstore cosmetics, perfumes, sunglasses off the rack, batteries, and condoms, always bringing something extra home for me, like lipsticks or nail polish. Or he'd go into a bookstore with an empty backpack and leave with it full of new novels. Sometimes he would be more ambitious and try his luck in a department store, walking out with shirts and jackets right on his back. He never got caught and often tried to convince me to join him.

He said I had the right kind of face for theft, inconspicuous and forgettable.

"Nobody expects anything from you, Reina. Nobody notices you when you walk into a room. You're like the air people don't realize they're breathing."

I didn't like the idea of stealing even if our mother never asked where all the new things that turned up in our house came from, probably because my brother also kept her supplied with gifts.

One day I told Mami what Carlito had said about me, and how it bothered me that I was a girl he was certain nobody gave a second thought to, as inconsequential as a flea.

"Don't worry, mi'jita," she told me, caressing my face with

her slim hand. "It's to a woman's advantage to pass through life desapercibida. Better to be underestimated."

"Why?"

"Because it's only in pretending to be cross-eyed that a woman is able to see double."

FOUR

Nesto says it was Yemayá who held my brother up to the surface after our father threw him into the ocean so that Cielos Soto could save him, and he's sure Cielos had already made a pact of his own with Yemayá before casting his line off of the bridge that day, asking her to deliver fish to his bait and hook. Instead, Yemayá made him a hero. And my brother was saved.

But there lies the debt, Nesto warns. Neither Carlito nor anyone in my family ever paid Yemayá back for her blessings, and nobody, especially the orisha, likes an ingrate.

Yemayá only punishes when deeply offended, he says. It's the reason why, when Carlito's mind filled with madness and he dropped Isabela's baby into the ocean, Yemayá did nothing to stop him and instead let the baby fall through her waters down to Olokun's realm on the ocean floor.

"That's why you need to make friends with the sea," he tells me, as we sit together on the beach behind my cottage one sunny morning. "The sea is the origin of all life and the tomb of all death. Before Obatalá claimed the land, oceans covered the earth. So all of life has aquatic origin and we need to honor it."

"You think we were once fish?"

"Only Olofi knows."

He runs his hand through the sand at his side, grabs some into his palm, and lets it slip out through his fingers.

"Babies breathe amniotic fluid until birth. It's a kind of seawater. We grow into our lives on land and lose our connection to the water, but we are of the ocean."

Nesto takes my hand and leads me into the water stepping sideways like he says we should always do when approaching the sea.

As we walk in deeper, he holds me, lifts me off my feet like my mother used to do, letting me float over his arms, dipping my head backward into the water.

He asks me to hold my breath, to see what kind of lungs I have. Then he teaches me exhalations and ventilation patterns, what he does each time he goes spearfishing or down on Lolo's line off the float, the way a body can fill itself with oxygen beyond the throat and lungs, down to the diaphragm, through the muscles between the ribs and chest, even into the muscles on top of your lungs and under your shoulder blades, packing and stacking the oxygen through tiny gulps, then how to do purging and cleansing breaths.

We practice in the shallow water where he can stand and I dip my head under the surface, holding my breath, gripping Nesto's waist for support while he watches over me counting time, tapping my shoulder at intervals so that I'll lift a finger to signal that I'm okay.

He teaches me how to clear my ears. Not the way you'd blow out through your nose like during the pressure change of an airplane ride, but by moving the jaw to release air through the eustachian tubes, contracting the cheeks, or moving the back of the tongue upward like a lever.

On the surface, I feel the air move around my head, a gentle clearing of pressure, and as we go deeper, the pressure intensifies until I manage to pop out the air.

I practice for days until Nesto says I'm ready to try it in the open water.

I trust him, and want to try, not because he's prepared me with a safety protocol, to prevent blacking out below and at the surface, sinking, or swallowing water; not even because I want to go deeper into the sea; but because I want to go deeper toward him.

On Saturdays and Sundays, the waters off the coast of the Florida Keys become a liquid turnpike, filled with weekend boaters, fat-bellied fisherman down from the mainland, those who own second homes lining canals, or people with trailers parked on campgrounds.

Nesto prefers to go out to the blue during the week or when it's cloudy and the waterways aren't so congested. But on this day, we decide to hitch a ride with Lolo even though he's taking a group of scuba divers out, two married couples overloaded with expensive gear Melly convinced them to buy at Lolo's shop.

Nesto and I keep to ourselves at the front of the boat. He drops coconut rinds and berries into the water, ebbós to both Yemayá and Olokun of the deep, for protection once he goes under. He hands me a few berries so I can make my own offering, and rather than let them turn to mush in my hands, I toss them to the waves.

I've never had trouble forcing hope, even when there was none to speak of. But faith has always seemed much more dangerous.

I watch the Atlantic break along the side of the boat as awareness pushes through me of its dark, unknowable depths.

I think of baby Shayna, see her small golden body fall through the air, hear her soft bones shattering as her body carves its way through the water down to the bottom of the sea.

How is it that one baby thrown to the water was saved and the other, thrown off the bridge in the same way, died?

Was it really a matter of winds and currents or could there have been greater forces at work?

I wonder if it's true when Nesto says I've inherited the debts for both a life saved and a life taken.

The divers take longer to suit up. Nesto and I are already in our wetsuits, of a lesser buoyancy, so that we can sink with less added weight on our belts. I've got my own suit now. Lolo cut me a good deal on a secondhand one at his shop. It had a tear on the thigh but Nesto patched it with some neoprene and duct tape. They lent us low-volume masks and long-blade fins too. Nesto goes in first, and sets up the float and the rig line while Lolo and his assistant tend to the scuba divers. I jump in and meet Nesto on the line.

We start by floating together, hands on the rig, adjusting to the dips and falls of the waves, the coolness of the water. For real divers, not just those breaking the surface like me, Nesto told me about the mammalian dive reflex—how the farther down one goes, the body enters negative buoyancy and begins to sink in free fall, swallowed by the ocean; the heart rate slows and the blood shifts from the extremities to the center of the diver's body to feed the organs so the chest won't collapse. The competitive divers go even deeper, submitting to a meditative and sometimes hallucinatory state as the brain slows down and the lungs compress, fighting the urge to breathe.

Why would anyone subject him or herself to that? I once asked Nesto, but he told me that when I got a taste of the blue, I would understand.

It's not about the depth. He never agreed with that. It's not about testing limits. When he was a kid, one of his friends came up from a deep dive bleeding out of his ears and throat, and another boy, trying to beat a friend's depth, became permanently paralyzed on the right side of his face.

You just want to go deep enough to arrive at that moment when your thoughts stop and all you feel is the water and your heartbeat, he says; you let the ocean possess you, and return to the surface connected to your instincts, enraptured by the mystery of life and of creation.

Even with our suits on, the water is cold, but somehow feels warm, comforting. Nesto guides me through the ventilation patterns as we hang on to the rig and though we don't say much, he nods and tells me it's time.

We rehearsed the steps aloud on the boat. After a succession of meditative warm-up breaths to first relax the mind, which Nesto says also burns oxygen, all our energy connected, until the final deep inhale, when I'll pierce the membrane of the surface to go under for my downward turn, my pulling myself down the rope, which he set with a weighted plate at the five-meter mark. I have to focus on the constant clearing of my ears, or else the pressure of water that is eight hundred times denser than air will be unbearable. Before I know it, I'm down, touching the plate at the mark, and turning back up to the surface while Nesto watches me through his mask.

Nesto moves the plate farther down at each interval as I rest on the rig, regaining my breath. But as I try again, reaching for the fifteen-meter mark, the weight of the ocean presses against my skull, the clearing of the ears is hard to maintain with each pull down the rope, and I notice, maybe for the first time, the astonishing openness of the ocean from the small space I occupy on the line, neon blue slashed with sugary sunlight.

I see the divers float below me, their attention on schools of fish and a couple of curious stingrays flapping by. It's an entire world, and I take it all in within a second or two before my body forces me upward, breaking out of the shell of water. I gasp for air in Nesto's arms and he asks for the safety check to show him I'm okay and responsive.

I understand now why he says that he and his friends took to the ocean as kids because it was the only place they could feel free. Even being limited by their breath and by their human forms wasn't as limiting as the life that waited for them on land.

I watch Nesto take a few dives himself, dropping under the surface so I can watch through my mask, the ease with which he moves. The conversation he seems to have with himself down there, or with those gods he says take care of him while he's at their mercy.

He's told me that at around forty feet, the ocean starts to break open, and instead of pushing you back up to the surface, it pulls you into it and you sink deeper and deeper.

When he's back on the float, his face creased by pressure lines from his mask, he looks changed, and I wonder if I look changed too.

We don't say anything. He's still catching his breath.

I remember he once told me the secret to going deeper is you have to think of the other ocean animals as your companions; you have to believe you're one of them while never forgetting that you are different and still need to come up for air.

A week later, Lolo lets me join one of his weekend scuba courses. I read the book, do the swimming pool dives with the tank on my back, stuff the BC into my mouth, pass the exam, and complete the certification with some shallow dives with the dive group. Out on the boat, I struggle to get into the water, but once I'm in, with Nesto as my dive buddy, we drop foot by foot under the surface and I watch from a seated position as the ocean lifts its curtains and its creatures come into view.

We descend to see a purposely sunk wreck. Above us, a single loggerhead turtle pushes past, and just behind it, an enormous spotted eagle ray, with its odd face, almost like that of a dolphin, yet winged, with a whipping tail.

I let Nesto guide me around the wreck, pointing out the eel tucked into a corner of the deck, the fat grouper passing through, while the other divers go through their own drills.

Marine civilization surrounds us, fish I've only seen in aquariums or on television, sharks I've only heard about on the news after a splashing surfer or swimmer gets attacked.

It's easy to get lost in the show, to forget to look at the dive computer, to realize all of this is a kind of experiment of technology and the body. It's all so beautiful, but the sound of the oxygen in my ears, the taste of plastic in my mouth, the bulky stream of bubbles that follows me at every turn, the clearing of the mask, the weight of the tank on my back, and the steadying of my fins are all exhausting, and somehow, confining.

Despite our enchantment, the awareness of our invasion never dissipates. The animals try to get away from us. I understand now why Nesto prefers to rely on his lungs and not the tanks. He prefers a few minutes on his own breath as just another creature in the ocean rather than a much longer dive burdened by all that gear; he says the noise of our breathing, our bubbles, must echo like a helicopter for all the animals in the ocean.

I can't wait until we ascend, go back on the boat, unload our tanks, log the dive, then are free to go back in the water with nothing but our wetsuits, to push below the surface with only our breath.

And we do.

The other divers come up in pairs, taking their time to adjust their eyes to open sky and sun once again, but Nesto and I are lost in the water, and I now understand why he brings me out here. The voices on the boat fade behind us and for a few moments it's only us, floating, drifting, dipping, and kicking under.

My mask in my hand, I open my eyes wide under the water, surprised to discover it doesn't sting at all.

When I come back up for air, Nesto is waiting, reaching out his hand, telling me it's time to return to the boat, but I don't want to go.

I want to stay out here.

Nesto smiles, content to see I've been converted.

"The best thing about her is that she's always there, waiting for you."

It takes me a moment to realize he's speaking of the ocean and not of me.

Winter in the tropics betrays. Despite the radiant sun, a sky faintly feathered with clouds, there are days of biting cold when winds from the north bring frost, leaving nature confused, with reports of iguanas falling from trees, lizards frozen to the pavement, turtles and manatees congregating in the warmer waters around sewage plants. Farmers panic over losing their orange and pineapple harvests. We put on our warmest clothes, and at night, since the cottage isn't meant to hold in heat, we burrow into blankets, pull out spares Mrs. Hartley left in the closet, and use the space heater she lent me from the main house. But the chill leaves us as abruptly as it arrived, and we step out of winter into a taste of summer. The sun holds strong for weeks without rain, warming the waters, and in the morning, instead of feeling our bones stiff with cold, Nesto and I wake to humidity, the pale winter sky returned to its cloudless blue.

Nesto sleeps over most nights now, and I sleep better with him here. But I often wake up to the darkness and when my eyes adjust, I watch him, the heaviness with which he sleeps, the way he always seems to find my body, even in his unconsciousness, and curl around me. I've never slept like this with anyone else.

Even when I had entire uninterrupted nights with other men, I never had this sort of closeness. I never had the same face meeting mine across the pillow morning after morning. I never had someone who didn't tire of me, who didn't eventually find me uninteresting. Who didn't decide someone else was more worthy of his time.

I always handed myself over. I let them turn my body into the thing they wanted. My mind left the scene, floating in space where they could never find me.

I told Dr. Joe about this once. He said I was "dissociating," imagining myself in a happier place. I told him he was wrong. There was no happier place. I was just not there.

Sometimes I wake up and I expect Nesto to tell me today is the last day we'll share, a switch signaling my time is up. But every morning he's there, and at the end of the day, when it's time to go to sleep again, he's there too.

I think I'm pretty good at living in the present now, when each day is just as good, or better, than the one before. But I still haven't broken my backward gaze and sometimes, when even my own history becomes boring to me, I take on Nesto's past. I try to picture him as the man that belongs to a tribe, not the solitary man I know.

I think about the woman with whom he made a family. The closeness they shared. The routines. The love for their children that bonds them even now. I try to picture them in the life they had together. The home they lived in, which had belonged to her parents.

I saw her face once, quickly, in a photo he showed me of a birthday party they'd had for his son when he turned five. She was much younger then, pretty, with long dark hair tied back with a bow, but her face was sad. He was to the side of the frame, looking serious too. Nesto later told me it was a Cuban habit not to smile for photos, a leftover Soviet trait just like the synchronized applause at government speeches. A communist thing.

He never asks about my past. Not in the way of boyfriends or lovers or aventuras.

"Don't you want to know about me?" I asked him once, curious and half-insulted, but he shook his head and reached for me with his lips, and between kisses told me, "I don't need to know about other men. For me, you were born the day I met you. Nothing before that counts."

"What about you? Does that mean you were born that day too?"

He nodded.

"And nothing before that counts?"

He looked thoughtful, then uneasy.

"What do you want me to say, Reina?"

"Nothing. Don't say anything."

I was relieved he listened, and I was out of my head and back in my body, feeling him above me, enjoying the pressure of his ribs against mine.

I watch him, shrouded by the night, blueness almost like the one that swallows us when we go out into the ocean. He must feel my eyes on him because without waking, he reaches for me, pulls me to him, and I mold my body to his, kiss him until he kisses me back and I learn the lesson again that I've learned every night I've spent with him, that I will find in his body, and not in his words, the answers to all my questions.

On a late March morning, Nesto leaves me to go to Cuba. He hasn't been there in more than a year and wanted to go for the holidays, but didn't have the money to pay his monthly bills and didn't want to miss out on any jobs that might come up. Now that he has the full-time gig at the dolphinarium it's easier, and he bought a ticket home for the weekend. I offer to drive him to the airport but he insists on taking the bus. I take him to the stop, wait with him, and watch as he pulls his backpack, full of gifts and encargos for his family—medicines, vitamins, and shampoos and soaps since they say there's an island-wide shortage—over his shoulder.

"I'll see you soon," he tells me the same way I've heard him say to his children so many times over the phone. He kisses me one last time and walks away.

This is a good exercise, I tell myself, to remember life before Nesto. I've gotten too used to the way we've built each other into our daily routines.

But I miss him. Nights alone, the dark hours before dawn when I sometimes turn and stir him from sleep with my lips.

One morning I go out to the dock on my end of the Hammerhead property with my coffee and see the bearded man from down the canal come out on his boat. He waves to me like he usually does but this time he slows down and gets close enough to my dock to ask me, without having to shout it, if I want go out for a ride with him.

"I have to go to work later," I say.

"I'll bring you back in time. Promise."

He pulls the boat up to the dock and I leave my coffee mug on the floor planks before climbing into his boat with him. He gives me a hand to shake and tells me his name is Jojo, his family is descended from the original settlers of Key West, and being a genuine Conch is a thing not many people can claim.

"How do you like living on the Hartley land?"

"It's not bad. You know Mrs. Hartley?"

"She was friendly with my wife till she got sick. Then she kept away, like she was afraid of catching cancer. She sent some nice flowers for the funeral though."

He's smiling but still has a sad face, kind of like that old shrink they made Carlito and me see as kids. The guy who told Mami I was considered "at-risk" and Mami kept saying, "What does that mean? At risk for what? Look at her. She's *fine*."

"You must miss her a lot," I tell Jojo as he pulls out of the coastal stream beyond the last row of buoys.

"You ever lose anyone?" he asks me once we're in the valley of open water, still desolate because it's a weekday and the fishermen are probably starting the morning on the hump.

"Yes."

"Then you know how it is. Only thing to do is take life one sunrise at a time."

He makes a turn, cranks the speed on the boat, and after a few minutes he points to breaks in the water line, clearly dolphin dorsals—half a dozen of them.

"Look back there." Jojo points, and in the boat's wake I see another group of dolphins weave and leap over the foamy mounds.

After a bit, Jojo slows down and turns the engine off. The waves we've made calm, and the boat glides along the soft current.

At first, it seems the dolphins have disappeared, but they reemerge, swirling around the boat, pulling off into pairs, then returning to our spot on the water. I lean over the edge, trying to follow them with my eyes as they rush under the surface. I've never seen anything like it. Jojo sits back in his driving seat, amused by my wonder.

"You'll only see them when it's quiet like this. Once all the boats are out, they keep a low profile. They don't like the engines."

"How did you know they'd be here?"

"I know all the spots."

"How?"

"I was practically born riding these waterways. My pop brought me out since I was a kid. He was a catcher. Long time ago."

"He was a fisherman?"

"No, a *catcher*. Of dolphins. It was the business back then. There wasn't much work around here besides deep-sea fishing. Lots of guys got involved. My father was one of the better ones."

"Catching them for what?"

"In the sixties, all the aquariums decided they needed dolphins. The animals don't just show up and volunteer. Somebody has to catch them. That's how it used to be, anyway. The laws changed in the seventies, Marine Mammal Protection Act and all that. Just a few big companies got permits to catch now. It's not a free agent's game anymore."

"He'd just come out here and get one?"

"Not only him. He had a team of guys. Takes lots of strong men to wrangle one from the water, maneuver the nets and such."

I'm silent, but it doesn't matter. Jojo is happy to keep talking.

"I had my own for a while. My pop made a pen for her behind the house, on the canal. I trained her to do some tricks.

We were doing twenty-minute shows twice a day for a while. We got a little famous too. As famous as you can get around here."

"How did you train her?"

"Same way you train anything. Even a human. Take away its food. Feed it when it does what you want. They learn."

"What happened to her?"

"Oh, she was my baby. Monica was her name. We all loved her. My wife and I never had kids so she was our little girl. But a *big* girl. A strong girl. I nearly went broke feeding her. When my pop passed, I started to feel it wasn't right keeping Monica, as much as we loved her. But you can't just let a dolphin go once you got her eating out of your hand, you know. Takes time."

"So, how did you do it?"

"Had to undo everything I did. Stop loving her. Stop talking to her. Stop touching her. Stop feeding her and using that dang whistle on her. Stop giving her a schedule. I put live fish in her pen to get her used to hunting her food. Even though she was in a sea pen and not a tank, she was out of shape compared with a wild dolphin. Those animals are meant to swim fifty miles a day, not bob around a pen. After a couple of months, I opened up the fence to get her to go out but she didn't want to leave. Till one day she finally did. For a long time I wouldn't come out here, in case she was around. She knew me and my boat. I was afraid she'd follow me back home. But I never saw her again. People tried telling me she probably died out here on her own, but I know she made it. I'm sure of it."

"You know I work over at the dolphinarium," I tell Jojo.

"You do?"

"They say those aren't market animals."

"Sure, that's what they say *now*. But at least ten of their original acquisitions back when they opened came out of my pop's nets."

"They say the ones they have now are rescues and retirees."

"It doesn't matter. Whether they're purchased or born captive, they're still market animals because whoever's got them is making plenty of cash off them."

When Jojo delivers me back to the dock, I hope to find Nesto waiting for me at the cottage since I know he returned last night.

I offered to pick him up at the airport, but he insisted on taking the bus down to the Keys. I thought he'd call when he arrived, and when he didn't, that he'd show up to see me before work, but he's not there.

The dolphinarium is buzzing when I get to work. Everyone is excited about the new dolphin I'm only hearing of now. I join the small crowd of trainers and techs on the dock by the new pen they've constructed at the end of the row of the ones that are already occupied, watching Nesto, almost chest deep in water with a scuba tank on his back, as he makes sure all the fences are securely bound to the poles that frame the enclosure.

He sees me and waves, then goes back underwater.

Rachel, one of the trainers, comes up beside me. She's my age, from Tampa, with long blond hair she wears in a high bun. In a colder climate, Rachel's complexion might be a pearly rose-gold, but the tropics have made her pink and rubbery, like bubble gum, her lips chapped and peeling and coated in Vaseline. Like most of the trainers, she was a star swimmer in college, but when they aged out of competing, they found that few job prospects could keep them in the water beyond lifeguarding or giving swimming lessons to kids.

Here at the dolphinarium, she works with new arrivals, teaching them the ways of pen life, though Nesto says there's not much to teach about living in a cage; it's a process of submission, which any animal can figure out on its own.

"I can't wait to meet our new girl. I hear she's a sweet thing." Rachel is grinning and giddy.

"Who said that?" I ask.

"Her handlers. They sent us her files."

"How do you know if a dolphin's being sweet as opposed to one that's not?"

"By its general attitude. The way it interacts with us. Since they got her, they say she's been gentle as can be. And she'll be so much happier here than in the tank."

It's like she's talking about a stray kitten, not a three-hundred-pound six-year-old dolphin, washed up from the oil spill in the gulf off Louisiana, one of the few animals that emerged from the fields of tar sheens with a remote chance of survival.

They took her in and named her for the lab in Biloxi where she's been held until being transported here. Roxi from Biloxi.

Rachel tells me she and the other trainers were assured Roxi has potential to perform and even to breed.

"How is it you teach them tricks and flips and all that?"

"We don't teach them *tricks*. We encourage them to learn new behaviors."

I don't really see how you can call getting a dolphin to beach itself on the dock, deliver a rose in its mouth to an audience member, and offer its fin for a "dolphin handshake" anything but tricks, but I keep that part to myself.

"Okay, the teaching of behaviors. How do you do that?"

"We practice operant conditioning." I can tell she likes the taste of big words in her mouth. "We change or create behaviors by using positive reinforcements, like food, as a reward."

"Do you ever punish them?"

"Of course not!" She laughs at my misstep.

"What if they don't do what you want them to do?"

"We just don't reinforce the behavior until they get it right."

"So you don't give them food till they do what you want them to do?"

"We don't acknowledge them until they demonstrate the desired behavior."

"You ignore them?"

She shakes her head at me. "It's not that simple, Reina. There are decades of research behind what we do."

With that, she finds a reason to get away from me, and walks out on the platform extending from the dock between the new pen and the older one, holding two females, Belle and Bonnet. Roxi from Biloxi will live alone till they add her to another pen with resident female dolphins or find her a new companion.

I watch Nesto work on the pen and think of when I started working full-time and Mo told me how happy the animals were. So much so that even though the fence keeping them in extends barely a foot above the water, and the dolphins can easily jump over it to get out, they never even try. Even during hurricanes, when the enclosures sometimes broke open, Mo told me, if the dolphins swam out into the gulf, they were easily coaxed by their trainer's whistles to return to their pens the next morning.

I remember when Carlito and I were kids, an early summer tropical storm once ravaged the local aquarium, busting open the bayside wall of the dolphin cove so the six dolphins inside were released to the open water. They were quickly spotted by people on the same bridge where Carlito and baby Shayna had both been dropped, doing their routines at all their regular showtimes, flipping and tail-walking and pirouetting, waiting for their rewards. People gathered on the causeway and adjacent beaches to watch the show. The dolphins, accustomed to the sight of a crowd, came closer to shore and it wasn't long before the aquarium people arrived in boats to collect them.

There was some noise about leaving them free, but the aquarium people used the footage of their routines in the wild to show that the animals were desperate to return to the aquarium. They *loved* performing, their minders told the reporters, and the aquarium was their home.

That was all it took.

Now it's just a story that locals tell: the case of the escaped dolphins performing in the ocean the routines that humans had taught them.

I still remember Mami's face watching the news coverage, the way she shook her head and said it was pathetic how those dumb animals had missed their one maldito chance to be free.

I don't know when it happens.

The moment when I can no longer just go about my job and walk past the dolphins in their pens, thinking of them as our gentle and docile residents.

Maybe it's after Jojo takes me out on the boat and I see the others swimming long straight lines, diving deep, not in shallow narrow loops like these dolphins, contained by fences.

Maybe it starts long before, when, during my rounds, I pause by their pens, wondering about their assorted histories that usually only go as far back as their previous ownership.

I think the point of rehabilitation is to let them go, and maybe use a place like this as sort of a halfway house on their journey back to the open ocean. But as with Rachel, whenever I ask too many questions, the trainers, techs, and vets just walk away from me, and I have to go back to my work, circulating through the facility, asking tourist families if they're all having a good time, trying to convince them to sign up for the Swim with Dolphins program, a big moneymaker for the park, telling them how it's a great opportunity to have "a natural experience" with the animals, just like I've been prepped to do, even when, if they stopped to take a look at the larger picture of all this, they'd see there is nothing natural about it.

The trainers use the dolphins that were born at the facility, not the ones who once knew life outside these man-made lagoons. And when the hour is over, the people come out of the pen with a look of enchantment. They don't notice it's a one-sided solace. The dolphins are hungry, working for each reward of water-injected mackerel popped into their mouth.

Sometimes a visitor will get mouthy on the trainers, having seen a documentary or read an article about the cruelties that can happen at marine parks or how the dolphins are stolen from the ocean, but the trainers never lose their show-grins, responding that the dolphins love their home here at the facility, and then they point the visitor to Oliver, a dolphin who washed up near Sarasota, bleeding to death after a shark chomped away half of his dorsal and fluke. A dolphin like that would never last in the wild, the trainers say. And it's true. Here at the dolphinarium Oliver has a chance to live a safe life, even if the dolphinarium has recently received citations for not providing enough shaded areas for the animals in their enclosures, which the inspector said violates the Animal Welfare Act.

"But if this is really some kind of refuge," a teenager once asked Rachel, "why do you breed them?"

"Breeding is part of our commitment to conservation." Rachel gave her standard reply, even though the bottlenose dolphins bred here aren't considered endangered.

The park visitors remark what a beautiful dolphinarium this is, where the animals swim in real seawater, not in the chlorinated clear water of aquariums around the country, with concrete and glass tanks.

Mo and the staff talk about captivity like it's the best thing a dolphin can hope for, but that kind of talk just makes me think of Carlito and all the years he spent trapped by the routines of prison life in a six-by-nine-foot prison cell, the size of a parking space, and what Dr. Joe used to say about inmates like my brother who were also sentenced to solitary confinement: "It doesn't have to be violent for it to be torture."

We are back at my cottage. Nesto is exhausted from his day on the fence, eager to shower and wash off the sweat and saltwater and rest his back before having to get up to do more of the same work tomorrow. I don't ask why he didn't come to see me the night before or even that morning. I only ask how his trip went but he offers few words in response.

"It was *normal*," he says. "Just normal," adding that everyone is having as hard a time as ever and all he accomplished by going home to Havana was to refresh his ever-broken heart.

I watch as he steps out of his jeans, pulls off his shirt, tosses them onto a pile on the floor, and walks into the shower, singing, "*Parece que el ciclón ya se fue y ya se pueden ver las estrellas, parece que la vida cambió y yo cambié con ella . . .*"

When he comes out, a towel around his waist, flopping onto the bed, his eyes closing with fatigue, I climb onto the bed and straddle him over his towel, not because I missed his body so badly while he was away—I did, very much—but because I can't wait to tell him about what happened while he was gone, how I went out on the boat with Jojo and what he told me. But when I'm through with my story, Nesto can focus only on the detail that I climbed onto a boat with a total stranger.

"You could have gotten yourself killed, Reina."

If my eyes had been closed at that moment, I'd have believed it was my brother scolding me.

"You can't just get on a boat with someone you don't know. It's dangerous and irresponsible."

"That's how I met *you*."

"At least we were on land. But I still could have hurt you. And this guy could have strangled you and dumped you in the ocean without any trouble. You would have disappeared and nobody would have ever known."

I crawl off of him and let him be. But an hour or so later, when he finally decides it's time to eat rather than sleep, and we sit on the sofa with plates of arroz con pollo on our laps, I try to bring up the matter of the wild dolphins again.

"You think it's true what Jojo says? They stole them from the waters out here?"

"Why not? In Cuba and probably in most places, when a dolphin dies, they just send people out to catch another."

"Do you think it's true the animals are content in their pens because they're fed and don't have to worry about predators?"

"That's a lie they tell so they can keep doing what they do."

"You don't think they lose their instincts?"

"No animal does. That's why they're called *instincts*. Everything that is learned can be unlearned."

"Even if they've been captives for years and years?"

"Yes."

"Even if they were born in captivity and have known no other life?"

I'm thinking of the babies in the pens, born from forceful semen collections and inseminations—the babies that the dolphinarium advertises with a sign outside the entrance reading Come See Our New Additions!

"Yes," Nesto says with some hesitation. "Even after generations have passed and their ancestors were the last ones to taste freedom."

He stands up, takes our cleared plates to the sink, and rinses them off.

When he's through, he goes back to the bed, collapses atop the covers, and shuts his eyes.

A few minutes of silence pass and I assume he's fallen asleep, but then I hear Nesto's voice call to me one more time.

"Believe me, Reina. There is not an animal on this earth that if given the choice between freedom or captivity, would not choose to be free."

Nesto sleeps and I try to sleep next to him, but wake up every hour until I finally pull myself out of bed and walk out the door to the beach. I go barefoot, which I don't think much about until I'm halfway across the wooden floorboards that lead to the shore, noticing the planks are populated by roaches, worms, and snails out for midnight grazing. Around me, I hear the song of the night creatures, owls, the wrestling in the brush of what are probably raccoons or possums.

I walk until I'm on the beach, sit near the water's edge, and stare out at the murky sky, the flat sea shining like a razor under fractured moonlight.

I feel a distant disorientation, as if I am no longer myself, living my life, but a stranger, an unknown, living in a world entirely unfamiliar to me, as if I'm watching it in pictures, snapshots from a life that might be torn from me at any moment.

My brother wouldn't recognize this woman sitting curled into her knees on the beach in the darkest point of night. He would only recognize me as the girl I was when he was alive, in that brown house with the bars on it, on that street where people avoided conversation with us.

I wonder what he would think of me down here, on this island, of the sight of me out on the water, throwing myself into the ocean with only Nesto to protect me should anything go wrong. He would likely warn me not to trust him, say that I have no reason to believe Nesto would do me no harm. He would say you shouldn't trust anyone but your own family and even then, it's a risk.

I am mourning my sadness.

I feel it slip away through the tranquillity of these islands, this new life, this ocean, this never-abandoning sun.

I never expected that I would miss the pain of all that came before.

My eyes drift near my feet where crabs stir from half-covered holes in the sand, and a little farther off, the curved silhouettes of hermit crabs drag themselves toward the dunes. The beach is rumbling with life even if nobody is around to see it.

Again, I think of Carlito. The years I tried to serve his sentence with him, and how he let me. Maybe it was wrong of me, but sometimes I hoped that he'd see in my eyes how I'd stopped living for anything and anyone but him, and that he would tell me not to come back.

Another memory comes to me.

When I was a girl of maybe twelve or thirteen, one of our neighbors put the word out that a special saint was coming to her house for a week and all the mothers of the block were invited to bring their daughters to visit her. I didn't know what this meant but Mami took me over, and the señora had all the girls sit around the tile floor of her living room while she stood beside a huge statue of the Virgin of something or other, dressed in a jeweled cloak with real human hair on her head, and told us that we should pray to this statue to bring us our future husbands, ask that they be good men, and to help keep us pure on the journey of waiting for this blessed man to appear in our lives. I remember looking all around me. The girls, some who were probably as confused as I was, quickly went for it, lowering their heads to pray. The mothers got on board too, even mine, who was as hopeful as ever in those years that she'd marry again. But I knew there was no reason for me to pray for something like purity when I'd already done things the other girls in that room hadn't. I'd already shown my body to boys, let them touch me. In a year or so, I would be pregnant for the first time. I already suspected there was nobody above looking out for me. I knew there must be a reason people in the neighborhood, and even my own mother at times, called me La Diabla.

As the lady at the front led the group through a round of Hail Marys, one of the girls sitting on the floor near me touched my ear.

"What happened to you?" she said, tracing my mark of the abikú.

"A fishhook caught me," I lied, because I'd just heard a story about a kid who lost an eye that way.

Before we left the lady's house that night, she had each of us girls write on a piece of paper our deepest wishes and prayers for the Virgin, which we were supposed to fold into tiny bits and leave in a basket by the statue. I watched the girls and our mothers think carefully before they wrote down the words of their prayers. I pretended to write but the paper I left folded at the Virgin's feet was blank.

Mami wasn't satisfied with laying out her wishes to only the traveling Virgin. She went to the top husband-finder of all the saints, San Antonio, and asked her statue of him to bring her someone wonderful. She tried all the tricks: she removed the baby Jesus from the saint's arms and hid him in a drawer until her prayers were answered and San Antonio delivered a new husband for her. When that didn't work, she tied the statue upside down to a post on her bed, but when one of her boyfriends was over, he hit his foot against it and when he looked under the bed and saw the statue there like a secuestrado held for ransom, he knew exactly what Mami was up to and didn't come around again. But she kept praying, and told me the story of a girl, a prima of a prima of a prima back in Colombia, who also prayed to San Antonio for a husband, but one day she got so angry at him for not producing that she threw the statue out of her apartment window and a few moments later a young man came knocking on the door with the saint in his hand, saying, "Excuse me, miss. Did you lose a santo?" And of course, the guy became her husband.

After I came to know Nesto, I learned Saint Anthony was another face of Eleggúa, whom Nesto regularly asked for assistance; the wise one, the trickster who, as a boy, was the only orisha able to cure Olódumare when he was ill, and for that reason, the Great One made him the controller of destinies, the one whose blessing must be sought at the opening of every prayer to any other orisha.

"You have to give yourself permission to believe," Nesto once told me. "The orishas are forces of light, and you don't have to look far to find them. The sun, nourishing us with its warmth, is Olorun. Mars and Mercury are Ogún and Eleggúa, guardians over their warrior sons. The moon is the queen Yemayá, keeping vigil over her children on earth. They're watching over us even when we don't think they are."

I smiled, because my mother would often, in her way, with her own santos and prayers, say the same thing.

When the sand becomes too chilly for my feet, I walk back to the cottage. I left the porch light on and moths gather in the glow, and I see what I haven't noticed by day, that star spiders have been at work on a few webs under the lip of the cottage roof. I'm near the door when I look down and see what at first glance looks to be an especially huge cockroach at the threshold, but when I bend in closer, I see it's a scorpion.

Mami raised Carlito and me with her own childhood habit of checking our shoes for scorpions before we put them on since scorpions like to hide in small, dark places. But I've never seen one in Miami. Even when Carlito and his boy gang said they were going out hunting for scorpions, they never found any.

This scorpion is dark brown or black, with large hook hands and an upward-coiling tail. I've heard they can jump. Mami was bitten by one as a girl and said it almost killed her, and other times just said she *wished* it had killed her.

I stare at this scorpion for a few minutes.

It doesn't budge.

I don't know how else to get past it or at least nudge it on its way so I call for Nesto.

He finally turns up in the doorway, rubbing his eyes as they adjust to the porch light.

"Don't come any closer," I warn, pointing to the scorpion between us.

"What the hell are you doing out here?"

"I couldn't sleep."

He goes back into the cottage and returns with a broom, a glass, a magazine; leans over; in one swift movement, uses the broom to scoot the scorpion into the glass, covering the opening with the magazine; and walks far from the path, liberating the scorpion in the land extending behind the cottage into the rough edges of what used to be the plantation.

I'm still on the walkway when he comes back, and he pushes past me, tugging my elbow, mumbling, "Reina, por Dios, I really wish that when I close my eyes or I'm not around, you would just be where I think you are."

When we're back in bed he lies flat, staring at the ceiling, the fan above making slow, nearly airless rotations.

"Reina. I have to tell you something."

I expect him to say that the scorpion is a bad omen, because that's what I was thinking until I reminded myself I don't believe in omens, ever since my father decided that my very birth was the worst omen of all since some say that when abikús come back to life, the deal they make with the spirits, in order to remain among the living, is to send another person back to the death world in their place.

"Something happened when I was in Cuba."

He turns his head to me. I'm almost afraid to look at him.

"You were with someone."

"No."

I would be more relieved if I didn't sense something just as bad behind it.

"I decided something while I was there. We decided something."

"*We?*"

"My family and me."

"Decided what?"

"I have to get married."

I try my best not to react but my eyes must give me away.

"Let me explain. You know the problems I'm having bringing my children over here. All the delays. There's a way around it. A much faster way. Through the Family Reunification Program. But we have to be a complete family. If I remarry their mother, I won't have to wait for the children one by one. And they won't have to leave their mother. She has relatives in Miami they can live with. I'll be able to see them when I want. I can move there to be closer to them. Everything will be better. It's the easiest thing. We won't have to wait as long. It's the waiting, Reina. It's killing me."

"You'll be a family again." I want to sound like this is a great thing.

"I'll be able to be a real father again. Not a long-distance one. But it won't be a real marriage. It's just to get them all out of there."

He's told me many times before how people are casually married in Cuba to ease the way for any kind of paperwork, from visas to car exchanges to housing permutas, and just as easily divorced, while people who live as married couples are often not married at all. Yanai herself went on to marry a German, hoping he'd take her and the children to Europe, but she hadn't managed to pass the required language test, so her visa never got approved and the German divorced her to marry a Dominican girl. But even if marriages can be transactional, this doesn't seem like one of those cases to me.

"She doesn't want to be with me any more than I want to be with her. It's for the children. That's it. Once they're all over here and she gets the political asylum, we agreed we'll divorce right away."

I don't know if I should be joyful that he's finally come up with a way to accomplish reuniting with his kids, or disappointed because one way or another he'll be married to someone else.

My silence must convey this, because he touches my arm and repeats, "It won't be a real marriage. But it is a real family. That's why I have to do this."

"So when is it going to happen, this wedding of yours?"

"Don't call it a wedding. It's not going to be at El Palacio de los Matrimonios or with a party or anything. It's just an appointment at a government office. We sign papers and that's it, we're married. I don't know when it will be."

"Soon?"

"I hope so. The sooner we do it, the sooner I can bring Sandro and Camila over here."

Nesto has told me he's most worried about Sandro because he reminds him so much of himself, once a great student in his aula, who the teachers now report doesn't seem to care about anything and if he keeps it up he'll end up in an Escuela de Conducta. He's becoming restless, intranquilo, disillusioned like Nesto was at that age, even if they've raised him to be a good pionero too, just as Nesto says all parents do—the typical doble-moral, patriots in public, dissidents in their hearts—so the State won't give them a hard time. But the Revolution is old, Nesto told me, it means nothing to the young, and now Sandro sees the great Nada that awaits him if he stays on the island. Nesto fears his son falling in with las malas compañias in Buenavista, or worse, going from a reform school to El Combinadito, the jail for minors. Or maybe even ending up like one of Nesto's best friends from childhood, a guy named Lenin who started selling Jamaican marijuana that came in through Oriente to foreigners in order to provide for his family, and was quickly turned in by the CDR, both his legs broken by police and sentenced by the court to fifteen years in prison.

"I know I can't ask you to wait for me, for all this to pass," he tells me. "You have your own life to think about."

We are both quiet.

"I will miss you, Reina, but I will understand it."

I don't know what else to say because I know if I were in his place I would do the same, just like I would have done anything to be under the same roof as my brother for one more day before I lost him forever.

"I will miss you too," I say. "But I will understand it."

"So what do we do then?"

I want to say *this will end,* the same way that everything in life does, and we will both begin again the way we've both done before in order to bring ourselves to this very night.

Instead, all I say is, "I don't know. Tonight is tonight. Tomorrow is tomorrow."

The new dolphin arrives the next day. They close the dolphinarium because I guess they want to keep the truth of how animals come to the facility a mystery to the public. And you'd never know it if you were driving along the Overseas Highway, that next to you, in that big white truck that looks like it should be moving furniture or fruit from Central America, there is a dolphin lying on a stretcher, its fins poking through holes cut through the canvas, with water being poured over its back by its human handlers, having just been flown from Biloxi to the Key West airport.

They keep us lower staff on the sidelines, far from the commotion of the dolphin being carried in, the trainers anxious and excited, the vets and techs leaning over their clipboards, comparing notes. Nesto and I find a spot in the shade below the stilted hut that looks over all the pens.

We didn't talk much this morning at the cottage. Normally he wakes up full of energy, but today he moved about heavily, and instead of showering like he usually does, he just dipped his face under the bathroom faucet and put on his clothes from the day before.

He had to come in early again for the final once-over of the fencing. In the case of the other dolphins, Mo once told me, even the time activists came in at night and cut out a part of the fence, the dolphins hardly budged, unable to understand they could swim through the gap in the fence and be in open water. But the new dolphin isn't so far removed from her wild days so they aren't going to chance her ability to free herself.

When the dolphin handlers get to the pen, Mo asks Nesto to come help them. He's not even in his work wetsuit but ends up in the water in his jeans, helping steer the stretcher to the center of the pen until it's announced they can lower it and help the dolphin swim out. It takes a bit for her to move. She seems reluctant, with all those people watching, holding their breath like she's a child about to take her first steps. But then she squirms enough to be out of their circle and as the handlers retreat to the edge of the pen, they watch the new girl slowly take inventory of her new surroundings and everyone starts clapping and whistling, as if they've all done something amazing together.

Later, when I'm sent to help out the interns in the fish house, separating the mangled mackerel from the pretty-looking complete ones that are used for shows, fattening them up by injecting them with water, Mo comes in to get a fresh bucket for the new dolphin and I ask how she's doing.

"Good," he says, sliding his hand onto my back. "We're going to change her name though. We already had a Roxi here who passed away in ninety-four. We want something new for this girl. Any ideas?"

I shrug. "It doesn't really matter what you call her. I mean, the names are for us, not for her."

Then I let slip out something that Jojo told me: mother dolphins imprint a name on a baby dolphin with a language of sounds and the baby can recognize it with its sonar from miles away.

Mo and the interns watch me, surprised.

"Well, she needs a name we can pronounce," he says, now, clutching my shoulder. "We're her parents now."

For days they keep the new dolphin's pen cordoned off from the rest of the walkway so visitors can't check her out, but sometimes I wander in, lower myself onto the dock, and watch Rachel or one of the other trainers in the water with her, rubbing her side when she lets them, and trying to get her attention when she swims to the edge of the pen facing the gulf. They're still excited about her, even if a little worried that she's not as sweet as promised, as eager to engage. In fact, she doesn't seem interested in them at all.

When they leave her alone, I stay behind. The dolphin never leaves the fence, only letting herself drift along its periphery, and I'm not sure at first, but then it becomes clear to me that she's pushing her head against the wiring, softly, and then with more force, as if trying to get out.

Years ago, when I was sitting across from Carlito in the visitors' room at the prison, he told me about the orca at the aquarium in Miami, that, so miserable in his tiny pool, so far from his northern Pacific home and family pod, took to bashing his head against the walls of his tank so hard he sometimes cracked the glass, and eventually caused the brain hemorrhage that killed him. I was too young to remember when it happened, but it was local lore, like our family's crimes.

That day during our visit, Carlito said he understood why the whale did that to himself. He told me he, too, had the urge at times to throw his own head against the walls of his prison cell, against the bulletproof glass window on the steel door that contained him, and if all the pain in his heart could be translated to physical strength, he knew he would have been able to break free.

But it wasn't the case. The glass and the walls were too thick.

There was no way home.

Not for the whale. Not for Carlito.

When I got the call about Carlito's suicide, I remembered how Carlito had told me, because he was the smarter one who'd read philosophy books and learned about so many things I hadn't, that the great minds of the world say the instinct of any living being is to survive. But Carlito had another theory; he said once freedom is taken away along with one's basic dignities, a living being either has to deny its own instincts and surrender to the oppressor, or be consumed by a new instinct: to reach for its own death.

I watch Roxi, or whatever they're going to call her, since they've decided to let the public submit names, then put it to a vote. Rachel comes up behind me and sees me with my eyes on the dolphin, still trying to push her way out of the pen.

"Don't worry," she says, though by her tone, it sounds like she's trying to reassure herself more than me. "She'll settle in here in no time. They all do."

"I guess she doesn't have a choice," I say, but Rachel is already lowering herself into the water to try her work again with the dolphin, cooing toward her. The dolphin doesn't respond and remains with her back to us, by the fence, eyes on the water on the other side.

At my old job, I could face clients, listen to all their problems like their disintegrating marriages, horrible children, financial debts, and feel for them as I looked into their eyes. But when an appointment was up and the next client sat in the chair opposite me, I'd forget about the one who came before. By day's end, I'd shake off all their troubled words like dirty water down the sink drain and return to my little life.

I don't understand why I can't do that anymore after my days at the dolphinarium, why I can't accept what I'm told about how well they care for the animals and how they're better off here than in the big, bad wild.

I used to be able to walk past their pens. Now I linger beside each one, feeling guilty every time I have to peel away to move on to the rest of my day's duties.

I don't need the burden of caring. I want to turn away from them, forget them when I punch out on the time clock to go home, clear my mind of the conditions and rituals of their confinement.

When I do manage to put thoughts of the animals aside, it's only to think of Nesto, the confession of his upcoming remarriage, still an abstraction like those predictions they give out at the start of every hurricane season speculating on either a mild or a vicious summer.

No matter the statistics, no matter how precise the science, they're always wrong.

It's a Sunday. Nesto and I are up early because we plan to meet Lolo and Melly to go out for some dives on the line and maybe stop to fish at the hump on the way back. We're at Conchita's eating breakfast on the small patio outside her shop when we hear the thunder of helicopters above us. Choppers often pass over the islands, low enough for us to see what color they are and if they're blue news copters or orange medical airlifters. But the helicopters today are that familiar green and white and I know, even before Conchita comes outside to tell us she's just heard from her husband, who heard it from a friend fishing on Barkley Beach, that some migrants have landed, and there are probably more still out on the water.

Nesto wants to see for himself. Every now and then we catch a story on the news about rafter sightings, sometimes a capsizing, some people abandoned by smugglers and found clinging to tubes on the water, and others lucky enough to touch ground. There was even the story of the guy who made it to Key West floating on a windsurf board without a sail. But it's not like any migrants ever show up on Hammerhead or in front of his motel on Crescent Key, so we jump into his truck and head down to Barkley Beach, and Nesto parks on the side of the road right behind a news van.

We make our way down to the curve of coast where dozens of locals have already gathered, Ryan among them, though we don't acknowledge each other because we're already in the habit of ignoring each other all around town. I feel his eyes on me, but I'm watching the scene before us.

Three men and a woman, all dressed up as if they'd been planning on going to church or a party and not out on a boat for five days, though their clothes are dirty, pressed against them with sweat and water stains, their complexions parched and sea-lashed. The Border Patrol guys talk to them like they're just regular tourists, and some other beachgoers approach and offer water and sandwiches. There's snickering from the wall of people behind us that it's because they're Cubans that they're being treated so well, not like your average migrant. We hear them tell the police there were supposed to be more of them on their boat, but at the last minute, several got scared and changed their minds. One man says another boat left at the same time from the same beach in Puerto Escondido, but they lost sight of it after the first day on the water.

Nesto watches them. He presses his lips close together, holds his arms tight across his chest, and stands with his legs wide apart, as if guarding over the spectacle on the shore. I look at the crowd around us. Pale folk with expressions of curiosity and shock at the sight of the vessel these people arrived on, a wooden thing the size of a hot tub with a cobbled-together engine, rope and tarps, cans of food, and empty water jugs littering its tin floor.

The new arrivals look happy, despite their fatigue, grinning with shriveled lips, faces toasted by days under the sun, ringed by the salt of sea spray.

I remember the boy under the banyan tree, his eyes burning with terror, so different from the expressions of the four before us, telling the police they each have family members in Florida who will claim them and come for them when called.

Nesto and I stand together among the crowd but somehow apart, and when the police have the new arrivals board the white-and-green Border Patrol vans so they can be taken for processing and then released to their relatives, we begin the walk back to his truck in silence. He puts his hand to the image of Elegguá on his dashboard, starts the engine, and we head up to the marina where Lolo and Melly are waiting, though we will have a somber dive, wondering in our brief suspension in the blue-violet twilight of the ocean, where it's easy to confuse your way back to the surface, what it must have been like for those travelers, spending days and nights alone on the water, with little beyond hope to guide them.

That night after we've eaten dinner, as I straighten around the kitchenette, I look over to find Nesto standing by the sofa, looking anxious as he watches me.

"What's wrong?"

"I'm going to sleep at my place tonight."

"Why?"

"I need to be alone."

I don't say anything, so he quickly adds, "Please don't be upset."

"No problem." I mean it, too, even if we haven't been adhering to what we set out to do, enjoying day by day. Instead, we count on each other's presence each morning, and I can easily forget that while he sleeps at my place every night, he hasn't stopped paying rent on his efficiency at the motel.

"I need to think about things without you next to me. Please understand."

He comes up close and holds me in a sort of half hug. He leaves my cheek with a soft kiss, turning away without meeting my eyes, and walks out the door.

Let him go, I tell myself. *This is something you need to learn to do.*

Let him go.

I expect him to come back later in the night. He doesn't. The next morning he calls.

"I have to go home, Reina."

"I thought that's where you went last night."

"No, I mean my real home. I have to see my family."

I'm back in Miami with Nesto. He's trying to find a way back to Cuba since, for now, he can't afford the airfare. I knew I'd be back one day. But I didn't expect that once here, I would feel so uneasy, as if at any moment I might be discovered and asked to leave.

We make our way off the turnpike onto the main artery of Little Havana, Calle Ocho, driving slowly past parked buses waiting for tourists photographing the viejitos playing dominoes in the park, and shopping for made-in-China guayaberas. We hit travel agency after travel agency—around here, there are tons—to see if Nesto can sign up to fly to Cuba as a mula; he'd trade his forty-four-pound luggage allowance for a free plane ticket to be a courier for people using the agencies to send packages to loved ones on the other side.

Most agencies tell Nesto they've already got all the mulas they need for the year, but at the last agency we check out, a woman takes him to a desk near the back to sign him up. I wait on a folding chair by the door, taking in the posters of Havana all over the walls—faded images of the cathedral, the beaches of Varadero, the hills of Viñales, CUBA ES AMOR printed in curly letters across the bottom.

On the drive up to Miami, I pointed Carlito's prison out to Nesto, where the main road splits and I'd turn onto a bumpy path that never seemed to get paved, toward the first gate where I'd give my name and the guard would check the approved visitors list and my ID before he'd let me through the high walls and past the gun towers.

Seven years. Both eternal and as swift as a blink.

I closed my eyes until the barricades and barbed wires disappeared behind us, but felt as if I'd been at the prison just yesterday, spending a Sunday morning with my brother, holding his hands across the table, unaware it would be the last time I'd ever see him alive.

"I never told you about my uncle," Nesto began, maybe to ease the silence until we were out of prison territory and back within the ordinary coastal landscape. "He was in prison too. Not like me. They always let me out after a few days. But they kept him for good."

"What did he do?"

"He didn't do anything. It was before I was born. He was my mother's older brother. His name was Guillermo. He wasn't as welcoming to the Revolution as my mother and the rest of the family. They started rounding up subversives. They ordered them to El Jardín Botánico and he was among them. They called it 'social purging.' Purging! Like they did to us as kids, giving us aceite de ricino to shit out our worms. A neighbor denounced him for being *flamboyant*. In those days they would arrest you for anything—having long hair, listening to yanqui imperialist music—anything they considered undermining to the Revolution. So the family had to go to the public assembly and repudiate him. Then they transferred him to the UMAP."

"What's that?"

"It was a reeducation camp. A labor prison. They put the prisoners to work building new neighborhoods for people the Revolution brought in from the campo. People said those new buildings had blood mixed into the cement and plaster."

"What happened to him?"

"The family lost track of him. They didn't try to visit him."

"Why not?"

"That's what the Revolution does. It ruins families. Parents and children each accusing the other of being traitors. Years went by. Maybe he died or was killed in prison. If he was released, we never knew it. When I came here I thought about looking for him. I like to think he got off the island when they let the prisoners onto the boatlifts. Maybe he was the lucky one and made it out before things got so much worse."

I hear the woman at the agency explain to Nesto that he can get on the mula waiting list but if he doesn't go when called, with as little as two days' notice, he'll lose his slot and have to go to the end of the line because there's no shortage of people wanting to travel on the agency's dime.

Nesto agrees to her terms, hands over his Cuban passport, and signs some forms.

There was a gringa I once knew from work who earned herself a Christmas bonus by flying to Cuba every December. She'd stop in Mexico City, where she'd be given a purse as heavy as a bowling ball and a ticket to Havana—all of it arranged and paid for by some unknown individual. There, she'd breeze through customs where everyone was paid off to let her through, meet a guy outside the airport where they'd give each other a pretend hug as if they were family. After a handoff of the bag and a night in the Habana Libre Hotel, she'd get on a flight back to Mexico the next day with the bag full of a different kind of weight to hand off to her contact in Mexico. She was warned never to look inside the bag, but one day she did and saw heavy bundles shrouded in black plastic. It was only after she stopped making those trips that another girl involved in the same smuggle told her what was in them: gold bars on the way into Cuba, and cocaine on the way out.

When he's through with the final errand, Nesto and I walk back to his truck. I assume he'll want to hang around Little Havana for a while, take in a little of the painted nostalgia, check out the shops on Flagler, or maybe get some Cuban food, but he doesn't.

"Is there anyplace you want to stop before we head back down?"

I think for a moment. An unexpected urge comes over me.

"There is a place. Actually, there are two."

That's how we end up at the old house. Or what's left of it.
I thought when the realtor told me the new owners planned to renovate and remodel, they'd at least leave the walls, but there is nothing left. No trace of the rooms where my brother and I once slept, the tiles I learned to walk on. Just the foundation, the grass pulled out all around it leaving a kind of moat. All that remains that is familiar to me is the cypress tree at the front of the yard, with roots that still seem to boil up from the earth, the tree my grandfather climbed with a shaky ladder to hang himself from one of its long branches.

I don't want to get out of the truck. I don't want any of the neighbors to see me, and I think if I keep my feet off the ground of the old block, it's like I'm not really here at all.

Nesto leans over me from his spot in the driver's seat to get a better look.

"So this is your house."

"It was. *Our* house."

I anticipated sadness at the sight of what became of the only home I remember living in before the cottage. Instead, I feel emptiness, as if the wind ruffling the tops of the palm trees could blow right through me, no flesh, no bones, no heart in its way.

Nesto senses it's time to leave and starts the truck without my asking.

The house, and everything in it, is behind me now.
Gone.

*　　*　　*

And then we come to the bridge.

Nesto parks in the lot meant for fishermen and beachgoers on one of the flat ends of land joining the bases of the bridge. I remember the last time I came here with my mother. As I did then, I try to feel the footsteps on the concrete pathway, try to conjure a piece of my brother, and of my father, on the walk they each took to catapult a small life over the railing, sending so many other lives into the water with it.

I remember standing at the highest point of the bridge's arc with my mother, half our family's ashes in our hands. Two lives reduced to dust.

This time, I stand with Nesto.

He looks at me as if to ask if this is the place where it all happened and I nod.

The sea below us is a foggy green, dotted with a few small sailboats trailing each other. The bay stretches for miles, until the two strips of land lining it fade and the horizon becomes all water, the sun dipping toward it.

"Nesto, what do you think happens to us when we die?"

"I believe what the diloggún says. Life feeds on life. For every life that ends, a new one begins."

"Do you believe in souls?"

"Yes."

"Do you think they go somewhere else?"

"I do."

"People say if there's a heaven, Carlito wouldn't have gotten in."

"Nobody can know those things."

He points straight ahead of us.

"You see that out there, where the sky meets the sea? When the world was made, there was no separation between heaven and earth. There on the horizon was the gate to heaven and it was wide open so humans could go into it whenever they wanted. These were the first generation of humans. They were still immortal. They didn't yet know death. One day a man and a woman noticed that the animals were different from them. They couldn't walk into heaven whenever they wanted but they could create life from their own bodies, and make babies. So the man and woman told Olofi they didn't want to be divine anymore. They wanted to be like the animals and make life too. Olofi said if he gave them the power to make life from their flesh, their child would be of this earth, not carved by the hands of Obatalá or given the breath of life by Olódumare like they were. The child would have flaws and failures. It would be able to create life, too, but it would one day have to die. The man and woman wanted to have their own child more than anything so they agreed. Then Olofi broke the open path between heaven and earth so that humans could only cross into heaven in death."

"You believe that?"

"I believe the message."

"What is it?"

"We can't be both human and divine. To be human is to be imperfect."

When we were children, I was terrified of losing Carlito, even before I learned that he'd already almost been taken from us. After our mother went to bed, I would sneak into his room, and if he didn't let me into his bed with him, I'd sleep on the floor beside it, to make sure that nothing happened to him in the night.

"Don't worry, hermanita," he would say. "I will never leave you in this world alone."

As we got older and he grew reckless, drag racing his beat-up car on the empty roads of the Redlands he and his friends used as speedways, I would make him promise that if he died before me, he would give me signs to let me know his spirit was still with me even though our mother warned us it was mala suerte to talk about our own deaths.

When he was arrested, we stopped those types of conversations, and instead I forced myself to believe that my brother's death would never come.

"There is something else the diloggún says," Nesto tells me. "'Death is but a journey into life, and life is but a journey into death.'"

He reaches for me. I think he's going to hold me, but he just touches my arm and tells me to wait there, he'll be right back.

I am alone at the top of the bridge for what feels like a long time.

Me and the metal railing, smooth under my fingertips, the whistle of the salty high wind in my ears, burning my eyes, tangling my hair, with just the occasional jogger passing behind me, admiring the view on the other side of the bridge of the crowded Miami skyline, the bank where Carlito once worked folded somewhere into it.

I stare down at the water rushing beneath me, its swirling silver-crested tide pulling against both sides of the bay and out toward the mouth of the Atlantic. I become dizzy, leaning against the railing, close my eyes, and see the image of my own body falling over the railing into the ocean just as the words fill my ears and leave my lips:

"Forgive me," I say over and over. "Forgive me."

When he comes back to me, Nesto has in his hands a bouquet of flowers, which he says he bought from the vendor selling them at the underpass just before the turn to the bridge.

He gives them to me and I tell him they're beautiful: a mix of sunflowers, a few purple roses, and birds-of-paradise.

"They're not for you." He touches my hair gently. "They're for you to offer to the sea."

I don't believe in these things the way he does, but I'm grateful because now I can leave something nice behind in remembrance of Carlito.

Nesto whispers some words I don't understand and then repeats, several times, "Yemayá awoyó, awoyó Yemayá," and tells me to say it too.

I whisper the words, take the flowers, and hold them over the railing.

It's hard to let them go. I feel Nesto's hand on my back guiding me, until I'm able to release my fingers, let my knuckles splay wide like a starfish, and the flowers fall from my palm to the water below.

We watch them fan into the current, some stems pulled under and others floating away from us above the waves.

That night Nesto and I don't tear into each other like we normally do. We lie close and quiet, letting the sound of the tide fill the cottage.

For the first time in my life, I fall asleep and don't wake until morning. And when I do I feel different, not lighter but heavier, as if the pieces of myself I've left behind at the bridge over the years, that which had been left there for me by others, have been restored to me.

FIVE

During a visit to see Carlito, I noticed his prison suit looked kind of dirty and realized I never thought to ask before how many changes of clothes he had, or how they got cleaned. He said the prison laundry didn't use detergent and clothes came out smellier than they went in. So he, like a lot of guys, used shampoo bought from the commissary to wash his own clothes in his cell toilet. Another inmate had explained things like that to him a while after he arrived on his cellblock, how to make life a little easier on the inside.

If he'd been a regular lifer, Carlito would have had a cellmate, but as death row cases, he and the others in his wing were in isolation. Most of the time, the only noises they heard were of the metal doors opening and closing on their corridor, or inmates screaming and banging on their cells' walls until guards came in, deeming a rebellious inmate violent and buckling him by the arms and legs to the four corners of his concrete bed where he would be left for hours.

But the inmates could also call to each other through the hall between security checks, press their ears against the slots in the steel door through which their meals were served, and when everyone else was quiet enough to let the echoes carry, they could even have what resembled a conversation.

Sometimes Carlito got advice like that he should consider converting to Judaism in prison because the kosher food was better than the standard fare, and sometimes they even let you have a bar mitzvah party with a cake and guests. But Carlito told me even a friendly inmate, a guy you'd swear wouldn't try to kill you if he had the chance, could turn on you in a second. Sometimes guards showed up in the middle of the night to search his room, cuffing him, pressing him hard against the door while they stripped every photo and magazine cutout he'd taped to the walls, ripping covers off books, checking every thread in that tiny cell even though they did regular room searches three times a week, just because some other inmate claimed he was hiding a weapon; if Carlito got caught with a shank or a blade or any kind of contraband, the snitch could earn favor points for ratting him out, and maybe have one of his own discipline charges or grievances against him dropped.

The only time he got to socialize, Carlito told me, was when he got taken to a civilian hospital for pissing blood after a guard punched him in the stomach a few times, though he couldn't tell the hospital people the truth or other guards would retaliate later. And another time, when his colon was so backed up from the prison food that he wailed in pain in his cell for three days before they agreed to send him out for tests. You had to be near death to get to go from the prison medical unit to a hospital, Carlito explained, because inmates had this idea that with only two officers to a prisoner on hospital grounds, it would be easier to take them down to escape. Some guy had pulled it off years ago and ran free for a full three months before they caught him up in Jacksonville and brought him back in.

Some inmates just tried to get to the hospital to disrupt the routine of prison life; to see people other than the guards and shrinks and religious they were used to; to have a doctor or nurse look at them with kindness; to be touched for reasons other than being handcuffed or shackled, flesh to flesh; and to be able to look out a real window without seeing prison walls and watchtowers and barbed wire surrounding them.

They would do anything it took to get there. Scraping an arm against a wall until they broke the skin, cultivating an infection until holes burned through their flesh warranting medical intervention. One guy Carlito met in the hospital had even chewed off his own toe.

There in the civilian hospital, on gurneys parked in the blocked-off prison ward, Carlito would hear from other inmates—inmates awaiting treatment for tumors growing out of their bodies like new limbs, late-diagnosed cancers, necrotic wounds from neglected diabetes, pneumonia, or even organ failure from hunger striking—about death warrants already signed by the governor up in Tallahassee and those prisoners recently executed up in Raiford.

When a nurse came by to puncture the fold of Carlito's elbow with a needle so he could receive intravenous fluids, he'd panicked, fearing they were going to shortcut his execution and do it right there, and instead of giving him electrolytes and nutrients like they were supposed to, they'd flush his veins with chemicals and cook him from the inside out.

He began to hyperventilate and they'd had to sedate him.

When he woke up, Carlito told me, he was in a room alone. Then he saw the two corrections officers at the foot of his bed.

"Am I dead?" Carlito had asked them.

One officer looked to the other and laughed.

"When it's your time, Castillo, it won't be as pretty as this."

Carlito fell silent and stared at me across the table. He looked down at my hands cupped around his.

"When you get out of here you can tell everyone about this place," I said. "They should know what life is like in here."

"*If* I ever get out, I'll never talk about this place again."

"What are you going to do when you get out then?"

I was still playing at a more hopeful game, and so was Carlito. We'd had no luck getting his death penalty overturned as "cruel and unusual punishment" and therefore unconstitutional.

But we were working on getting another appeal on the grounds that the jury was prejudiced by the media and the trial should have been moved to another county. The new lawyer who filed the motion told us, you never know, maybe his sentence could be commuted to life so Carlito could get paroled after twenty-five or thirty years. He'd be in his fifties and still have a chance to build a real future on the outside.

He'd be a free man again even if he might not be free in this country. By committing his crime, Carlito risked being denaturalized and potentially deported, forced onto a flight back to Colombia, which wasn't so bad since Carlito's plan had always been to go back to Cartagena anyway—make enough money in Miami to buy a condo facing the beaches of Bocagrande, eat in restaurants where the ricos ate—and Mami and I could join him, he said, and he'd make sure we lived like queens.

Sometimes we'd fantasize together about what he'd do when he got out of prison because it was better than talking about what he'd request for his last meal or what he'd say in his final statement before being locked into the death chamber.

"If I ever get out," he'd say, "the first thing I'll do is go home, chop down that fucking tree in the front yard, and set the house on fire. Then I'll go to a restaurant and order myself a cold beer and a big, bloody steak."

Other times I'd ask the same question and he'd just shrug.

"Maybe it's better if they keep me here. I have no money, and they don't give you a pension for completing your prison time. There's nothing for me on the outside anymore. I'll have nowhere to live. They'll stick me in a halfway house with a bunch of lunatics."

"You'll live with me."

"Nobody will give me a job. People treat parolees worse than shit under their shoes. How is a man expected to turn his life around under those conditions?"

"I'll help you, Carlito. And you're so smart, anyone with a brain would know they should hire you."

"To do what? Clean toilets? Or to pick avocados twelve hours a day at some farm in Homestead?"

"Whatever it is, it's just a beginning."

I reminded him of all the people we'd see around, so often it was like we didn't see them at all: ladies selling fruit at intersections, guys who came knocking at the door offering to pull weeds for a few bucks.

"There's no shame in any work," I told Carlito. "Those people don't have education to fall back on like you do, and they probably get even dirtier looks than murderers when they go out looking for work."

"I'm not a murderer, Reina," was all he'd answer, and I'd feel like a failure because, as usual, I'd managed to hurt him.

"I'll take care of you," I tried again. "Just like you always took care of me. I promise."

But Carlito didn't want to listen to me anymore. His eyes were already darting around the room, the way they often did when we were near the end of our visiting time.

Dr. Joe once told me that one of the effects he'd observed in his subjects in solitary confinement was concentration problems, due, he suspected, to the lack of stimulation.

Carlito would start looking past me, as if cracks in the prison walls held some code, and I knew I'd lost him for the day.

We'd sit together in silence for the remainder of our hour together until the guard led him away.

Mo informs me the consensus among the vets and techs is that the new dolphin, who they're now calling Zoe, has psychological problems. They say she might even have brain damage or trauma that's left her unable to tend to basic needs like feeding herself.

"Maybe she's just depressed," I say.

"Depressed? This place is paradise for dolphins."

We're looking over the dock as Rachel stands in the pen, which is shallower than the others, no deeper than a swimming pool, and tries feeding the dolphin some fish, but she won't take it. I know they've had to supplement with force-feedings through a tube. The dolphin still refuses to leave the fence. She's worn the front of her head with the lines of the metal chain links, and turns away from Rachel whenever she approaches. Instead of just roping the area apart from the other pens, Mo had Nesto erect a huge curtain rod to wall it completely out of sight of the park visitors.

I'm technically off today but came in to work because I wanted to see how the new girl is doing. Weeks have passed since her arrival and everyone is getting impatient. Rachel is still trying all sorts of things to catch the dolphin's interest. Inflatable toys, hoops, mirrors—the 99-cent store stuff the staff members call *enrichment tools*. They've even brought in Coco, a gentle, older female from one of the adjacent pens, but the new girl isn't interested so they've separated them. They need the new dolphin to bond with Rachel, I am told. They need her to understand that Rachel is her source of food.

When Mo gets called on his walkie-talkie to another part of the park, I slip off my sandals, put them on the deck next to me, and drop my feet into the water. I see right away that the dolphin notices. Maybe it's the sound of my toes breaking the surface that alerts her. She lifts her head up. But then she moves away from the fence and comes a little closer to me and Rachel starts encouraging her, trying to lead her in the direction of her own open arms but instead, the dolphin makes its way over to me.

"Can I get in the water with her?"

Rachel looks surprised that I'd even ask, but with the dolphin at my feet now she relents. "Okay. Go suit up. And tie back your hair."

I always keep a swimsuit in my bag now, for days when Nesto and I steal away from work at lunchtime or after we finish the day and go for a swim at Hemlock Beach before sunset. I go into the locker room to change and take one of the spare wetsuits they keep on hangers in the corner, and walk back to the pen as fast as I can, hoping Mo or any of the vets won't stop me to ask questions.

The dolphin is back by the fence when I get there, and when I lower myself off the deck into the water at the shallow end, feeling the mushy sand under my feet, she turns again and comes directly toward me.

"You're not pregnant, are you?" Rachel asks.

"No. Why?"

"Sometimes they're attracted to pregnant women. They can sense it with their echolocation."

Now the dolphin is in front of me, dipping her head into my side. I let my fingers run against her dorsal fin, along her rubbery back.

"Just relax," Rachel tells me, though she doesn't need to. I feel the power in the dolphin's body, the way the water parts at her slightest movement and rushes against me, but I stand there, letting her swim circles around me, weaving through the water, kicking up her fluke, and back to my side again.

Rachel steps back toward the deck and returns to the spot I've claimed with the dolphin at the center of the pen, handing me a bucket of fish, telling me to try feeding her. I take one fish at a time out of the bucket, offering them to the dolphin, and she pulls the fish out of my fingers with her teeth until I go through all of them and leave the bucket empty. I expect Rachel to be happy with this, but she watches me with her hands on her hips, her lips tightly screwed. She says she next wants to see if with my help we can get the dolphin interested in some of the toys, and we take turns tossing an inflatable ball to each other. But the dolphin goes underwater, shooting to the deeper corners of the pen, only to reappear in front of me, tossing her head up, making clicking noises.

"She's showing off for you," Rachel says, sounding even more annoyed.

By now, a few others from the staff have gathered on the deck, including Nesto.

Mo comes to the front of the group on the deck, eying me with disapproval.

"I think you should get out of the water now, Reina. Leave Rachel to get back to her work with Zoe."

"I got her to eat a whole bucket of fish," I call back to him.

"You're not trained to be in the water with the animals. Do me a favor and get out of there *now*."

I make my way toward the ladder in the corner of the pen, but the dolphin follows me, and when I am all out of the water, standing on the floorboards, she takes a last look at me before turning around and heading back to her spot by the fence.

Rachel tries to lure her from the edges of the pen again, but the dolphin won't move.

Nesto walks with me back to the locker room, giving me the same look he gave me when he found out I'd gone off on the boat with Jojo. I don't want to hear him tell me I put myself in danger again so I walk quickly, avoiding his eyes.

When we're far enough from the rest of the crowd, he says under his breath, "You're going to give them a reason to get rid of you."

"I was just trying to help her."

"This is a job, Reina. We come here to work. Nothing more."

On Saturday and Sunday mornings, I sometimes go out to the beach behind the cottage, remembering that I would be with my brother at the prison for that hour if he were still alive. I sit on the sand facing the ocean, trying to conjure Carlito's memory, inviting him to sit with me. I hold my palms open before me, close my eyes, and try to remember the weight of his hands on mine, his voice before his crime, before bitterness set in, when he would throw his arms around me for no other reason than to tell me he loved me.

There were guys in his prison who'd killed several people and instead of death sentences, they received multiple stacked life sentences. Carlito told me he wondered what was worse: knowing your life was running on a short fuse and you could be called to your death any day, or having your lifetime and several more spread out before you for another two hundred years, an illusion of immortality even if it's to be endured within prison walls.

We all have to show up for our death, but maybe it was a gift to know the date of your last day. Unlike those with eternal sentences, my brother was promised an early escape, even if, in the end, he decided to flee in his own way.

Nesto says Carlito was probably a son of Changó, who, in his mortal days, was an impulsive king and, haunted by regret, hanged himself, later ascending as an orisha. His sons on earth are said to be born with inner violence, war upon their heads, like Changó, who always carries a double-edged ax, ready to fight and to die in battle. But they are also protected by Changó's wife, Oyá, patron of the dead, who Nesto says will help Carlito on his journey through the afterlife.

"Carlito," I whisper, the sound of my voice buried by the tide.

In my mind, I tell him about the dolphin, how she came to me, chose me over all the others, how I felt her skin and the enormousness of her body pushing the water between us.

I have felt insignificant all my life, but in those moments with the dolphin, I was special.

I remember when we were children and Tío Jaime and Mayra bought a pet store poodle that wouldn't let anyone touch her except Carlito, not even Mayra who tried to love her into submission. But around Carlito, the dog went limp, curling into his side, licking his hand, begging for his attention. When I put my hand near the dog, she grabbed my fingers between her teeth until Carlito pulled her off me. One day, while Carlito played with the dog in the living room, I wandered to the back patio where Mayra kept her parakeets and budgies in small metal cages arranged on shelves, mostly ignored except for when she took them in to fly around the house until they wore themselves out.

I went to each cage and opened the latch, reaching in as Mayra once taught me to do. The bird stepped onto my finger, and I pulled my hand out and shook it off into the air.

I let all eight birds go.

That night, when she realized what had happened, Mayra called our house to tell Mami. They figured it was me since I was the only one who'd gone out there, but I denied it just like Carlito had always taught me to do.

Mayra told Mami there was something wrong with me. I was worse than your ordinary fresca and way more chinche than my brother ever was. She said I had no conscience.

"Calm down, Mayra," Mami said. "They're birds. Where else do they belong but in the sky?"

Mayra and Tío Jaime grew so frustrated by their dog's behavior, the way she rejected them, that they took her to a vet and
had her put down. Carlito was furious. He said they didn't give
the poodle a chance to adapt, that you couldn't blame her for
being upset she got stuck with such shitty humans like Mayra
and Jaime. He cried for days and told me he should have done
like I did with the birds and smuggled the dog out of there.

Once, on the phone from prison, one of the rare times
Carlito spoke of his death sentence, he mentioned the poodle.

"They're going to do that to me. They're going to euthanize
me like a dog."

"Don't say that."

"I wonder what it will be like," he continued. "I think about
it sometimes. The walk from the cellblock to the death house. I
wonder how it will feel when they push the drugs into my veins.
You don't always die right away, you know. They say the whole
thing is supposed to take less than ten minutes. But it took one
guy an hour to die. His skin started to slide off his body while
the poisons fried him. But he wouldn't die, so they kept having
to pump him with more."

I remember feeling so sickened by his words that I couldn't
speak.

"They give you three injections. One to anesthetize you,
one to paralyze you, and one to stop your heart. The anesthetic
is supposed to keep you from feeling, but nobody knows if it
really works because even if you're still awake and your body
can feel pain like you're on fire, the paralytic keeps you from
screaming and crying, until the last drug finally suffocates you
and you go into cardiac arrest."

"Who told you all this?"

"A new guard in here. A young guy. He stands outside my door and talks for hours. It's like they shot him up with truth serum or something. You know what else he says? All the people who go into the chamber with you wear masks. Even the doctor whose job it is to stand over you and make sure you have no pulse left. That's so nobody outside finds out that in here, they're paid to be serial killers."

"Carlito," was all I could manage after several moments.

"I'd rather be shot by a firing squad. I'd rather be gassed or dropped out of an airplane. All those people sitting on the other side of the glass, waiting to watch you die in a chemical experiment, like it's a fucking magic show. They should save the money and just take me back to the bridge and throw me over. That's how I was supposed to die anyway."

The line started to beep the way it does when a prison call is down to its final seconds.

"I have to find a way out of here, Reina. I can't let them kill me."

I thought he meant through the appeals process or our petitions for clemency, how plenty of death row folks, especially women, get their sentences lifted and are resentenced to pure life.

But now I know he meant something else.

They don't let me back in the water with the dolphin. Whenever I go to her pen, to get a look at her progress, just like the other staff members often do, Mo comes by and tells me I'm a distraction and to get back to my work minding the park guests. The dolphin is still despondent, *nonreactive*, ignoring Rachel and all her attempts to entice her with fish or toys, instead remaining by the fence for hours, sometimes so still she'll roll onto her side only to set herself upright again, until the sun sets and all of us go home.

They're consulting with experts at other aquariums to see if they've dealt with similarly resistant cases. In the worst-case scenario, she'll remain alone in a pen indefinitely, subject to more force-feedings, and still the staff maintains this is a better fate than releasing her to the wild. But they're hopeful she'll observe how the other dolphins around her have adapted to life in their enclosures, respond to scheduled feedings and human contact, and understand surrender is her means of survival.

It reminds me of Carlito's prison days when Dr. Joe told me that even though most inmates fantasize about the day they'll be released, a lot of them don't actually want to be freed; they've been in the system too long and in some cases, through generations, the claw of the law present from the cradle.

"Incarceration is contagious," Joe said. "It becomes a state of mind, and once it penetrates a prisoner's psyche, it's very hard to remove. Inmates will become so emotionally destroyed that they will internalize their surroundings and forget about the world outside, and where they came from. They start to believe prison is their natural habitat."

"I don't think prisoners ever forget where they are."

"You would be surprised, Reina."

"You try living the rest of your days in a cell. See how natural it feels to you."

"That's exactly the point. Isolation is designed to break a person's consciousness. For some, the only way to endure it is by losing one's mind."

I wake earlier and earlier, dreams pulling me out of sleep. I dream of the Santo Toribio church, of the muralla where I used to hide from my mother and grandmother and slip off to with Universo. It is always night in my dreams and I am always alone.

I shake awake to find Nesto beside me. In the morning, I've gotten into the habit of telling him my dreams, which he says come through Olokun, orisha of the deepest part of the sea, who brings messages from the ancestors.

Then I think of my mother, who believed it was no good to ponder dreams. "It's like looking for hairs in your soup," she'd say. "You'll never be happy with what you find."

Cartagena. Always Cartagena.

After his sentencing, Carlito made me promise to go back to Cartagena for him, so I could tell him about the colors, the smells, and the sounds, and he could close his eyes and pretend for a moment he'd been there with me.

"Maybe your dreams are telling you it's time to go back," Nesto says.

"I guess it would be nice to see if it's as I remember."

"Nothing is ever as one remembers it. That's the point of memory. So you can keep the pictures of your life you want to keep and forget what you need to forget. The only reason to go back is to see the place as it is now, and to see how you feel in it."

On our next Sunday phone call, I ask my mother if she'd be interested in going back to Cartagena with me, tell her it's something Carlito always asked me to do. I hope she thinks there might be something special about taking that kind of journey together, maybe it could give us peace to move forward with, but she says she won't leave Jerry alone to go on vacation anywhere.

I tell her she can bring him along though the last thing I want is to travel with the guy, but Mami dismisses me and finally admits Jerry refuses to travel to a country he considers "uncivilized." Maybe in the future we can all go, she offers, after they're married.

"What about you?" I ask Nesto. "Would you go with me?"

"I would. But I have to go home first."

He's still waiting to hear from the agency if a slot has opened up for him to go as a mula. Mo agreed to give him the days off without pay.

Mornings my dreams wake us up, Nesto and I don't go back to sleep. We lie in the cool predawn darkness, listening to the morning birds make their calls, waiting for sunrise to lift away the night.

On one of those mornings, I tell Nesto to come with me out to the dock. Dawn has broken and I know Jojo will be coming around the bend of the canal any moment on his boat. Nesto kicks his feet around the dock impatiently.

"What are we doing out here, Reina?"

"Just wait another minute with me."

Sure enough, there's Jojo, turning out of the canal passage. I wave him down and he comes closer to the dock. I ask if he can take both of us out with him. I want Nesto to see what I've seen the few mornings I've gone out with Jojo.

Nesto and I sit together on the bench at the back of the boat while Jojo drives out. The morning sky swirls with orange and pink. Jojo calls to us to look to the right and there, just like the first time, a group of dolphins swims against the waves to keep up with the boat. Jojo finally cuts the engine and the water slowly flattens, the dolphins turning over the surface, their backs glowing in the light of dawn.

Nesto stands up to get a better look and I see his tired face brighten. We watch for a while as the dolphins vanish underwater, reemerging on the other side of the boat, and rushing against each other.

The sun is higher now, and we know it's time to go back so we can make it to work on time.

While Nesto gets his things together to head to work, I lay out the morning grapes for the iguanas, something he always laughs at. There are no iguanas left in Cuba, according to Nesto, because they were all skewered during the Special Period along with the banana rats, squirrels, and just about every other edible species one could catch and slaughter to feed one's family. Even the zoo population thinned out in those days, pigeons and tortolas picked off park grass, manatees pulled out of canals to feed a whole barrio, and the pasteles sold on street corners were rumored to be packed with vulture and totí meat. But it happened a long time ago. These were things people didn't talk about over there anymore.

"Then why do you talk about it over here?" I asked.

"Because if I don't tell you, you will never know. And I think it's important that you do know. It's part of who I am. I had to eat things I never thought I'd eat too."

A pair of red parrots fly over the cottage and land atop a high palm leaning over the roof, birds that might even have come from as far Colombia, before they could be stolen from the rainforest, wrapped in newspapers, stuffed into suitcases, and smuggled out of the country to be sold for thousands in North America: exotic pets turned escapees.

When Nesto finally comes out of the cottage, keys in hand, to head for the truck, I reach for his arm to stop him on his way and tell him what I've had on my mind for days.

"I think we should let her go."

"Let who go?"

"The new dolphin."

He looks at me sideways, his brow high. "Let her go where?"

"Set her free."

"What are you talking about?"

"She's not trained. She won't even eat. She hits her head against the fence all day and all night. She knows where she is and what's outside the pen. She knows the gulf is her home. She wants to get out. We just have to give her the way."

"She's their property, Reina."

"She's nobody's property. She belongs in the ocean. You know that."

He takes a few steps away, turning his face from me to the path that leads to the beach.

"And how are we supposed to get her out of there? Build her a ladder?"

"You put that fence up. You know how to take it down."

Nesto sighs so long it turns into a whistle.

"I'm not a citizen yet. I can't commit crimes. If I got arrested, I'd risk everything."

"Just listen," I say, walking toward him, reaching for his hand so he'll come back to my side by the porch railing. "During one of your maintenance checks, all you have to do is unscrew the clasps from the fence to the poles. Then, at night we'll take Lolo's boat, drive around to the back of the pen, and we'll dive under and pull it apart so the fence wall falls down and she can swim out."

"You know they say they won't swim through anything. They can't tell it's an opening."

"She will."

"How do you know?"

"I just know it."

"What if she doesn't come out? We'll be wasting our time."

"I'll swim with her. You saw how she was with me in the water. I know she'll follow me. When she's out far enough, she'll know to go the rest of the way alone."

Nesto shakes his head at me. "I don't think so."

"Listen, just like you walked across that border in Mexico, that dolphin is going to swim through that gap in the fence."

As I say the words, I realize how silly I sound.

"Estás loca, Reina."

"If we don't get her out of there, either she'll starve herself or she'll be tortured into accepting she has to live in that pen forever. That's no kind of life either."

"The other dolphins seem to be doing okay there."

"They've already been made into zombies."

"They don't try to escape."

"Some people are better at being prisoners than others."

"They're not people, Reina."

I turn from him. The biggest of the iguanas, with a high ridge extending from its head to its tail, swallows grapes a few feet away.

"Reina. Did you hear what I said? They're not people."

"Imagine they build a fence around this property we're sitting on and tell us we can never leave it. Never, for as long as we live, only eating the shitty little food they let us eat after we perform whatever stupid chores they want us to perform. This tiny patch of land has to be the only world we'll know forever. How would you feel?"

"I already know a place like that."

"Then you know why we need to do this."

"Look, we can talk about this later. We're going to be late for work."

When we're in the truck, before he turns the key in the ignition, I say, "If you don't help me, I'm going to cut a hole in that fence myself. It will be much harder to do alone. But I'll do it."

He covers his face with his hands, fingers long and cracked with calluses. His body looks especially tired to me that morning.

I start to feel bad for what I am asking but don't stop myself.

"I've thought about this for a long time. I'm not going to change my mind."

"Reina, por Dios santo. Can you just let this go?"

"I can't. She's not like the rest of them. She knows where she belongs."

Later, at work, I see Nesto by the new pen. I'm talking to some visitors by Belle and Bonnet's enclosure when he passes me, and ducks behind the curtain dividing the new dolphin from the dock. When I finish with the visitors, I go to the other side of the curtain and see him, his eyes fixed on the dolphin, her head still pressed to the fence, while Rachel and some techs sit on the dock nearby with clipboards, discussing new strategies to get her to integrate.

At night, back at the cottage, Nesto throws himself onto the bed without any dinner. He pulls off his beaded collares and places them on his handkerchief on the bedside table. I climb onto the bed and kneel at his side. He runs his hands on the fabric of my jeans, over my thighs down to my knees, and reaches for my hand.

"If we get caught, I'll take the blame for everything," I tell him. "I'll say you were just driving the boat and had no idea what I was planning. But we won't get caught. They don't have any security cameras out there. They can't afford it. And we can make it look like an accident, like the fence just came apart."

"I did not come to this country to free a dolphin, Reina."

"Neither did I."

"What about the dolphins in the other pens? And what about all those other parks in these islands? There are dolphins just as miserable as that one *everywhere*. Letting one go isn't going to make a difference."

"It doesn't matter. I can't leave her there. I have to try."

"It's like trying to block the sun with a finger."

"Two fingers," I say. "There are two of us."

He closes his eyes and shakes his head. When he opens them, he touches my hair, lightly, as if it's made of light rather than my messy strands.

"I'll help you. But only because you have a debt to pay to Yemayá for your family. You're going to settle it by returning that dolphin to her waters."

"I don't know about debts, but I know it's still the right thing to do."

"We should wait until it rains. Just before or after a storm. Or even better, *during* one. So the guard on duty won't hear the boat coming."

"So we'll do it?" I just want to be sure of what he's saying.

"We'll *try*, Reina. That's all I can promise you. We'll try."

I put my arms around him and whisper my thanks into his ear, though it doesn't seem like enough, not because of what he's agreed to do, but for what it will mean to me if we are able to pull it off.

"You're not scared?" he asks me.

I shake my head and smile though I feel heaviness in my chest, knowing the real reason I have any courage at all is that I have so little to lose.

The spring sun flames out later and later, but even on cloudy days when underwater visibility is poor, we go in for a swim. Once out in the blue, Nesto says, there is no way you can refuse it.

It's there, while Nesto makes his own offerings to the ocean—watermelon, fruta bomba, or just a banana peel he casts off into the current with a question for Yemayá and Olokun, waiting to see if it floats or sinks—that I make my own petitions to the water, asking for help to guide me through the darkness, find my way through the night tide past the metal fence, so I can clear the way for the dolphin, lead her through the path to her freedom. Most of all, I ask the ocean to keep us all, Nesto, the dolphin, and me, unafraid.

A week or so later, two guys from Switzerland turn up at the dolphinarium and when I stop to ask if they're enjoying the place like I'm directed to do, they start asking, not about the animals or the facility, but about my life, how I got lucky enough to end up working here, and where I'm from since I don't look like any of the other girls around Crescent Key.

They ask what there is to do at night around here and if I'd like to go out with them.

"You look like you know how to have a good time," one guy says. When I decline, they become even flirtier, playing the clown for me.

Mo stops me on the walkway as soon as I part from them.

"What was that all about? Looked like they were trying to pick you up."

"They were just asking about the place."

"Asking what?"

I realize I have an opportunity.

"About the new dolphin mostly. I guess word's out she's not doing so good here."

Mo's empty hairline shoots up and he looks back at the Swiss guys who've moved onto Dottie and Diana's pen. Mo studies them, and I know I've planted a seed of suspicion that will serve me later.

It's maintenance day. I walk over to the new dolphin's pen and see that Nesto is already underwater, checking the bearings on the fence like he does on all the pens, and he's doing what we agreed he'd do—instead of tightening the bolts holding the clamps to the corners and support posts, he's actually loosening them. He works around the dolphin, still at her place along the fence. Rachel is out in the front lagoon working one of the shows. I notice Mo has followed me.

"What do you supposed she finds so fascinating about that fence?" Mo says, though I'm not sure if he's posing the question to me or to himself.

"What's on the other side. The sea."

He pulls his hand out of his pocket and cups my shoulder, his palm warm through the cotton of my shirt.

"Let me explain something to you, Reina." He points across the fence. "That out there is the *gulf.* Behind us is the *ocean.* And way down there, south of the Florida Straits, is the *sea.* We use the correct terminology around here. You got that, doll?"

"Got it."

I don't tell him there are no fences out there marking where the oceans end and the seas begin. It's the same water flowing free. I read in one of the cottage magazines that a single wave can travel around the whole world before it hits shore. There are no borders, no security checkpoints to inhibit a wave's journey. The world's oceans are one body of life. Only land separates water, but land, too, is rooted in the ocean.

I don't tell him that a few nights ago, as we sat together watching a storm from the cottage veranda, lightning filling the sky like arteries over distant columns of rain, Nesto told me Yemayá's realm in the ocean is the greatest energy conductor, able to absorb the temperature of Changó's lightning strikes, each one hotter than the sun.

"It's power beyond our understanding," Nesto said.

Then he added that the only things we can count as truth are two prophecies of the diloggún that rest against each other:

No one knows what lies at the bottom of the ocean.

And the next prophecy:

Blood that flows through the veins.

It's a simple plan. Nesto is slotted by the agency for a flight to Havana next weekend. We have to do it quickly or risk having to wait until he returns.

We know we are breaking laws starting with trespassing and vandalism.

We have a cloudy moonless night and a cold rainstorm on our side, though without wind, thunderclaps, or lightning.

This, Nesto reassures me, means that Olódumare, the Creator, owner of the world's secrets, who pours rain, is offering us cover.

We've had Lolo's boat for a few days after taking it out for some dives. During this time, Nesto and I practiced, running it slowly down the canal along Hammerhead, each of us suited up and jumping off, to time how long we thought it would take to undo all the clamps on two poles, for both of us to pull the sheet of fence fabric down into the sand and clear the way for the dolphin to come out. It was faster than having to cut a hole with pliers, a bolt cutter, and a saw. We'll have our wetsuits, fins, masks, and gloves, because Nesto knows the fence is already scabbed with sharp barnacles. We won't take oxygen though, because we know the noise and bubbles would probably make the dolphin even more apprehensive.

The night we go out, we do ventilation patterns to open our lungs, to oxygenate, and to relax our bodies. I've looked forward to this night, imagining the dolphin swimming out of the pen and away from us. But the journey from our dock, around the island, under the bridge to the gulf side of the Keys, feels especially long. Nesto promises that with our lights off and rain muffling the sound of the boat's engine, we won't be noticed by anyone onshore.

We've rehearsed aloud many times. Nesto made drawings of what the fence looks like underwater so I could memorize it because we can't use a big flashlight and risk attracting attention. We know there is only one security guard on duty at the dolphinarium at night. We're banking on him tiring of his rounds by three in the morning, taking shelter from the rain under one of the canopies at the front of the facility.

As we get closer to the pen, Nesto and I try not to speak to each other. In the darkness, we rely on the silhouettes of hand gestures, touching each other, or whispering deep into each other's ears if we have to be heard. He stops the boat about twenty meters from the pen and I lower myself into the water, cold seeping through my wetsuit. I slip my mask over my face, and as I fear, I see only blackness. We'll have to use the tiny flashlights we've brought with us that only illuminate the span of a hand. I swim ahead, feeling for the fence, setting my intentions in my mind the way Nesto taught me to do whenever we approach the ocean for a dive. And because Jojo told me he learned dolphins can sense our motives, we have to make it clear to them, articulate it to ourselves so they can read it in our being, that we mean no harm.

It's a matter of minutes, my breath shortening the more I try to push it longer, and I struggle to keep myself from gasping loudly every time I come up for air. I work on one pole, the tiny lights guiding us through the unscrewing of bolts and clamps, cutting the fence ties with the wire cutter while Nesto works on the other, but he finishes before me and slides over to finish my part of the job. The fence begins to wobble and falls over us. Nesto warned me we'd have to back up quickly to pull it down from the top or it could pin us under.

We've prepared for this in his drawings and I do as I was instructed until the fence hits the sand at our feet. I swim over to the dolphin, still in the same spot she claimed when the fence was up. I go to her, hoping she'll smell me or see me or sense me with her sonar the way she did that first day I went into the water with her. I fear she won't recognize me in this darkness like she did before, or she won't follow me. But then she starts moving and I do, too, while Nesto clears out of the way and heads back to the boat.

I swim away from the fence slowly, looking back to make sure she's behind me. In the night I can only see the occasional gloss of her dorsal, feel the water moving around me. But then I feel the pressure of her slipstream and know she's beside me and I swim a little faster, careful not to kick up water with my fins. We push farther out, past the boat, toward the small mangrove islands dotting the bay until it unfolds into the gulf. She doesn't touch me, but I feel her through the water, her weight moving against the current, and then, when we are so far out that my body starts to feel much heavier, my breath even shorter, I have to let her go.

I turn, make my way back to the boat, trusting she won't come back with me, refusing to look behind me so she won't think to follow. I feel something near my legs and hope it isn't the dolphin. When I come to the back of the boat, I give Nesto my fins and he reaches out his arms to lift me in.

We don't speak. We don't say a word. He starts the boat and we head back for the cottage.

It's only later when we stand on the bathroom tile and peel out of our wetsuits that we each take in the stunned look on the other's face.

I am certain we've done the right thing, but we can't know until the morning if we've been successful. For now, we have to wait.

I don't know what to say to him, how to thank him for helping me do what I asked. I reach my arms around him and put my face against his chest. We don't shower off. Tonight, we go to bed as we are, sticky, salty with the sea.

By the time we get to work the next morning, the dolphina-rium is erupting with scandal. Mo's been calling Nesto for more than an hour already, telling him to hurry up and come in to work though he won't say why. A local news van is parked out front, along with several police cars. The employees, from the gift shop ladies to the maintenance workers to the trainers and vets, are in disbelief. Nesto and I approach the crowd at the end of the walkway, where the curtain stood, though it's been removed. Charlie, one of the techs, tells us the fence collapsed and the dolphin escaped out of the pen. Rachel and some of the other staff members are already out on the boats trying to find her, so far with no luck.

Mo, the park owners, and the cops take Nesto aside, since he was the one to erect the fence and was in charge of making sure it was sound. I watch as they question him for their police and incident reports, asking him to explain the exact procedures he used to build and check the fence. Nesto tells them on his last check the fence was in perfect condition, not a screw out of place.

Soon, Mo tells everyone to get back to work. He says he's sure it wasn't an accident that the fence collapsed; it's too un-likely all the hinges would come undone at the same time and it would fall uniformly to the ground. That's how he knows it was a deliberate breakout and not that the rain or winds pulled the fence open, or that the dolphin pushed the fence down herself.

The only suspicious activity Mo can think of to tell the cops about is the Swiss guys who came the other day, asking questions about the new dolphin.

"Goddamn," he says. "They probably came here to scout the place."

In the afternoon, I overhear Rachel telling Mo that maybe they should try taking me out on the boat with them to look for the dolphin. They're standing in the shade under the observation tower and don't see me coming down the stairs behind them.

"She's the only person Zoe let get near her," Rachel reminds him.

"She doesn't know the first thing about those animals or how to be in the water with them. We don't need that kind of liability right now."

Then their talk turns to Nesto.

"We'll have to get someone to double-check the Cuban's fence work from now on," Mo says. "Got to make sure he's not the one getting sloppy on us."

Nesto and I stay late that afternoon. He's rebuilding the pen we've taken apart, working diligently to ease the day's chaos, and I'm talking to the last guests to leave before closing, Iowans wondering if it's true what the news said that afternoon, that a dolphin escaped.

I give them what Mo said would be the official story: the fence broke open during the storm and the dolphin probably got disoriented, but will surely return to her home here.

"They always come back," I say, hoping that I'm lying.

At home, Nesto and I don't speak of what we've done, as if, even by admitting our culpability to each other, we'll be discovered.

Paranoia sets in. Nesto feels eyes on him everywhere. The police call him in to question him again and he always gives the same answers.

The trainers still go out on the boat, believing their own tale that the dolphin has just lost her way.

The investigation turns up no evidence. The security guard who was on duty that night swears he did his complete rounds, checked the pen several times, and didn't hear anything unusual out on the water.

Nesto and I float together in a strange state of hyperawareness.

I feel no regret or pride, just relief and a quiet satisfaction, as if Nesto was right after all—I've begun to settle my debt, and somehow things are falling into balance.

One morning, I see Jojo's boat come up the canal and pass me on the dock where I sit with my legs hanging over the edge, dangling above the water. He slows down, waves to me, and cuts the engine as the boat bobs a bit closer to the dock.

"You still working over at the dolphinarium?"

"Yeah."

"I heard about the animal that got out. They recover her yet?"

"Not yet."

"What are they saying about it?"

"The whole fence came down. Looks like it toppled over in the rains."

"We're talking about a hundred-thousand-dollar animal here. That's the going rate for wild-caught these days. No question somebody broke her out. Maybe even stole her for another facility."

"But she was a rescue."

"It's animal laundering just the same," he says, touching his beard, starting the engine up again. "Secondhand dolphins are still worth a pretty penny."

"Where would somebody hide a dolphin?"

"There are houses on water all over these coasts. Somebody would just need to build a pen. It's easy. And it's been done before."

He stares at me so long I wonder if my face is giving anything away.

"They think it might have been activists," I tell him.

"Could be. Last summer a couple of them tried to free a dozen manatees that were stranded from the red tide and held in a pen up in Islamorada."

"Did they get away with it?"

"Only two or three manatees made it out. But someone turned the folks in. They got arrested. I think they got probation and had to pay some fines. No matter. I'm sure if you'd ask them, they'd say it was worth it."

"I'm sure they would."

"There's also the chance the animal died and they're saying it's stolen so they don't have to report the death."

"Why wouldn't they want to report it? Aren't the animals insured?"

"Sure, but they also want to keep down their official animal turnover numbers. Lots of places do that. Nobody likes hearing about dead dolphins, or wants to draw attention to the fact that captives are lucky if they live ten years, and wild ones can easily live up to fifty."

"How do you get rid of a dead dolphin?"

"How you think? You wrap it in a net, drag it out on a boat, load it with big rocks and sink it far out in the ocean." He points toward the horizon. "You'd find yourself a dolphin boneyard not too far out there if you only knew where to look."

The dolphin doesn't return.

A few nights later, I hold on to Nesto tight, put my mouth to his neck, and whisper as softly as I can into his ear, "Nobody will ever know it was you and me."

He nods, kissing me. Then he tells me a story, a pataki, of the Ibeyís, los jimaguas, the divine twin children of Changó and Ochún who were raised by Changó's mother, Yemayá. The twins, a boy and a girl, were playing in the forest when they encountered the devil who set traps for humans and, after catching them, would eat them. The twins were trapped now themselves, and one of them hid while the other stepped forward and made a deal with the devil that if the child could dance longer than the devil, the child would be freed. But the devil didn't realize there were two children, and the twins played their tambourine and danced and danced with the devil, and when one child became tired, they switched places and danced and danced until the devil grew so exhausted he had to give up. With the devil on the ground gasping, barely able to speak, the Ibeyís made him promise to stop his hunting and trapping of humans and let them roam the earth free as they wished. And so the Ibeyís became known as the protectors of all creatures, forever revered as the two young ones who, with their cleverness, together outsmarted the devil.

Tonight, hours before he's due to leave for Cuba in the morning, Nesto does an ebbó to Elegguá, asking for assistance with his plan to reunite his family. I watch as he arranges four coconuts on the edge of the mattress, places a card with Elegguá's image on the table beside the bed, and lowers his head before it, making the sign of the cross. He takes a coconut in hand, rubbing it along his body from head to foot until he's done so with all four coconuts, asking Elegguá, controller of paths, to change his fortune and bring his family to him. Then he goes outside and I follow, watching from the veranda as he places a coconut on each of the four points of the Hammerhead property surrounding the cottage. He starts in the east, facing the ocean, smashing each coconut with a hammer until it's a mess of meat and juice, jumping over the broken shells until he finishes the last one, and returns to the cottage, careful not to look back over his shoulder or he'll break the ebbó. Thunder rolls over just as he passes me on the veranda, and I know Nesto is pleased because thunder is a sign from Elegguá's friend Changó, galloping through the heavens on his white horse, that his petitions have been heard and will be answered.

We are both at the airport in Miami, after a long bus ride up from the Keys before sunrise, about to board flights to opposite ends of the Caribbean.

My trip was planned on impulse, another piece of restitution, the final trip my brother was never able to take to witness for one last time the first home we both knew.

I am also leaving because I don't want to be alone in the cottage wondering what's on the other side of Nesto's journey.

A representative from the travel agency meets Nesto and the other mulas outside the airport, handing him a duffel filled with parcels to be dropped off with its agent in Havana for delivery.

We stand in the check-in area, halfway through the crowd of passengers waiting to have their luggage weighed at the counter, enormous packages shrouded in plastic, overstuffed suitcases, store-boxed television monitors, and toasters. In front of us, a man pushes along a metal airport cart with a plastic car tire on it, and when Nesto asks what he's going to do with only one tire, he says he's already brought the other four over and this one is just the spare.

I stand with him in the convolution of lines. Airport taxes to be paid, forms to fill out, before they give him a boarding pass.

"It's like this every time," Nesto says. "It's harder to get out of this country than it is to get in."

He once told me about when he arrived at the Matamoros border crossing into the United States. He was told it was a dangerous city, full of trapaleros and paqueteros eager to scam or rob anyone passing through. He called some friends of friends, Cubans who'd settled there and made a living renting rooms to migrants getting ready for the crossing. They warned Nesto it was best to walk over with nothing on him but his Cuban passport because border guards were as bad as bandidos and would confiscate his money, clothes, whatever he had on him. He should leave his things with them, they told him; they'd keep it all safe till he called from the other side with an address, and then would send his stuff over to him. When he made it into Brownsville—no thieves at the gate, no hostile Border Patrol agents—then to Miami, he tried to call the friends in Matamoros to give them his uncle's address, but the number was wrong and he never heard from them again.

His arrival in Miami was full of similar deceptions. The amigo who helped him open his first bank account, write a check, and use an ATM machine also stole his pass code and robbed him dry. That blue truck he drives now isn't the first one he bought in the United States. The first, purchased from an acquaintance, died a day after he brought it home. And during his first year here, when he went out looking for work, he was shocked to hear employers tell him without hesitation, without asking as much as his name, "I don't hire Cubans," which is why he decided to start working for himself.

I see Nesto is embarrassed when he tells me these stories. I can't picture him so vulnerable. Until I see him at the airport this morning, his eyes nervous and uncertain as they search mine when we stand by the security checkpoint before we part ways to catch our separate flights at different ends of the airport.

He pulls me into his arms. I close my eyes tight, wishing us back to last night, in the cottage, when we lay close and quiet, neither of us speaking the truth that he will return from this trip married to someone else.

"I hope everything works out the way you want it to," I tell him.

He closes his eyes and nods.

"I hope you find what you're looking for in Cartagena."

There is already an appointment for his marriage at some government office, where the person in charge will ask a bunch of questions, like why, if he and Yanai divorced years ago, they've decided to remarry, and they'll say they fell in love again on one of his visits home, realized they can't live without one another, and want to make their family whole again. The way he rehearsed it aloud in the cottage, peppering his story with details like that being far away in Los Yunay Estey made him understand he can only ever love her, the mother of his children, even had me convinced. But then Nesto broke character; shook his head; looked down at the floor, moaning as if suddenly ill; then tried the monologue all over again, trying to sound even more authentic.

"I can't ask you to wait for me."

"I know."

He steps out of my embrace. My arms fall off his shoulders before I understand this is the last time I'll touch him and these will be our last words to each other before we part. He's turned away from me and become a part of the crowd drifting toward the security X-ray machines. I don't want him to see me watching him, so I walk away quickly, and if he turns back to look at me one last time, he'll have found me gone.

The taxi drops me at my hotel, a former hostel upgraded to a boutique hotel on Calle de la Soledad. I wash my face, change out of my jeans and into a light dress that won't stick to me with humidity, place myself on the street, and try to see if by memory I can lead myself to my grandmother's home, back to the first bed I slept in as a newborn, cradled by my mother's arms, while my brother slept beside us.

The streets are even more colorful now than years ago when Carlito and I came with our mother to see Abuela through her final days. A basket of fuchsia, turquoise, and banana yellow, with dark wood balconies dripping with bougainvillea, stone streets pounded by horse-drawn carriages like the one Carlito and I once saw turn over right in the Plaza de los Coches. One second the horse shuffled along mechanically, and the next, it collapsed, flat on its side, the carriage buckled over. Shopkeepers and street vendors rushed over to help the passengers to their feet. The horse was dead. Its ribs and pelvis protruded and tourists asked when was the last time the driver fed the horse, talking about animal abuse and fair labor. Others just blamed the heat.

I was quiet the rest of the day and Carlito laughed at me for being so sentimental, said nobody was going to miss a ratty old horse that was probably diseased anyway. I was surprised he could be so callous. He'd always been nice to animals, not like some of the weirder kids from the neighborhood who used to kill squirrels to give them shoebox funerals in their backyards. Carlito even saved a rodent or two from certain death at those kids' hands, but that day he was strutting new teenage macho heartlessness.

"How would you like it if somebody said that about you after you're gone? Ese pendejo comemierda. We're better off without him.'"

Carlito laughed arrogantly. "Everybody knows I was saved from the water by angels. Nobody would dare say something like that about me."

When my mother was a girl, the whole neighborhood knew when a norteamericano set foot in El Centro. Now, there are so many tourists beyond the moneyed folks who stay at the fancy hotels, a daily extranjero flood of cruise ship passengers doubling the population between the city walls. Street vendors toss around English and Italian phrases to get their attention, and even the kids rapping verses to tourists sucking on fruity drinks at the café tables in the Plaza Santo Domingo conclude their performances with "Come on, amigo, a dollar for my song."

I find my way through the pedestrian crowds to Abuela's building, which I remember as whitewashed, rain-stained gray where its fachada merged with the pavement, now painted the color of guava, fresh tejas on the roof, its balconies newly honey-stained. A sign beside the door that once led to the stairwell spiraling to the apartments above reads, INQUIRE WITHIN ABOUT SALES AND RENTALS.

Above the street, the window where Abuela used to sit at her sewing machine table is open. I can ask the building's new management if I can see the home that belonged to my family. See how it's changed, maybe take some pictures to show my mother. I'll tell Carlito about it too. I still report to him. I don't believe in much, but I believe he hears me, still see his face across from me at the prison listening to me as I'd describe the feeling of being drenched by a sudden rainstorm, the warm sizzle of sun on my skin, the sweet and tart smell of the orange and pineapple groves I'd pass on the drive down to see him.

I want to see if I feel the same as I did when I saw the house in Miami ripped out of its soil.

But I hesitate. I'm not ready to step within those walls, identify myself to the new owners, say the words *this was once my home.*

I used to blame my mother for having taken us away. I imagined that if we'd never left, the darkness wouldn't have found us, and even if my brother had grown up to be a killer just the same, at the very least, because there is no capital punishment in Colombia, Carlito wouldn't have been sentenced to death, and probably not even to cadena perpetua, which is not even a life sentence like the name implies, but a maximum of sixty years. But Mami told me I was wrong, even if in Colombia it seemed like a person could get away with more for less. She said there's another kind of justice down here and sooner or later, the streets would have made him pay for his crime.

I step away from my grandmother's building down to the tree-lined plaza at the corner, still glistening from fresh afternoon rain. The Parque Fernández de Madrid has been cleaned up, but the same old guys stand in the shade at its fringes selling candies and frituras out of carts, arguing about fútbol teams, a solitary vago fishing for scraps in garbage cans. When my grandmother's hand joints stiffened and she became too old to care for the beauty of other women's nails and hair, she sold mamoncillos and ciruelas de campo from baskets to passersby. In this park, I used to spend hours with my brother and the neighborhood children because anywhere was better than the stiff heat of Abuela's apartment, which always smelled of her tobacco and the incense she used to camouflage it. Here, I met Universo and came with him often when we were older, listening to him talk about his plans for his life, how jealous he was that I was lucky enough to grow up far from Cartagena and how one day, even though his mother forbade it, he'd leave too.

Besides the tourists, the foreign men with preening local girls, the slouching backpackers, are the ordinary faces of tired people whose names I may have once known, who may have known me when I was still considered una hija del barrio even though my parents had taken me to the other side of the Caribbean, because back then people still believed, for a long time after you left, that you might still come home.

An old man sits with a paper bag in his hands, tossing crumbs to the crows and pigeons and sparrows at his feet. There's a commotion among birds between the benches. A furious chirping grows louder near me, a pair of sparrows split from the hungry swarm, pecking each other with their beaks, wrestling against each other, rolling on the ground, their claws joined, until one rises above the other, jabbing at the other bird's beak and back. I stomp by them so they'll separate, but they go back at each other with more fury. I shoo them with my hands, but they meet in the air and pull each other down into the dust, and it's clear these birds are fighting to the death.

"Déjelos, mi niña," the old man with the crumbs calls to me. "You'll never stop one animal from trying to kill another. Nature is wiser than we are."

I leave the birds to their massacre, the old man and the park behind me. I walk until I pass the cafetería on the corner of Calle de la Universidad where Mami would sometimes escape to, usually a few days into our visit every summer, after a standoff with our grandmother. Mami would always threaten to pack up and leave, though she never did. I'd sit with her, chewing on a pan de bono as she sipped aguardiente, saying she never belonged here and it was a mistake to keep coming back.

Though we came to spend time with Abuela, Mami often had dates with men she knew from her girlhood who were already tired of their wives, or she'd go for a drink at a hotel bar and find a tourist or businessman to take her out that night. She never brought men home, but on nights she stayed out, Abuela would sit by the window and watch over the street to see if she was coming. If she stayed out all night, Abuela would lock the door, refusing to let Mami in the next morning, making Carlito and me swear to do the same because Abuela said we had to be unified in our punishment.

Mami would plead to us through the door. Carlito always caved in first, slowly undoing the lock. But her shame was complete and she'd move around our shared space careful as a mouse, going into the bathroom for a long shower until one of the neighbors screamed that the building water tank had run out.

"Don't ever become like your mother," Abuela warned me regularly, whether Mami was out of sight or right in front of her.

My mother would look at me with hurt eyes, but would never argue or defend herself.

Years later, when it was me who disappeared with boys, mostly Universo, sometimes not coming home until sunrise while Mami slept because she didn't get as many dates anymore, Abuela would taunt her daughter, tell Mami it was obvious she was jealous of me because she couldn't attract quality men, just the barrio bums.

"What would a decent man want with a trash dump like you?" she'd hiss. "Only pigs like garbage."

Abuela had a way of silencing us. Carlito and I watched as she humiliated our mother, never sticking up for her, never mentioning that it didn't matter how flawed she was, she was our mamita and we loved her.

Once back at our house in Miami, our mother would make me hand over the dresses Abuela spent all summer sewing for me with the best fabrics she could find at the shops on Badillo, taking scissors to them, ripping the seams, slicing the dresses into long rags she'd put on the end of a wooden pole and use to wash the floors.

If my grandmother could know me as I am now, she'd say I missed my golden window in life. She'd say I threw it all away to look after my brother, the years I should have been busy making my way in the world. She'd say I squandered my feminine currency by hanging around a prison for so long.

She advised me when I was still a teenager, instead of going back for another year of school, to stay with her in San Diego and marry Universo so I could get marriage and children out of the way. Abuela had faith Universo was a good boy raised by good women, and wouldn't grow up to be the typical sinvergüenza husband who disappears Friday through Sunday. Even so, at the time, I couldn't imagine a worse fate.

It's a wonder Universo never got me pregnant since I was never more careless than with him. He might have loved me. He never said it, but it's possible. But he was a boy a bit like my brother, wild with loyalty to his mami. Universo's vieja never let me beyond the front rooms of their house on Calle del Cuartel. I pass by it now and see it's been converted into a hotel too, the front sala where the tías once crocheted and gossiped made into a lobby, the wall that once held a cabinet of their finest china now studded with room key slots behind a bulky reception desk. But every now and then, when his mother and all her sisters were out visiting parientes in San Pedro, he'd sneak me inside and we'd do it all over the house.

"That malparida Castillo girl," la vieja would tell Universo, her sisters, and anybody from the neighborhood who would listen, "she's more dangerous than a bullet to the ear."

To keep her son busy and away from me, Universo's mother would send him on endless errands. She didn't trust the modern supermarkets popping up all over the city, selling packaged meats and imported shined-up fruit. She preferred to send Universo outside the city walls to Bazurto. Sometimes I went with him. We'd make our way through the maze of vendors, pinch our noses through the odors, until we arrived at the shaded section where they kept the live animals. Universo would pick out a chicken, watch as the vendor broke its neck, dunking it in a pot of boiling water to loosen the flesh, making it easier to pull out the feathers. I'd hide my shock so I wouldn't have to hear from Universo how sheltered I was by my North American life, and how what goes on in those big gringo meat factories was far worse than this. Behind us, rows of cows and pigs hung on hooks for people to pick out their cuts—not a single part going to waste, down to the eyes, tails, and hooves. I'd stay with him until I couldn't stand it anymore, then wander out through the fish stalls to the road, crossing the traffic of trucks and horse carts to the polluted lagoon, and watch the scavenging seabirds until Universo came to find me.

I remember the look he gave me every time he found me after I'd slipped off into a crowd. Relief, happiness, a kind of peace. I felt it too.

Sometimes Universo took me with him on the back of his motorcycle all the way to San Juan Nepomuceno, through hillside roads scattered with guerrilla checkpoints, past marshy ciénegas bleeding into green and blue mountains. When we arrived, we'd sit at the bottom of the church steps for hours, waiting to see if Universo could spot his father, who he heard lived there now with his second family, but we never saw him.

On the way back into Cartagena's city walls, we'd stop at the feet of La Popa, the white monastery on the mountain that hovers over the city like a cloud, where Universo's mother, who we all called La Cassiani, told her son the Karib and Calamarí Indians worshipped Buziraco, the devil in the form of a golden goat, until the friar who wanted to build the monastery and shrine to la Virgen de la Candelaria showed up, confronting the devil and his worshippers, throwing the golden goat off the side of the mountain. The devil retaliated with hurricanes and storms until the church was completed, and then relented, moving deeper into the continent. It's for that reason, Universo's mother told him, that Cartagena has always remained protected, and the rest of Colombia so troubled, already half a century under the thumb of its latest civil war.

Our grandmother told Carlito and me a different story: After Buziraco was thrown off the mountain, the devil of La Popa had lingered in the shadows of the hills, so quiet people didn't notice he was there. But when our father took us away from Cartagena, the devil followed our family across the Caribbean, waiting to see how he could make us fall. She'd meant it to scare us into being good children but Carlito and I only laughed at her story, though it turned out to be the same warning I'd receive from the blue-haired bruja so many years later.

I climb the muralla steps up to the wall where I used to sit with Universo, where I can still hear my brother's voice echoing against the stone corridor calling for me to come home, watching the sun fall like an orb into the dark ocean.

Carlito wanted to bring Isabela to Cartagena. He planned to marry her and the day he went to the bridge with her baby, he was already close to having all the money he'd need to buy her a nice engagement ring. He'd been saving for a year, and before that, even longer, for a down payment on a home. Isabela said she would take his last name, but told Carlito she wouldn't give him a baby until after the wedding. On their honeymoon, he'd take Isabela to Cartagena, where Carlito predicted, his eyes shining with hope, they'd conceive their first child.

"But Cartagena is *ours*," I'd insist.

I hated when he talked about a future with Isabela, but hated even more that he'd peddle our past to her.

"Don't be jealous, Reina. One day you'll love someone as much as I love Isabela and you'll want to share everything with that person too."

Years later, I'd try to understand how Carlito had once wanted to give Isabela so much, yet had still managed to take everything away from her. But Dr. Joe told me the prison was filled with guys like Carlito, who'd committed terrible crimes against the person they professed to love the most.

"It's a mixed-up, messy sort of love," Dr. Joe said.

I remember wondering if there was any other kind.

I don't go to my grandmother's grave. But for three days, I walk the narrow passages from Santo Toribio to what was her home. I lean along the wall of the building across the street, watching to see if anyone goes in or comes out of the doorway. Her window is open and I stare at it for a long while to see if I can will the image of my grandmother's figure into the frame, how she'd perch there to check on my brother and me playing in the park. I look down the block, see a pack of young boys walking together, and, as they press past me on the narrow sidewalk, I check their faces, aching in that way I've lived with for so long, trying to see my brother as he used to be, exploding with youthful curiosity, wrestling with the best and worst parts of himself.

If not today, I may never have the chance to see my grandmother's place again.

I ring the bell beside the door and an intercom voice answers.

"I'm interested in a property," I say.

The door buzzes open and I let myself in.

The ground-floor apartment, which used to belong to a guy everyone called "El Viejo Madrigal," a retired army captain who liked to sit around in his old uniform drinking whiskey, is now an office and a slim woman, speaking Spanish with a French accent, welcomes me in. I planned to lie, tell her I'm looking to rent an apartment, but I try honesty instead, tell her the apartment on the fourth floor had been in my family for generations.

She doesn't seem to believe me, or maybe she thinks I've come here to make a claim on the place, so I drop the name of the guy Mami sold it to, a lawyer from Medellín whose name I remember because she had a fling with him before transferring the deed.

"I'm leaving tomorrow," I say. "I won't be back again. I would be grateful if you would let me see it for just a minute. Then I'll go."

She looks around the office, maybe looking for an excuse to say no, but it's otherwise empty beyond the two of us, not even a phone ringing.

She sighs, a little embarrassed, and stands up.

"Follow me. Just a few minutes though. I've got to mind the office and I can't leave you up there alone."

The stairwell and landings have been painted and retiled; our footsteps are the only sounds in a building that used to vibrate with voices. But the aroma of locked-in dusty moisture on the third and fourth floors is still the same—a smell my mother hated and said was full of spores that would one day kill us.

My grandmother's door is no longer blue but tangerine, and the woman tells me the apartment has been recently vacated and is available should I want to live there again.

Without furniture it should appear larger, but the apartment feels so small. I can't believe we lived here, the four of us.

The walls are a fresh white, the splintered wooden floors sanded down and varnished. The agent waits in the hall as I walk through the rooms, stand in the places that used to hold beds, where I slept and where my grandmother died.

I don't know what to feel. I long for some sort of sensation that will bring all my lost pieces together, but I only feel the inertia of the space, the light breeze coming in through the window I've been watching for days from the street.

"Carlito," I whisper his name, but I am overwhelmed with solitude.

There is nobody here but me.

Here on the equator, darkness falls evenly for twelve long hours of night. I don't take myself to restaurants or to the champeta or salsa clubs the front desk guy recommends to the other hotel guests. I buy a bakery sandwich and a soda, and settle into my room, the sounds of the horse carriages and music of the Plaza Simón Bolívar reverberating against the terra-cotta tiles and stone walls the color of burned bone.

The TV news talks about a homeless man set on fire near the university in Bogotá, about the peace negotiations between the guerrilla forces and the government being carried out on neutral ground in Havana.

I think of Nesto.

By now he would have gone to the appointment from which he would have left a newly married man. I wonder if they kissed or took photos. I wonder if the children looked on with renewed hope at the sight of their parents together again.

My mother, despite all her boyfriends, never managed to make a new father of anyone for Carlito and me. She longed for a handsome and rich gentleman to show up and marry our whole family, give us a new last name. I think she still dreams of it.

I wonder what Yanai thinks of their reunion. I wonder if she'll be willing to let him go in the end and if he will be willing to walk away.

Nesto gave me the number of his mother's place the last time he went home because his American cell phone would be blocked from working on this island. He said to call if I needed him. He said to take that any way I wanted.

I consider it for a while before I dial.

He told me he never would have left his family if he hadn't had to. He would trade everything to be with his kids again.

Would you trade me? I thought, selfishly, though I knew better, because not so long ago, I would have traded anything and anybody in my life, even my own mother, to have Carlito walking free beside me.

It takes a few tries, sorting out the tangle of numbers and country codes on the hotel room phone.

The buzzy ringing, the voice of an older woman answering.

"This is Reina. Nesto's friend," I say, feeling foolish.

She responds as if I'm just a neighbor calling from around the corner, "Oh, yes. Hold on, hold on."

I hear her footsteps, as if she's walking with the phone, other voices in the background, and I try to pick out who they are from how he described his family members to me—could that girl's voice belong to his cousin, or his niece? The man, maybe his stepfather, or an uncle? But then I hear only Nesto, telling me to wait one more moment, he's going somewhere quiet. The other voices fade, and he says he's taken the phone to his bedroom at the back of the house, which, no matter how many years he's been away, has remained his room, as he left it, the same way we maintained Carlito's room for him until Mami occupied it with her saints and crucifixes.

"I hoped you'd call. How did you find your city?"

"Not really mine anymore. How are things over there?"

"You know. The same."

We are both quiet.

"It's not the same though. You're married now."

For a moment, I think the line has gone dead. I hear nothing, not even his breath, until the line comes alive again with his voice.

"No. It didn't happen."

"Why not?"

I imagine another case of postponed appointments, bureaucratic delays.

"Let's just say that plans have changed. But I can't talk about it on the phone. ¿Me explico?"

I know he means that over there you never know who is listening in on a call.

"I'm sorry. I know how much you were hoping this would work out."

"It might still. It might not."

I don't know how to respond so I just listen.

"I wish you could see how things are here. I wish you could experience life as a Cuban. No, I take it back," he laughs. "Nobody deserves that."

He stops himself and I hear him take a deep breath.

"I wish you could come, though. See my house. Meet my family. You would see that everything I've told you is true."

"I've always believed you."

"You can hear about it from me all day long, you can read about it in your magazines, watch it on *TV Martí*, but you won't understand until you see it for yourself."

He pauses.

"You could come here. You have the two passports. You could postpone your ticket and fly into and out of Havana from Colombia. You'd face no issues when you get back to the States."

"I'm supposed to go back home tomorrow." But the word *home* feels odd leaving my lips and even stranger sitting heavy on the airwaves between us.

"Reina, I'm inviting you. Come see my island. I would be so happy if you came."

Nesto has never asked me for anything. And until now, I've never felt there was anything I could give him.

"I'll think about it," I say.

"Don't think about it. Just come."

I tell myself, it's not a big deal, simply going to visit a friend for a few days, but of course it's more than that; it's to carve out another space in whatever little time we may have left together, to meet him at his origin, the way I returned to Colombia to meet myself in mine.

Now, to go to him in Havana seems like the only choice, continuing on the same path that brought me back to Cartagena:

The only way to hold on.

The only way to let go.

A few nights before we left for our separate journeys, Nesto and I went out to the beach and saw, on the path illuminated by the moon, the long tracks left by a turtle that came ashore to lay her eggs. We followed the lines until we found her nest far from the tide in a knoll at the foot of the dunes. Nesto marked the area with coconuts and seashells. There were times he and his family were forced to survive on turtle meat and now that he was no longer hungry, he said, he'd show his gratitude by looking after this turtle's babies in her absence.

In Florida I dream of Cartagena, but here, I dream I am lost among night waters trying to swim back to the cottage, to Nesto, gasping, my limbs fatigued. But then I feel myself buoyed from underneath by a giant loggerhead turtle who carries me on her back. I hold tight to her shell as she breaks through the current, and though I feel safe in her care, in my dream the moonless night is unending, and we never reach the shore.

There are no direct flights from Cartagena de Indias to Havana. Less than a thousand miles separate the cities but, instead of heading north across the Caribbean, I'm on a plane heading south, over the rippling cordillera of the Andes into the city built on the savanna, Bogotá.

I remember making the same stopover with my mother and brother. Mami always seemed nervous and said it was because she didn't like being so far inland, the singsong accent of la costa with its swallowed syllables, the sweet air fresh with salt and sun, so unlike the guttural voices of the capital and the thin air high on the plateau, the atmospheric pressure change we felt upon touching ground that made our heartbeats jumpy—the same fluttering I feel in my chest now—and which, if we'd ever stayed longer than our layovers, would cause headaches and dizziness until the body and blood adjusted to the altitude and the soroche passed.

The man sitting in the seat next to me, a guy in a wrinkled suit who so far hasn't spoken a word, gathers his things to get off after we land.

When he sees I haven't budged from my seat by the window he turns to me.

"This isn't your stop too?"

"I'm staying on until Havana."

"¿Y qué se te perdió por allá?"

"I didn't lose anything over there," I say, smiling, because it's true, I haven't lost Nesto yet, "but you never know what I might find."

A short while after the first man leaves, another old man arrives in his place. He settles into his seat, pulls a worn prayer book from his bag, and sets it on his lap, gently caressing a small photograph between his fingers. It's an image of the same young boy with a staff I saw on Nesto's dashboard the first night I climbed into his truck under that full moon. The one I recognized that first night as El Santo Niño de Atocha, rescuer of victims of circumstance, safe keeper of travelers, but whom Nesto claimed as Elegguá, opener of paths, so living beings can accomplish their destiny.

SIX

I exit the José Martí airport terminal and make my way to the corridor designated for arrivals through a crowd of waiting families and friends. At first, it's as if everyone has his eyes, his broad smile. But then I see a hand reaching above all the others. He pushes through the wall of shoulders and elbows toward me, his long hair pulled off his face, temples and collarbones shining with sweat, pulling me close to him.

"I can't believe it," he says between embraces. "You're really here."

As he pulls me out of the crowd, Nesto looks different to me. Something in his eyes. Or the way the sun here has turned his skin a deeper amber than our sun back in Florida. I can't place it, but before I say anything about it, Nesto turns to me and touches my face.

"You look different to me, Reina. Something happened to you in Cartagena."

"The only thing that happened is that nothing happened."

"Maybe that's what you needed."

Nesto rented a car from a neighbor, a discontinued miniature Korean Daewoo Tico left behind by Soviets in the nineties. He drives among other cars, Fords, Chryslers, and Pontiacs, most from the middle of last century, down a long road lined with billboards of socialist slogans: ¡Más Socialismo! and ¡La Revolución Sigue Adelante! splattered under images of Fidel Castro, Che Guevara—Nesto's namesake—or Camilo Cienfuegos, and sometimes of the three men together.

Entering the city through Avenida Salvador Allende, I see peeling building facades, sun-bleached the color of ash, broken

balconies, boarded windows, crumbling columns—some struc-
tures already imploded with only posts of their original foundation remaining, no fresh paint to offset the decay. Nesto tells
me this is what happens when there is no money for repair and
you take everything away, leaving a city to defend itself against
time, storms, and the salt of the sea.

He turns onto narrower city streets in the direction of the
hotel I've arranged. He's invited me to stay with his family in
Buenavista but I insist I don't want to impose myself on his
clan, show up as proof of his life on the other side of the Straits
when he's come to be with them, not play tour guide to me.
Any time he has left over, we can spend together, but I don't
want to be a burden.

"But you'll at least come over and meet them."

To that, I agree.

Nesto parks the car and comes along so I can check in at
the hotel and unload my bags.

Once in the hotel room, small with wooden-paneled walls and
colonial furniture, Nesto says, "You know, it wasn't so long ago that
I wouldn't have been able to walk into this hotel with you, or even
walk on the street with you without getting stopped by police."

"Why?"

"Because you're foreign."

"How would they know?"

"They *know*. They have a file on every person that enters
the country. You just got here and I'm sure they've already got
a file started on you."

"Why are you whispering?"

"Remember where you are, Reina. The archipelago has ears."

We leave the hotel, where Nesto eyes the employees, sure everyone is a chivato, an informer, and walk down to the Malecón,

finding spots on the seawall under the last golden bits of daylight, the city at our backs.

Below our feet, young boys splash in the balnearios where Nesto says he learned to swim, shallow pools carved out of coral and stone buffering the seawall from the whipping waves of the open sea. There are no visible boats, there is nothing to indicate that anything exists beyond this island or that the sea ever ends.

Nesto says the Malecón is a city unto itself. Around us, Cuban families and tourists stroll; vendors offer peanuts in paper cones, and raspados of red and blue sugared ice; clusters of teenagers pass glass bottles around, sipping rum or matarata, moonshine. There are pairs of embracing lovers, the sounds of laughter, conversation, the music of guitars and tambores and voices singing songs to which everyone seems to know the words.

I've been waiting for him to explain. I don't want to probe, but I can't hold back the question I've been carrying with me from Cartagena.

"Are you going to tell me what happened with the marriage plans?"

"It's like you said. Nothing happened and everything happened."

"What does that mean?"

"It's Yanai. She doesn't want to go."

"I thought the plan was her idea too."

"It was. But she changed her mind."

"I don't understand. All this time I thought she was trying to leave. The marriage to the German. The plan to marry you again."

Nesto takes a deep breath, eyes fixed on the ocean.

"It's not that simple, Reina. I had chances to leave this island before I finally took the step. In the nineties there was the

Maleconazo right along this wall down by the port. There were boat hijackings and people protested so much the government said anyone who wanted to leave could leave and they wouldn't put you in jail for trying like they usually do. I was nineteen or so. Sandro wasn't yet born. I was young enough that I could have started a life somewhere else. It was the time to leave. But I was too scared. The boats were getting intercepted on the water by the Americans and the people on them sent to camps in Guantánamo or Panama. I couldn't do it. I couldn't risk leaving just to end up in an army prison. I finally understood what my mother always told me. It's hard to leave, to be the one to rip apart your family. *So hard.* No matter how much you hate where you are, no matter how much you curse your government or desire something better, leaving your home, your country, is like tearing off your own flesh."

"You never told me that."

"It would take a lifetime for me to tell you everything there is to tell."

He sighs.

"There were other chances after that too. You know marriage is a negocio here. People come from other countries offering to marry a person. At that time, it was five or six thousand dollars for a European or Mexican. Two or three thousand for a Peruvian or Costa Rican. Men, women, it doesn't matter. Sometimes they disappear with the deposit, but sometimes it's a legitimate transaction. I never considered it but I know plenty of people who left that way. After the Maleconazo, life became even more difficult. With the Special Period, we were all the thinnest we had ever been in our lives. I was at Santa María del Mar with a friend. People would go there hoping a tourist on the beach would buy you lunch. I was just there to swim, to forget about things for a while. But a woman swam over to me in the water.

She said she'd been watching me. She was from Barcelona. She liked me, it was obvious. She was a pretty good-looking temba, at least forty-five. I wasn't interested but she kept talking. She told me she worked with a theater company and could send a letter of invitation for me so I could get a visa to travel to Spain. She said she had a big apartment and I could stay with her. She didn't want money. She said she didn't want anything except to help me because she saw how miserable things were for us here. She would pay for everything until I got settled. She would give me a job at her theater or help me find work doing something else. I didn't believe her but she later sent the letter and the money for the plane ticket and I was lucky and got the tarjeta blanca and permission from the Spanish embassy to travel. Even Yanai wanted me to go so I could send for her and Sandro later and we could have a new life together in Spain. But people kept telling us horrible stories about Cubans who went to Europe and ended up sleeping on the streets, in bus stations, how people abroad hated them and mistreated them and wouldn't give them jobs so they had no choice but to become criminals or prostitutes. They said the cold weather would kill us and we'd beg to come back home to Cuba but by then, maybe the government wouldn't let us in. They terrorized us. We didn't sleep thinking about it."

"So what happened?"

"I couldn't do it. I couldn't leave. In the end, I was too scared. Things were so bad on the island in those days, but I still believed it couldn't get worse. By the time I realized how wrong I was, it was too late. Yanai had opportunities to leave too. She had a cousin in Chile who said he could bring us both there. He had a restaurant and said he would put us to work. But Yanai was afraid to go so far away, almost to the end of the earth, so she told him no. And then, after we divorced, she married the

German. She said he was a good man and all he wanted was companionship and that he promised he would send the kids to a good school and they would live in a beautiful house in the countryside. Sometimes I think she didn't study enough for those language tests on purpose. But when she said she'd marry me again herself so I could bring her and the children over together, I believed she was serious. Now I see she never wanted to leave and she's only being honest about it now. She says she'd rather live in her family's house, keep up with the daily lucha because she already knows how to survive here. She's afraid of the world out there, even in a place as close as Florida. I understand because I was afraid for so many years too. Everyone here is."

"Didn't you tell her you'd help her?"

"She knows I can only help so much. She'd have to get a job."

"What's wrong with that?"

"Here she can go to her job at the women's clinic and earn the equivalent of twelve dollars a month, but she would spend more than that on the buses or almendrones she'd have to take to get there. So she is able to not work and earn the same, which is to say, nothing."

He points across the dark water and night horizon.

"There, everyone has to work and *hard*. Nothing is free. You get a small amount of help through the Adjustment Act but beyond that, you are on your own. She's scared. She says she doesn't want to drown out there. She prefers to drown at home even if our children drown with her. I tell her, 'Yanai, there is nothing for them here,' and she just says, 'Look at you. What have you accomplished there in La Yuma? You're a nobody over there just like you were over here.' I don't have anything to answer to that because she's right. I am a nobody. But I only want for my children to be what they want to be, say what they want to say, have what they want to have. It's a small ambition for anyone else, but for me it's everything."

I know there are no words that I can offer to comfort him, so I slip my hand over his as it rests on the smooth stone wall and we sit together a while longer in silence as the Malecón of the night begins to take form: pale Europeans walking by, arms draped around much younger local girls provocatively dressed; foreign women marked by sunburns and tan lines, elbows linked with dark, muscled young men. Farther down the road and a little deeper into the night, Nesto tells me, the real body commerce begins.

We start the long walk up Paseo del Prado to my hotel, passing prostitutes in arched walkways, the shadows of joined bodies in dim alleyways between crumbled buildings, behind graffitied barricades under signs indicating reparaciones, though Nesto says it takes an eternity for anything to get repaired, and often a building simply collapses, taking the lives inside with it.

The hotel bar is full of foreigners and a few locals among them. Once in the room, Nesto flops onto the bed as if it's already his and I lie beside him, kissing him. He won't stay the night. He wants to see his kids in the morning to walk with them to school. We enjoy each other for the part of the night we do have together.

"I have to admit, I didn't think you would come."

"I told you I would."

"I thought you would change your mind, or you would lose your way somehow. I didn't think there would ever be a day when I'd see you in Havana, with me."

That night, my first on Nesto's island, I dream of walking at dusk through a thick green forest where trees burn down to their roots, each one spiraled by smoke and fire. In my dream, I don't run or panic, but remain still, heat on my face, watching the forest burn until all that is left is seared earth.

Two days in Havana. Nesto says he can take me where the tour groups go—to see the lovely painted and restored plazas of Old Havana where musicians perform "Chan Chan" and "Guantanamera" on street corners, where tourists drink daiquiris at government-run cafés and buy communist memorabilia from government-licensed vendors running shops out of their living rooms. The Havana of illusions, he calls it, packaged for foreign consumption.

"I'd rather see your Havana."

"You will. Tonight I'll take you to dinner at my mother's house."

"What do they know about me?"

"That you're important to me. And that I invited you here."

"Okay," I say. "But what can I bring? I don't want to show up empty-handed."

"You won't. You and I are the ones bringing the food."

Today Nesto has borrowed another car from a friend, a boxy brown Russian Lada with windows that don't roll up or down, and a backseat that slides off its rails hitting the car's unpadded and oxidized metal shell. We are on our way to the tree-lined streets of Vedado, on what Nesto says is the daily mission of every citizen on the island, to put food on the table that night.

We start at an agropecuario, a market built on a lot amid mansions in varying states of disrepair and decay, abandoned by the rich who once inhabited them. The better-maintained ones are government offices or foreign firms, but most have been split from single-family homes into tenements holding up to twenty families. Nesto buys a plastic bag from a lady selling them on the curb and inside the market, and we make our way down rows of produce piled onto crates and tables. Nesto picks onions, yuca, malanga.

"Are there potatoes?" Nesto asks a vendor.

"No, amigo. Maybe next month or the month after."

"How about lemons?"

"No lemons in the markets since November. Only for tourists."

At the back of the market, Nesto buys several pounds of rice and beans.

"I thought you got that stuff free," I say.

"The State gives just five pounds of rice and beans per month, and it comes full of pebbles and worms. Even the coffee they give us is cut with peas."

We pass the butcher stand where a man with blood on his apron swats flies gathering around thin slabs of beef hanging on hooks and fillets resting on his splintered wooden counter, Todo Por la Revolución painted in red across the front.

Outside the market, as we walk back to where he parked the Lada, a man approaches Nesto with a stack of egg crates on his shoulder. Nesto negotiates for four dozen eggs and the man helps him arrange the cartons on the floor of the Lada so they won't crack.

"Do you really need that many?" I ask.

"With the Libreta, a person is only allowed five eggs a month, but right now there are no eggs in any dispensary or market in all of Playa or Marianao. So we have to get them here while they have them. Next week or next month, there might not be any."

Just as the egg vendor walks off with the money Nesto paid him, another man arrives at Nesto's side whispering that he has in his possession potatoes, which only tourist restaurants have had access to in months.

"Bueno, amigo," Nesto says. "Show me what you've got."

The man disappears around a corner, reappears a few minutes later with a paper sack in his arms, and presents it to Nesto, who pushes down the flaps to get a glimpse of what look to be real potatoes, fat as fists.

"Give me a dozen," Nesto says, and the man is thrilled to be paid in CUCs.

"Black market potatoes," I say, once we are in the car and on our way again.

"Black market *everything.*"

We hit three supermarkets where you can buy food, clothes, furniture, and appliances at inflated prices in the tourist currency, but are unable to find milk for Nesto's children beyond condensed or the powdered kind. Finally, at a diplomercado out in Miramar where the expats and diplomats shop, we find real boxed milk and Nesto buys an entire case along with a few other luxuries—cheese, salami, pasta sauce, cookies, and crackers—food he says will hold up after he's gone and won't spoil easily in the tropical heat. We wait in line to pay among foreign-looking shoppers, their carts full of bottled water, wine, and packaged meats.

"You do this every time you come here?"

He nods. "This is what I save up for. I try to leave my mother's and children's refrigerators as stocked as I can. They go through it quickly though. When you live with rationing you panic because what remains uneaten today might not be where you left it tomorrow."

Nesto takes me into the hills where a forest folds around the Río Almendares, the river that slices through Havana and pours out to the ocean through the end of the Malecón. Here in the bosque, spreading into a grassy field curtained by trees feathered in Spanish moss, air lush and clean, as if we've traveled very hard to get here, away from the noise of the city and smell of diesel and petrol, Nesto tells me people come to meet with the orishas, for a limpieza or a despojo, bathing for purification in the waters of Ochún, laying down offerings of fruit and flowers on the riverbank, gathering stones, beating drums, singing alabanzas for the orisha's continued blessings.

Others, he says, come to conjure Ogún who dwells in forests like this one. Some come to place ofrendas at the feet of the Changó's Ceiba trees—the only tree resistant to lightning and left untouched when the great flood covered the earth, giving shelter to mankind and animals so that life would endure—with bark so potent it can cure infertility: a tree so sacred one should not dare cross its shadow without first asking permission.

Nesto says the bosque is a popular place for small sacrifices, under trees dripping with branches and vines. People arrive to feed the saints with live chickens in cloth bags, leaving behind bloody ones, and nobody, not even one of the guards at the military post across the road, looks twice. At our feet are pieces of broken animal bones, even some chicken claws intact, shards of broken pottery, knotted ropes of all colors, decomposing fruit, and small pools of dried blood staining the soil. In dusty patches on the forest floor are painted white lines and circles among branches and twigs, which Nesto says are interpretations of the cowries, and in the gentle river current, I see sunflowers from upstream glide past us.

It's because so many come here to meet with the orishas that Nesto says nobody would ever suspect we've actually come here to meet with the beef broker.

We watch a man walk down the hill sloping evenly like a set of stairs and make his way toward us on the edge of the river. He's an older guy, maybe in his fifties, who Nesto told me is a trusted manager of one of the government slaughterhouses, running his negocio by slipping cuts of beef into a briefcase or satchel and taking them on the three-hour drive back to Havana for distribution. There are other men who run the same enterprise for fish, which comes from Africa, unavailable in the island food dispensaries for months, and another guy who brokers the plump chicken breasts meant for tourists, since the only cuts available with the Libreta are bony thighs or legs, and each person is only entitled to up to a pound per month.

The man arrives at our side and presents a newspaper-wrapped bundle to Nesto, who peels back a corner to get a look at the quality, counting six fillets.

"You're looking at Fidel's best," the man tells Nesto. "Canadian Holstein crossed with Indian Zebu."

A few vultures gathered around a chicken carcass farther down the riverbank seem to have noticed the smell of the steaks and move toward us.

"Not bad," Nesto tells the meat man. "I'll take them all."

He slides a few bills of CUCs into the man's palm with a handshake.

The beef broker heads back up the hill to his car, but Nesto stalls a bit, wrapping the bundle in a plastic bag he brought with him.

Through the trees I see the afternoon light is starting to dim, casting the forest in a pale golden film, similar to the forest of my dream. I try to picture the fires I saw last night in my sleep, try to feel for a connection.

Nesto walks to the edge of the riverbank, handing me the bundle of beef as he slips off his shoes and steps into the water, getting wet up to his knees. He leans over and dips his hands into the current, pulling smooth round stones off the river floor. He rubs them on his arms and neck, and places them on the ground by my feet.

"Many years ago in Africa, when the orishas watched as the first slaves were being packed into ships to be taken across the ocean, Ochún asked her mother, Yemayá, where they were going and Yemayá told her to a faraway island called Cuba. Ochún begged to be allowed to accompany the Africans on their journey. She didn't want them to travel alone. This is why we love her so much. And they say if you are alone and wait patiently next to her rivers, you can hear her sing the song her father, Obatalá, taught her, which holds the secret of life. To hear it with your own ears is a special blessing."

"You and your stories, Nesto."

"I prefer this history to the one they force on us."

"So, what's the secret of life?"

"You don't know? It's so simple."

I shake my head.

"Love."

He stands in the river, his legs haloed by the current. He waves me over to him. I step as close as I can with my feet still on the hard earth. He cups water into his palms and lifts it to my face so the water drips off my forehead and cheeks.

"For protection." He lets his fingers linger on the curves of my face, cool with water, running them over my lips, down my collarbone, and over my heart.

With the day's errands out of the way, Nesto says it's time to go home. He drives along Quinta Avenida, past former residential palaces turned-embassies and ministries, where police monitor street corners. One has to drive fast, Nesto explains, since the early eighties when a bus crashed into the gates of the Peruvian embassy, killing a guard and opening the doors to thousands of asylum seekers, setting off the events that led to the boatlift. If caught slowing down suspiciously in this area, one can be fined. We pass through Miramar and Nesto points out the aquarium where he worked, and the cafeteria down the road where he says young girls hang around, selling themselves for a few dollars to anyone who comes in for a coffee so they can buy minutes for their cell phones.

"Every time I see them I think of my daughter," he says. "And I think I have to do whatever it takes to get her out of here before she starts getting offers for her body."

Soon he turns onto another road and up a long hill where the neighborhood has clearly changed, turning from slick and smooth paved avenues to broken, potholed streets. A barrio of colorless buildings wasted by time and neglect to their original plaster and concrete tones. Houses like blocks haphazardly arranged by a child, built one on top of the other. People walk in the middle of the street. Children carry smaller children. Skeletal dogs sleep belly up in small patches of shade under tin awnings. Garbage accumulates on street corners. There are few trees around here and the salty ocean air doesn't reach this far up the city slope.

"This is it," Nesto says. "This is Buenavista."

We're not far from the famous Tropicana, where Yutong buses drop hundreds of tourists each evening for a show, or even from the neighborhood where El Comandante is said to live beyond gates in a no-fly zone. But Buenavista is one of the forgotten pockets of the city, Nesto tells me; some sections didn't even have electricity until a year or two ago.

People wave to him as he rolls the car slowly down the broken road, until he pulls over, parks, and points to a house with metal bars over the front door and windows that reminds me of the house I grew up in.

"This is my home."

Nesto opens the front door for me and we stand in the entryway as he calls to his mother until she comes down a dark hall toward us. She looks much older than my own mother, more like the sweet abuelitas of kids I knew from our neighborhood in Miami, grandmothers who lit up when their grandchildren came around, so different from my grandmother, who, in spite of her affection for me, often snarled that it was too bad I had the misfortune of being born my mother's daughter.

Nesto greets his mother with a kiss, then pulls back to introduce me to her.

"This is Reina, Mamá."

"Reina," she pulls me to her chest with an embrace, then holds me by my shoulders to get a better look at me as if I'm a long-lost relative and not a total stranger. It's a warmth I'm not used to. "Welcome, welcome. Estás en tu casa."

I see Nesto's smoky eyes in his mother's. She's dark as melao de caña like he is, though her face is dotted with freckles. She ushers me into a sitting area with a door open to the patio while Nesto goes out to the car to bring in the food we bought for dinner. I look out to the patio and see the prized trees Nesto has told me about, which fed his family through their toughest times. Beneath the mango tree, the long-haired white cat sleeps: Blancanieves, who Nesto told me he rescued from a dumpster years ago, before someone else could trap her to use or sell for brujería.

This is the house Nesto was brought to as a newborn, the long-awaited son; the space in which he'd grown up as a fatherless boy, through hungry years when he had to find a way to help feed his family, the home of the young man who left when recruited for the military; the house he returned to after marrying and divorcing the mother of his children, the house he'd remained in until he gathered the courage to leave that final time, crossing the ocean to the other shore where he eventually met me.

I see pieces of his former life everywhere, relics of stories he's told me back in our new life together in Florida. Opposite the sofa where I sit is the fish tank Nesto built into the wall as a teenager from glass panels of abandoned windowpanes and concrete he mixed himself, full of tropical fish swimming over pieces of coral and painted rocks; the shelves Nesto told me he built from a disassembled table to hold his mother's ceramic figurines and a few pieces of bone china, the only things she had of value, inherited from her mother; other things Nesto made for her when there was no money to buy gifts: a box made of seashells gathered in Isla de la Juventud, a rose carved out of the wood of a fallen chaca tree with his mother's name, Rosa María, inscribed at the base.

On the wall above the chair where his mother sits facing me, three pictures hang: a royal portrait of the king and queen of Spain beside one of a young Fidel in a military cap; on his other side, a depiction of the island's patron saint, la Virgen de la Caridad del Cobre, the other face of the orisha Ochún.

I notice on the table next to her armchair a framed photograph of Nesto with his children standing by a small roller coaster, the same photo he has taped to a wall in his room at the motel on Crescent Key, which now feels so far away along with the cottage and the life we share on those small distant islands.

Nesto arrives at my side, sits beside me on the sofa, tells his mother all the places we went to get the food for tonight's dinner.

"Can you believe it?" his mother says to me. "The things we have to do in order to put a decent meal together in this country?"

I nod, though I'm uncertain of what to say because Nesto has always told me that despite her disappointments, having given her life and her faith to a revolution that gave so little in return, she still feels a conflicted loyalty to it.

Nesto tells his mother we are going to go to Yanai's house to collect the children and bring them back here while she prepares dinner. By the time we return, he says, the others—his stepfather, sisters, nieces, and aunts—should be back too.

We walk along the broken road. Every now and then we're interrupted by people calling to Nesto, saying they're glad to see him back in Buenavista, and he pauses to wave back, telling them yes, it's good to be home.

"Nesto," I begin when we're a few blocks along. "What have you told your children about me?"

"That you're important to me."

"That's it?"

"That's all that matters, isn't it?"

"When my brother and I were kids, we hated when our mother brought somebody new to the house. She'd send us to the kitchen to get the guy a beer and we'd spit in it before we brought it back to him. Then we'd watch him drink it and try not to laugh."

"Why would you do that?"

"I guess we were afraid of someone taking her away from us."

"Didn't you want a father?"

"No."

"Didn't you want her to find happiness with someone?"

"I didn't understand why she couldn't be happy with just my brother and me."

"What do you want me to tell my kids about you then?"

"Tell them I'm nobody special."

"I'm not going to lie to them, Reina." He points to a house a few feet away with a wide stone terrace behind a high metal fence. "That's the house."

A body rushes Nesto from behind and he reaches around him, laughing, knowing his son's weight and touch on him, pulling Sandro into his arms. He's as tall as his father and already growing out of his chamaco body with new muscles. He's in his blue school uniform, carrying a nylon book bag I remember Nesto buying for him around Christmas. They hug and wrestle for a moment until Nesto breaks up the laughter and motions to me.

"Sandro, this is Reina. My friend from La Yunay. She's eating with us tonight."

Sandro says hello and kisses me on the cheek. In his face, I see their bloodline, his grandmother's eyes, his father's grin, canela-skinned, a blend of his parents on the spectrum of mestizaje.

"Go get your sister," Nesto tells him, and Sandro disappears through the gate, leaving us on the sidewalk outside the house.

"You used to live here," I say, taking in the facade, trying to picture Nesto living within its walls with his wife and family.

"Yes, for many years. You see that terrace? I built it myself. It was a narrow wooden thing before. I brought each one of those stones and laid them with my own hands. I built the columns for the roof canopy, and I built that front door after a cyclone blew out the old one. And this fence?" He fingers the metal wiring. "I put it up too."

"You're good with fences." I slide my hands over the rusty links, remembering how we freed the dolphin together, on a night that already feels so long ago. "Putting them up, taking them down."

I look back up to the house and notice a slim figure in the front window watching us. She leans on the edge of the window frame, arms limp at her sides, dark hair pulled tight off her pale face.

Nesto notices her too and gives a small wave.

"That's Yanai. She knows about you too."

She raises her palm slightly, gives a faint wave, then leaves the window and our sight.

Their daughter is smaller than I expected, even from older pictures. She runs to Nesto when she steps out of the house and sees him waiting for her outside the gate, swings her legs when he pulls her off the ground into the air. She's changed out of her school uniform into a dress that Nesto sent her from Florida and shows it off proudly, twirling at his feet. Her hair is braided, similar to the way my mother used to braid mine every morning before school, gently dividing my hair with the comb, in a way that I loved, even if later other girls would pull on those braids. I can't help thinking of my mother now and what she would say if she knew where I was, with Nesto at the foot of his ex-wife's door. She would remind me there is no stupider woman than one who takes up with a man between lives.

"Look, Cami," Nesto says to his daughter. "This is my friend Reina."

She stands behind him, covering her face with a flap of her father's shirt.

"Hi, Camila," I tell her. "You're even prettier than your papi told me."

"Say thank you." Nesto nudges her, and she mumbles, clutching her father's waist.

We walk back to Nesto's mother's house. Camila drops her father's hand to walk ahead with her brother, his arm protectively draped over her shoulders. She leans into him and he tilts his head toward hers as if they're sharing secrets.

I remember how Carlito and I used to walk together the same way, how I felt when I was by his side that nobody in the world could hurt me.

I would give anything to feel that way again.

Nesto says there's no way the rest of his family will miss dinner tonight, not because a guest is coming but because they've all heard he was bringing home steak from the broker. As we wait for his mother to prepare the food we brought home into a meal for twelve, the others begin to arrive: his stepfather, Juan Mario, who was out having his bifocals repaired, a small husk of a man with a hollowed face, trails of pigmentless patches up his arms and across his neck including one on his shin he swears is the exact shape of Cuba; then Nesto's two older sisters, Bruna and Galina, women with thick bodies and tired faces who bear little resemblance to him, probably because they have different fathers; Bruna's daughter, Clarilu, nineteen, with her boyfriend, Yordan, and her baby daughter, Lili, in her arms; and Galina's daughter, Cassandra, twenty-two and wearing an engagement ring Nesto tells me was given to her by a British guy she hasn't heard from in a year.

We're crammed into the living room, spilling onto the patio, Nesto's sisters and Yordan leaning on the walls because there are not enough chairs to go around. Nesto tells them I used to paint nails and Cassandra rushes off and returns with a bottle of polish—a gift from Nesto—and asks if I'll paint hers for her.

"Of course," I say, and when I'm through, Clarilu and then Nesto's sisters each ask for a turn. Nesto pushes his daughter forward.

"What about you, Cami? Do you want Reina to paint your nails?"

She clenches her fists and hides her hands behind her back, shaking her head. Nesto smiles at her and then at me. He looks happy, though it's a kind of happiness different from the one he shares with me: joy with confianza, among the people who know him best. The room is small and hot, the metal fan in the corner barely moving the air, but I envy this family's closeness and think of how vacant my childhood home felt in comparison.

Nesto's mother has taken the steaks we brought, sliced them down, and added them into a stew with rice, potatoes, and fried eggs. She arranges the food on a table near the kitchen and we eat with plates on our laps, Nesto and me on a corner of the sofa with his children on his other side. Nesto's sisters ask me about life in Miami, if it's as beautiful as they see on the telenovelas they catch from their neighbor's illegal satellite dish. Nesto's stepfather, after hearing I arrived from Colombia, asks if it's true that all of Venezuela's shortages are to be blamed on their neighbor because that's what the Cuban news reports.

"I can't say for sure," I tell him, "but I really don't think so."

Through it all, I watch Nesto's children. They eat quietly, his daughter's head resting on her father's thick arm. I remember being her age and trying to claim ownership of my mother every time she brought a new man home to meet us. I would cling to her, wedge myself onto her lap until she pushed me away or told Carlito to take me out to play. I remember the men I saw as intruders, invaders of our territory. Carlito was never as threatened or bothered, with an innate awareness that each man was just passing through.

There is dessert of flan and by the time each of Nesto's family members has been served, there is none left. They give me the biggest piece and I see Nesto's daughter eye me with envy. I offer to share with her but she shakes her head, hiding again behind her father, tugging his shoulder down to her level.

I hear her whisper into his ear, "Papi, will we ever see her again?"

"Yes, mi amor. She's a very good friend of ours."

"Will she come back with you when you come back?"

He tries to distract her, offering her what's left of his own slice of flan, but she's undeterred and now asks her father when his next visit will be, and makes him promise to return before her next birthday because her mother has promised to throw her a big party.

After dinner, Nesto walks his children home and I stay behind, offering to help his mother and sisters clean the plates, put away what little food is left, but they don't let me and leave me to wait for Nesto in the living room as his stepfather watches a news program describing Venezuela as the role model for the future of the Americas.

When Nesto returns, he tells me to follow him down a narrow hall past the kitchen and a row of small bedrooms, to a cave-like room at the back of the house, the bulk of the floor taken up by a mattress and a small stereo system on a metal stand; the only window covered by a thin sheet to block out light.

On the wall, a solitary print of Fidel hangs upside down.

"This is your room?"

"What's left of it. I sold almost everything I had before I went to Mexico."

We stand quietly as I look around. In the distance, the sound of somebody striking together a pair of palitos, like the opening pulses of a guaguancó. I hesitate to touch Nesto in his house, afraid he doesn't belong to me here, and maybe not at all anymore.

I wonder how it would have felt if I'd ever had the chance to stand with him within the walls of what had been my room in the old house in Miami, or in the first room I ever lived in, the one I just left behind in Cartagena. I think I would never have felt more naked.

I touch his hand, as if that is all that's permitted. He takes hold of my fingers and leads me down to the mattress and we rest facing each other as I try to picture the years and nights he spent on this very bed, more than thirty summers, winters, and springs, waiting, waiting, waiting, and how I slept on a similar bed on the floor across the ocean, and though I didn't always know for what, I was waiting too.

In my dream, I lie on a crest of beach where sand meets water, my body pressing deep, carving its form into the earth; when I stand and look down, I see my silhouette has hardened despite the current rushing over it, filling the space where my body rested until the water recedes and my form in the sand fills with blood; water washes over it again, and with each wave, an exchange of blood and tide.

I tell Nesto about my dreams when he calls me at the hotel in the morning, how they've changed since I arrived in Cuba.

"I'm going to take you somewhere so you can make sense of them," he tells me.

"No brujas, please."

"She's no bruja. She's the best reader of dreams in Havana."

The morning sun is hot, the air heavy with moisture. Nesto picks me up in a 1952 Chevrolet, borrowed from a cousin. He drives through Centro Habana, down cracked roads, stray dogs scampering to avoid being kicked or chased off; men hunched over popped-open car hoods trying to diagnose the day's malfunction; buckets and baskets full of fruit or food being pulled from the street up to balconies full of laundry lines; old men sitting around improvised tables and overturned crates playing dominó; ladies young and old, some with babies in their arms, lingering in windows and doorways mirando y dejando, watching the world go by.

We come to the enclave of Cayo Hueso, webbed with wires and antennas, where Nesto parks on the corner of a tight street, asking a group of shirtless boys kicking a ball around to watch the car so it's not stripped of any parts while we're gone.

He calls up to a building, "Zoraida! Zoraida!" his voice filling the small avenue.

A woman pokes her head out of a third-floor window, turns her face upward to yell the same name too. Finally, on the sixth floor, another head emerges from some curtains. A man calls down to Nesto to catch, and tosses a key down to the street for him. Nesto opens the building door to a foyer wall painted over with a portrait of a dreamy-faced young Che, and we start the long walk up several flights of broken stairs, sweat gathering in the crevices of my collarbone and dripping down my spine. I stop and lean on the banister to catch my breath while Nesto flies past me, teasing that I have no stamina, until we both arrive at the top floor, which opens into a small cinder block single-room apartment on the building's roof.

Zoraida sits in a wooden chair at the center beside an altar to Santa Barbara—Changó—with her long sword watching over a glass of white wine and a red apple. Zoraida is a small woman, her head wrapped in a ruby scarf, wearing a long white dress that reaches the floor. The door behind her opens to a concrete garden. Nesto greets her, bowing to her slightly, and introduces me; and Zoraida, who Nesto says is at least one hundred years old though nobody knows for sure but she looks about seventy, waves me over to her, takes my hand in hers, rubs it gently with her thumbs, and says, "So you are the one having trouble with your dreams."

She turns to Nesto. "You leave us alone. Go outside. Wait in the shade until I call you."

Nesto obeys and I see him settle onto a metal chair out on the azotea while Zoraida tells me to sit on the stool close to her.

"I've known Nesto, since he was a young boy. His grandmother used to bring him to me because of his nightmares. Now you, mi niña, it's your turn."

I begin by telling her the dreams of the past, of Cartagena until I returned, of my father, my brother, babies going over the bridge, though I don't tell her the reason for these dreams, how they come from real memories. Then I tell her of my dreams here in Cuba, unlike any I've had before. The burning forest that looked so similar to the one I visited yesterday. And the most recent dream: my body in the sand, my figure form filled with blood and water.

She watches me as I speak though I have the impression she's not really listening, but reading into me a different way.

Once I'm done talking she says sternly, without a trace of speculation, "You have been haunted by shame. You have been shackled. You have known violence and you have committed violence unto yourself. You must try to understand why you have placed yourself in a prison. To dream of fire is an indicator of change. You will have to let go of all that came before. You will feel an end to great pain, but only after trials of despair. To dream of sand, water, and blood shows that you feel impermanence, but it's the opposite; something in you is taking root. Listen to the voice of your instincts. The spirits are guiding you."

She pulls back and eyes me with sudden suspicion.

"You don't believe in our santos or even the ones you were raised with."

I shake my head.

"But you are a daughter of Yemayá. You must know this. She claimed you long before you were born. You must feel it. You watch the moon. You follow its glow. She is the universal mother. You are in her special favor. Anything you ask of her, she will give you."

She calls to Nesto who comes in from the patio and stands at her side.

"Nesto, take her to see Yemayá. She will bring peace to her dreams."

She takes Nesto's hand, enormous next to hers, and he lowers himself onto one knee at her feet.

"And you, have patience, my dear boy. The Great One hears you. In time, you will have all that you want."

"Gracias, Zoraida." Nesto leans over and kisses the top of her hand.

He tries to give her some money but she refuses it, pushing his hand away. He walks to the altar of Santa Barbara and places the bills under the apple.

"For your santa, then," he says, and she doesn't protest.

Nesto says he wants to show me the view before we leave Zoraida's place and leads me out to the azotea, all of Havana spread out before us in concrete cubes, homes upon homes, water tanks, electrical chords, antennas, barking dogs, and pigeon coops on nearly every rooftop.

I feel heat pressing against my chest and become breathless again. I've felt nauseated all morning but haven't said so because I don't want Nesto to think it's caused by his mother's cooking. I could hardly eat my breakfast at the hotel. I feel my stomach cramping, my body both burning and suddenly chilled.

"It's so hot," I tell Nesto, shielding my eyes from the sun as he points to where the Malecón begins and to the fortress of La Cabaña across the harbor.

Everything becomes dark but I feel his hands on me, hear him say my name. Then he's above me and I'm not standing on the azotea looking over the city, but lying on the dusty concrete rooftop with Nesto fanning my face with his shirt, which he's taken off, Zoraida slowly coming toward us through her doorway, one hand on a cane, the other carrying a glass of juice. He helps me prop myself on my elbows, resting my head against his knees, taking the juice from Zoraida, holding the glass to my lips until I taste mango.

"She's more overheated than a hot dog!" Zoraida says, and returns a moment later with a wet cloth, handing it to Nesto, who slips it onto my forehead. "What have you done to this poor child? Can't you see she's not used to our heat?"

I sit up but my head feels heavy and I have to lie back down for another moment until Nesto helps me up and toward the door. I thank Zoraida, though I'm almost too dazed to speak.

"Take her straight to the ocean," she tells Nesto. "Make sure she covers her whole head with water."

When he sees me hesitate to go down the first flight of stairs, cautious with my footing so I won't lose my balance, Nesto takes my arm, ducks his head into my chest and throws me over his shoulder, carrying me all the way down to the street where the boys wait beside the car for Nesto to pay them their chavitos.

We head east, outside the city perimeter toward the beaches. I close my eyes as Nesto drives, feel air rush past my face through the open window, the smell of gasoline and exhaust giving way to the aroma of the sea and greenery of the city outskirts.

I think of the last time I fainted, as a teenager when Universo took me to San Basilio de Palenque because he was obsessed with Benkos Biohó, the cimarron king who founded the refuge for runaway slaves like him high in the hills, surrounded by jungle, the only community in the Americas to resist colonization. We had to hitchhike out of Cartagena and caught a ride with a truck driver on his way to Mompox. He left us at the bottom of the muddy trail and we hiked through thick humidity until we came to the dusty clearing of the village plaza. Universo told me the Palenqueros were known for being reclusive, untrusting of outsiders, and reluctant to come down from their hill.

An old man came out to meet us by the road, asking what we were doing there.

"We came to see that," Universo said, pointing to the statue of Benkos in the center of the plaza, an iron man with arms extended, broken chains hanging from his wrists.

We walked over to the statue, sweat slick down my back and my legs, sun reflecting on the white dust at our feet.

I remember telling Universo, "This must be the hottest place on earth," and then I was on the ground.

When I came to, Universo and the old man had dragged me into a patch of shade by the church, laying me on some grass. I felt my skull crushing, heard the man shouting in Palenquero until a young boy appeared with a gallon of water that they poured over me.

"This girl doesn't belong up here in the hills," the old man told Universo. "She belongs at sea level. Take her back to the water."

Nesto pulls off the highway down a winding road to Bacuranao until we are at an arc of beach, sand fine as flour, water turquoise and transparent.

"When I see this beauty, I think, *How could I have ever left my homeland?*" Nesto says. "Then I go back to the city, see the conditions in which the people live, and I think, *How could I have stayed as long as I did?*"

The beach is desolate except for a lone horse tied by a long rope in the shade of a coconut palm.

We walk to the water and Nesto reaches for me to turn my body, reminding me to always approach Yemayá with humility, from the side, never head-on.

I go into the water as far as my thighs, gathering my dress so it won't get wet. Nesto doesn't care, though, and goes in with his jeans on, dunking under the surf, and holds me so that I can dip my head under the water too, feel the cool foam run down my neck and chest.

We find a coconut palm for ourselves and lie on the sand, salt and water hardening onto our skin, my head cushioned on Nesto's chest and his in the pillow of his arms.

I'm tired, I tell him, *so tired*, and let myself close my eyes for a little while to sleep.

When we leave the beach, Nesto drives from Bacuranao on the Vía Blanca through the clapboard houses, cuarterías, concrete cube apartments, and colonial buildings of Guanabacoa to neighboring Regla until we come to the tip of the peninsula facing Havana across the bay, at the gates of a white church on the bluff. There is no service happening but the church is busy with people coming in and out, scattered in pews facing the altar where a black Virgin holds in her arms a tiny white baby Jesus.

Nesto leads me to an altar on the side of the church where believers have placed dozens of blue, white, and violet flowers, girasoles, candles, and candies, kneeling before the statue of the Virgen de Regla in prayer. One woman carries a baby dressed in blue and white, presenting her child to the statue, whispering the name of Yemayá, then leaning forward to kiss the baby's cheek.

Nesto takes a turn kneeling before the altar and I kneel beside him. I don't know what he's praying for but I hope his prayers are heard. I hope everything he and Zoraida say is true, that our desires echo through the heavens and that faith will bring them to completion. I close my eyes, feeling the petitions of all those around me.

"Yemayá, estoy aquí," a voice says from behind me.

And beside me, Nesto, "Yemayá awoyó, awoyó Yemayá."

Outside the church, a few Santeras sit on the wall lining the harbor road beside improvised altars of dolls surrounded by flowers, seashells, paintings on wood of a tongue with a dagger piercing it, arranged on handkerchiefs and blankets at their sides, calling to passersby, offering clairvoyance and blessings.

"Oye, muchacho," one calls to Nesto. "Come let me tell you about your future."

Nesto ignores her and I follow him to the water's edge where passengers of a ferry from across the harbor disembark, and we sit together on a flattened piece of stone.

"You don't want to have your fortune told?" I ask him.

"Not here. Not like this."

"When is the last time someone read the shells for you?"

"Before I left for Mexico."

"What did they tell you?"

He shakes his head. "It wasn't good."

"Tell me."

"A few days before I was supposed to leave, somebody left a dead chicken at my mother's door. Its chest was pinned with a paper with my name written on it. It made me nervous because nobody knew I was planning to defect outside of my family."

"What did you do with it?"

"I called a friend, a Santero, to take it away. He buried it somewhere so nobody would be tempted to cook it. They say the worst maleficio is the one you eat. But that friend told me to go to see an iyalocha to find out what was going on."

"Did you go?"

"Yes. And the iyalocha told me someone from my past, maybe a jealous or bitter ex-lover, did a trabajo on me. She said this person was in communion with Paleros because the hechizo was so strong it couldn't be broken no matter how many limpiezas or polvos she mixed for me. She said the purpose of the spell was so that I would never find peace in my life. Not with my family and not even within my heart. She warned me not to leave the country under those conditions. She said I would never find the better life I was seeking. She said the only way to undo this trabajo was to become full Santo, but not just anywhere. She said I had to go to Santa Clara because it's in a sacred place at the center of the country, the crossroads of aché and benevolent energies. But it would have cost me thousands. Money I didn't have then, money I don't have now. And if I did, it would be money better spent on my family and my children."

"Do you believe her about the trabajo?"

"Sometimes I do. Sometimes I don't."

I tell him how the blue-haired bruja in Miami told me that the only way to break the curses I've inherited was through some cleansing ritual that involved bathing in honey, milk, oils, and rose petals, surrounded by seven seven-day candles every night for a week. At the end of the week she said I would sleep as if I'd returned to the womb and would be free of all the dark powers plaguing me.

"She wanted to charge me three thousand dollars. She even said I could pay in installments."

"Did you consider it?"

"No. I was taking care of Carlito in those days. Any extra money I had went only to him."

"The iyalocha told me I would always be alone."

"The bruja told me that too."

"Do you think it's true we're both doomed to solitude?"

"If I believed that, I wouldn't be here with you."

I often think, if only Carlito had lived another three months, he and Nesto could have met each other.

But then, if Carlito had lived, and everything in our lives hadn't gone so wrong, neither Nesto nor I would have ever found our way down to those lonely islands, into each other's lives.

I feel tethered to Nesto in a way I've never felt with anybody else.

Like family but not family because we weren't tossed to the tides of life together but instead found each other, adrift.

"I need something to change," Nesto says, eyes on the Havana skyline across the water, pale and blurry in the afternoon haze. "When I was young and I got so frustrated I punched walls, cursed everything about this country, locked myself in my room for days without speaking to a soul, my grandmother would tell me, 'Cálmate, mi'jo. Not even sadness is a permanent condition.' She thought she would be alive to see the end of the regime, but of course, she was wrong. Those men are immortal."

"Nobody can live forever."

"The thing is, they can all die and it still won't matter."

"Why not?"

"Because where there is a dead king, there is already a crowned prince."

"What do you mean?"

"We're not looking at the relics of a revolution anymore, we're looking at the beginning of a dynasty."

It's a half-moon night, a breeze from the trade winds ruffles against our skins. On my last night in Havana Nesto and I sit together on the same stretch of the Malecón that he took me to on my first night. He's quiet beside me, until we part so that he can go back to Buenavista, see his children for dinner again, and for one last time before returning to Florida, try to reason with Yanai, convince her to change her mind so they can carry out their plan to marry again and get her and their children out of here.

Later, I dream of my brother in prison.

I confuse stories he told me when he was still alive about how the guards would often abuse inmates, especially the mentally ill ones. He'd learn about these accounts when he crossed ways with them in the infirmary or hospital, bruises on their faces, gashes on their heads. He'd hear about it from other inmates on the prison "radio," echoes down the death row corridor between security checks, how guards withheld toilet paper and meals while writing in their reports that those prisoners refused them, taunting the most vulnerable ones until they banged their heads against the walls, tied them to their beds or cuffed them to their toilets for days, then punished them for soiling themselves by sending them to the hole.

These were guys, Carlito said, who you couldn't imagine being fit for trial, men who could barely speak full sentences, who cried in anguish at the faces of demons they saw within the shadowed corners of their cells, burrowed in the crevices of the walls; men who ended up in prison when they should have been in a psychiatric hospital somewhere. The prisoners could do nothing but endure the mistreatment because the guards would only deny their actions, lying and covering for each other with their own kind of brotherhood loyalties.

I told all this to Dr. Joe once, everything Carlito had described, and was surprised when Dr. Joe didn't even argue or try to convince me it was an exaggeration.

"And you just let this go on?" I'd said.

"I'm only one man, Reina. Prison is too big a system."

"Then you're complicit. And you're as bad as the rest of them."

In my dream, it's Carlito who is being tormented, starved so that his body looks as dry and shriveled as the bark of a tree.

He cries, screaming for our mother, for me, to come save him, while a faceless guard laughs, mocking him. He covers Carlito's head with the sheet of his bed so that my brother can barely breathe and, in my sleep, I feel myself suffocating, slapping at my own face to tear the cloth off my mouth. I see the guard grab Carlito by the neck, thrust his face in the toilet, leave it there until water fills his nostrils and Carlito is certain he is drowning.

He can't cry anymore. No sound comes from his throat, but I feel him scream from within, calling for Mami, calling for me.

In the morning, Nesto meets me at the hotel, his eyes ringed with fatigue, and I know he hasn't slept. He will take me to the airport though he won't leave on his flight to Miami until tonight.

"She said she'll *think* about it," he tells me, once we are in the car, yet another borrowed Lada, on our way to the airport. "I asked her how much more time she needs. It's been years already. By the time she's done thinking, the kids will be grown and have their own children to struggle to feed or Sandro will have already thrown himself to the sharks to bring himself over. I know she has a new boyfriend. My sister told me he works in the kitchen of a paladar. But Yanai says she's not staying for him. She says this is her country and it breaks her heart to think of leaving it. She blames me. She says I should never have left. She says, 'If you love your children as much as you say, why don't you come back?'"

"Do you ever think about doing that? Of moving back instead of trying to bring them over?"

"Every day. Even my mother tells me maybe Yanai is right, and the children are better off here. They won't know the pain of leaving their country. They know only the pain of being left behind. She says to let it be, to let time take care of everything. But just look around this island. Anyone can see time is our enemy. We are already four generations deep into this mierdero of a revolution. I was born into it. I didn't have a choice. But am I supposed to surrender my children and all my descendants too?"

We slow at an intersection and Nesto turns to face me.

"This island causes blindness. I know because I was blind for a long time too. But I can't let things just be. I have to keep trying."

At the airport, we say good-bye though it's only for a matter of hours because we will meet tonight back at the Miami airport, after my detour through Colombia and his short flight from Havana, and take the bus together back to the cottage in the Keys.

When I came to Cuba a few days ago, the airport arrivals area was a scene of ecstatic embraces, loved ones reunited after years, maybe decades. Here at the entrance to the departures terminal, the long hugs are accompanied with tears, a feeling of families breaking apart for who knows how long.

I tell Nesto what I've never told him before.

"I'll wait with you through it all. As long as you want me by your side. I believe you when you say you had to leave in order to help your family. But I want you to know, I will also believe you if one day you tell me you have to stay."

SEVEN

We've been back on our island a week, in the routine of days at our jobs, watching the dolphins surrounded by metal fences, and the pen where the wild dolphin once lived, now occupied by a veteran performer, quarantined with dolphin pox that's left her marbled with lesions. Sometimes Nesto and I talk about trying again. We'll wait for the right kind of rain, monitor the wind, make sure the current will help carry the dolphins out rather than push them deeper into their cages. We just have to wait a bit longer. Nesto and I have become good at this kind of vigil-keeping together.

Our nights in the cottage are quiet. Nesto has been solemn since our return, though I sense his restlessness. We've been looking forward to a day out in the blue, but when we go to meet Lolo at the marina on a Sunday morning, he tells us the boat is having engine trouble and we'll have to wait another few days.

Nesto and I decide to go to the beach instead, and head south to an unnamed wide arc of gray sand on the Atlantic side of the islands that only locals know about. A few families have already set up their towels, pulled out the plastic pails and inflatables for the kids. There is splashing in the water and the drone of laughter. We find a spot on the edge of the cove, near the barrier of sea grape trees. There aren't many words between us, but I'm comforted to look at him as we lie on our backs, see his eyes shut to the sun, veiled in a momentary calm.

I don't know who on the beach spotted it first; I'm only aware that soon after I've fallen into my own nap, I hear the voice of a child on the beach say, "Look at that boat, Mommy."

A few seconds later, an adult voice comments that no boat should be coming this close to shore. I hear a putting sound, like that of an old car on its last drops of gas, and open my eyes. Just past the buoys, a run-down blue boat scrapes toward the beach, a black tail of exhaust rising from its engine, now as loud as a mower, reverberating against the flat edge of ocean.

"Nesto." I nudge him awake. "Look."

He props himself on his elbows and as we take in the sight, the sharpening figures of the boat's passengers, more people on the beach rise to their feet and approach the water. Nesto gets up too, and I follow.

The boat seems stalled, the dark plume of fumes thickening behind it. There's commotion on board, bodies moving from one end of the vessel to the other. Nesto waves to the people on the boat, as do some others on the beach, while a few in the wall of voices warn that the boat had better not come any closer or somebody could get hurt.

"Do you suppose they're refugees?" someone asks.

"If they are, they'd better move fast," another voice answers.

Nesto turns to me, his face strained with anxiety. "There's something wrong with the boat." He rushes to the shoreline and shouts across the water, "¡Tírense! ¡Tírense al agua! ¡Naden! ¡Naden!"

They don't hear him, or maybe they're too frightened to swim as he says. It's only a matter of minutes though each second feels suspended, the smoke cloud growing larger, Nesto's voice louder and more urgent as he lunges deeper into the water so they'll hear him.

A Coast Guard boat materializes as if conjured by the waves, silent yet swift, encroaching on the blue boat while the passengers push themselves to one side of the vessel and Nesto screams louder than I ever knew him able, "¡Tírense! ¡Naden! ¡Los esperamos! ¡Naden! ¡Naden!"

Only one man does as Nesto says and throws himself into the water, the chorus of beach voices cheering for him, but as we watch him struggle even in the stillness of a sea on a day with virtually no wind or current, it's clear the man is much too weak to clear the distance between the boats and the shore. But Nesto is already swimming toward him, body against the tide, and he doesn't stop, even as a smaller Coast Guard boat we didn't even notice, pulling in from the other edge of the coast, intercepts the man.

For a moment we lose sight of him and then see, even with the sun shining into our eyes, he's being pulled from the water onto the boat and any chance he had to touch ground is gone.

Nesto remains in the water, treading, his head just above the surface, watching as the officers on the larger Coast Guard boat round up the rest of the passengers onto its deck, outfit them with life jackets, and prepare to tow the blue boat behind it. Behind me, the beach chorus is silent, but quickly gives way to exchanges of empathy for what's just occurred. One woman tells another what a shame it is that these people traveled so far, coming so close, but will be sent back to wherever they came from, *repatriated*, which sounds to me like such a painful word.

There is no doubt one among us called the police to report the arrival of the migrants.

The local news van arrives and people in bathing suits line up to be interviewed. In a few hours, we will see them on television, describing how the boat appeared suddenly on the horizon; the pity they feel that those people, having braved a week at sea, came within a hundred yards of Florida soil only to be turned away.

The reporter on the scene will show images of the blue boat, and describe in a voice-over how it was cobbled together with different metals and a car engine that failed its passengers on the final stretch of their journey.

He will wrap up his report facing the camera, saying the thirteen migrants, now in protective custody, were rescued by the authorities, though I think the real rescue would have been letting them make their way to shore.

Then he will turn it back over to the in-studio broadcaster who will offer her own commentary and statistics about how it's only June and the number of asylum seekers has already surpassed last year's figure, approaching the records of the nineties boatlift exodus, before cutting to a commercial for a used car dealership in Florida City.

On the ride home from the beach, Nesto stops to buy a card to call his family. He wants to tell them what we've just witnessed, how this is the future that awaits the children if they don't find another way sooner. When Yanai comes to the phone, I hear him beg her to reconsider marrying him as he paces the parking lot, saying it's their best chance to give them an opportunity at a better life, then it grows to arguing, though he turns his body and steps away from me so I can't make out much more.

When the call ends, he kicks the back fender so hard that the truck shakes with me sitting inside it. Then he drives us up to the lagoons on Card Sound Road, where he parks along the marsh and spends an hour chucking stones through clouds of dragonflies and across the water as if trying to crack glass.

I won't ask what she said. I want to leave it between them, but Nesto tells me anyway.

"She will only marry me if I can promise her a house over here as good as or better than the one she will leave behind, and a car to get around in. She says even if she'll be a refugee on paper, she refuses to live like one."

"She's scared. She feels safe there. She isn't ready to leave."

"I don't think she ever will be. I can hear it in her voice. All her excuses. It's like she's telling me to forget it, to stop hoping because it will never happen; I'll never bring my family here. At least not in the way that I want, and not for a very long time."

He throws another stone with the force of his whole body behind but it seems to drop out of the air into the water only a few feet away.

"Until then, what do I have?" He motions to the swamp and sea oats surrounding us.

Maybe he expects me to say *nothing*, and not so long ago, I probably would have.

"You have me. And this small life we have together. I know it's not the same, but it's something."

He drops the rock in his palm and walks over to where I stand, leaning on the back of the truck.

"Reina, I don't tell you so because I don't want you to think of me as a burden, but since the night we met, you have been the only thing keeping me from drowning."

On the drive back to Hammerhead, along the Overseas Highway, I notice a pale rainbow emerging from the ocean through the golden crest of sunset. I point it out to Nesto, its fractured prisms deepening in color for only a few moments until the clouds hide it from our side of the sky.

He smiles in a way I haven't seen him do since I saw him with his son and daughter.

"Do you know what a rainbow is?"

"The crown of Yemayá." I want him to know I've listened to all he's told me about the world as he sees it.

"Yes, but there's more. The seven colors of the arcoíris are the manifestations of the Siete Potencias, the seven tribes brought from Africa to the Americas, the spirits that remain to guide humanity through the troubles of life. It's how Yemayá and all the spirits show they are watching over us, and that we are exactly where we are supposed to be."

In the evening, Nesto and I sit together on a mound of sand on the beach beyond the cottage, facing the low tide, water pulled from the earth like a curtain. Faint white boat lights scatter in the distance, and fat beams of helicopter searchlights fan edges of the coast—the custom whenever migrants land or are pulled from the ocean—looking for others still out on the water.

It's still nesting season but Nesto says the female turtles will be confused with so many lights and, unable to find the beach to make their nests, they'll drop their eggs in the ocean. A generation, maybe even an entire bloodline, lost in one night.

"I hate the ocean sometimes," he says. "I hate what it does to us, and what we do to it. And I hate that I was born on an island. I've had nothing else to look at but that same blue horizon all my life. I'm so tired of it."

He grows quiet. The only sound is of the helicopters echoing against the tide.

"I should have swum to those people sooner. I could have helped them. They weren't that far out. I could have pulled them off the boat myself and carried two or three of them to the beach."

I want to find the right words to comfort him, to say there was no other way things could have gone, but the same feeling haunts me; I'm a good enough swimmer now, I could have gone out and carried someone back with me too.

I picture the boaters in some holding facility or detention center, maybe even a jail like the first one Carlito got taken to before he was sent to the federal prison. Or maybe they are already on their way back home.

"There wasn't enough time," I say, perhaps trying to convince us both. "It happened so quickly. Those police boats would have cut us off no matter what."

"We could have tried. We might have failed. But at least we would have tried."

Lighting flickers in the distance and dark clouds cover the moon's halo. We head to the cottage as a thin rain begins to fall.

We lie on the bed, Nesto curving himself around my body, wiping my hair from my face. I feel his heartbeat against my back. Despite the wreckage between us, the voids we carry of the missing and of the lost, though it's just the two of us here in the darkness, tonight it feels like enough.

The phone rings just as Nesto and I have found our way into sleep.

"Oye, where have you been?" my mother wants to know. "Why haven't you answered any of my calls?"

"I've been busy," I say, because I never told her I was away. "What's going on?"

I step outside with the phone, leaving Nesto in the cottage alone, and sit on the last plank of the walkway before it drops off into soft sand.

"Bueno, the truth is I can't say it was a surprise."

"You're getting married." I try to muster a tone of enthusiasm.

"No, mi'ja. That's out of the question now."

"What happened?"

"I knew about her. A woman always knows. I thought it would pass. I ignored it. But she's smart. Very smart."

"Who?"

"La otra, Reina. Who else? She was a patient of his. He gave her a mouthful of crowns. He says he's in love with her. He wants to be with her. He went to stay with her while I pack my things."

"He's leaving you?"

"Don't say it like that. I'm the one leaving."

"But he's making you move out."

"We're not married. My name isn't on anything here. I have to leave so she can move in."

"I'm sorry. I know you had high hopes."

"Así es la vida. There are no guarantees. Now I have to find somewhere else to live and soon."

"Where are you going to go?"

"Home," she says, and I know she means Miami. "I'm sure I can get my old job back. Maybe you want to move in with me. We can get an apartment by the water like we always wanted. Or another house. We can start over together."

"I've already started over."

"What kind of life do you have down there? You take care of fish and live in a choza on some woman's property. You need to progress, Reina. Look for opportunity. Y el muchacho con quien andas, what's his name?"

"Nesto."

"What does Nesto have to offer you?"

I want to think of something specific to answer her, something she can understand, but all I say is, "I just want to be here."

"For *now*. Until one of you decides to leave the other. That's what always happens."

I'm quiet so she moves on.

"I'm going down next week to stay with Mayra and Jaime while I look for an apartment. You think about it. It will be like the old days but completely different. We'll reinvent ourselves. Mother and daughter, together again."

It's not hard to picture us reunited, living in a beachfront condo in Miami Beach, one of the high-rises she'd point out to Carlito and me when she took us for long drives up and down Collins Avenue. Sometimes she'd pull into the sloping circular driveway of one and make Carlito and me get out of the car and look around the lobby so we could describe it to her, tell her about the bronze and marble and leather lobby furniture, the flower arrangements on glass-top tables, the chandeliers, and all those mirrored walls. She once had a boyfriend who lived in a condo on the Intracoastal. He invited us there a few times to swim in the building's pool. "What do you think, Reinita? Wouldn't you want to live here?" she asked me as she helped me float in the chlorinated water. I told her I would love to, because it seemed that's what she expected. But then we didn't see the guy anymore and when I asked Mami what happened to our moving plans she said she didn't know what I was talking about.

It would be different now. Two grown women. Without the anchor of Carlito in prison to divide us.

We could live on the water like she always dreamed. The people we know, who know us, all live in the same inland pockets on the other side of the city.

By the sea, we can take on new identities. We can be the mother and daughter who are more like sisters, like best friends.

We've both already done our running away. Maybe we belong together.

Like Nesto says: family belongs with family.

And my mother is the only person on this earth who shares my blood.

Carlito and I once ran away together. It was his idea. He was around eleven and I was on the verge of nine. He was mad at our mother because, one night at our uncle's house, after Carlito tried out new curse words he'd heard from other boys in the neighborhood, Mayra had slapped him, an openhanded bofetada across the jaw that left his lower lip swollen, and Mami had done nothing to defend him in response. She was always extra sensitive when it came to Mayra, who she said suffered so much from her childlessness that she practically tried to steal Carlito from her when he was born.

"You can't talk to people like that, especially when you're in their home," Mami had explained, smoking a cigarette out the car window as she drove us home.

Carlito protested from the passenger seat beside her, but she only turned up the radio and started singing along with El Puma.

When we got home, Carlito told me to pack my schoolbag with clothes and anything I could sell for money. I didn't have anything worth anything except the gold cross Abuela had given me for my First Communion so I brought that. Carlito stole all the cash out of Mami's wallet and after we were supposed to be sleeping, came to my bedroom for me.

We sneaked out the back door and walked to the end of our street together but couldn't decide where to go so we returned to our backyard, lay down on the grass, heads on our knapsacks, and fell asleep until Mami found us out there in the morning.

She wasn't even upset. She just said, "Go inside and get ready for school," and then served us our breakfast silently.

When I was fifteen or sixteen and Mami and I entered the era of vicious fights, I sometimes threatened to leave. By then I had older boys and even grown men I could call who would come for me in their cars and let me stay with them as long as I played along in the ways they wanted.

"I'm running away!" I'd shout at my mother from my bedroom door, and she'd answer, "It's not running away if I help you pack!"

I could never leave her. Even as I visited Carlito in prison and he urged me, as if I were the one who needed consolation, to have the courage to move out of our house into a place of my own.

"You could decorate it yourself," he told me. "You could buy new furniture, better than that garbage shit we grew up with. Buy yourself a real bed and some nice pictures for the walls."

He was no longer insistent that it was our responsibility to look after Mami, the way he'd always been until he went to prison and she turned on him. But I couldn't picture our mother on her own, as if, without the gravity of children, she'd become so weightless she'd be carried off by the wind.

When we lost Carlito, after we delivered his and Hector's ashes to the ocean below the bridge, I asked my mother what happened to the body of the daughter she'd lost between Carlito and me. I wondered if she'd been buried or if Mami had held on to her ashes too.

We were in the old house in Miami. I was helping her pack what she'd take with her to her new life with Jerry, separating it from the things she no longer wanted, everything that would be left for me to keep or to throw away.

My mother was quiet for a few moments before answering, then said, "I don't know what happened to her," as if surprised by the fact herself.

"You don't know or your don't want to remember?"

"I was alone in the hospital when I delivered her, just like I was alone when your brother was born and when you were born. Hector was here in Florida. My mother was working so she couldn't be with me. It was in the afternoon, so that was enough to scare me because my mother told me strong babies are always born before sunrise. It was so quiet in there. I knew she wasn't alive before they told me. They let me hold her for only a minute or two. They said any longer would make me go crazy. Then they took her from me. I was crying so much I couldn't speak, not even to ask where they were taking her. And they never told me. I started having visions of what the hospital people could have done with her. Left her in a refrigerator, or just thrown her in the garbage, or sold her remains for brujería. It was torturing me. But then your father told me it didn't matter where they took her because her soul never wanted to belong to that body. And she was still in heaven with other babies, waiting to be born. A year later, we had you."

And then, without my asking more, she said, "I should have buried her. I should have given her a name."

Carlito told me he looked forward to hurricanes. He would watch from his cell's narrow window slat as wind twisted palms and curled rain, flooding prison grounds so that Carlito could pretend, if only for a moment, he was looking at the sea, imagining Colombia on the other side.

He said those storms were the only times inmates and guards were close to equals, both held captive by the prison lockdown, unable to flee, taking in with fear and awe the great power of nature surrounding them. It was the only time the guards seemed human to him, not like the guys who regularly taunted inmates, forcing them to fight each other like dogs for their entertainment, placing bets on who would win.

"How can they get away with such a thing?" I'd asked Carlito. "There are cameras everywhere." I pointed to the one in the corner of the visitors' room that monitored all our interactions.

"The guys who work the control room know how to blow out a camera for a few hours, make it look like a short circuit or a digital glitch so the other guards can do whatever they want. They're a fucking pandilla, Reina. They've all got each other's backs."

But on those hurricane nights, after the power went out and even the generators stopped working, and prisoners howled through the blackness, the guards suffered confinement right along with them.

As a family, we'd been through plenty of bad storms. We endured the blurred, watery edges of hurricanes' outer bands as they passed over and around Florida and even a few direct hits that blasted out power lines and flooded the streets.

But never a storm like Andrew.

Rosita from next door came over asking Mami if she was worried. She was from Puerto Rico so she understood a hurricane's potential to destroy. But Mami was from Cartagena, where hurricanes hadn't hit in centuries, so she waved off Rosita's concern, said we were too far inland to be affected by storm surges and it would just be a matter of heavy rain like every summer. They ended up smoking cigarettes and sipping agua de Jamaica in the kitchen, chismeando about the other neighbors until it was dark and the wind started to change.

We spent the night in a closet. Mami, Carlito, and I huddled as far into the corner as we could get, behind an old trunk and the vacuum cleaner. Carlito had boarded the windows as best he could with cardboard and plywood he found in the garage. He blocked the front door with the coffee table turned on its side. When the house started shaking we went into the only windowless space, holding each other through the whistling and clapping and crashing of the wind.

We fell asleep in one another's arms, curled over one another's knees, until after daybreak when we heard people out on the street shouting, wanting to know if the Castillos were safe.

Rosita's roof peeled and popped off like the lid on a can of sardines, but ours remained sealed to the house without even sagging where a fat palm tree fell onto it. Our windows blew out. The back door shattered. But the front door stayed intact, and this kept wind from filling the house, churning the contents like it did to many of our neighbors' homes, splitting swimming pools, rolling cars halfway down the road. We heard on the news about people who found sharks spit from the ocean in their yards; marina boats washed onto land; houses ripped off their foundations, walls folding in like wet paper, televisions and furniture hurled miles away; trees torn from the earth; dead animals everywhere.

Our neighborhood went weeks without electricity and water but that was nothing compared with communities farther south where few homes were left standing.

Mami was celebrating because we were among the blessed and living. She said this time the santos were looking out for us.

When I go up to Miami to meet my mother, she brings up the night we spent in the closet during the hurricane.

She's been staying with Mayra and Tío Jaime, but I told her I don't want to see them, so we agree to meet at a restaurant on the Miami River, with a view of warehouses and passing cargo ships, saturated in the stink of the nearby fish market: a restaurant she likes because Jerry used to take her there and she wants to make it her own now. She told me on the phone she hoped I'd bring Nesto with me so she could finally meet him.

"I don't know why you're being so mysterious about him. Are you afraid I'll steal him from you?"

She laughed, but I didn't.

"He has other things to do," I told her, and it was true. He's officially given up his room at the motel, moved in with me, and convinced Mrs. Hartley to let him give the cottage a fresh coat of paint inside and out.

Today I find my mother sitting alone at a table by the water, sipping a cocktail. She's cut her hair so it barely touches her shoulders, and has lost so much weight she had the nerve to put on a flamingo-pink dress with a buttoned bodice she bought twenty years ago, and a pair of strappy silver heels that I borrowed from her a few times as a teenager, before I had the cash to buy my own. Seeing her there, all dressed up and sitting alone at the restaurant, I remember how she used to say her beauty would have been better served in some other life.

A young waiter approaches the table and the way she throws her head back in laughter at something he says makes me sad for her. She doesn't stand up to hug me when she sees me, just wraps her arms around my neck when I lean down to kiss her, and I feel the stickiness of her lipstick streaking my cheek.

When I sit down, she holds my hand across the table like she's afraid I might make a run for it.

I hold her fingers tightly too. I've come prepared with things I want to say.

She starts with talk about an apartment she saw up in Aventura with two bedrooms, so I can move in whenever I'm ready. It's on the ocean, with a pool and a tennis court, she says, and I wonder when she's going to stop torturing herself by looking at places she can't afford on her own. She's started seeing another bruja—the one on Brickell all the celebrities go to, had to wait a month for the appointment and pay four hundred dollars for the hour—who predicted better fortunes for her, advising Mami that taking up tennis would be the key to meeting the next man in her life. But just as quickly as she gets excited describing her future as a lady with a condo, she becomes nostalgic for the old neighborhood, launching into the barrio gossip she picked up from Mayra and her posse of lenguonas, about people who are divorcing or having affairs, second families discovered or secret children showing up.

Then, through the appetizer and even the main course, she moves on to her list of the sick, dying, and dead.

"I almost forgot," she says. "You know who died? La Cassiani."

"Universo's mother?"

"Esa misma. They took her to the hospital with chest pains and the doctors finished killing her with some infection. The son went to bury her in Santa Lucía. Mayra heard it was a beautiful funeral with a vallenato band and everything."

She moves on to another story, about some fulano de tal, a male neighbor of Mayra and Jaime's, who asked her on a date, but I can think only of Universo's mother, who wasn't much older than mine though she always seemed more aged by her life's disappointments; how she'd stare me down as if that were enough to keep me away from her son, how she brought the daughters and granddaughters of her friends to her house, niñas de buena familia, hoping Universo would choose to be with one of them over a mala like me, as if she knew something about both my past and my future that I didn't.

Mami stops herself in the middle of a thought about whether or not the guy is as completely divorced as he says, as if suddenly disoriented, glancing around the restaurant, then back at me.

"Listen to me. I go on and on. I'm becoming one of those viejitas who talks to themselves. Soon you're going to find me having conversations with the television."

She looks embarrassed, something new for her. My mother is a woman of congenital confidence, armor built into the rust of her complexion. I watch as she rearranges herself in her seat, looks down at her breasts, adjusts the straps of her bra. When finished, she reaches for my hand again, pulls it close to her mouth, and kisses my knuckles before letting go.

"I want to tell you something. Do you remember the night we spent in the closet together during the hurricane? You were both big by then, but I held you to my heart as if you were two babies. Do you remember?"

I nod. But more than that, I remember my brother and me, with all the force and strength we had, mooring her with our child bodies, holding on to her as if the gusts might tear her away and then we'd be left with no parents at all.

"I never prayed as hard in all my life as I did that night," she says. "I prayed the wind would spare our house and the roof would stay on tight. I didn't think it would. Your father and Jaime built that roof themselves. I thought, *Tonight, Hector will succeed in killing us all.* But I prayed with everything I had, Reina. I told God if He saved us that night and kept a roof on our house so we would have a place to live the next day, I would never ask for anything ever again. After that night in the closet, I believed my faith saved us, even if my prayers, enough for several lifetimes, weren't enough to save your brother later, when he really needed them. You remember how much I prayed and prayed when Carlito was arrested. I made so many promises. But Diosito had already saved Carlito twice. Once from your father, and then from the storm. And maybe my prayers aren't worth much after all. I'm just a stupid woman. I've made so many mistakes of my own. What I'm trying to tell you, what I've wanted to say to you for a long time, is that a mother can't always save her children. That's what I learned from everything that happened to us. You each had to save yourselves. Your brother couldn't, but you did, mi Reina. You did."

Her eyes are watery and she puts a napkin to them before her eyeliner has a chance to smudge, then dips her fingers into her water glass, dabbing droplets along her neck as if it will be enough to cool her off.

"Mami."

She lifts her hair off her neck and fans herself. "Why did we come to this restaurant? It's so hot. We should have gone somewhere with air conditioning."

"Mami," I try again. I want to reach for her hands as she did with me, but I can't bring myself to do it. We are sitting at a tiny table for two, but she feels so far from me, as if I have to shout for her to hear me.

"Mami, please listen to what I'm going to tell you."

I pause to make sure I have her full attention but am afraid if I wait too long, the words will slip back down my throat to the place in my gut where I've been holding them for so long.

"It's my fault Carlito did what he did. I'm the one who told him about Isabela. It was me. And it wasn't true. I *lied*, Mami. I lied and he believed me."

I lean back, letting the truth rest on the table between us.

My mother watches me without a trace of surprise in her eyes, though I know this doesn't mean much. She isn't one to give anything away; emotions are as valuable and as vital to her as money.

"Why?" she finally whispers.

"He loved her so much. I thought he would choose her over us. I didn't want him to leave us."

She sighs and closes her eyes for several seconds. When she opens them, it's as if we are somewhere else, not at a restaurant on the river with me confessing, but back in the old house, sitting across the wooden kitchen table, me still carrying the secret of my regret.

Maybe if she were another kind of mother she might offer solace, words of comfort; tell me something that could release me from my shame; say something like, *Reina, you could not have known he would take what you told him and do what he did. You never could have known.*

But the woman across from me is Amandina de Castillo, wife of Hector and mother of Reina and Carlito.

The only thing she knows to say in response is, "We should make a promise to each other never to speak of those days again. No matter what."

"I'm not going to promise that."

"I don't want to remember those things anymore. Please, if you love me at all, Reina, let me forget. Have mercy on your poor mami. I beg you."

We watch each other until she breaks her gaze, looks to the water and to the sky, darkening with granite clouds.

"It looks like rain is coming."

I nod. "I've got a long drive south."

"I wish you would stay."

I don't know if she means this afternoon, waiting out the rain together, or if she means longer, maybe forever, starting yet another life with her here in Miami.

"I can't. I have to go home."

We stand together on the street outside the restaurant, not far from the coil of lots under the interstate, once a tent city that housed Mariel refugees. My mother hugs me, her arms falling around my waist, her cheek hitting my shoulders.

I remember when I was a child and could only reach as high as her hips, how I'd cushion myself against her thighs, lean on her as she talked to people, how she'd grip my hand tight through crowds, hold me on her lap as we watched her telenovelas and she dreamed up other lives for us.

She seems so fragile to me now, unsteady in her heels; even her bangles and earrings look too big for her. In her face, I see traces of my grandmother and I suspect, by the way she looks back at me, as if I am a photograph and not her daughter in the flesh, that she sees one of her old faces in mine too.

She is so small in our embrace that I feel as if I am carrying her, but when I let go, I feel her arms tighten and strengthen. Then it's as if my mother is carrying me.

A few months before he died, Carlito was in one of his moods. We faced each other in the visitors' room at the prison and he waited a long time to speak to me. I did all the talking, telling him about my dumb life painting nails. He stared back at me, his eyebrows dipped, nose wrinkled, lips tight like he was ready to spit. When I finally shut up, he shook his head at me as if I were some pitiful thing.

"I should have died the day Hector threw me off the bridge. That fucking Cuban should have let me drown. We all would have been better off."

Sometimes I wondered if the reason Carlito never took the blame for his crime was that he didn't blame himself, but blamed me, for sending him off in a rage that day. I didn't know what he was capable of. If I had known, I would have tried to stop it. I would have called Isabela and told her Carlito was on his way to her house and not to open the door. His fury would have passed. He would have returned to his normal self and nothing would have been lost.

That day in the prison, with my brother's dimmed face in front of me, I said something I'd never said in all the years I spent visiting him, or through any of my letters or phone calls.

"Forgive me, Carlito."

I thought he would pardon me for failing him, for failing us, but the brother I once knew, who even in his brutality could be tender, loving, and gentle, looked away from me to the guard standing by the door, and to the clock on the wall behind me.

"What do you want me to say, Reina?"

He shrugged so abruptly his handcuffs dragged against the metal table, making a grating sound I'll never forget.

I don't know if he knew what I meant with my request, or if it meant anything to him. I wish I could have said more that day. If I'd had the right words, maybe I wouldn't have felt so exposed yet smothered by the filthy starkness of the prison walls, the guard taking in everything we said to one another.

We were quiet until Carlito said he had a headache. The bright lights of the visitors' room burned his eyes too much and gave him a migraine.

"You don't mind if I leave our visit early, do you?"

"No," I said, though it hurt me since we had half an hour left and it would be lost time we would never have the chance to make up.

He looked to the guard to signal that he was ready to leave me. This guard was an extra rigid one, so instead of hoping for a contraband hug, I kissed my fingertips and quickly pressed them against my brother's cheek before the guard could pull him away and reprimand me for making physical contact with a death row case.

A few days later, he called me. I'd just gotten home from work and kicked my shoes off in the foyer. The house was quiet, lonely but familiar, and after a day of making conversation with clients, I longed for its muteness. But then I heard the noise of the prison behind Carlito's voice and all I wanted was more of his chaos, more of him.

"I only have a minute but I wanted to tell you, in case you're still wondering, and so you never wonder about it again, there is nothing to forgive, hermanita. You're my Reina. You're my guerrera. Your brother loves you. Remember that when I die."

He hung up the phone, probably because he knew I would say he wasn't going to die, not as long as I had anything to do with it.

He could rely on my denial. I was the only one who listened when he said that even if he deserved to die, the state didn't deserve to kill him.

The only sort of death that seemed possible for my brother was his execution, but maybe by then he already knew he would take care of things himself.

He used to ridicule other inmates who took their own lives, calling our father spineless for slicing his own throat rather than facing the rest of his days in prison.

"And he wasn't even in solitary," Carlito said, like Hector's life sentence was some kind of vacation.

Carlito thought of himself as a prisoner of conscience, victim of legal prejudice, saying there were gringos who committed way more heinous crimes who got out in fifteen years or less.

Sometimes he said if he'd really meant to kill anyone he would have just gotten himself a gun and gone after Tío Jaime, who Carlito always suspected of being the original guilty party: the one who lusted after our mother so much that he deliberately infected his brother Hector with the jealous psychosis that sent him to the bridge that day with baby Carlito.

"I would have made that motherfucker get on his knees and sing for his life," Carlito said. "And then I would have killed him anyway."

Carlito and I were both in high school when some delinquents started a trend of jumping off the bridge into the bay at the very spot where Hector had launched his son into the ocean. Groups of teenagers gathered by the railing to see who was brave enough to climb the wall at the bridge's highest point and jump over. People claimed it probably wasn't high enough for a person to be instantly killed by the fall. In most cases, people were known to shatter a bone or be so shocked by the impact they forgot to breathe and others would have to dive in after them before they drowned. It was part of the thrill, seeing if you had the instincts for survival.

For a while, I tried to convince Carlito that we should try it. I thought it might undo his trauma and get him over his aversion to water. I thought there was something poetic about it—Carlito returning as a grown man to the location of his almost-murder.

I pictured us climbing over the railing one leg at a time, finding our balance on the slim concrete ledge of the bridge, hands on the rail behind us, our bodies dangling over the ocean.

We could throw ourselves off the bridge as a pair, and when we came up through the waves, taking our first breaths, we'd each see the other waiting, and find our way back to land together.

Carlito refused.

I knew he went back to the bridge on his own though, walking the length of it. He knew that bridge well, long before he returned to it with the baby in his arms.

Witnesses said she was crying desperately. She'd loved Carlito like he was her own father, but that day it was as if she knew he was stealing her from her mother forever, and the thick hands that held her would soon let her fall.

When they found Carlito dead in his cell, his prison suit was rolled down around his waist. That's what they told us anyway. Carved across his chest in a fine and shallow yet bloody line was an arc he only could have dragged through his flesh with a pen because Carlito wasn't allowed to have any sharp objects in his cell. The line bowed from his rib cage up to the base of his collarbone and back down on the other side. The prison people first described it to my mother and me as a mutilated attempt at a rainbow, just another improvised inmate tattoo. But when we arrived at the prison morgue and were given a few moments alone with Carlito, gray and cold, his soul departed, we saw for ourselves the bloody bend he'd scrawled across his heart and knew we were looking not at a rainbow but at the bridge.

I still have her phone number. I've come close to dialing it many times but always stop myself, unsure of what to say. I know the white house with the brown door she grew up in with her parents, where she and I sat on her bedroom floor as girls and traded secrets, where Carlito would later sneak to at night because she always left her window open for him. She's remarried now. She must live somewhere else with her new husband and new children. I sit in my parked car long after my mother drives off, until I finally have the courage to call.

I don't know if she recognizes the number but she answers quickly.

"Isabela. This is Reina Castillo."

I wait for her to respond but she's silent.

"I'm sorry to bother you. I know you must be busy. I was wondering if I could talk to you."

"We're talking now," she says gently.

"I moved away but I'm in town today. I was wondering if we could meet in person, if it's not a problem for you."

"We can do that," she says slowly. "I have my kids with me. Can you come to my house?"

I tell her yes and she gives me the address, just a few blocks from her parents' place.

I drive south, ahead of the rain, through our old neighborhood, though I avoid the lot where our house once stood.

When I arrive at Isabela's, I see evidence of her family's world: small bicycles in the driveway behind a minivan, balls and toys scattered across the front lawn.

This, I can't help thinking, could have been my brother's life.

I step out of my car and ring the bell. I hear voices within, then see her silhouette behind the frosted glass of the front door. She opens it and we take each other in for a moment. Isabela, as beautiful as ever, though thicker in her face and body, luminous even with her mussed wavy hair and none of the makeup she used to wear so much of.

"Reina," she says, stepping outside with me, closing the door behind her. "What a surprise to hear from you. You look good. So where did you move to?"

I see that she's barefoot, hear the kids laughing in the house behind her.

"Down south. The Keys."

"Must be nice."

"It is."

"We're always talking about taking the kids down but we never make it."

I remember Christmas when I saw her at the hotel.

"Have you been down there at all lately?" I try to sound casual, despite the strangeness of our being face-to-face.

"Not in years." She looks suddenly wistful. "Not since Carlito took me down there when I turned twenty-one. We rented Jet Skis. I kept falling off."

I study her hair, the way she still tilts her head for no reason, and I am sure it was Isabela I saw that day in the spa, though I realize now, it couldn't have been.

"So what is it? What did you want to talk to me about?"

I take a deep breath, as I would before a dive with Nesto watching me on the line to make sure that I'm safe, that I come back up for air without blacking out.

"I have to tell you I'm sorry. For everything."

"I know you are. We're all sorry."

"No, there is more you don't know. I'm the one who told Carlito you were cheating on him and who made him go crazy that day. It's my fault he took Shayna from you. I didn't tell him to do it but it's my fault. I'm the one who started everything."

I can't face her. I stare at our feet but feel her eyes on me. Then her hand grazes my shoulder, soft as a feather.

"I knew that. I've known for a long time."

I look back up at her. Her face hasn't changed. Still calm, full of mercy.

"How?"

"Your brother told me."

"When?"

"I tried to visit him in prison. It was a while after the trial ended, after the sentencing. I didn't know visits had to be planned in advance and you had to be approved. I just showed up so they turned me away. I wrote to him and asked if I could come see him, just to talk to him, just to see if he was okay because I worried about him being in there all alone. But he never answered me. I kept writing to him anyway. A few times a year. For his birthday, Christmas, things like that. A few weeks before he died he called me. He said it was you who pushed him to do what he did to my baby. I always imagined it was something like that. I didn't tell you because I didn't want to upset you."

"It's my fault," I say, though my voice has gone faint.

"No, it's not. You're not the one who took her to the bridge. He did."

A small boy opens the door behind Isabela and pokes his head out from behind it.

"Mami," he says. "Who's that?"

"This is my friend, Reina. Dale un besito."

He steps toward me, also barefoot, in his small blue jeans and T-shirt, and I bend so he can kiss my cheek. This child and the one inside, babies whose innocence Carlito stole before they were born because there will be a day when their mother will have to explain to them what happened to the older sister they will never have the chance to know.

"This is Rafaelito," she says, slipping her hand onto his back. "Go inside and watch your sister for me, papi."

When her son is gone, Isabela sighs.

"I knew how you felt about me, Reina. When Carlito and I got together you thought I was going to take him away from your family. He said you were jealous. But I was the one who was jealous of you. I never had a brother or a sister to love me the way your brother loved you. I felt so alone in my childhood. But Carlito would do anything for you. He told me so many times."

She lowers her voice and steps in a bit closer.

"I blamed myself for a long time too. I told myself that if I hadn't let him take my baby girl with him that day, if I had just kept her home with me, she would still be alive. I thought if it was anyone's fault it was mine, because I am the mother, I'm the one who was supposed to protect her, and I am the one who let my daughter go."

She looks around and checks the door behind her to make sure it's shut tight.

"I found out I was pregnant right after Carlito was arrested. He never knew. Nobody knew. Only my parents. They said God wouldn't want me to have his baby, and they were afraid that if I showed up pregnant to the trial it would influence the verdict. They even took me to see a priest and he said my case was an exception because nobody should have to give birth to the child of a murderer. They made me get rid of it. I didn't want to. I tried to fight them but I was so weak in those days. I thought I would die of sadness. I was sure I wouldn't live through the pain of it all. And the trial hadn't even started yet."

Both of us have tears in our eyes. She pauses, draws in her breath, and looks all around us, as if searching for someone to stop her from saying more.

"I can never tell this to anyone except you. I still love your brother. He killed me along with my daughter. He broke my soul into pieces. He destroyed the happiness of my family. But I still love him because I remember the boy I knew, the Carlito I fell in love with."

I can't manage any words so I reach for her hand, as if asking permission to hold her.

She takes me into her arms and I feel her tremble against me.

"I'm so sorry," I whisper into her hair.

We pull apart and she gathers her breath, her eyes drying and brightening as I wipe mine with my hands.

"I forgive you for everything, Reina, like I forgive your brother and I forgive myself. You and I are the ones still standing. We've outlived our penance. I'm free. You're free too."

"I don't feel free."

"But you are."

Rafaelito pries the door open again and checks on his mom. She looks back at him and then to me.

"I have to go. It's almost time for the kids' dinner. My husband will be home soon."

She reaches for me and we embrace again for a long time.

"Take care of yourself, Reina. This time, when you leave, don't look back."

The long blazing days of summer grow shorter. Nesto and I take in what they call an acoustic or electrical storm. A song of thunder with no rain. Torches of lighting ignite the black night. Fiery veins rooted in both sky and ocean.

We've already lost power in the cottage. We open the windows to let air through and sit on a mound of eroded beach. These storms are our night symphonies. We watch sparks and flashes thread the horizon, traveling along the water, knowing there are others who also watch and wait for Changó's strikes from the other side of the sea.

I dig my toes into the soft sand, eyes on the ocean like a blanket covering the earth. Nesto reaches for me, and leads me by the hand to the water's edge where he raises his palms to the white light of the moon, both of us stepping sideways into the shallow tide.

I feel the Atlantic pool at my ankles, soft sand cradling my feet, embracing my legs and torso as the water pulls us in. I lean into Nesto's arms and he dips me under the tide, seven times, whispering an oriki to Yemayá, protector of maternity, asking for her blessings. Then we swim together as the ocean floor drops out from below.

All my life I have wondered if I am the true abikú, as predicted and as marked by my father with the cut in my ear, unworthy and inhospitable to life.

I wondered it as recently as yesterday, before I learned that within me I've been carrying a hidden being, something I didn't know I could want this much.

It was this temporary magical state, this biological trick, that, as suspected, likely made the wild dolphin look to me with recognition and led her to follow me out of her pen to open water. I thought I was special that night though I didn't yet know how.

Of course there were signs all along. But we didn't see them, because they weren't the signs we were looking for.

When I found out, I couldn't stop myself from offering Nesto a way out, but he wouldn't take it. He said we belong to each other now.

He told me he knew from the first time he took me out to the blue—when I showed him the sea horses in the water, because they're solitary creatures and to see them in courtship is extremely rare—that we would be together for a long time.

Maybe I wasn't aware of it, but I think I knew then too.

I hear Nesto's breath, the sound of his body breaking the waves behind me as I swim ahead, and I know he will never let me go too far.

It's no longer just the two of us out here in the water.

He watches as I give myself to the current, the way my mother taught me to do when I was a child in her arms, and let the water ease me back to shore, back to him.

A few nights ago, Nesto called me out to the beach. He pointed to the turtle nest he marked months ago with coconuts and shells, and that he's looked over to make sure it remained undisturbed. The sand was beginning to move. We watched from behind the dune as hatchlings climbed their way out of the nest their mother made for them, following the path marked by moonlight, leaving behind them a tiny trail of prints like stars in the sand, dipping into the tide, struggling to swim against it until finally carried out by the ocean.

Nesto and I were quiet, amazed at their instincts, the way the celestial compass of nature and the night guided them home.

Nesto stands on the edge of Lolo's boat, hands on his hips, afternoon sun burning his back. When he gets that look about him, I wonder if one day he'll carry out the fantasy he's told me about, sailing a boat across the Straits to collect his children himself.

He reaches into a bag we've brought along and pulls out a round watermelon, a hole carved in it, filled with molasses meant to hold his deepest wishes and plugged with white flowers. He places it carefully in the water below.

He lifts his palms to the sky in alabanza, watching the offering roll above the waves away from us.

I wait for him on the back of the boat so we can fall into the water together.

He comes to me, giving me his hand, and we toss ourselves into the ocean, feeling ourselves sink into the current, heavy yet weightless.

I take my time coming up for air, even as the water wants to push me to the surface.

There was a period during my brother's years in prison when I'd wrestle with the long nights by walking aimlessly along our neighborhood streets.

Many times, police cars pulled over asking if I was lost or needed a ride.

I'd tell the officers, most of whom knew me by name or by face from Carlito's trial, that I was just out for a walk and they'd urge me to go home.

"You're a girl alone," they would say, as if I were unaware. "Ask yourself how many hours or days or weeks would have to pass before anybody notices you've disappeared from this earth forever."

I never had an answer for them, but the question has always remained with me.

I take too long to come up for air and Nesto reaches down into the water and pulls me up to him.

I'm blind with salt and sun but feel him hold me, waiting for my eyes to open to him.

Only then does he let go.

I drift into my own space of ocean, a small chasm forming between us.

Across the growing bulge of waves, I see him reach for me again, hear him call my name, telling me not to slip away.

Acknowledgments

My infinite gratitude to the many people on these and other shores who have been a part of this journey.

On this side of the Florida Straits, I thank E.Q.R for sharing so much with me and for Buenavista; the Marine Animal Rescue Society, and Ricardo Paris for his excellent freediving instruction out in the deep blue.

In Cuba, my thanks to Genaro Bombino, Paquito Vives and Alicia Pérez, Pamela Ruíz and Damián Aquiles, Tom Miller, Elvia Grisuela, Ofélia Riverón and Cáritas de La Habana, Bibiana Barban and Carlos Rodríguez, María Josefa Rodríguez, and Gabby Mejía, who was there that first trip; the community of La Casa de los Orishas de La Habana and La Asociación Cultural Yoruba de Cuba with whom I visited and consulted many times over the years of researching and writing this book; and Adolfo Nodal and Peter Sánchez, masters of logistics. Special thanks to Gustavo Bell Lemus.

In Cartagena, my thanks to Álvaro Blanco and to San Basilio de Palenque.

To my stellar agent and first reader, Ayesha Pande; my editor, Elisabeth Schmitz, for her passion and precision; Katie

Raissian, for her keen editorial eye and kindness; and the tireless team at Grove, especially Judy Hottensen, Morgan Entrekin, Deb Seager, Justina Batchelor, John Mark Boling, Amy Hundley, Becca Putman, Charles Rue Woods, Gretchen Mergenthaler, Julia Berner-Tobin, and Cecilia Molinari.

For their generous support, I thank the National Endowment for the Arts; C. Michael Curtis for publishing "The Bridge" many years before it would grow into a novel; David Mura for important advice early on; my colleagues and my students at the University of Miami; for their friendship and encouragement, my thanks to M. Evelina Galang and Chauncey Mabe, Edwidge Danticat, Chris Feliciano Arnold, Mark Powell, Claudia Milian, and Daniel Samper Pizano. I am especially grateful to Stella Ohana, who read the manuscript on a moment's notice and provided crucial insights.

I thank my family and the many friends who remain constant companions no matter the distance or how far I disappear into my work; my nieces and my godchildren, and the memory of my grandmother Lucía, and my uncle H. Above all, I thank my parents, for their faith and for more love than could fill an ocean.